# BREAKING
## FAITH

# BREAKING FAITH

## Blood Kin Book 1

# M.S. ABELL

ISBN: 978-1-7333095-0-9

Book Cover Design & Formatting
by JD&J Design

Printed by Kindle Direct Publishing

# TABLE OF CONTENTS

# DESCRIPTION

The landscape has altered after the 2020 riots stimulated by the controversial Mayan calendar predictions of global doom. Increasingly more powerful shifts in energy waves in the Universe coupled with the cumulative thought forms of humans throughout history have transformed the world giving physicality to psychic phenomenon, or in other words, magic. The leading edge of cosmic particles from a massive solar explosion millions of light years ago is transforming human evolution in as yet unknown ways. Covens have risen from the ashes gaining prominence, respectability and influence in the economies, religions and governance of all countries. A central government, a World Government, oversees the welfare of Earth.

Tempest Duvayne Phillips loves her grandmother, Gloriana Duvayne, Ryniah of the Council of ParaHumans, Beldame of Coven Duvayne, and member of the Enclave for World Governments, even when Glory has put her in perilous and sometimes demeaning situations. When a fourth task novae, Tempest faces the realization she must sever contact with Glory to protect her heart family, including Rogan Branaugh, her closest friend and co-owner of Branaugh Security. Caught in the struggle among CEOs of Covens with political and governmental power, Tempest battles to create a new future with otherworld possibilities. Her heart family has finally found the buried medpod containing the body of the Blood Lair Patriarch, a thousands years old FolKin Elder, who inadvertently bonded with Tempest in her pre-teens.

Tempest must work with Daire D'eath, one of the richest and most powerful men in the world, to extricate the Elder. The immediate attraction between Tempest and Daire has the potential to grow to something more if only Tempest can survive the obstacles facing her: the arrival of a Mistress with her Tonal Mates from the Patriarch's homeworld, a death challenge from a Coven CEO, the dimensional invasion by Kin and Flairs, and arcane magic in the guise of a shapeshifting sword as well as aggression from various Earth military and secretive agencies. Dimensional gates, aliens, demi-Folk, Kin, and military... oh, my!

# ABOUT THE AUTHOR

Sue Abell has been writing since early childhood – short stories, novels and even a play. Her style of writing is organic … rarely does a novel form from an outline. Most often, her novels come from the dreams she has while sleeping. Sue lucid dreams: she is aware she is dreaming and either participates in the action or watches what is happening. Can you stand by and watch when something you can control is taking place?

Sue spends her time reading, working full-time at a law office, and, of course, writing – currently with 36 additional novels in various stages of progress as well as the next Blood Kin novel in the works.

She lives in North Carolina with her cats: SemperPawz Shogun ("Sho") and SemperPawz Cazimeer ("Kaz") (Maine Coons).

In memory of Sassy and Tia (part Manxes), Budd (black and white tuxedo shorthair), Teegrr (part-Maine Coon) and CongoCoons Cooprr (Maine Coon).

For more information about Sue Abell, please visit www. marthaabell.com. Send an email to Sue at sue@marthaabell. com.

# CHAPTER 1

Family sucks. But family of the heart, even though overbearingly protective, were much preferable to her genetic family who were treacherous, agenda-driven and power hungry. Tempest Duvayne Phillips would maintain ties to her father, mother and siblings but she was going to have to cut her ties to the Grand Dame of the Duvayne Family.

Glorianna Duvayne, Ryniah of the Council of ParaHumans, Beldame of Coven Duvayne, member of the Enclave for World Governments and her grandmother had impressed on Tempest since she was born that her Fate was bound to the Covens. She was collateral, to be used for the good of the Covens, at the Beldame's discretion. If Tempest wasn't in such a precarious position, she'd let the evil-sounding laugh stuck in her throat freedom. Currency for the Covens? Not since Rogan Branaugh freed her from Glory's compound years ago. Fables, legends, myths and history stated that Fate was the playground of three women, and The Duvayne was not one of them, no matter how much Glory thought otherwise.

But Tempest found herself confronted with stark facts while watching the HWV parked in the loading bay behind D'eath Towers for the last five minutes. The lack of emotions and movement from the men she sensed sitting inside the vehicle didn't match with the small amount of information Glory provided to ensnare Tempest into making the meeting in Glory's place. Arriving at the location early and observing the stealthy arrival of the heavyweight utility vehicle, had spun Tempest into a montage of short videos of doing Glory's "little favors", and agreeing to the gentle requests to appear at certain Coven meetings "to show family solidarity." Disillusionment about herself filled her as the memories flowed.

Crap. She was Coven currency. Glory was a master at getting what she wanted and Tempest had allowed her grandmother to use her despite all Tempest's protests to her heart family that she was her own person. Her laughter would be bitter if she allowed it voice. But reviewing her life now, in a critical situation, was beyond foolish. She had to get her head in the game.

Her hand inched down to the small purse anchored at her left side by the strap crossing her breasts to her right shoulder. Her intellect said, "Pull out the digi-mic and call in backup." But the good little Coven Witch, even with Tempest's sudden revelation, said, "You promised your Grandmother to follow her instructions and when she said 'alone' she meant alone." For the last time, Tempest would follow her Coven leader's instructions.

Drawing in a deep breath, she wrapped the shadows in the black corner formed by intersecting shadows of several buildings more closely around her, fumbling the energy draw for a few seconds. Cursing to herself, she hated using methods she didn't completely control, she moved along the side of the building hugging the steadily decreasing shadow. It was possible she was wrong about Glory's intentions, but Tempest wasn't kowtowing to Coven bastards or bitches, even her grandmother's. Just before the shadow ended, she stopped, drew in another deep breath, released the energy and strode into the alley projecting strength, confidence and kick-ass attitude ... and froze. In her peripheral vision, a figure appeared on her left. Well, shit.

Another errand gone bad. She ... was ... done. It was the final straw in the long line of coincidences involving her grandmother. Coincidence was just another word for deception and deception meant trap. She was definitely having a long overdue discussion with Beldame Duvayne. It was time her grandmother gave Tempest some direct answers.

If Glory was in trouble, Tempest had to know the full particulars and, with the aid of her heart family, she could work with Mikuh, Captain of Glory's security team, to develop a protection plan. Continuing to allow Glory to shove her into supposed insignificant situations that evolved into life-threatening events ended now. There were too many people depending on Tempest. Acknowledging her grandmother might have a different agenda which didn't take into consideration Tempest's welfare left a bitter taste in her mouth.

Tempest swung away from the grabby man. His fist closed around the strap of her purse. He yanked and it broke, the purse falling away. Damn it. Her only means of protection plopped onto the concrete out of her sight.

"Get off me!" The Assholes-R-Us agent quickly grabbed her, binding her arms at her sides which totally ticked her off. She slammed her head back, ramming the man's nose and jammed her heel into the top of his foot. The smell of his sweat, and the garlic wafting from his mouth beside her ear, made her angrier. She couldn't even hold her breath to escape his foul scents.

She let her body go slack waiting for the slightest change in his grip. The man grunted and bent slightly but held on. Men tumbled out of the HWV in the delivery bay of the D'eath Towers administrative building – reinforcements. She wrenched left then right. Her opponent stretched her body back. As her feet lifted from the concrete, she snapped her knees to her chest. The NuSkin along her ribs ripped and a small warm wetness trickled free. The man lost his balance staggering several feet, but maintaining his grip.

She eyed the trio strutting like roosters away from the black HWV. Light from the security lamps positioned at regular intervals around the dock glinted on a pressure syringe held in the fist of the man on her left. Time to go! She turned her head and bit deep into the arm across her breasts, jammed the heel of her shoe into his thigh, and threw her weight to the side. This time his grip slipped. She screamed and with a deep inhale, exhale tore free ... landing on hands and knees on the concrete. The left seam on the skirt of her little black dress split and her thigh high nylons shredded. Shit! She just bought the damn dress and nylons that morning.

Scrambling upright, Tempest kicked the heels from her feet and ran backwards until she thudded into the side of the step-filled wall. With a hunch of her shoulders, the beaded jacket fell to the ground. The cool early evening air raised goose bumps on every inch of exposed flesh. "What the fuck are you doing? I'm The Duvayne's proxy."

Fury ate her control. She wanted to wade into them hitting, punching and kicking until they were moaning on the ground. She searched the ground for her purse. It sparkled at the edge of a pool of light. With a rolling flip, she launched her body the few feet, her hand catching and tightening around the satin and velvet fabric. She ripped the top open. Relief cascaded down her spine as her fingers closed around a short wood and metal rod. She shook the cloth away and thumbed a hidden button on the rod.

Clink, clink, clink, clink.

She twirled the fully extended staff behind her shoulder dropping into a half crouch. She should be at the front of the damn building watching incoming traffic not in some back alley tussling with her grandmother's supposed minions.

She eyed the six foot six inch giant in the center of the half circle of men recognizing him as the leader when the others stopped at a twitch of his hand. The aura of self-confidence, arrogance and power was another indicator he was the head jerk. The hip-length black leather jacket he wore bulged at the left shoulder, a sure sign of a weapon.

"The Duvayne instructed us to escort you to her Virginia estate. As soon as you arrive, you are to call her for directions to some restricted papers she needs for an important meeting tomorrow with one of the President's advisors. We're then supposed to take you to her."

Tempest tipped her chin towards the man on the leader's right. "What's with the syringe?" She should have followed her first instinct, pulled out the digi-mic stuffed in the now damaged purse and called Rogan Branaugh, her business partner and first member of her heart family. She really wanted that digi-mic.

The hair on her neck and arms vibrated caution and danger, but the leader didn't fidget and displayed no urgency to remove her from the area. "Where's Mikuh? I don't recognize you as being part of his teams. What's your name?"

"Captain Braeden is with The Duvayne and we were hired a month ago. You haven't been at any of your grandmother's properties for over three months so of course you wouldn't know our faces." The smile on his lips didn't reach his wintry grey eyes.

She snorted at the obvious attempt to distract her and snapped the pole forward protecting her chest. She gave him a toothy grin. "Mikuh emails me when he adds new people. No waiting in line. No delays. Now ... this is what's going to happen. You back up, get in your vehicle and drive away. No harm, no foul. You push this and I'll set hounds on your trail. I'll watch them play with you and, when I feel like it, I'll break you."

She infused her words with confidence and arrogance – the only emotions she was sure he could recognize. She settled into her center, reaching for the pool of detachment she used to protect her soul when faced with deadly decisions. And she would follow through on her assertion. It would be difficult, if not impossible, to stop her people once they heard about the confrontation.

The leader flipped back the right side of his jacket. "Just reaching for my bona fides, Ms. Phillips."

His fingers inched into the inside pocket. A two-inch dragon emblem coin spilled out to dangle from his fingers on a gold chain. "Our credentials."

From this distance, it appeared real. Her grandmother's sigil. Re-evaluating her recent insights, she tried to work out Glory's reasoning for sending trigger-happy, volatile minions. Was this only another test? She had thought they were past the need for continual assessments. The tear which had formed in the fragile trust she had in her grandmother widened. Glory was Ryniah and Beldame and Tempest knew the majority of her responses to situations were from worldview. But would she deliberately sacrifice her granddaughter? She struggled to boost her shields.

The setting sun flashed across the surface of the golden coin. It spun around and about … a little at first then speeding up until it twirled madly. The attack when it came was subtle. The low mesmerizing tone reinforced with power, and the glittering light from the motion of the coin, snared her attention. She strained to hear the voice.

She nodded her head. Yes, his response was logical, reasonable. The last time she saw Mikuh he had said he would be hiring men. The glow of the medal spiraled out, warming her. Her muscles released their tension bits at a time. She tilted her head; a faint hum with throbbing peaceful undertones lulled her inherent barriers. She had no reason to be suspicious. Her grandmother had sent these men. Her fingers relaxed on the rod in her hand. She couldn't remember the last time she felt so safe.

"I thought she was supposed to be so powerful. Ooooooh, stay back. She's dangerous. She's just a fucking little bitch with ideas above her station."

"Shut … up!" The deep voice was low, even. Saffron Gibraltar took a step forward maintaining the spin on the medallion. "Crayton, move in on her from the right … slowly. When I tell you, use the syringe."

Tempest shuddered. HyperRealm, the dimension she accessed in her astral body, shimmered in and out of focus. Her light body appeared in the altered state construct. "Danger" pulsed in giant red letters on a billboard jutting into a roiling grey sky. In the center of the space, a rock wall surrounded the well from which her energy flowed. Her innate power bubbled and boiled, spilling around the edges of a black plug covering the fount. This was wrong.

She shook her head … once, twice – struggling to focus in the physical reality. She concentrated on the smooth surface of the wood on her palm, the roundness of the pole in her fingers. Black well-formed brows framing maroon and silver eyes swelled in her mind. The ring of silver melted outward, the maroon receding like tidal waters in a bay. A shot of silver light struck the intruding force, releasing the hold on her mind and body. "Thank you, Bastian." Her silent acknowledgment held worry for the ancient being.

"Rogan is coming. I have pushed your location into his mind." Weariness appeared briefly in the gaze before the image disappeared.

"Now, Crayton! Move in now! She's breaking the spell." Gibraltar shoved more power into his hand, down the thin metal cord and into the coin. He added more torque to the talisman.

Shit! The hypnotic lure was a simple technique but the spellmaker had invested a tremendous amount of power in the object and there was a faint hint of familiarity about the designer. She swayed as a wave of dizziness threatened to take her to the ground. If she fainted, she was lost. She split her attention, sending most of it inward, only retaining enough to track the men who had her cornered.

In HyperRealm, her extended body approached the shield overlaying the node from which her power emerged. She pried at the edges with the tips of her fingers. Scooping up handfuls of the small amount of escaping power she saw as a yellow liquid, she created a lever with will and intent. Thrusting it beneath the black lid, she shoved as hard as she could.

A roaring engine echoed through the alley. Figures charged inward from every direction.

Gibraltar snapped the coin into the palm of his hand and spun on his heel trotting to the HWV. "Leave her for now! Our orders were to get out if a confrontation appeared imminent."

The attackers piled into the HWV — front, middle and rear. The driver gunned it. Judah Brightarrow raced ahead of the closest group. He grabbed Tempest at the waist, tucked her close and tumbled away from the speeding vehicle. Glass flew from shattered windows as weapons fired at the fleeing vehicle.

"No I.D. pulse!" A voice yelled from the shadows.

Beneath Judah's protective shield, every muscle in Tempest loosened for a few seconds before stiffening. She struggled against the automatic reaction to escape the trapping body. He had saved her from more pain and she didn't want to repay his shielding her by hurting him. She silently cursed the Covens, and Nelson Treadaway and his sycophants in particular, for the emotional scar. Rogan dropping beside them was the final push needed to toss bad memories into the deepest hole she could make.

Men surrounded the three of them facing away, scanning all directions. She followed Rogan's lead letting him turn her over, Judah sitting up to help him. She placed her palm against Rogan's chest feeling his heart thumping hard enough to break out of his body. Fear etched extra lines in his face.

"Agh." Tempest nearly bit her tongue off from the pain blossoming throughout her body. It was the fourth time something went wrong, damn it. She refocused on the present moment as the teams moved into battle positions, Judah and Rogan dropping over her causing her breath to whoosh out. A black van skidded past the alley, reversed and backed in. The rear doors burst open and a man jumped out swinging a bulging backpack.

"No, Jake." Rogan waved him back. "It's not safe here. Help me, Judah."

Lorcan Wykes, Rogan's First, stepped close, covering their withdrawal. "Are we returning home or continuing with the op?"

"We're continuing with the op." Tempest wanted to return home and crawl into bed, but making contact with Daire D'eath was a key component in their plans.

"We're heading home." The deep baritone of Rogan's voice glazed Tempest's lighter tone.

"Rogan ..." Tempest raised her arm reaching out to her friend.

He shook his head. "Give us a minute, Lorcan. Now, Judah."

Together, they lifted her, completely ignoring her 'I can walk,' and carried her to the van, gently depositing her on a portable stool Jake wheeled into position and locked into place.

"Listen, Jake, you've got to patch me up and help me do something with this dress. Someone grab my jacket and purse and bring them to me. I have to make first contact with D'eath tonight. He's done his homework and he's organized this fundraiser knowing it benefits one of Glory's pet projects."

"Why can't you just make an appointment to tell him we need to expand our excavation into part of his land? It's not necessary to make everything a big production filled with convoluted plots and goals like your grandmother, Tempest. Why can't this be simple?" Frustration sent a fresh wash of acid to eat at Rogan's stomach. The woman was giving him an ulcer.

She snapped at him. "I'm tired, sore, and I hurt. I want to go home, but I have to do this before I can. I called multiple times to make an appointment to see him without any results until the person who answered the last time agreed to a date two months from now. We can't wait that long. If a direct appeal for a time to talk in the next couple of days doesn't work, we'll move forward without D'eath's consent."

She felt Rogan slide the zipper down the back of her dress. The material slipped off her shoulders pooling at her waist. She bit her lip holding back her smile as she considered the picture the three of them made ... her upper body naked except for a black demi-bra, Jake bent over her lap and Rogan tucked against her back in the cramped space. The grin slid off her mouth at the double glare from the men.

She hissed and half rose from the stool when Jake tore the NuSkin from her ribs. "Damn it, Jake, you could have used the releaser." She sissed through her teeth at the burning pain of disinfectant on the half-open slash.

"This wound was made at least a week ago, Tempest. I read the reports my colleagues write about the medical issues they handle. I read them daily. There's been no mention of you being in the clinic. Why is that, Tempest?" Jake pushed the words out through gritted teeth.

Tempest wiggled to loosen Rogan's fingers flexing on her hips. She huffed her exasperation. "Glory wanted me to pick up some things for her from the shopping center and some punks jumped me when I came out."

"She has people to do those things for her, Tempest. Why did she choose you? What did you get for her?" Rogan clenched his teeth. He respected the Beldame, but she took advantage of Tempest's love and affection, placing Tempest in dangerous situations without backup, justifying her request with the admonishment it was Council business or a surprise which must be secret.

Ow!" She pinched one of Rogan's hands to get him to ease his grip. "Her personal assistants were busy with other tasks. I liked helping Grandmother, Ro. I went to her favorite shoe and dress stores and picked up her packages. When I was walking to my car, three young toughs came out of nowhere. One of them got in a lucky slash. Mercy Research was close so I stopped and asked my friend, Tom Cavanaugh, to look at it."

"You should have told me, Tempest. What if an infection set in?" Jake readied a patch and pressed it over the four-inch slash spraying the edges with the fixative. He waved away her response and glanced out of the side of his eyes noting the same worry in Rogan's. Glory Duvayne was going to get Tempest killed. "All right. You're back together. You're going to be sore tomorrow, but other than reopening the knife slash, it's mostly nicks and bruises." He gave her a stern look. "I want you in the clinic first thing tomorrow morning. Now, let's see what I can do about your dress."

Rogan edged the straps back over Tempest's shoulders and helped her into the noisy jacket. He stepped out the side of the oversized vehicle, turned, grabbed her at the waist and lifted her to the ground. He had noted her use of the past tense for working with her Grandmother. Maybe she was finally going to wipe the blinders from her eyes. "Move everyone back into position, Lorcan. We're finishing this tonight ... one way or another."

The teams melted away.

Jake sat at the edge of the floor of the cargo space his feet planted on the concrete road. He twirled his finger at Tempest. "The split makes the dress sexier. The seam should hold as long as you're finished with the gymnastics."

Rogan walked to the passenger door and swung it open. "We'll park a couple of blocks from the front of the building and you can walk down from there." He was shaking his head as he lifted her into the seat, circumventing the argument he could see her preparing. "I'm staying close. If D'eath's guards check us out, I'll blow the deal." His head pounded from the vampire's tap, and his nerves jumped like rabbits chased by a pack of wolves.

He checked to make sure all her body parts were safely inside the vehicle, slammed the door and climbed into the back settling into the chair in front of the shelves of keyboards, laser screens and digi-boxes. The van eased to the mouth of the alley and out onto the street.

# CHAPTER 2

Declan Tath approached the small knot of people, planting a fake smile on his lips. "Councilmember Johnson, Ms. Farmer, I need a few minutes of Daire's time. A few leftover details from today's business just won't go away. I'm sure you understand."

The pencil-thin woman wrapped her arm around Declan's, snuggling against his side. She peered upward measuring his reaction to the white silk dress poured like cream over her body. Her nipples were hard and pressed against the thin material. She licked her lips renewing the shine to the scarlet red gloss. "Barney was just about to give us the real story about that dust up at the current session of Parliament." She sent an air-kiss to the rotund man stuffed into the black tux, his chin double-stacked above the too-tight collar of his white shirt and bow tie.

Declan detached the feline from his arm raising her hand to his lips for a quick kiss. He held his breath heading off the pending sneeze from the overpowering perfume coating her skin, clothes and hair. "Ms. Farmer. As always, it's been a pleasure. Brent and Jasmine are going to escort you to one of our private rooms so you can freshen up." He dipped his head and spoke in a low voice beside her ear. "The rules were very specific, Ms. Farmer, and all media outlets were advised that digi-links are banned from D'eath Towers. You'll step into a reader and Jasmine will confiscate all of your little tools. Brent and Jasmine will then escort you to your hotel."

"You bastard!" She retained enough control to keep the

smile on her lips, her voice low and even, but anger and hate sparked in her eyes. "I'll sue your ass for violation of my First Amendment rights."

A grin, showing strong white teeth, flashed. "I'll advise our attorneys of your imminent lawsuit. In the meantime, you will leave this room as a lady or a squalling cat. I'm banning you and your news organization from all DD Research & Security properties. I will personally review all guest lists of events Daire plans to attend and advise him to bypass every one where I find you or your news organization's names. Good evening, Ms. Farmer." With a tip of his head, he motioned the guards forward.

Cherie Farmer's face whitened, her blusher red slashes across each cheekbone. She sneered in contempt. "Henrik Goudrey will laugh when I tell him what you've said. You're blowing smoke. No one shuts out Henrik." She leaned forward hissing in his face like the cat he called her. "No one." She jerked away from the hand of the tall, swarthy, red-headed male guard, her nose wrinkling at the thought of the genetics required to produce the combination.

Declan whispered in his digi-link. "Cherie Farmer is leaving. Check a three-block radius for her news van. Remove the occupants and pulse the hell out of the vehicle. I want everything they might have recorded erased. I don't care if anything else is expunged at the same time." He glanced over his shoulder noting the faces a little too interested in the exodus. He fixed the visages in his mind with a mental note to have threat level dossiers prepared on each of them.

"What did the little birdy do to have her wings clipped?" Daire slid a hand into one pocket of his black dress pants as he slipped up beside his First. He gave a brief nod to the Australian leader in a nearby clump before allowing his eyes to track around the room.

"There's something you need to see." With a nudge of his shoulder against Daire's, Declan strolled among the guests, his gaze forbidding and focused on the far wall, forestalling any attempts to interrupt their progress. "Farmer brought in at least one micro digi-cam and two digi-links. I said you wouldn't attend any events her news organization, or she, might cover in the future."

Daire smiled and patted a slender white hand reaching for his arm, deftly shifting around the thin, perfumed, barely clothed body. "There's an emergency I must handle, Madeline. You know how it is, but the European ambassador recently received an award. I know he'd appreciate your time." He lifted his free hand, drawing one of the guards to his side. "Please escort Madeline to Jons Charbonneau." He hoped his friend would forgive his siccing the black widow onto him.

He air bussed the model's cheek and turned away, lengthening his stride to leave the room quickly. "How long do we keep the ban in place? Henrik is going to be on us like flies on molasses and he'll aim as many detrimental stories our way as he can make up until he's reinstated with full access."

Before exiting the ballroom, Declan motioned with his fingers, aiming additional guards to rotate throughout the space. "My preference is forever. We don't need his support. The Media Truth and Damages Act requires that there must be a kernel of truth in all reports before they can be broadcast. He can stomp the hell out of the truth, but something has to be at the center of his tirades. Are you worried about what might be said?"

Daire chuckled. "Not with the techs we have at our disposal. Have our PR department reach out to Henrik's opposition and give them some extra sound bites. Run hostile-level dossiers on Henrik, his backers and all his reporters. Find me something to use against him to mitigate our ban." He followed Declan into the security booth. "We both know he's dirty; it's just a case of finding the information, but don't reallocate resources to the effort. I'm not worried about him if nothing turns up."

"I'll talk to Winston. He can use the search as a learning tool for some of his junior techs. Here. Lachland was sampling the feeds from the outer digi-cams." Declan placed a hand on the man's shoulder. "Run it, please."

The air inside the small room cooled as the images flickered on the screens. The three men and one woman seated behind the bank of monitors shivered. They glanced out of the side of their eyes at the stiff figure of their leader and his First. They jerked when Tath's deceptively mellow voice ordered, "Again, please. And slow it down ... now."

Declan's finger traced the path of the fleeing HWV, the windows exploding. "Watch." He tracked the trail of three bullets coming from a different direction barely missing the woman cradled in the grasp of the man. "He must be wearing armor. You can see where the bullets graze his back. In this turmoil, no one has realized yet there was a sniper shooting at their charge."

"Too bad we didn't have voice recorders on those cams. What is Tempest Phillips doing alone in a deserted area near our empty garage? I'm guessing all our security teams are front and center on this building."

"With the World President and one-third of the Enclave's members here, I decided focusing on the immediate area was the best use of our forces."

Daire nodded. "No one could have predicted this little tête-à-tête. I don't like this, Dek. Who's the target of this action — Tempest, us, or both? It's suspicious considering how close we are to beginning the move to Jericho and our declaration of independence."

"Do you want to contact Tempest Phillips' security?" Declan turned and motioned toward the door. He threw instructions over one shoulder. "Watch all of the cams around the perimeter. Report immediately on any activity."

"Let her contact us."

"You think she will?"

"Oh, yes. She'll show up here tonight." There was certainty in Daire's voice.

"Uh, Sirs." Lachland cleared his throat, shrugging away the poke in his side from Mara, the unspoken admonishment for noninvolvement with the upper ranks. His shoulders hunched, sensing the combined focus of his leaders. "I'm sure you already know …." He paused.

"I may have been inattentive at the time whatever information was brought to me and failed to realize its importance. I listen with both ears and all senses, Lachland." Daire infused encouragement into his voice. He hated when his employees hesitated approaching him.

"I ran a search of the digi-audios in the archives with 'Tempest' as a parameter. She called your office five times in the last two months requesting a meeting."

Daire stiffened. "Do you know who was in the office at the time of the calls?" He tried to modulate his voice to hide his anger, but Lachland's stillness gave testament to his failure. Should he make physical contact for reassurance or would that make it worse? He sighed.

"All three of your assistants were on duty at that time, Sir. It came in on the main digi-link and it wasn't transferred to a different station." Lachland wished he had kept his mouth shut like Mara wanted.

"Unhelpful since any of the three could have answered. Check the digi-cams around those times and see if any of them were alone in the suite." A traitor. He pinched the bridge of his nose between two fingers. For a moment, the weight of protecting the thousands of his people across the country and in small undercover groups around the world was too much. He bolstered his sagging spirit with the knowledge that tonight the first groups were migrating toward Jericho and within a few weeks, he would pull in the undercover men and women.

Declan edged Daire aside. "When was the last backup from our main system to Jericho1?"

Mara glanced over her shoulder. "We make nightly updates to the backups, but it's been three months since we tuned up Jericho1 ... all according to protocol." She scanned the maintenance logs. "Our hackers have been busy deflecting a series of attempts on our systems which isn't unusual, but the decision was made to delay synching Jericho1 until tomorrow to allow for deeper scrubbing of the data."

"Run the update to a backup secure server at Jericho and assign techs to make sure there aren't any viruses or hidden Trojans before meshing with Jericho1. Cut the hard lines between Jericho1 and the main system now. Initiate blockers for the wireless connections. We'll run dual systems starting now. Get your heads together and come up with a plan to compare all future data. Find a way to check the last three months. Maybe we'll get a clue about what our opposition wants ... other than our immediate and total destruction."

Daire snorted. "You're a pessimistic bugger, Dek. Since we're the hosts of this gig, we need to get back to the hordes. Thanks, Lachland, for bringing us this information." He paced to the door with Declan at his heels.

"You still believe she's going to show up. Even after a dust up like that you don't think her guards are going to talk her into going home." Declan slid through the door. When it closed, he checked the knob to ensure the locks had engaged.

"No, she's not going home. She's tried to schedule an appointment with me five times. Whatever she wants is very important to her and I think it has something to do with the extra activity on Brace Mountain. I thought I was providing a neutral venue for her to contact me personally."

"So, this gala was just a ruse? How did you know the girl would attend and not The Duvayne?"

Daire shrugged. "It was a calculated risk. Even if the old woman came, we'd still come out ahead. She'd get some free publicity, more funds for her pet charity and she would owe me a small favor. Download the visuals of the attack to a digiport. Pass it along to Tempest's associates." He stopped in the hallway far enough from the rotunda to inhibit listeners. "Have the aerials given us any information about what they're looking for on the mountain?"

"Disrupters and something else are planted all along the ridge. When our hovercams get within one mile, a weird code enters their system and sends them off to another location. We don't know how the code is infiltrating our software. We can't even find the bugger. It's driving Winston crazy. He has a few techs working on it night and day. Are you planning to offer her an alliance?"

"I want to wait to decide that until after we meet face-to-face the first time. Alert George to hold her at the entrance until you come for her. Oh, and move Lachland to a position with more responsibilities and higher security clearances. His initiative brought a potentially disastrous flaw in our protocols to our attention in the face of approaching the two most important people in the company. I don't want that type of talent to go to waste." He drew in a deep breath, forced his shoulders back and ambled through the doors into the midst of the circling sharks.

# CHAPTER 3

Well. She was back in the shadows, staring at assholes full of their own self-importance parade around watching to make sure the teenies on their arms, and their contemporaries, paid homage to their bloated egos. She snorted silently. Glory would use her coldest, harshest voice to instruct Tempest on protocol and respect. She snorted again. What Glory didn't understand was Tempest didn't care anymore.

Tempest still loved her grandmother. And Tempest valued the many times during her teenage years when Glory interceded in the fights between her father, Glory's son, and Tempest. But the last few years Glory had stepped with hobnail boots on the respect that had grown between them during those years. Only tatters remained, and it was those tatters which had pushed Tempest to continue to help her grandmother – against Tempest's better judgment and Rogan's admonishments.

Yes, some family sucked. It was indeed time to cut the wispy strings that still existed between them. No more doing the favors which devastated Tempest's soul based on Glory's entreaty that her request was for the greater good. She would find a better way to protect her heart family and allies from Glory's machinations.

Giving a final tug to the new thigh-highs, she let the hem of her dress fall into place. It was a good thing she had included several extra pairs when they were loading the van with the digital equipment despite the teasing glances and comments of the men.

D'eath Towers was an impressive remodel of a one-time forty-story building. The change in the New York cityscape during the 2020 riots was beginning to disappear thirty years later as new buildings replaced fire blasted concrete rubble. She eased more tightly into the darkness as several black, security luxury vehicles rolled to a stop at the entrance of the armor glass, steel and concrete building. Bodies poured out of the front Tower, surrounding the SLVs and opening passenger doors. Men in dark hand-tailored suits, the crème-de-la-crème of Enclave power brokers, stepped out of gloomy interiors and turned to hand out their female companions all of whom were wearing sparkling jewels, and sylk, velvet and satin gowns of every color and design.

The government structure worldwide had also changed, ushering in the perfect environment for takeover by people with other than normal abilities. "That scientific prognosticator who's courting the World President just arrived. He's got a small cortege of assistants. I wonder if he plans to orate about his predictions for the next superflare."

The digi-casters had swiped the word from an interview of one of the mainstream religious figures who was proselytizing the end of the world. Men and women with all kinds of scientific degrees had their thirty seconds of fame, as behind the scenes advisors attempted to forecast if and when a third superflare would hack the earth with cosmic energies from exploding universes thousands of years in the past.

Digi-casters had added physicians and psychiatrists to their lineup as the Covens rose to power. The doctors pontificated their ideas about the reasons for "normal" people suddenly showing signs of so-called psychic abilities. Physicians pointed to MRIs displaying new pathways burned through many people's brains, while the mind specialists described them as schizophrenics and urged the few remaining government agencies to force them to take medications for the good of all.

A small chuckle escaped Rogan Branaugh as he leaned forward in his seat in the rear of the surveillance van. "He may be the smartest scientist in the world, but he's not going to stay alive much longer if he continues irritating the Covens. Kraftt winning the election for World President was quite a shocker to many people, including me. Everyone knows he's forthright and independent. The special interest groups are in trouble because they can't influence him. He'll give the science guy the boot if the man is too outrageous in his theories. By the way, Treadaway is on the guest list for tonight and where he is so are Valmont and Parkes."

A shudder worked its way along Tempest's spine. "I'll keep an eye out. I can handle them." Barely. The mere mention of their names was more than enough to curdle the milk in her refrigerator not to mention dumping gallons of acid into her stomach. She barred the doors on the bad memories trying to escape and focused on reading the arrivals' auras, deciphering relationships by analyzing how the invisible shells blended. "There're only a few Covens vociferously against Kraftt. Grandmother likes him and she's head of the Council so the majority is going to vote with her to stay in her good graces. I see some corporate bigwigs, a few members of the World Enclave, and a bevy of military brass fluttering into the building with their women."

Rogan tapped a screen on his left. "We've got good pictures from the cameras Lorcan and Judah secured on the building above your head. Winston will have one of his juniors print still photos and add them to our dossiers. For the new faces, our researchers will hunt down all the open and hidden connectors between them and prepare our usual reports. Our new profilers will add their information and we'll get together with Lorcan, Judah, Strider and the team captains in a few days to review everything."

He studied the area, easing the cameras back and forth for

as many views as possible, keeping the motion slow. Hovercams would have been the better choice, but the D'eath security teams were alert and watching everything. Anchoring the dotcams into place yesterday had been tricky while the D'eath teams searched a five-block radius around D'eath Towers at random intervals throughout the day, but Lorcan and Judah had managed with only a few close calls. "I don't like you out there by yourself. Kosh and his team will close in."

Kosh Galveston and his eight-man team were from the military's elite, black ops groups. Rogan had offered Kosh, and advised Kosh he could pass along the offer to any others he completely trusted, a refuge with Rogan's security business. Kosh had passed along the information and several teams had accepted, but Kosh's men had wanted to remain active for another tour. They were a week away from being required to re-enlist when a mission imploded due to deliberately faulty intelligence. Kosh had managed to get himself and his men out of the situation with minimum damage but one entire team died and two other teams were broken, with members physically impaired and released from duty. Rogan had pulled in the members of the broken teams along with Kosh.

"No, Rogan. D'eath recruits from the same sources we do and his people will have almost the same training we do. Besides, Grandmother RSVP'd for one ticket. As her surrogate in Duvayne charity matters, no one will question my presence once I'm inside." Tempest inched backwards. One of D'eath's men was too interested in her section of the building.

"I agree with Rogan. You are the heart of this Family, Tempest. Many people depend on you." Sebastian Bloodhawk's weary voice was barely a whisper in Tempest's mind.

"Sebastian! You should be resting. Rogan is watching out for me." She tried to hide her anxiety. "You must conserve your strength."

"I will stay connected with you until you are back within the circle of your fighters."

Her energy level dived with the finality of his decision then returned higher than before as Sebastian overcompensated for his inadvertent pull on her strength. Her adrenaline ebbed and flowed so fast she was dizzy. She carefully hid her reaction from both men and leaned on the brick wall behind her, the beads on her black jacket crackling as she collapsed against the concrete.

Sebastian would sever his link with her if he thought he was endangering her even as she fought to hold onto him. A Folkin Elder over five thousand years old had more juice than she did even in his current depleted condition. She had duct taped the back of the bag shredded in her fight. She slipped her fingers through the top and withdrew a tissue carefully dabbing the cold sweat from her forehead. The dainty purse had room for her dotmitter, collapsible rod and Glorianna Duvayne's invitation, much more important items than makeup.

"Tell me again why we're skulking around in the dark." Rogan's gruff voice in her ear helped steady her. "Shit! That's why you were out of place. You added some secret bullshit thing for The Duvayne to our mission tonight! Who were those men? What the fuck has she gotten you involved in?"

She rubbed her forehead with the middle finger of her left hand knowing cameras were on her and swallowed a heavy sigh. "There were some anomalies that came up at her Monday meeting in the area. She wanted me to check it out and the main guy said he was Glory's representative."

Suspicion deepened his tone. "Did she suggest you do this alone?"

Her eyes flicked around the area seeking movement among the lengthening shadows as the sun set below the surrounding skyscrapers. She gave him honest responses whenever she could, but it was difficult balancing her commitment to Rogan and heart families with her responsibilities to The Duvayne. "Do I look alone? I've got you and several teams as back up."

"And we were almost too late as it was to give you reinforcements. I don't like this, Tempest. My back is itching like I'm in the crosshairs of a scope. We should abort now and contact D'eath again. We have his direct link code. Use it this time, Tempest. Does The Duvayne know about Bloodhawk?"

"Shit, no, Ro! Do you think I'm crazy? If she knew about him, he would already be out of the ground and in some research laboratory somewhere. I love Glory, Ro, but I'm not blind to her faults. Bastian would give her a major bargaining chip within the Covens as well as in the World political arena. She'd use him in whatever way gave her the best advantage. She wouldn't care about his welfare."

"Once we dig him out of the ground, she's going to know. What are you going to do then?" His voice was normal, at least as normal as the current situation allowed.

"I'm going to complete the bonding process, Ro." She sensed his immediate negation of her statement. "Bastian said when he recovers his strength he'll have the power to protect himself and us with enough left over to help out with our commitments to our clients. Once Grandmother knows whatever affects him will hurt me too, she'll back off." She hoped it would make a difference for Glory, but then it wouldn't make much difference from now into the future.

"She's never been altruistic when it involves her view of how to run the World, Tempest. You can't get in her way." A feeling of foreboding dug its claws into his stomach.

"I won't let her drag us down, Ro, but I have had to give her a minimum amount of my time and attention to keep her happy." And Glory's focus away from her friends, she silently added. But that was at an end now. During the assessment meeting with her people, she would lay everything out and they would decide ... together ... how to protect everyone.

A flicker at the edge of her eye caught her attention. "Hold it. There's a patrol heading this way. I'm going silent for a few minutes." She inched backwards into the doorway, jamming her body between the framing, and tapping a gem on the jewel-encrusted silver cuff on her left arm. Bands of light intertwined projecting the image of an empty door.

A roving band of four guards worked down the sidewalk heading in her direction. At every alley entrance, one advanced and took a quick look with weapon ready. A nod and the others disappeared into the dark only to reappear a few minutes later, their bodies loose but alert.

The flickering light from her side of the projection lulled her into a slight trance enticing memories to bubble up. Wonder flooded her again that Sebastian's subconscious had chosen her when she was ten years old, out of the billions of people on Earth, to link with in the first of a three-step process. His presence in her mind and soul as she grew up had been like standing in front of a pot bellied stove filled with fiercely burning coals, adding strength to her backbone during the times she felt like giving up. He hadn't had the physical or mental resources to do anything more than cushion her soul during the roughest circumstances and his inability to do more to help drained his finite energy reserves.

She held her breath listening to the crunch of boots only a few feet from her hiding place. The projection flickered as the two searchers turned away. One of the men stopped and looked over his shoulder. Tempest let the air in her lungs siss out soundlessly a little at a time. She should be thinking about her approach to catch Daire D'eath's interest, but her mind wandered backwards while the guards argued in the mouth of the alley.

# CHAPTER 4

Her screams of terror woke her parents and brought Tempest's nanny, scrabbling into her robe, running from her room on the lower level of the mansion.  Robert and Anna Phillips had returned to their rooms leaving Doris with the effort to calm and quiet Tempest.  The second superflare had struck earth, wakening the damaged lifepod which cradled Sebastian's body in a suspension chamber.

For six hours, Tempest had screamed while the diagnostics worked through the pod shutting down unnecessary systems before evaluating whether Sebastian's essence was viable and activating the healing mechanism.  With the revival of his base consciousness, self-preservation had kicked in connecting his lifeforce to the most compatible healthy being, while the healing element worked on reviving the cells and tissues in his body.  The link solidifying into a permanent bond had jabbed Sebastian's consciousness into action.  He set up heavy duty shielding around the small tie before blacking out again, effectively shutting down the sharing of thoughts and emotions.

Tempest periodically felt his guilt about the bonding.  She had told him many times that action taken during basic survival was excusable ... if any justification was necessary at all – which she didn't think it was.  She would have done the same at a conscious level if she had been him and it was within her power and knowledge.

During the chaos which had reigned while power grids,

communications, and transportation recovered, reports flooded the airwaves about the awakening paranormal talents in millions of people with dormant, nascent or active abilities. Hospitals were flooded with people seeking chemical neutering of the unwanted senses. Martial law was mandated as groups, bound by fear and hatred of the unknown, rioted in the streets.

The roar of a three-car convoy screeching to a halt in front of D'eath Tower spurred the security team down the sidewalk and returned Tempest to the present. She remained still, noting one guard lingering slightly behind his teammate. He was still suspicious.

A four-star general emerged from the middle vehicle across the street. He jerked his jacket straight. Lights glistened on the gold and silver medals pinned on his chest, the stars on his shoulders.

"Ro, Sebastian is on alert. He said he could give you a push if he thinks I need help." She subvocalized, just loud enough for the electronics to pick up but not loud enough for human ears. She appreciated the team's concern. As leader, she often quashed her initial reaction to take action and allowed the men and women to step in front of her in dangerous or stressful situations. She didn't like them using the trump card of her responsibilities as their leader. She needed them to understand that she treasured their lives as much as they valued hers, but that message had to wait for a different time and place.

Rogan grunted. He didn't want the alien entity near his mind again, until the headache from the last connection dissipated, but he could live with it to keep Tempest safe. They had discussed as many scenarios as possible and the current plan was the best course. Damn it! He gritted his teeth. "Give Bloodhawk a heads' up. Ask him to use a lighter touch on his taps."

"How's the move going?" Tempest threw out the gambit to distract him from second-guessing their strategy. Relief flooded her as the general's presence pulled all the guards across the street. "Whenever we're responsible for one of these events, we need an extra person at the arrival point whose sole responsibility is to stay on the door. It appears dignitaries have their own ideas about why there are people checking them in which doesn't include doing a job."

"I'll make it part of the prep instructions." He shrugged to relieve the unease skittering down his spine. "If it had been possible to continue with the original plan, just a few more months would have had housing for everyone finished. With half the team and their families already there, and the rest being escorted to the compound tomorrow, there's going to be some bunking together. Margreet and Thomas are coordinating the living arrangements. They'll settle everyone until all of the houses are completed."

The logistics of moving over two hundred team members with their extended families ... mates, children, brothers, sisters, and a few parents and grandparents ... was a nightmare. His eyes flicked restlessly from screen to screen, his fingers teased the controls on the counter. "We'll have twenty fighters with us until we pull out."

"I'll be okay, Ro." Tempest's voice was solemn.

The hushed tone stirred his memory of their first meeting. Word had spread through the military that The Duvayne was hiring men who had specialized training. The information had arrived at a propitious time: just like Kosh, he and the remains of his eight-man team had barely survived their last mission. He had needed to get them out before their betrayer succeeded in whatever dirty plans the brass had agreed to. The security team had cleared him through the gate at the Duvayne East Coast Estate.

Tempest bounced off his chest as he walked the driveway to the main house. Black circles beneath tired, haunted grey eyes had stared at him from a sharply defined gaunt face. Dirty blonde hair hung dull and lifeless to beneath her breasts; a taupe shapeless dress with a square neckline framed the distinct structure of bones below her throat. The too thin body shivered and shook in the cold air. Chills had hopscotched down his spine.

Several men had charged from between manicured shrubs lining the pathway. Rage, pain and despair had morphed the grey eyes to almost black. Seeing her escape cut off, her body shuddered beneath the supporting grip of his hands. Her face shut down and she stepped away turning to face her trackers.

He blurted an offer of allegiance. She blinked. Her hoarse "yes" was barely audible over the angry shouts of the men. Her voice jerked him back to the present.

"Uh, oh. Reverend Paul is here as well as Bishops Dornan and Klopak. D'eath needs a new social assistant. Combining mainstream religious personalities with Coven leaders is dry tender waiting for the match to start the firestorm. If those mainstreamers had been more open-minded about the woo woo stuff, they wouldn't have lost their flocks, status and power to the Covens. Here we go." She pushed away from the brick wall. "Congressman Lovett has arrived with his entourage. I'm heading across the street."

Tempest deactivated her 'link, stuffing the tiny earbud and mouthpiece into her purse. She threw her shoulders back and added an extra swish to her hips. As she approached the small group surrounding the Congressman and his ladies, draped one on each arm, she studied her own reflection in the windows. The white blonde shoulder-length mass of curls had been gelled into submission. The pulled back style on the sides emphasized rather than softened the determined angle of her jaw line.

The black, spangled, waist-length jacket over the knee-length black dress concealed the muscles in her arms which pampered ladies avoided. Her faux-leather low-heeled ankle boots covered in Swarovski crystals in the shape of intersecting small and large squares, with quartz crystal points centered in several larger squares, were out of character for the occasion, but she could run in them if necessary and the crystal points were loaded with extra energy ... a backup, just in case. She had bypassed the crystals in the back parking lot going direct to her innerscape because of the threat level. The starkness of her outfit confused the color of her eyes to a grey green.

Smiling into the quizzical look from one of the Congressman's attendants, she followed the group. At the door, the woman on the Congressman's right arm handed a white and gold invitation to the stern guard, who turned and handed it to a man behind a carved cherry wood pedestal. The man looked at the Congressman, checked the monitor just visible over the front of the tall desk and nodded.

Tempest moved into the vacated space handing her card directly to the second man. "Mr. Dawkins." She tried on a polite smile.

A fleeting grin raised the corners of his mouth: she was the second person to read the nametag and call him by name. George Dawkins entered the name into the computer. A red flag window pulsed on his screen for several seconds before disappearing. He flicked a small switch at the edge of his board and motioned to a man standing in a pool of grey shadows behind him to take his place. Walking around the small podium, he offered her an arm. "Ma'am, if you would step this way for a few moments?" He escorted her to a grouping of chairs and sofas.

Tempest settled onto the arm of a chair noting the slight shrug Dawkins made. He must have a new weapons harness beneath his left shoulder. A faint query in Tempest's mind distracted her. "It's okay, Bastian. Security is very tight. Grandmother decided at the last minute not to attend so her assistants wouldn't have had time to call the D'eath organization about the change. It would be her photo attached to the invitation, not mine. They're just being cautious with the President of the World Enclave here."

His presence faded to an imperceptible ghost. She flinched as acid flooded her stomach from rising fear and tension. The hibernation pod designed to save his life was turning on him and slowing draining his essence. She sensed he was close to self-termination to keep from dragging her with him when he died. Until he tasted her blood, he could sever the link without much harm to her. Tempest took a few seconds to direct a slow, surreptitious stream of comfort, warmth and healing energy to him.

# CHAPTER 5

An increase in the volume of voices from behind the partition separating the huge foyer into entrance and ballroom drew her from her reverie. Three men stood at the edge of the frame. A pale feminine hand held onto the arm of the leader. As she watched, he detached the importuning hand, raised it to his lips and air kissed it. He said a few words, bowed and stepped back. He turned away and, for a brief instant, his face reflected distaste. She read the flicks of his fingers held waist high sending the men behind him into defensive positions nearby.

The black formal wear was expensive and tailored for his body. His long stride was more suited for denim and boots or a figure-hugging stealth suit made of soft, supple faux leathers. His tanned face implied long hours in the sun or a mixed heritage. Her guess was a mixed heritage. His amber gaze locked onto her. It was a stare meant to threaten and control. She held her amusement inside. Living, training, and fighting beside over two hundred testosterone-laden, strong-willed men had inoculated her against the best intimidation tactics, not to mention Glory Duvayne's patented glare.

Declan Tath accepted the white card from Dawkins without looking away from The Duvayne's granddaughter. The overhead lights bounced among blonde curls, picking out strands of silver, gold and bronze. The white skin on her face, neck and arms was either an indicator of an indoor existence or heavy sunscreen. The cameras hadn't paid justice to the vibrancy of her personality, an allure he was sure Daire would find irresistible, a complication they didn't need right now with the upcoming split from the Enclave which governed the majority of the countries of the world. A voice rattled information into the transceiver in his ear. "We're disappointed Beldame Duvayne was unable to attend tonight, but you are a welcome substitute, Ms. Phillips. I'm Declan Tath." He stepped to her side and offered the bend of his arm. "Allow me to escort you inside."

Tempest rose and snuggled against his side, her hand lying limply on his arm. Seeing a hint of censure in Declan's look at her out of the side of his eyes, she dropped the helpless, fluff-brained pretense and straightened. "Thank you, Mr. Tath. Something came up at the last minute requiring Grandmother's immediate attention. She was very disappointed she couldn't be here. When her assistant mentioned the gathering, I offered to be the Beldame's representative."

"A granddaughter is a more than acceptable substitute, Ms. Phillips." His chiding tone brought a faint flush to Tempest's cheeks.

"I don't exploit my grandmother's status, Mr. Tath. It can too easily backfire – on me or someone else."

He nodded. "My apologies, Ms. Phillips."

With a gasp of surprise, she stopped at the edge of the temporary wall. "This is spectacular! I've read the reports about the design, but I've never had the opportunity to visit D'eath Towers." She presented him with her brightest smile. "I'm sure you have other matters you need to see to. I'll just walk around for a while so I can see everything. I can meet Mr. D'eath after the initial rush subsides."

"Allow me to escort you until Daire arrives, Ms. Phillips. I can answer any questions that might arise while we walk."

The surroundings did deserve a long walk. Exotic birds chattered in the confines of floor to ceiling cages containing small trees with lush foliage providing an abundance of hidden nesting areas. Water murmured and splashed in rock-strewn fountains on tables, large earthenware crocks in corners, and soaring metal sculptures. Colorful fish in many sizes swam through a maze of transparent tubes attached along the walls at intervals among a profusion of trees and plants. Small tea lights lined the mantel of a walk-in fireplace; candles in heights varying from three feet to mere inches grouped near several container waterfalls. Earth, air, fire and water shared the space in many and varied ways. It was a Coven leader's wet dream.

Daire smiled, providing a neutral answer to Harrison Baines, the majority owner of the mega-corp BaneTrust, while removing Nancy Baines' hand from his ass ... again. Handing off the expensive suit he was wearing to Margreet with instructions to burn it was the only viable option for it. The women rubbing against him like sensuous cats left the cloth permanently infused with the aroma of their perfumes. No dry cleaner would ever be able to remove the scents. He could barely endure the cloud of odor he carried with him as he moved from group to group.

He walked the Baines to the cluster surrounding the World President, Martin Krafft, eased them into the conversation, and, at a wink from Marty, he drifted away. He acknowledged the wave of Gus Peridon, Minister of the North European Coalition, with a nod and slipped behind and around a mixed crew of independent island and continent officials to escape the military general heading toward him with a fierce, intent expression. He had nothing to say to the military at this stage of the game.

Daire moved into place beside his surprise guest. Declan turned, stepping away several paces: he was close enough to hear the conversation, but far enough to act as a temporary barrier to the other people in the room.

The vitality of a new personality moving within her personal space pulled Tempest's focus from the meditative state fostered by the green growth, flickering candlelights, and murmuring water. Turning her head, she fell into soft shadow eyes, the grey of a sky at dusk, edged with the black promise of night.

"Ms. Phillips, I'm ..."

"Daire D'eath. Everyone here knows you by presence and name." She was curious. "Did your motto come first," she nodded to the heraldic crest on one wall, "or your name?"

He laughed. "D'eath is a family name." He sobered. "My mother was shot during the 2020 riots. I was born in a deserted warehouse." He was surprised he was sharing a painful personal story with a stranger. "She and I almost died before Dad was able to find us. Mom said she looked into my eyes and knew I had the willpower to dare death." He shrugged. "And that's what she told Dad to name me if she didn't make it." He moved away a few steps attracting the attention of several men around the room.

Nelson Treadaway, CEO of Coven Darksylk, stiffened. Tempest Phillips ... alone with D'eath. He ground his teeth. His new associates had promised to divert Glory Duvayne. They said the young bitch was out of the City and wouldn't return for several days. He would need to re-evaluate the efficacy of the group's network. He had arrived on time so he could speak privately with D'eath for as long as possible. But Tath had intervened ... repeatedly ... making sure no one was alone with D'eath. What did D'eath want from the Bitch Queen and her treacherous understudy?

He caught Glendon Parkes' and Artur Valmont's eyes, tilting his head toward the isolated trio. Covens Embras and Stonehill had the same goals as Darksylk: break the Duvayne women and take control of the Covens. Secret signed alliance documents locked in Darksylk vaults would change the face of the ruling Council at the next Convocation. Then he would supervise the transport of the Duvayne bitches, old and young, to reinforced rooms where they would stay ... for however long it took to re-educate them. Contain or destroy Duvayne and the power was his. He eased out of the swirl of people around him and used a small spell to blur his features.

Tempest stiffened and slammed her heavy-duty rock

shields into place. She inched around until a wall protected her back. Someone was using magic in the room. She scanned the crowd ... Parkes and Valmont! Treadaway ... where was Nelson Treadaway? She swayed back and forth searching the crowd, looking around Declan Tath standing in front of her.

A memory rose, like Minuteman missiles exploding into the sky from underground bunkers, drawing goosebumps from every surface of her body: cuffs gripped her wrists and ankles holding her naked body open and vulnerable to the eyes and hands of five men. A special gag bottled her screams in her throat. She twisted and fought the restraints, the men laughing and jeering while drinking ritual wine. Disillusionment, humiliation and rage were a potent brew sending her further within herself than she had ever been, finding a reservoir of unlimited raw power. She gulped the energy, writhing as it burned new pathways inside her. She slammed all of it against the magic holding her, but the men, all Coven CEOs with years of experience and ability, controlled the centuries of blood magic woven into and around the altar.

A hand physically surrounding her wrist pulled her back into the present. She sent a vague smile at Daire and Declan closing around her, forming a protective barrier. Alerted by their movements, guards moved into predesignated positions, weapons unslung, but not yet at ready.

Treadaway dropped the small spell as he joined Parkes and Valmont several yards from D'eath.

Ice blue eyes loosened Tempest's shaky hold on reality sending her back into the memories. Treadaway approaching the carved stone, running his hand over her breasts pinching her nipples. Valmont moving in on the opposite side, attaching clips tightly to her bruised nipples sending pain shooting through the nerves. He stepped back, his eyes following Treadaway's hand down her body, licking his lips. Treadaway's right hand rose into view clutching an athame. Other figures closed in. At the first cut of the blade on her lower stomach above her womb, her back arched.

Blood welled from the cuts, running down the sides of her hips. A bead dropped onto the altar. Power exploded like the blast of a bomb, hurling the men away. White bolts stabbed erratically around the room like arcs of electricity.

The bolted door shattered and Glorianna Duvayne, followed by Mikuh Braeden, her security captain, and his team, burst into the room. The Duvayne waded through the uncontrolled turbulence. Seeing the partially carved rune in her granddaughter's skin and the way the bastards had staked her out like a sacrifice to bloody gods, Glory came close to losing control of her own magik. She swallowed her rage, ripping off her jacket and pressing it on Tempest's abdomen. With the blood staunched, the wild energy faded and she easily contained what remained. Only she had the right to determine how Tempest was used.

She called Tempest to sanity with a soft hand on her face. Turning from the altar, The Duvayne stared at the men kneeling on the floor in front of Mikuh's team, hands behind their heads, legs crossed at the ankles. Fury shot from her eyes daring Treadaway to express aloud what his body was reflecting about his treatment. Her voice was calm, quiet. "Come near Tempest again without permission and I will destroy you, your friends, and all your family lines. I'll neuter you and every male with even a drop of your blood in them. Your descendants will cease to exist."

With Mikuh carrying Tempest, and his men protecting their backs, Glory stamped from the room. The Duvayne moved Tempest onto the East Coast Duvayne Estate that night. Tempest assumed the men had obtained her parents' consent to perform the ritual based on Glory's performance. Glory's actions since that incident had clarified things in Tempest's conclusions. Yes, her parents may have known, but Glory had had some hand in the affair. Tempest just hadn't been able to find the smoking gun.

Tempest fell into the now with the help of Treadaway's

arrogant smile and Sebastian zinging her with small bursts of power. Bastian had been unable to help her during most of her growing up years. The machines around him had misfired several years after the initial bonding, putting him in deep sleep. Their essence connection provided some support, but with his body in stasis he was unable to directly affect the physical reality. Even though it wasn't something he controlled, guilt plagued him when periodically her traumatic memories escaped her control cascading into his consciousness. It was the second superflare rolling through which ignited a different system shunting the deep sleep controls into a slow awakening.

"Tempest! I am sending Branaugh!"

She twisted her arm, loosening Daire's grip, before sliding her palm down, clutching his hand, soaking in the strength he was emitting. "No, Bastian." Deep breath in ... let it out. "I'm okay."

Frustration formed a knot in Sebastian's chest welling into his throat and threatening to choke him. He wanted to search her mind for his own reassurance, but it would be a breach of trust, which he couldn't justify to himself. "I'm here when you need help."

A circuit flickered. Fear stabbed him like a knife to the heart. He thanked the Lady and Consort the activities at the gala were distracting Tempest. There wasn't much time left. His plans were in place if she and her people were unable to get him out of the pod. When he reached his limit, he would cut Tempest free. He would not take her with him into the Shining Star.

# CHAPTER 6

Tempest drew comfort from Daire for a few seconds before releasing him. She leaned in and whispered near his ear. "I know you're curious about the excavation near your upper property line. I need to talk to you. I'll call tomorrow to schedule an appointment."

"I'll look forward to talking with you again." He deliberately made his response as bland as possible. He made direct eye contact with the leader of the trio invading his space and interrupting his time with Tempest. He had hoped to give her his private number but that was impossible now. He forced the other man to shift his gaze. Daire raised an eyebrow at the snarl Treadaway allowed to escape his throat. It was apparent the man wasn't used to losing a contest of wills.

Hearing the promise layered beneath his words, Tempest slid away from Daire and Declan, standing on her own. A changing pattern in the flow of people in the room snagged her attention. More guards, their weapons in view not hidden at their sides, left the protection of hidden alcoves and entered the main space. They shifted a little at a time without any overt movements, placing more bodies near and around Daire and the World President.

She let the edges of her mouth twitch up but held back the full grin she wanted to make. "Treadaway." She took the offensive, enjoying the flash of temper breaking through his control.

Dominance and submission were the underpinnings of the hierarchy in most Covens. She would never address another as "Master" or "Sir" and she now had the will and juice to enforce her position. He had tried to break her once. She knew he would try again. Bring it, bastard! She wanted to hurl the words into his face.

Tempest moved away from the men and sidestepped one of the servers circulating the function with drinks. A sharp pain sliced across her left forearm. She glanced down and staggered forward as a woman bumped her from behind.

"Excuse me, mamselle. I am so clumsy." Cherie Farmer ducked her head and kept her body turned away from Daire and his overprotective subordinate. Henrik's money in the right pockets had given her another chance to find some meat for her next expose. It had taken some finagling to find the right person and it had to be another guest. None of the damn guards would betray either D'eath or Tath. A small niggling drip of admiration forced its way out of her conscience before she dismissed it. Doing a favor for one of Henrik's associates, a little bump to some unimportant woman, was a minor blip on her landscape.

One of the roving guards grabbed Tempest's upper arm dragging her upright. She grinned and nodded her thanks. Treadaway's maneuvering had done more for her in that brief exchange than she could have accomplished by herself. It had roused Daire's protective instincts. It was an effective icebreaker, a chink in his usual standoffish business persona.

Daire's eyes narrowed, noting the convergence of action around Tempest. The lights flashed on something in the server's hand. A few flicks of his fingers sent four guards to corral the server and the woman who bumped Tempest. He inserted a hand into his jacket pocket and pressed the second button on the device hidden there, activating full alert.

Protectors entered the room, the silver design on their black armor-padded jackets glittering in the overhead lights. Voices began to rise as the crowd noticed the influx of heavily armed men and women. Extra personnel moved into place near security monitors on strategic floors providing backup eyes and ears. Tacticals spread throughout the building and garages, and outward to a two-block radius of the Tower.

Treadaway was an irritant, but a wealthy, powerful contact. Daire didn't like the hostility the man was showing to Tempest, but he didn't know enough about the Covens, Treadaway, or even Tempest, to risk alienating anyone at this stage. Until he had more information, the break with the Enclave was public, and with most of his people at the Jericho sanctuaries, he had to be circumspect in his actions, whether he wanted to or not. But he would now treat as suspect anything Treadaway said until other sources confirmed the intelligence.

He shifted his stance and the air currents lifted Tempest's light scent to his nostrils from where she had rested against him a short time ago. Her scent barely made it past the stale perfume coating his clothes. He normally kept his emotions under tight control, but Tempest stirred many buried feelings and opened new pathways he wanted to explore ... with her. His body throbbed and ached as he inhaled her, feeling her slide into a place deep inside he hadn't known existed. Rich vibrant urges ran straight to his groin. He moved uneasily as his member stiffened making him glad the jacket was long and concealed his loss of control.

Daire felt Dek move from his side. "Nelson." He nodded to the two other men. "It was good of you to come tonight. Have you made your donation yet for Beldame Duvayne's charity? I'm sure she'll appreciate your generosity."

"Why was Tempest Phillips here? What business do you have with her?" With the withdrawal of D'eath's main bodyguard, Treadaway pushed power into his words stepping forward several paces to add physical intimidation to the mix. His own energy flashed back at him as it touched D'eath's aura. Unbelievable! There were no records that the D'eath family had supernormal abilities.

Treadaway's brashness and audacity temporarily stunned

Daire into silence. A squelching set down was leaving his mouth when Dek appeared. He swallowed the abrasive reaction.

Declan smiled and tipped his head. "Gentlemen, please excuse us. I believe President Krafft is ready to make his appeal. I know you don't want to miss it." With a twitch of his shoulder, he directed Daire to the back of the room. They meandered through the chattering crowd moving in the opposite direction.

Martin Krafft's booming voice and hearty laughter filled the air inviting a response.

George Dawkins dropped into place beside his employers and friends, opening his hand to show a small plain box. He pressed a button on the side jamming any digital cameras or audios. "We've got the two people sequestered. You're not going to like it."

"I already don't like the fact that someone decided he, she or they could come into our place and accost one of our guests. And that they had the confidence they could do it without consequences."

Declan finally let Daire feel the rage he was hiding. "The woman who bumped Tempest Phillips was Cherie Farmer."

"What?" Daire stopped, giving them an incredulous look. "How the hell did she get back on the premises? Without one of our guards seeing her? I hope you have our traitor."

Dawkins shook his head. "Relax, Daire. It wasn't one of our people. We know Jeffers smuggled her back in during one of the rotations. I'm already working on new protocols to close that hole in our defenses. She'll only say to talk to Goudrey, that we're stepping on her rights and to let her go immediately. The server is still silent. We confiscated a needle exactly like those used by the black ops groups to dispense drugs or poisons. I've sent it to our labs for analysis."

"Fuck!" Daire jammed his fingers through his hair. "Do we have any idea where Tempest Phillips is?"

"She walked down the sidewalk to a black HWV parked three blocks from here. There were men in hiding following her like we were, as well as a group gathered outside the HWV waiting for her. She got in. They drove off. The others we knew were nearby disappeared, too. We heard some engines starting up in the distance. We're not sure if they were with her or stalking her."

"Shit. She said she would call. I don't want to wait. See if you can get her digi-number. And find out which one of the assistants in my office is our betrayer." He glanced toward the stage and met Martin Krafft's eyes. Daire lifted a hand, received a nod in reply, and stalked to the door. "Make sure everyone gets out of the building, George, then lock us down. Hang onto Farmer and the server. We'll make Goudrey come to us looking for his songbird. And let's see if anyone comes for the server. I'll decide what to do with him the day we move to Jericho if something doesn't happen before then. Come on, Dek. I need a drink. Christ. I need several."

# CHAPTER 7

The regular flashes of light from the streetlamps were mesmerizing. Tempest rested her forehead against the cool glass of the passenger side window. She licked her lips and swallowed often in an attempt to coat her suddenly dry throat. Her right hand absently smoothed the scratch on her left forearm. She coughed to clear her throat. "Daire said he would take my call. I'm worried about Bastian, Ro. I don't know if we have the time to play nice with Daire. I think we need to speed up the excavation."

Rogan snatched a look at her profile before returning to the road and the vehicles in front and behind them. The flush on her cheeks added to the concern he already felt. He activated the link to Jake who was behind the solid panel separating the front seats from the cargo space lined with computers, weapons cases, and medical equipment. "We could do that. Is the equipment breaking down faster than estimated?"

"No. I don't think so. I ... I don't know. I get occasional images and feelings of pain from him, but his mental abilities are so much stronger than mine. He hides a lot of what's going on. He's so lonely and he has such a deep-rooted sense of what's right and wrong." She slid a glance out the side of her eye at her best friend, without turning her head away from the comfort the cold glass offered. "Just like a few people I know."

A smile ghosted across her dry lips. Her body collapsed further into the molded seat. The ache in her head began to pound like a hammer hitting an anvil. Her focus shifted. "I don't want Daire making an impetuous fatal decision. He's got too many people to protect. Maybe we should just go ahead without his permission. It would give him plausible deniability in the future if things escalate out of control."

"Is that what you want to do?"

"I don't know what I want to do other than get Bastian out of that damn pod that's killing him, protect our people, and find out what the hell Grandmother's doing. I'm afraid, Ro. And that's not a good place from which to make rational decisions. Treadaway and his sycophants being at the gala, moving in on Daire the way they did, those men at the back of the Towers claiming Glory sent them. And Grandmother deciding not to attend at the last minute."

She rolled her forehead back and forth across the glass. "This whole situation reeks of Coven power plays. Do we have a leak, a traitor, Ro? Someone who's divulged information about what we're doing, not just with Bastian, but our other plans?" She felt like she was betraying her friends just thinking much less talking about such a thing, the thoughts a consequence of her own insecurities learned from childhood and teenage years of treachery before Rogan saved her.

Rogan set the turn signal and slowed, following the HWV in front of him onto the side road. The leaf encrusted branches of old-growth oak and maple trees formed a green roof over the hard-packed gravel, blocking the stars and half moon. "Our core group would never betray you, Tempest. And those in the second circle I would vouch for without hesitation. But we do have a few new recruits and the people we are training for the corporations and military have noticed their instructors are from the second tier."

Tempest straightened in her seat. Her overheated body abruptly turned cold. A shiver worked its way down her spine, Goosebumps charged along her arms. "Have you been getting complaints? Do I need to step in?"

"We always have people roving the offices, training facilities, and our private properties. There's been an increase in the reports from our ramblers about overheard conversations where questions are being raised about why they haven't seen certain people."

He nodded, anticipating her question. "Yeah, they wonder about you, me, Lorcan, Strider ... and the rest of the core group. Not only that, but the rovers have found people in places they shouldn't be and don't have access to, and the techies have digis detailing the same information. There's also been an increase in false alarms on certain doorways. It could be just the usual testing of our security, but the escalation is substantial. We don't need to change our plans or routines. If we did, it would only give credence to their imaginations. Our people are working it. We should let them do their jobs without our interference ... for now."

The headlights followed the curve of the road to a stone wall. Laughter and voices floated from the open windows of a small wood-frame house two hundred yards from the wall. Several figures rose from chairs and rockers placed at intervals along the porch across the entire front of the home. They moved into the shadows at the edges of the lights from the windows. The merriment from the interior died.

Two men appeared from small structures on either side of the gate composed of lengths of reinforced rebar. The three-car cavalcade stopped, engines idling.

Tempest watched four people, three men and a woman, approach the vehicles from the back. A man and the woman stopped at the back of the third HWV and the two remaining guards paced beside the line up, weapons up and ready. She heard the almost silent whirring of the window beside her lowering, knowing the same action was taking place in the other two vehicles. One of the guards was so young she swore she could see the newness dripping off him. The other guard had a big smile on his face as he strutted to her door. He had stopped at the trailing HWV for a good long look at the passengers before moving forward.

"Hey, baby." Strider allowed his weapon to drop to his side, the strap across his shoulder keeping it secure. He leaned over and crossed his arms on the edge of the window. The smile faded. "Well, shit! You look like hell." He quirked an eyebrow at Rogan, who shook his head. "These bozos aren't treating you right, baby. Next time we'll leave them at home and I'll go with you."

Tempest rolled her head against the seat to look at her friend. She forced a smile onto her lips. "It's been a long day, Strider. Rogan can give you a rundown of the evening's activities. How are things here?" She deliberately laid a trail away from her interaction with the unknowns. She didn't want another lecture about personal safety, Glory's actions, and bodyguards. She just wanted her fluffy, soft, comfortable bed. And maybe a hot shower, if she could stay upright long enough to get wet and dry off.

Strider stepped back and tapped the window ledge. "We've got everything covered here." He waved a hand at the men beside the gate after receiving a nod from the newbie beside the front vehicle. "My shift is over now that all of you are back. I need to update my replacement then I'll be up to the house." He leaned over and gave Rogan a hard look before gathering the young trainee with a glance and walking to the back of the cavalcade.

The gate split at the center, the panels retreating into the walls of the stone fence. The sections touched base and began to close without delay, locking into place with only inches to spare from the back of the third HWV crossing the border.

A mile from the fancy entrance, Rogan stopped in front of a three-story red brick mansion, white columns across the front, glowing in spotlights strategically placed to eliminate shadows. Lights in several windows on the second and third floors spilled across trees, the branches nearest the house lopped off.

Tempest waited while Rogan opened his door and left the idling HWV, talked briefly with the guard who appeared from the side of the house, and crunched his way around the front to her door. He had broken her of the habit of opening her own door and getting out of the transport she was in. It hadn't been an easy lesson to learn and even now her hand itched to grasp the handle, her shoulder leaning to push open the door. Safety first. Always. Safety first.

The door opened and she swung her legs out. She took Rogan's hand and let him pull her upright. Right then, she didn't have enough spark remaining to chide him. "One of those poor trees is reaching beyond its forced boundary again."

Rogan slammed the door and waved the vehicle away. "If we were staying here longer, I'd have Glory's gardener trim it again. It's not going to grow enough during the remaining time we're here to create a problem." He angled a look at the top of her head. "Unlike some people I know."

A soft laugh escaped her throat. "Us rebels have to stick together against you authority types." She poked him in his chest.

She called over her shoulder. "I want to shower, Jake. Any problems with the NuSkin?" At his soft "no," she walked through the door Rogan opened and continued up the stairs to her bedroom on the second floor. She waved fingers in the air over her shoulder to acknowledge Rogan's voice telling her he would bring her something to drink. Her feet shuffled along thick padded carpet which continued into her bedroom. She was almost too tired to wash off the grime.

The bed with its plush softness drew her limp body like a water-starved person to a stream. Hissing and screeching rolled toward her from the hallway. "Maggie! Stop chasing Gracie!"

Two tortoiseshell bodies flashed past her legs. Her foot caught the edge of an area rug and she stumbled against the vanity in her bathroom. Gracie crouched in the corner behind the trashcan spitting, the hair on her neck and back standing erect. Maggie sat on the bath rug several feet away licking her paw then washing her face. "Maggie, leave Gracie alone." Tempest walked to Maggie who glared at her snarling sister before running out the door.

Masculine curses filled the air followed by the crash of a table against the wall. Gracie charged out of the room seconds before Rogan appeared, his hands filled with bandages, a glass and a bottle. Tempest's eyes lit up and she moved faster than she should have. Grabbing the bottle, she twisted off the lid, shook the pills into her hand, selected two and dumped the remainder back into the container.

"Jake said he would give you a shot for pain." Rogan continued as she shook her head, "But I knew you would prefer the slower acting pills." He handed her a half glass of orange juice to wash down the capsules. "The rest of the juice is on the rug in the bedroom."

He dropped the medical supplies on the counter and opened the linen closet withdrawing a washcloth. He wet the cloth and walked out of the room. "Get in the shower while I clean up the mess."

She hissed as the water cascaded onto the scratch on her arm and the abrasions on her hands and legs from the fight, reviving her enough to wash her hair. A short time later, she stood in front of the mirror feeling squeaky clean. She applied salve to the scrapes deciding against bandages.

"Need any help?" Rogan called from her bedroom.

"Nope." She stepped into her favorite flannel pants and eased on the oversized shirt, hugging the soft, warm cloth against her. She padded into the bedroom and dropped into the chair in front of Rogan.

He slipped the socks in his hands onto her feet before checking the last message on the screen. "Tulsa and Smythe have the 'net up at Summerfield. Jack said they've received our money. He says Gene wants to invest the team's funds separate from yours this time. Morgan is printing the documents Gene says you need to sign for several more entities to mask the purchase of the shares. Gene also wrote, 'Next buy.'" Rogan raised an eyebrow.

She shook her head. "Not yet."

He hid his amusement as she stared at him. "The men spread out and talked to people in the area about the HWV driven by those unknowns."

"That man ... the leader ... had one of Glory's personal medallions, Ro. And it was bespelled to specifically capture me. I could feel the intent in the strands wrapping around me, lulling me to acquiescence with the belief I was safe and secure ... and I couldn't break free, no matter how hard I tried." She raised tortured eyes to Rogan's. She lowered her voice to a barely heard whisper. "Only two people know my insecurities enough to set something like that into play ... and it wasn't you." Her heart was breaking even though she had years of experience with her grandmother's ruthless and implacable decisions.

Rogan tamped his anger at Gloriana Duvayne into a dark corner. Allowing it physical expression wouldn't serve any real purpose other than to hurt Tempest more – which he refused to do. "Other people have her personal medallions. One of them could have been careless and left it where someone could 'borrow' and copy it then return it without them knowing it was gone."

"Yeah, it could have happened like that." She shook her head. "I appreciate you giving her the benefit of the doubt. I really do. But we don't have that luxury any more. I can continue to turn a blind eye to her machinations to our detriment or I can stop clinging to some unrealistic fantasy about our relationship and do what I should have been doing all along and protect the people who really love and care about me. And we both know that the medallion could be copied but not the spell bound to it ... that had to be put in place by a practitioner."

"It's not necessarily an all or nothing situation, Tempest." He didn't want her to cut herself off from all her family. It was bad enough she had to sever her relationship with her parents in her teenage years for self-protection. He was relieved to know Tempest had started to initiate contact with them the last couple of years.

"No." She shook her head back and forth. "No. The last few times I've done things for her something has happened." She flinched when his eyebrows shot up then lowered in a frown. "I would have told you, Ro, if I considered it more than just a coincidence. But that's all I thought it was until it was a third and now a fourth time. This latest incident has to be the breakpoint. It has to stop somewhere before the bad thing happens and something occurs which can't be fixed."

Her melancholy tugged at him. It was time for a topic change. "You mentioned in the car D'eath said he will accept your call."

"I think there was more he wanted to say, but Treadaway and his buddies appeared and it was downhill from there. There was no way I could have any private conversation with Daire at that point. Treadaway had an agenda and he wasn't going to leave before he completed it. You know how he is."

"Someone needs to kill that bastard." Cold rage settled in the pit of his stomach. He wanted to be the one to do it after the hell Treadaway put Tempest through and continued to put her through. He could stare the man in the eye and pull the trigger or swipe a knife across Treadaway's throat without hesitation. "Was that why Bloodhawk tried to contact me? The connection fizzled almost as soon as it began."

She shivered. "No. Bastian got a flash of an errant memory. Seeing the three of them together like that ... it just surprised me, that's all."

She eased around in the chair to relieve her stiffening muscles, the ache in her side. Her eyes drifted shut. Her head jerked and her eyes popped open.

He wanted clarification about the situation, but he let it go. It was time to pour her into bed. He regretted agreeing to let her go in alone. He had known it was a mistake when she made the suggestion, but the others had seen the logic behind her reasons. She had laid the trail and guided them in the direction she wanted to go. He snorted. He would have laughed at their stupidity if the result had been different.

"Are you calling D'eath tomorrow?"

Tempest scooted out of the embrace of the chair. She walked to the bed and pulled back the bedspread, raised the pillows and drew the blankets aside. "Yeah. Treadaway was actually an asset in a way. His fetching personality assures Daire will be more inclined to help us."

Tempest crawled into the bed turning onto her uninjured side and hugging a pillow to her chest.

Rogan wiggled his eyebrows. "You keep saying 'Daire.'"

She grinned and yawned. "I like pain pills. The light, fluffy kind of pills. They make my head all swirly." Her eyes drooped, but she forced them open. "Did they pinpoint the location of the pod?"

She should stay awake. Plans needed to be developed.

Rogan softened his tone. "Tulsa is making the final calculations tonight. We'll have it in the morning."

"Good." Her voice slurred. "I'll call in the morning to set an appointment …." Her eyes shot open. "Call Mikuh and tell him about the unknowns. Tell him grandmother is scheming again."

"I've got it." He skipped sideways as he walked to the bed just missing Gracie and Maggie running past. The cats scrambled onto the bed settling in different places beside Tempest. She shifted to accommodate the furry rascals. He flicked the blanket over the threesome, snapped off the lamp beside the bed and pulled the door shut leaving a small opening in case the cats wanted to leave.

"She's asleep?" Lorcan Wykes, Rogan's First, checked the lock on the window then looked at the monitor in his hand noting the light was green.

Rogan nodded. "She's depressed and disillusioned. I

wish her damn grandmother was a nurturing woman rather than the manipulative bitch she is."

Lorcan leaned against the wall. "So Tempest is finally acknowledging what we've always known. The Duvayne's objectives don't include our welfare, or more precisely, Tempest's well-being."

"Yeah. I hate to see her hurting." He set his shoulder against the opposite wall. "Where's that damn pod?"

"Good news, bad news." Lorcan shifted his hand back and forth. "We were definitely close where we've started digging, and part of it is on our lands, but the section which contains the medical bay is on D'eath's property. From the model the techies have managed to produce, there's no door from the piece on our side to the other segment. If we try to blow a hole, or try to cut an opening, we risk an explosion, which will take the mountaintop and anyone on the ground with it. We could put up rigging so technically we're on our side, but we're still going to have to open the ground and it's down deep. Judah and Rock are timing the digi-cams D'eath sends up the hill to watch what we're doing. The techies have succeeded ... so far ... in diverting them to other areas."

Rogan stared out the window rolling the information around. "Have we got any information on the unknowns who made a try for Tempest?"

"Tulsa said D'eath's people sent us a digi of the action." He nodded when Rogan's eyebrows shot up. "Yeah, it surprised us as well. I expected we'd have to go in and lift the recording from their servers. The interesting bit is at the end. It's a good thing Judah has fast feet. We have another potential problem. Someone shot at Tempest. If Judah hadn't covered her and taken her down, we might be having a funeral right now. If that's not enough, D'eath also sent along a needle which he believes was used to scratch Tempest."

Rogan jerked upright away from the wall. "The hell you say!"

"Yep. The bullet creased the back of Judah's armorvest. Jake has the needle and will get us a report as soon as he can. Stevie pulled out recordings from some other buildings in the area. Hawk's techies are still gathering information on the unknowns Tempest faced, but it wasn't hard to identify the bogies on the rooftop." He disliked saying the name as much as he despised the man himself. And he really hated being the one to stimulate Rogan's memories, re-igniting Rogan's nightmares which had dissipated somewhat during the last year.

"One of Treadaway's people?" He braced himself. The stress beneath Lorcan's matter-of-fact report meant a bigger blow was coming. His mind jumped through a list of other possible suspects, but no one readily popped up.

Lorcan shook his head. "Treadaway might be a peripheral player in this game. Stevie enhanced the stills as much as possible. Shit, Rogan. It was Sugarman and his crew. And where Sugarman is Busch isn't far behind."

The strike when it came almost took Rogan to his knees.

Rage. Sadness. Pity. Horror. Pain. Rage. Pain. Horror. The litany of emotions clicked into a continuous loop yanking Tempest from a drug-induced sleep. Fleeting images flashed in and out of her mind, mixed with the tendrils of her dreams, creating new horrific scenes. She pushed her body up and rolled out of the bed, landing on hands and knees on the floor. One of Gracie's claws blazed a trail across the scratch mark Tempest received at the gala as Gracie scrambled to stay on the bed and not follow Tempest to the carpet. Crimson and black blood trickled along Tempest's forearm to the top of her hand braced on the floor. She toppled onto her hip and braced her back against the side of the bed. Reaching to the top of the side table, she plucked a Kleenex from the dispenser and slapped it onto her arm. She staggered upright and stumbled to the door.

The emotional cacophony crescendoed as she dragged her bedroom door open. She squinted in the bright overhead lights in the hallway. "Ro? What's happened? Are you okay?"

Rogan hauled in his exploding feelings, slamming them behind the shields Tempest had helped him build. Whitman Busch. There was nothing Rogan could do then to mitigate the betrayal of his eight-man team, the pain and suffering of the families of the five dead members of his team, and the horror of his sister, tortured by Busch's business associates, dying in his arms, her last breaths absolving him of all responsibility, her fingers pressing into his hand irrefutable evidence of Busch's culpability in all of it. And the additional perfidy of their superiors who took the original evidence and destroyed it, refusing to prosecute the fair-haired media darling.

Rogan pulled himself together. That was the past. The time would come when Busch would make a mistake and Rogan would be there to get the retribution his sister and men deserved. He would recover the hidden copies of the original evidence and use them as background. With the originals gone, there was nothing he could do. For now, he had to concentrate on the present and near future.

He quickstepped to Tempest and scooped her up, carrying her back to bed. Jake had promised the low-dosage pain medication would knock her out for six hours. It was unforgiveable his loss of control pulled her from the healing sleep she needed.

"Go to sleep, darlin'." He tucked the blankets around her, making accommodation for the cats curled into the warm depression Tempest's body made before she left the bed.

The medication dragged at Tempest. She fought the pull. Rogan was hurting and she needed to make it right. He was her best friend, confidante, big brother, and protector. He was the only safety she had to cling to in the uncertainty her life had been and appeared to continue to be. Their relationship was set long before she became aware of how strong, virile and just plain hot he was. They had a very embarrassing talk one day about why they didn't take their relationship to the next level. The relief they both felt had turned into belly laughs, as they each realized the other was concerned about how to explain their nonsexual feelings.

She patted his cheek and managed to form a semi-complete thought. "Hurt?"

He pressed his hand over hers against his cheek, accepting her comfort for a few seconds. "It's okay. Bad memories."

She nodded. "Yeah. Bad memories all around tonight. We'll make things better tomorrow." She blinked rapidly holding onto conscious thought.

He nodded in agreement. "Yes, tomorrow things will be better. Sleep now." He ran a finger down her cheek, rose and backed out of the room, turning off the light and closing the door. He turned, almost bumping into the loitering Lorcan. He lifted his chin, motioning toward the staircase to the first floor.

They walked silently and quickly down the stairs through the foyer and into the open space of the combined family room and kitchen. Lorcan headed to the always-ready coffee dispenser. He pulled cups from the overhead cabinet, poured the dark brew and handed one of the mugs to his commander. "She's becoming more sensitive. Is it a side effect of the bond to the Elder?"

Rogan's voice floated over the door of the open refrigerator as he rooted around looking for the cream. "I don't know. I just wish he had connected with someone else." He backed away and slammed the door shut. "Of course, if we didn't have this situation, there would be something else."

He splashed the contents of the container in his hand into his cup, cursing as the liquid splattered onto the table. Grabbing several napkins from the holder in the middle of the table, he dropped them on the puddles and swiped them up. He crossed to the sink, tossed the crumpled paper into the trashcan hidden in the cabinet beneath it and returned the cream container to the refrigerator. "I just want that damn pod out of the ground now. I don't want to continue pussyfooting around waiting to get D'eath's permission. We should just go in, do the deed, clean up after ourselves and then ask for forgiveness."

He returned to the table and picked up his cup, blowing

on the creamy liquid before taking a sip. He hitched his hip on the edge of the table. "Tempest said she was going to take one more run at D'eath. Call the teams in. Now. I want us prepared to move in either event. Our people should have completed the majority of their assignments."

Lorcan tipped his cup up and took a hefty swallow. He grimaced as the bitter brew bit into his tongue. "Shit! You should have warned me it had been on the burner too long."

"That's why I got the creamer. The first pot is always the one left from the previous shift."

Lorcan turned, poured the liquid from his mug and the carafe from the coffeemaker into the sink, and rinsed the carafe. He opened the cabinet and took out a vacuum container, spooned coffee grounds into the strainer to his taste and started the machine. ""Blaisdel Corp. wants more guards for their upcoming event. Carson and Blake want out. Their assessment is that it's a media ploy and they don't want their faces in the digis."

Rogan frowned, reviewing in his head a list of the two-person teams still within range of a callback. "Pull Carson and Blake out diplomatically. Bronson and Rutledge are the most politically savvy senior team after Carson and Blake and they don't mind the shenanigans. We need to give the younger men on our teams more experience with our way of doing things. By pairing each of our youngest with a more senior fighter, we should be able to put together three six-man teams. I don't want to put any more than that into play, but it's a good training ground."

He paced back and forth, using the movement to stimulate his thoughts. "We must cater to our clients' requests up to a point, but we're stretched thin with protecting the families before, during and after the move to our new compound and liberating Bloodhawk. We're light on fighters. We need to up our recruitment."

"The construction crews are hurrying to complete all the houses while following our guidelines. The foreman wants to clear cut some spaces and bring in more people."

"No." Rogan was firm, explicit. "We won't sacrifice our environment to the dictates or wants of strangers, and no new construction people in the compound. We don't have time to perform more than basic background checks and I'm not putting our loved ones in potential jeopardy due to our lack of manpower."

He glanced at Lorcan propped against the counter, laughter in his eyes. "Yes, I do realize it's the company's way to justify going over budget. We'll deal with that headache when it's presented, and I might just make them submit their arguments directly to Tempest."

"Oh, no, Rogan, that's not just mean; that's diabolical." Lorcan was laughing so hard he had to hold his stomach. "Grace will personally have to make an appearance. She won't accept a substitute. Tempest will look at him saying nothing. He'll start stammering his explanations. Then he'll get mad and try to bluster his way out of his predicament. And he knows he better not get in her face. He will consider the guards posted inside her door, but since he hasn't done business with us before he doesn't realize she would hand him his balls all by herself. Oh, Rogan! I would need to be one of the guards. I'd have to see the confrontation."

Rogan chuckled but sobered quickly. "I wish Poppa Gammens and his sons were available."

"Actually, Bear Gammens called this morning. Poppa told him to let us know there would be crews available in about ten days."

Relief flooded Rogan. "Poppa understands our specific requirements and he won't use any new people he might have. Call and give Bruce Grace the five days' notice. He'll scream to his Coven representative, but he signed our contract and acknowledged upfront we had the option to terminate early."

Rogan chewed his lip. He turned to stare out the double French doors, blind to the scenery beyond the glass. "Send the Call. Put out word to the teams in the military and initial agencies. Run full background checks on whoever responds if we don't know them and basic checks on those we know. I'll tell Winston to shift the standby crew into full time for now. I hate working everyone so hard, but it should only be until we're at Summerfield."

Seeing the question hovering in Lorcan's eyes, he nodded. "Yes. I'm sure. It's dangerous pulling many Kin together in one place. We can offer them protection, which would certainly be safer in the current climate than going solitary." He shrugged. "We can only go forward."

# CHAPTER 8

Bullets thudded into concrete walls. A man jerked, red blossoming at his shoulder and spraying men crouched nearby as he spun around. Smoke drifted through the air. Yells and deep-throated rumbles from vehicles of all types overshadowed a screaming voice shouting indecipherable orders.

Tempest woke from the nightmare strangling a pillow against her chest. Fear skittering through her bones held her stiff and immobile. Cat paws climbing onto her leg released her locked muscles allowing her to take several deep breaths and push the dream away. The paws continued along her side, her skin twitching as unclipped claws dug in. A small body dropped to the bed and a fur-covered butt appeared in front of her nose.

She reared her head back, adjusting her position to curl around Maggie, breathing through the stiffness and pain of the previous evening's injuries. She fought her body's lethargy and swirling head, a result of how deep she had traveled during sleep. She grappled for something to think about to loosen the tentacles of the vivid, horrifying nightmare. Her fingers slid rhythmically across soft fur. Her mind drifted. A blood-splattered hand forced a pressure bandage against a white shoulder. A man's pain-filled groan obstructed low murmured instructions.

Branaugh Security. Tempest jerked her mind from the images threatening to overwhelm her, filling it with real-time data. The business was booming. Using Rogan's name for the company had been the right decision. It had brought companies with high-risk assignments as well as businesses like Blaisdel Corp., rooted in the technology industry, with simple, relatively safe requests. A smile flickered on her face. Good. That's good.

She concentrated on their work. Blaisdel and similar groups offered a low-key setting, allowing them to use the companies as a training ground for young recruits and providing a stress-free environment for the vets Branaugh Security was hiring, who were returning from violent military excursions, to re-assimilate into society. A frown furrowed her brow.

She needed to see the reports for their recent jobs and the intake information for new clients. Was the ratio of simple to dangerous increasing? Meeting the responsibilities to clients and protecting the extended family was stretching the company's resources beyond what she considered safe. Every husband, wife, child, grandparent, sibling, and cousin was part of her own family. Were too many, particularly dangerous, jobs coming their way? Or was she just being paranoid?

Tempest shoved the pillow away dislodging a purring Maggie, who hissed and jumped to the floor, displeasure radiating in every ponderous, thundering step out of the room. She swung her feet over the side of the bed, walked into the bathroom, took care of an overfull bladder, and turned to stare at her image in the mirror. Ugh. Day-old oatmeal had more appeal. And she detested oatmeal.

Swaying on her feet, her head spinning, she slapped her hands onto the sink steadying her stance. Her eyes flickered green, gold, green. For a few seconds, something shoved Tempest aside in her own mind and took control. She dropped to her knees, her head thrown back, a scream of rage echoed off the walls. The entity lost the hold on her body.

Rogan slid into the room in low position his weapon extended. Lorcan followed taking the high range. Tempest planted her hands on her knees, her body bending forward, her head hanging. She swallowed hard and fought to slow her breathing. What the fuck was that? Should she tell the men she was losing her mind – quite literally, losing her mind? They stared at each other for several seconds.

"You screamed." Rogan stood, shoving his weapon into his shoulder holster. He stepped closer offering his hand.

She shook her head and managed to pin a shaky smile on her face. Beads of sweat dotted her forehead and she swiped them away with trembling fingers. Gripping the edge of the sink, she pulled herself upright. An aberration – it was a one-time anomaly. No need to add more drama to their already over-full stage. "It's okay. I've got it. Sorry. Remnants of a bad dream."

The men shared puzzled looks. Rogan tipped his head toward the door and Lorcan backed out of the room.

"Is there something I should know?"

"I saw fighting, bodies falling, blood splashed everywhere. I thought I saw something out the side of my eye. I scared myself, that's all." She wrapped the issue with bits of the truth and offered it as a distraction.

Rogan turned the information over in his mind. He sensed she was telling him the truth, but she was holding something back. He would give her room and let her bring it to him when she was ready … hopefully, before it bit them in the butt. "Ready for breakfast?"

She sent him a grateful smile, turned the handles on the faucet and bent over the sink splashing cool water over her face. No food she could think of in any of the recommended groups was appealing. Even her favorite omelet and meat dish was unappetizing. Her stomach growled. She glared at it in the mirror, the traitorous organ. "I'd die for a cup of coffee."

Rogan leaned one shoulder against the doorway, arms folded across his chest. "It sounds like you need more than that."

Tempest grimaced. "Yeah, well, my mind isn't in synch with my body. One says 'yuck' and the other is rubbing hands together saying 'bring on the food.' The see-saw action makes me nauseous." That and the unfamiliar look in her eyes a few minutes ago. She barely lifted her shoulders, tossing off the eerie feeling threatening her composure.

Preceding Rogan into the bedroom, she walked to the bed and pulled on the lavender knit slacks and short-sleeved over-sized top in the same shade which she had chosen earlier. It was relaxed and cool, without being slouchy. Grabbing an unstructured red jacket and the leather strap wrapped holster and gun, she headed for the bedroom door. Whatever "it" was could wait until the next rainy day when events weren't smashing into her face. "How far down are we drilling on the background checks on our clients? Are we doing more than the usual business and financial checks?"

Rogan paced at her side. He tilted his head watching the side of her face. "Eighty-five percent of the checks are the basic runs. We choose about fifteen percent at random for a full in-depth review as a training exercise for the newbies and refresher for our experienced investigators. What are you thinking?"

"We've been getting a lot of clients recently – much more than usual. Is it an indication that our, well, your, reputation is growing, and people want the best, which I know we are without question?"

"Or?"

"Well, I know this sounds paranoid, but what if someone wants to distract us? What if these phantom 'evil perpetrators',", she tossed him a grin as she made air quotes with her fingers, "are directing business to us with a 'sorry, we're busy, but we know Branaugh Security is an excellent company and they can take care of all your needs?'"

She lifted her index finger. "To meet our current commitments, we've had to reduce the number of people on each job." She added a second finger to the one sticking up. "We always have feelers out for experienced people wanting to transition out of the dark arts military and law enforcement arenas." A third finger rose. "Our move to Summerfield is complicating everything as we have to pull off senior guards and send them to our clients to reassure them where our headquarters is located doesn't affect their contracts." There. Her nerves were settling. Concentrating on business was the stabilizing influence she needed.

He fingered his chin. "To what end? Lorcan and I were just talking about our need for more specialists. Some of our friends and contacts in the military and initial agencies here and overseas are already calling to ask about opportunities in our company." He hesitated before continuing. "I told Lorcan to make the Call." He hoped at least three Kin warriors would answer. With Judah, Lorcan and the three warriors at the points, and himself at the center, a Starburst could form. The resulting blast of energy would ratchet up their strength, speed and senses ten-fold or more. The risk of a Call was ... acceptable.

She forced him to stop with a hand on his arm. She turned to stand in front of him, staring up into his face. "Ro, if it's what you want, we can build more houses, do whatever is necessary to make them welcome." She infused her voice with sincerity and enthusiasm. She didn't want strangers entering her safe zone interfering with the relationships with her heart family. She had first dibs on their loyalty and love – not strangers who abandoned them for what amounted to political expediency on their world. Rogan refused to discuss the details, and Lorcan followed his lead, only letting small things drop in conversations, but she had pieced together enough to know she would have a hard time keeping her fists to herself.

"An expansion would be an excellent time for sneaking someone into our midst with orders to ingratiate themselves ... and more than one person could be inserted in case one of them is discovered. We could also find ourselves infested with moles on several different fronts." Rogan stepped to the side, using a hand to direct Tempest into the kitchen before him. He nodded to Lorcan standing at the stove with an apron loosely tied around his waist.

Lorcan waved a spatula at the line up of dishes and lid-covered bowls on the nearby counter.

Tempest allowed the change of topic. She took the plate Rogan shoved into her hands and with his hip bump she shuffled to the counter. She reached for a half slice of dry toast and watched her hand bypass the bread. Several slices of bacon and half the remaining contents of the bowl of scrambled eggs and platter of diced potatoes appeared on her plate. Her fingers selected a piece of bacon and the hickory-smoked flavor exploded on her tongue with unusual punch as she chewed it with gusto. Fear threatened to close her throat and choke her when she swallowed.

"I guess you were hungrier than you thought."

Rogan's dry comment helped her find her center, and she was herself again, but the hunger remained. She carried the plate to the table, curled up on the banquette and picked up the mug Rogan placed in front of her, refocusing on their conversation. She needed a distraction. She needed something to anchor her in the present. "Are we being too paranoid?"

Lorcan turned off the burners on the stove, picked up his cup and refilled it before turning and leaning against the granite cabinet. "Possibly. But it makes a good scenario and we should keep it in mind. So are we going to move more aggressively with the hiring?"

"We should have been doing it before now. Rogan, contact the men who have approached you. If you trust them, get them here as soon as possible. I want to start our relationship with them from a position of trust, and I'd like to say no need for background checks, but I don't want to be using possibly hindsight regret at some point in the future."

Rogan eased onto the leather cushion beside her, setting his plate, mug and utensils on the table. "It's alright, Tempest. The men we're considering understand caution. If we didn't do the checks, they'd question our business acumen and sanity and would look for work someplace else. They know their safety and the safety of their families depend on the leaders."

She forked some eggs into her mouth, giving her time to consider his words. "Sensible. Reasonable. Okay. We should also beef up the medical side. Jake should take the lead on that. I'll call Gene and Jack and ask them to liquidate some hard assets and drop the money into the operating account. They need to know there will be more people so they can adjust our investment strategies and raise the amount of money automatically transferred as well as lower the transfer threshold. Lorcan, you have access to the account so pull out as much as you need to update our weapons. Margreet and Thomas need to select more sites for home construction at the compound so I'll leave that up to you, Ro, once you know how many people we'll get in this initial recruitment. And include residences for Kin."

Tempest dropped her fork onto her plate and leaned back. She looked at the large round digital clock on the wall across the room. "So ... would Daire's general office hours start at 8, 9 or 10 a.m.? I want to call as soon as it opens and get the appointment scheduled."

Rogan lifted his mug and waited for Lorcan to fill it from the always-full pot. He nodded his thanks and cupped his hands around the cup studying the black depths. He usually got his own coffee, but any movement on his part would spur Tempest to leave. "We need to address the issues of Treadaway and your grandmother. And ..."

Tempest jammed her fingers into the sides of her hair. "Arghh, Rogan. Not now. Not again. I'm so damn tired of making educated guesses about their plans, what they're doing, how can we circumvent their antics, how to beat the Covens at their own game, yada, yada, yada. It's a never-ending cycle. Even with more information, unless we can read their minds, we don't have shit. And their mind shields are some of the best in the world so we're not going to have any sudden epiphanies."

Lorcan choked, spitting his coffee back into his cup.

Rogan settled into the curve of the seat, raised his mug to his mouth and sipped, eyeing Tempest over the edge of the cup. He took his time sitting the cup down. "During your encounter last night, ..."

"Damn, Rogan." Tempest pushed her breakfast debris away, crossed her arms on the table and dropped her head onto her forearm. "Do we have to have this conversation now? Can't the enumeration of the mistakes I made in my moves against each opponent wait until at least after I talk to Daire?"

He sat the cup on the table, lounged back into the seat, crossed his arms across his chest and his feet beneath the table. "Daire sent us a digi of the fight as well as a needle which he says was used to scratch you. And, yes, we will address – later – what I believe are critical lapses in your training. However, what we need to discuss is the shooter who targeted you and most likely would have killed you if Judah hadn't taken you down. And the second item on the agenda, we'll have to leave for later as well. At least, until the doc has had an opportunity to analyze whatever remains on the needle and what it was meant to do. Do I have your attention now?"

Tempest snapped upright. Images, thoughts and feelings whirled around her mind and tumbled together into a recognizable pattern. Who could bring such pain to Rogan? Rogan had a life before they met, but there had only been a few occasions when he talked about any relatively traumatic events, which she thought was bullshit since they seemed to discuss her crap incessantly and in great detail. She knew there was a tragic event which affected his life now, but he refused to talk about it and Lorcan and Judah always said, "Ask Rogan." The blighters. They should share everything with her since they now seemed to live her life with her. She couldn't remember the last time she had time alone away from the estate without demands from her grandmother or birth family, or out from under the protective clutches of her heart family.

"Is Judah okay?" If people were shooting at her, she preferred to take the hits herself not one of her friends. And the needle explained the scratch on her arm. Since that was in Jake's domain, she filed it away in the back of her mind.

"Yes, Judah is okay. The round skidded across the back

of his vest." He answered the unasked question in her eyes. "Stevie cleaned up the focus from one of the digis. We know the leader of the crew who took the shot. Brice Sugarman is a known associate of Whitman Busch. You wouldn't know him, but …"

"Well, shit!" Tempest leaned back. She was peripherally aware of Rogan's shocked look and Lorcan pushing away from the counter and walking toward the table. Well, if that didn't beat all. She remembered the little asshole from several Coven meetings she had to attend. He had enjoyed ordering her to fetch things for him and he had wanted more. She still hadn't forgiven her grandmother for bringing her in as an attendant and not as a member of Glory's family.

As a family member, she could have worn one of the uniforms protocol allowed – a black business suit comprised of a short skirt, sleeveless shell and form-fitting waist-length jacket. She had gone in wearing the transparent white sleeveless material which tied at the sides to give the illusion of a short dress, thigh-high hose and four-inch heels. The other women provided as servants had no choice but to wear the antiquated collar and chains and nothing else. She made sure none of her heart family knew what happened at the gatherings.

Yeah, her grandmother had later explained Tempest's presence as an attendant had helped Glory push through one of her important projects. It was just one of her schemes wrapped in words like "for the benefit of the people," "it will make our people's lives better." Well, Tempest hadn't seen much difference. She just saw the Coven leadership and upper echelons getting richer and the rank-and-file barely holding their own. It was several months before Tempest agreed to see Glory again. And with the last three … now four … errands for Glory going so badly wrong, it was definitely time to curtail the relationship … this time for good.

"Where did you go?" Lorcan pulled out the chair across from Tempest and sat down.

"Glory has had dealings with the little Napoleon for a couple of years. She contacted me when you and Lorcan had to go straighten out the design issues on the Raptor at the time of one of the quarterly meetings. Hmmm." Her finger tapped a beat on the table. She reviewed the events during that month-long separation with new eyes, from hind-sight. "That was awfully damn convenient now that I look at it."

"You told us you were taking the opportunity to spend some quality time with your grandmother. You said you didn't need any of our people as guards because Mikuh and his teams would watch out for you as a member of Glory's family. What didn't you tell us, Tempest?" Rogan uncurled from his lounging position, like one of the great cats readying for attack, and leaned forward, determination in his eyes. "As I recall, you were different when we returned, even though you denied it. You skittered away from friendly embraces you would normally return. There were a lot more showers. You disappeared into your room more often. Glory called many times and you were always too busy to take the call or out of contact on the training ranges. What happened, Tempest?"

She took a breath and heaved it out. "Not what you're imagining I expect. I wasn't hurt physically, Ro. And it … I have distance from those memories now and I don't want to give them more significance than they deserve. At the time, I didn't think Glory knew about the development of the new technology, but I shouldn't have been so naive. She separated us and got what she wanted. I should have been looking for the roundabout when she took my initial refusal to attend so well."

She shook her head. "It's fine. Everything's fine. So. Busch has been involved behind the scenes with the Covens for years." She tilted her head. "I can't see Treadaway working well with Busch or Busch with Treadaway. Their egos are just too big to allow any kind of compromise. That means there are at least two plans in play, or rather three or more if we consider Glory."

Lorcan pushed away from the table, stood and strode to the sink washing his mug and putting it on the drainer. "You were right earlier. Absent telepathic agents, and I don't know anyone who would admit to any such powers, we have no immediate way to determine what's going on. I know some recruits who would be willing to come immediately, and with more trustworthy people, I can set up surveillance on Treadaway and his cronies. We need more intel and I plan to get it."

"Good. That's good. I also need your help. Both of you. With the move to Summerville, it's a good time to break with grandmother completely. She has Father, my brothers and sisters. There have been issues with all of the last errands she's asked me to do for her. It's getting too dangerous to remain involved with her. We draw enough enmity through our own actions. We don't need Glory's crap as well. I'll tell her myself that I will be focusing all my time and attention on our plans for our future and she'll have to get someone else to help her. Your job is to make sure I don't falter during a weak moment."

She slid across the banquette and stood. "In the meantime, I'm going to call Daire then spend some time in the solaria."

"Tulsa and Judah will be your guards if you go into the City today." Rogan shook his finger at her. "Don't forget to take them."

Her laughter trailed her out of the room.

# CHAPTER 9

Rogan watched Tempest until she was out of the room, tilting his head to listen to her footfalls as she headed toward the office.

Lorcan, resting against the counter, eyed Rogan. He closed his mouth at Rogan's shake of his head.

Pulling his digi from his pocket, Rogan stared at it for several seconds. He activated the device, punched in a number from memory and waited.

"Mac, I've been waiting for your call. Did the last two teams get out okay?" Mikuh Braeden twisted around, wincing at the pull on the slashes on his back. It was worth the humiliation and pain. A couple more days and he and his teams were free. "Mac?" Dread snaked up his spine, a tell from his military days which he had learned not to ignore. He should have been more careful, checked the caller ID before talking. "Who is this?"

"Mikuh, it's Rogan Branaugh." Rogan's eyes flitted to Lorcan before returning to the digi in front of him. He sensed Lorcan moving, sliding onto the chair Lorcan had vacated earlier.

Clearing his throat, Rogan laid the digi on the table, tapping the speaker icon. "Lorcan is with me. Tempest just left to take care of a few things." He hesitated. "What's going on, Mikuh? It sounds like you're in trouble."

Mikuh gritted his teeth. "Just some unexpected business came up and I had to move some teams around. What can I do for you?"

Rogan's eyebrows shot up, but he decided to let the diversion go. He cleared his throat, unsure whether or not to continue. "I need to clarify a couple of things. I need to know what happened at the Coven quarterly meeting. Lorcan and I were called out of town to take care of some business at that time. When we got back, we found out Glory had demanded Tempest attend the meeting. Tempest just told us a little bit about Glory's meeting." He halted to collect his thoughts, debating about how to proceed. "She was different when we returned, Mikuh."

Mikuh couldn't deny the pain and anger he heard in Branaugh's voice. He wouldn't cover for Glory, not this time and never again. "Tempest was dressed, and presented, as an attendant at the meeting. You know what that means, Rogan. The dandy Glory was seducing into her trap became very handsy with Tempest, forced her into several uncomfortable positions. He pushed Tempest to the edge of what he saw Glory was going to permit." Mikuh stopped, heaved a big sigh. He rubbed the back of his neck, dropping his arm as pain shot through his body again. He continued his pacing around the outer perimeter of the wall surrounding the Duvayne's house.

"There was nothing I could do, Rogan. At the first hint of movement on my part, Tempest looked into my eyes and signaled me to stop." Antipathy coated his next words. "I looked to Glory but she was immersed in her role as Ryniah of the Council of ParaHumans and Beldame of Coven Duvayne." Self-disgust spilled out. "Tempest wouldn't let me do anything, Rogan. I felt her willpower holding me in place." His voice trailed off in a whisper. "Tempest wouldn't let me do anything."

Rogan heaved a deep breath. Tempest's will was off-the-charts strong. She wouldn't have wanted to drag Mikuh into the middle of a battle between her and Glory. "Not your fault, Mikuh. Don't take that on yourself. Do what you have to do to get Glory to accept your resignation, without harm to your body, emotions and soul. Do it now, Mikuh. Get out.

Tempest wants you here. So do I. Bring along any of your people who you trust."

Mikuh bowed his head. Tempest's absolution by wanting him as part of her House eased his guilt. "I've paid the premium Glory demanded to let me out of the remainder of my contract. She was quite amenable saying she didn't want someone protecting her back who didn't want to be there, using her most disdainful manner." Irony pulsed in his voice. "She certainly enjoys getting her pound of flesh." He stopped, thinking back to the scene.

Glory had demanded the termination of his contract be paid in a physical manner. He wasn't surprised. Satisfaction filled his eyes remembering the tightening around Glory's mouth, the tiny narrowing of her eyes, as he quoted the paragraph and section number of the termination clause which allowed for negotiating the extent and type of force if either of them chose a flesh repayment. Since Glory was the "employer", her man made the first five strokes on Mikuh's bare back with a whip.

The man went beyond the negotiated amount of force, the whip tearing into Mikuh's body, blood flowing freely. Mikuh had mentally thanked his friend, Cash Monroe, who he had chosen as his second, when Cash advised Mikuh to allow Cash to strap Mikuh to a St. Andrew's Cross for safety. Dr. Adam Rosen, selected as a neutral third party, had ended a continuation of the scene, advising Glory she had negated her contract by the brutality of the attack and Mikuh was only required to physically work for her through the next seven days. Two days remained and he still had to figure out how he would explain the fiasco to his teams and his reason for not allowing them to protect him.

"You know, Rogan, I didn't feel a thing when she turned on me. I saw her for who she was and she couldn't deal with it. Soon, Rogan. Tell Tempest … tell her thanks. She has my loyalty. I'll be in touch soon."

"Good, Mikuh. That's good. Your quarters will be in the main house. Your people will be housed according to their family needs in the compound. Let me know if things go south. We'll back you up." Rogan laughed. "You know Tempest will be the first to get to you."

Mikuh forced a laugh. "Keep her safe, Rogan. There's blood in the air. I feel it like I did when I was military."

Rogan listened to the dead air of an ended call.

"Well, that went swimmingly. And we still don't know exactly what Sugarman did. Plus, now we don't know what Glory did to Mikuh ... because from the tone of his voice and nuances in his words, she did something unforgiveable." Lorcan gritted his teeth, his hand clenched into a fist. "We don't need to know the details. We'll take care of Sugarman and Busch when the time comes but everyone needs to know what happened to Tempest as well as Mikuh."

Rogan looked up, thought about Tempest's right to privacy then nodded. "Yes. But no coddling. No treating her like she's wounded. We're all scarred in some way or another, emotionally, physically, spiritually. As for Mikuh, we keep it simple."

Rogan stood, his body protesting the amount of time he sat on the banquette bench with every muscle clenched. "Get Ben started on setting up a suite for Mikuh and some houses and apartments for families and solitaries. I'll tell Tempest in the morning that Mikuh will be coming onboard soon."

"How will you explain ...".

"With some part of the truth, Lorcan. In the meantime, we've got things to do."

# CHAPTER 10

The call to Daire passed through to his executive assistant after only a few seconds. Tempest was surprised she was given an appointment for that afternoon but confirmed the time and place. After notifying Tulsa of the appointment, she continued to the solaria, her favorite room.

Dark blue blackout curtains fell from ceiling to floor blocking light from windows covering three walls of the oversized room. The ceiling was the masterpiece of the space. A special translucent material covered the ceiling, capturing and mirroring on its surface the energies reflected by, and movement of, the stars, suns and other worlds within range of its sensors. Royalties produced from the patents on the processes, used in other industries by many different companies around the globe, poured into an account set aside as the group's security blanket. Their company, with all its subsidiaries, ranked as one of the top five richest companies in the world, and Gene Brody and Jack Scarlett, best friends and financial gurus, worked hard to continue to grow their funds.

Tempest pulled her double padded lounger from the huddle in a corner and dragged it to the center of the room. She threaded her fingers together, turned her hands palm up and stretched toward the ceiling stopping just before the cut on her side protested, slowly bent over and touched the floor. She released her breath and relaxed into the position, holding the pose for several minutes. A gradual return upright and she shook her arms and twisted in slow motion from side to side. She threw a leg across the end of the lounger and settled back.

Closing her eyes, she took several deep breaths. Starting at ten, she counted backwards allowing her consciousness to start the path to her doorway into HyperRealm, the portal she used for explorations of time, space, dimensions and other realities as well as healing, remote viewing and similar ventures.

Treadaway was usually more circumspect in his pursuit. Her refusal to agree to the pact he made with her father to be his mistress and a willing participant in her own debasement as a part of his darker rituals had set them on a path which could only lead to diminution in status for him or more likely death for one of them because she would never …

Well, crap. She wiggled deeper into the cushions using the movement to break the trail her thoughts were headed. She wasn't going to give the asshole more energy by thinking about him. She began again at ten and headed down. Nine … eight … seven …

What the hell did the Kin do to Rogan, Lorcan and Judah that made them split away? Were the same issues going to crop up if Kin answered the Call? She had to protect her men and if Kin didn't toe the line, she would kick their butts out of Summerville.

Tempest surged upright in disgust and rolled out of the now lumpy confines of the recliner. She stomped around the edges of the room, skirting the stacked chairs in one corner. Anger and exasperation spiked and crackled around her like a summer thunderstorm. Her thoughts tumbled in a chaotic mish-mash; no one thought gaining supremacy and locking her into a loop. On her sixth revolution, her breathing steadied, her mind began to slow.

Her steps took her further into the room. Her left arm rose, her leg moved forward in slow motion, her right arm followed through. One movement flowed to the next and she slipped into the long-form kata of Shu-Tai-Ree, the gentle side of the fighting movements Sebastian had imprinted in her mind. Transferring the knowledge from her mind to her body had been frustrating, maddening, but, in the end, rewarding. It was the energy generated by Shu-Tai-Ree she wanted to access for the healing Mandela she had in mind.

Her consciousness fragmented, one part reaching to the sun, coasting to a stop near a sun flare discharge. The fragment cautiously sent out a tendril, gingerly touching the edge. The chances of a second discharge in close proximity to her current position were very small. She began to channel the energy through her healing Mandela aiming it for a body-wide cleansing and healing.

Once the draw was on automatic, she lowered her body to the floor then flicked to the second fragment, the part of her that flew into the chamber containing Sebastian's body trapped in a gas-filled medtube. Dials, buttons, alarms and monitors covered grey metal panels lining the walls. Broken glass-like shards littered the floor. She floated to the six tubes in the center of the space. Some lights embedded in the thick, black, foam-like padding between the containers pulsed, others flickered slowly on and off, and several flashed brilliantly and died. Two tubes appeared to be the main source of the debris on the floor, their covers shattered. Two additional units tilted a few inches out of line, the boards dark and dead. The last two tubes were in one piece, most of the readouts and lights functioning.

Excitement brightened the fragment which was Tempest into a glowing ball as she floated closer to the container. It was her first look at Sebastian's physical body. She had an image in her mind created from vague memories Sebastian had of himself from reflective surfaces which he inadvertently passed to her at various times, but to see his actual body.

It was ... well, boondoggle! There was only a dark figure hidden by white gaseous fog. Her imagined hand and arm slid through the glass-like cover. She waved her insubstantial arm, accidentally touching his body. A sparkling Celtic-looking knot, with a turquoise blue rim and pulsing white gold strand threaded in the center, popped out of his body dazzling her eyes. It felt like a combination of his essence and hers. She wanted to touch the symbol, was drawn to touch it, but she backed away as fast as she could before she attracted his attention. That would be bad. He was in a deep trance and he needed to stay there until they retrieved his body.

She drifted away from the medtube to examine the empty one at its side. She noted the knot hovered in the air, continuing to beat for a few seconds, before disappearing back into the tube. The cylinder appeared to be untouched. She examined as best she could the boards controlling it. It gave her pause. Two, mostly undamaged, medtubes. It could be a bargaining chip with the D'eath organization. The tube holding Sebastian captive would go to her tech labs. The second cylinder and the remains of the ship would go to Daire. It was a win-win for everyone.

Her essence swirled around sensing the presence of something. Alarms shrieked, lights flashed and died beside one of the broken chambers. Worry slammed her. It was too close to Sebastian's enclosure. The sudden surge of emotion flung her back toward her physical form. Her body jerked as she thudded into it followed by a second jolt as she rejoined the third part of her, which had remained behind. Her mouth opened to scream, but nothing emerged. Insubstantial flames erupted all around her. Her fingers dug into the thick carpet covering the floor of the solaria, her body bowed.

She had to release her connection to the sun. The fragment attached to the Mandela had continued with her original purpose, but a solar flare had burst too close to her position. The power increased too fast. The energy was more than she had ever handled before. She attempted to break the bond, to count herself up. Her body writhed on the floor, fire scorching her skin, power forging new avenues in her mind.

"Gently, dearling." Sebastian's baritone voice eased into her mind, his spirit folded around her. He regulated the temperature of her body and severed the tie to the sun marveling at the unusual application she had created from the Shu-Tai-Ree energy. He worked to calm the shudders and assuage the shock spreading through her system. He felt his hold on his own consciousness and body slip another ratchet. Not much time now. It wouldn't be long before his disconnection was permanent.

Where would the next journey take him? Was there existence after this? In many ways, he was excited about finally learning the answers to the age-old question, but he was also saddened to leave the corporeal existence when it had just begun to get interesting. A new species! Their ingenuity was astonishing, their emotions so fresh and clean after centuries of living with the moral and physical disintegration among the denizens and citizens of his old life. He grunted, regaining the ground he lost and moving upward a little more as Tempest clutched his essence, feeding him some of the energy still coursing through her body, refusing to let him go.

"You're not taking the easy way out of this existence, old man. Sleep now." She used more of the energy to add emphasis to her suggestion.

Tempest sprawled in a heap, panting out the pain as Sebastian winked out. She knew he allowed her push to affect him; he was an Elder with more power than she would ever see in her lifetime.

She sniffed, smelling the stench of sweat and scorched cloth, rolled over and pushed to her hands and knees. Hunh. She stared at the outline of her body burned into the carpet. The outer edges of her pants and shirt were brown, with burnt holes. That wasn't good. She would need to bury the remnants of her clothes beneath a lot of trash along with hiding the carpet squares she would have to replace before she left the room. It was a good thing there were extra squares since they often had to swap them because of spills after one of their boisterous gatherings on full moon nights. It would be bad if Rogan, Jake or any of her heart family saw any of the remnants. They would ask questions and demand answers she didn't want to give and misdirection wouldn't be an option.

She pushed to her feet, her body coursing with vitality. Well, at least she had accomplished the main objective of healing her physical form with the bonus of knowing she had helped Bastian. She walked to the closet on the only wall in the room, opened the door and chose several squares. She dragged them out, used her foot to shut the door and hauled the pieces to the damaged area. Fitting the replacement carpet into place along with scuffing the edges to meld them with the original was the work of only a few seconds.

Tempest took a last look at the space, shaking her head. The carpet replacement was easily detectable. With a quick smile, there was no way anyone could conceivably blame it on her, she pushed the lounger back into the herd in the corner. The fried carpet pieces she shoved into the deepest, darkest side of the closet. Her next step – take a long, hot shower – she was rank from sweat, fear and fire.

# CHAPTER 11

Water dribbled down Tempest's neck into the neckband of the pink sleeveless square-necked shell she wore. Light green striped cotton knit trousers hung from her hips: old, well-worn and comfortable. She swiped at the water with the towel in her hand while studying the calendar displayed on the monitor on the table in the corner of her bedroom.

Her finger danced above the 'accept' button on the screen. Well, shit. She rested most of her weight on one leg and crossed her arms across her chest. She stared through the display, imagined conversations playing out in different scenarios in her mind. She knew, she just knew, if she went through with her chickenshit decision to schedule her training session with Strider instead of Rogan, she would be facing both men on the mat not just one. And ... and ... Rogan would be sure Strider was up to date on the digi Daire provided of her street fight so they could 'maximize' their time with her. And then wouldn't everyone just be having a fun time?

Tempest snorted. A chime flowed from the speakers at the same time a popup window overrode the button. No time now to switch things around. She would wait until she returned. She ticked the alarm off and skittered to the walk-in closet across the room.

Decisions, decisions. What should she wear to a meeting with one of the most powerful men in the Amalgamated Territories, the former United States, Canada and Mexico, and in the world? Sliding hangars across the bar, she shook her head at the small collection of skirts and jackets provided by her grandmother for Coven meetings.

She shuddered, the heat of embarrassment flowed down her face and neck followed by a burst of anger in the pit of her stomach. The memory of the last time she attended a quarterly meeting at the behest of her grandmother still had the ability to affect her. Arriving early as ordered, Glory's personal assistant escorted her to one of the dressing rooms. Even now as then, anxiety collected in a ball in her chest impeding her breathing.

"Beldame Duvayne requests that you change your clothes. You'll find your required apparel behind the screen."

Well, that didn't bode well. Tempest stepped to the divider and looked around the side. She was shaking her head before the words left her mouth. "No. Absolutely, unequivocally, no. Tell Beldame Duvayne I will not be attending the meeting."

She turned to leave falling back a step to keep from running over the assistant standing in front of her holding out a digi. Her lips tightening, she accepted the small receiver placing it at her ear.

"Tempest, I don't have time for your histrionics. Get dressed and present yourself in the next five minutes or there will be consequences I will initiate." Without waiting for a reply, the line closed down.

Tempest had considered ignoring The Duvayne's instructions and leaving the building. Mikuh would have interceded with the guards on duty to get her out since it was a different Coven's turn for providing security that month. And there was the rub – pitting Mikuh against his employer. He didn't like many of her grandmother's orders and projects, but he was bound to The Duvayne's service for at least another six months. His only out was if she released him, which wasn't going to happen, or Glory died. Tempest had offered to buy-out his contract, but Mikuh had refused – Glory would refuse to release him and it would cause animosity between all of them.

Tempest wouldn't trap an enemy between her and Glory in a pissing contest, much less a close friend like Mikuh.

She had dressed in the attendant's sheer fabric and stayed at the meeting as long as she could, stuffing her anger down deep. Her threshold between anger and rage imploded when Sugarman slipped a hand beneath the opening of the fabric at her hip and tried to go lower ... her grandmother watched and did nothing. She hadn't told Rogan or the others about the meeting keeping the humiliation to herself.

She had to let it go. Her grandmother had always had her own agenda and she moved people around like pawns on a chessboard. Remembering the same episode twice in one day was allowing more credence to it than should be allowed. She refused to dwell on the past. There was enough going on in the present which needed her full attention. When love turned bitter, it was time to get out. In sudden decision, she gathered the hangars together in one hand and unhooked them, dropping the clothes into an empty box in one corner. She knelt on the floor and flung heels into the box one at a time.

Closing and sealing the top of the box brought a lightness of spirit she hadn't felt in a long time. She stood and dragged the box out of the closet, across the room, pausing to write 'charity' on two sides, and into the hallway leaving it beside the doorway. She re-entered the room and the closet. A new day, an important turning point in her life, required a different attitude. She would dress for herself. Not business professional, not what the Covens expected, but what was an extension of her personality. She would save the leather-like apparel for another time.

After choosing a matching comfortable bra and panties set which didn't push out or expose parts of her body, she wriggled into black leggings, while contemplating the colorful array of oversized T-shirts. Her hand wavered between white and cobalt blue tops. A glance at the boots on the floor and she flipped the white from the hangar. Black boots today, she decided, sitting on the floor and pulling the shaft of the boot to just under her knee. She fingered the swirling patterns in the shaft, following the curvature of the tiny copper wires embedded in the leather, feeling her senses float upward. She hastily removed her finger and ran through a grounding spell. She needed to have all her wits around her and not be floating half in and half out of her body.

Twisting to the right, she selected one of several black cloth tubes from the shelf and placed it beside her. She pulled Velcro tapes open and unrolled the covering. The overhead light flashed on matte-finished handles, and ornate wood handles with sparkling jewels forming personally chosen patterns. One finger tapped a slow rhythm on her leg while her eyes slipped from blade to blade. She nodded and with a quick motion chose several knives, slipping them into pockets sewn into the inner sides of each boot and positioning one at the middle of her back in a sideways draw holster she attached to a belt she clasped around her waist beneath the shirt. All the excess material in the top hid the holster ... at least until someone searched her ... which she hoped wasn't going to happen.

Rerolling the tube, she replaced it on the shelf. Her hand hovered over another roll containing her wrist sheathes with specially forged blades. It would require wearing a jacket or changing the short-sleeved T-shirt for one with long sleeves. She shook her head. There would be two experienced, seasoned bodyguards at her back. If attackers got through them, she was already dead.

Standing, she paused in front of the full-length mirror on the closet door, absently chewing her lower lip. Was she being too informal for the situation? No. She wasn't going to backtrack on her decision to outwardly reflect her new attitude. With a rude gesture at her figure in the mirror, she swirled away and took several steps across the room toward the outside door. Between one step and the next, the hairs on the back of her neck rose and waved energetically, ants crawling down her spine. She kicked around and strode back into the closet, grabbed the tube with her wrist sheathes and left the room. She might not wear them but she would have them in the vehicle. Yeah. Her nerves settled. That felt right.

# CHAPTER 12

In the entryway, Tempest scooped up her backpack, flinging it over one shoulder, stepped out the front door and waited a few seconds to hear the automatic lock engage. She sensed the electronic net surrounding the house engage. Checking the watch attached to the strap of the backpack, she trotted down the steps and headed for the garages.

The sun was bright, forcing her to dig in the pack for sunglasses, slipping them over her eyes. A raucous breeze spun the curls around her head tripping a laugh from her throat. Daire D'eath's face, his long, lean body exuding vitality and alpha male testosterone, filled her thoughts. Yum! He was a walking, talking reason for battery-powered accessories if the real thing wasn't available.

The men and women in the teams were forthright and open about their sexual activities. Hearing the talk about orgasmic delight made her curious and wonder about her own sexuality. Her few liaisons had been pleasant but unremarkable leaving her with no urge to seek another partner and BPAs took care of the itches that inundated her periodically. The awakening of her libido now was as surprising as the target of her lust. She had enough strong males in her life as it was and Daire D'eath would never be one of the biddable, agreeable men who were her preferred choice.

She paced along the recently graded gravel road. Tempest paid a high price in emotional pain and turmoil and physical duties for the loan of the small thirty-acre estate from her grandmother. Traffic was a monster no matter the time, making the hour's drive from the City interminable. The City/County Development Agency wouldn't allow the construction of additional buildings on the land so several barns were remodeled creating barracks for the unmarried men and women, who used colorful screens to separate the floor and loft areas into individual spaces. Two and three families packed the few houses, with some older children sleeping in the main area of the barracks on cots and in sleeping bags in the evenings.

Overcrowding was the main reason for the accelerated move to Summerfield, but she and Rogan had agreed it was time to pull in all their operatives and only accept well-vetted jobs. Their decision had stuffed the rafters to the gills. They didn't have to take every job offer any more, not since Jack and Gene had managed, through a series of risky investments over time, to expand the funds everyone had thrown in the pile into a humongous amount of money which would take many generations to deplete if it was static – which it never would be. The second and more powerful reason for the urgency to move was the growing fear and unrest in the general populace and continuing changes in the World political system. She wanted to be in a position of power – on home territory, with shielding in place. Paranoid? Not in this situation.

Boisterous, unfettered laughter drew Tempest from her reverie. She rounded the curve in the road and stopped, grinning at the tableau in front of the main garage. Water streamed from hoses onto screaming, laughing men and women running and sliding around several barely wet HWVs. She dodged around the excited combatants and ran to the open door of the building before she was recognized and someone decided she needed to join the fun.

Benton Welles, master of transportation, walked out of the shadows at the side of the opening wiping his hands on a cloth. Dirt and oil stained his once white shirt. White hair cut short around a suntanned wrinkle-lined face showed his age, but his azure blue eyes were as warm and timeless as the oceans.

A grin burst onto his face. "It's a good day to be alive. What brings you to my door, pretty lady?" He raised his hands, backing up at her approach. "No, no, no! I'll not be staining your white shirt to match mine." The usually imperceptible burr deepened.

Tempest giggled, shaking her finger at him. "No cause for alarm, Ben. I don't have time to go back to the house to change." She watched three men scuffle over a hose. A few meaty thuds and numerous grunts filled the air. She scrambled backwards to avoid the spray of water arched in her direction.

"Here now, you young scampers! Quit your tussling in my door when I've got visitors." Ben's smile widened. Several women inched to the hose, grabbed it and pulled. "It's good to see them having fun."

Watching the spirited tug of war between the men now allied on the wet end of the hose and the women holding the middle of the rubber snake, Tempest nodded. "Yeah. It's been an unforgiving few months. Has the date been set for you and your crew to move to Summerfield? I didn't have time to check the revised charts before I left the house."

"We sent the kids with the latest group. It's just us old men to take up the slack."

The lingering sadness in his voice pierced her heart, bringing tears to her eyes. She rubbed her hand up and down his arm. "I'm sorry Rosie won't be a part of our adventure."

Ben's breath hitched, tears clogged his eyes. "Me, too," he whispered. His Rosie would have loved the hills and valleys around Summerfield. She had survived the surgery to remove the bullets from her body and lingered in the critical care unit during the arrest and charging of the robbers, but her physical heart wasn't a match for her spirit and it had stopped. It was Tempest, and his and his Rosie's four sons, who had kept him alive during the last few years. He had finally woken up and realized it was time to get on with life ... the life Rosie would want him to live to the fullest.

"Come up to the house tomorrow for supper. We haven't had time for a visit." She missed the gentle evenings with Ben, or the rowdy game nights with him, his sons, Rogan, and any of the other two hundred plus people on the estate who wanted to play.

She staggered back, her hand on her stomach. Acid rose in her throat. She fell to her knees on the grass verge gagging. Her insides roiled and cramped. She vomited uncontrollably.

Ben stared horrified. A column of white flames, with red lightning bolts, engulfed and sizzled around Tempest. "ROGAN!"

The tug-of-war stopped, water spilling onto the feet of the motionless figures.

Tempest convulsed, tumbling sideways onto the ground, rolling onto her back. Her breath froze in her chest, agonizing waves of pain smothering her. A vision of Sebastian slammed into her mind: the tube encasing him shook, sparks spilling onto the floor. Dials around the chamber flickered and died. Controls nearest the tube dimmed, surged brighter then stabilized.

"Don't touch her!" Kodiak Smythe yelled, running from the direction of the barracks.

Ben knelt at Tempest's side, his hands gripping his legs to keep from reaching out to her. He raised stricken eyes to Kodi. "Where's Rogan?" His breath wavered. Tempest was the daughter of his heart. He couldn't lose her, too.

"A call went out to him. He's only minutes away."

Tempest's eyes fluttered. She gasped ... once ... twice ... and inched onto her side, deep coughing erupting from her mouth.

The strange glow was gone. Ben smoothed her hair with a shaking hand.

"Well ... and wasn't that fun?" Her voice was raspy, her throat sore. She ran her tongue across her teeth. "I'm okay

… I think." She struggled to sit up, releasing a sigh when Ben slid behind her, offering his body as support. Being so close to another person didn't seem like a good idea, but the warmth of another body was comforting. She was at a loss for words.

Kodiak crouched on one knee, his fingers on her pulse. "Rogan will be here soon." He had some medical training during his stint with the military, but this was beyond his capabilities. Anxiety filled him. Jake Swanson, their doctor, had agreed it made sense for Jake to be at Summerfield with the families and he would be on the spot to make decisions about the new medical and research facilities. Jake had said Kodiak had more than sufficient skills to handle the common day-to-day bruises, cuts and sprains at the Estate. No one could have anticipated such a bizarre incident.

"A few more minutes on the ground would be nice," Tempest joked, clutching Kodiak's arm for reassurance and patting Ben's hand to comfort him. She checked her link with Sebastian, huffing a sigh of relief at his apparent weathering of the disturbance. "I think everything has stabilized for now."

An SUV the color of a storm-tossed sky skidded to a halt. The doors slammed open spilling out Rogan and Lorcan.

"What happened?" Rogan took in Kodiak kneeling beside Tempest with Ben at her back. Water dripped from men and women circling the trio with weapons at ready, eyes continuously searching the area.

Tempest coughed, clearing her throat. "The machine holding Bastian in thrall misfired. The feedback spilled over onto me."

"You never should have connected with that thing!" Kodi didn't understand what had taken place between Tempest and the alien, but the stranger was an unknown quantity and Tempest was the only priority. "He's killing you! You have to cut whatever hold he has on you!" He was scared. He almost reached out to shake her.

Tempest gazed earnestly into Kodi's eyes. "It's not

Bastian's fault. It's some quirk of my talent, I think. Bastian is already doing too much in his effort to protect me. If we don't get him out soon, he's going to slide too far into trance and he'll die."

Seeing fear leap into Kodi's eyes, she tried to reassure him. "It's unlikely he'll take me with him. He'll be doing everything he can to make sure he doesn't." She didn't know how to feel about that. She had grown used to having Bastian as a warm presence in her mind ... nothing overt, only a seedpod in a small corner. She reached up, placing a hand on Kodi's cheek. "Listen to me, Kodi. You and your friends are not to take any precipitous action. Do you understand? Yes?"

She saw the blank stare the men used when they were hiding, or didn't want to discuss, something. "Talk to me, Kodi. Tell me you understand." She released her breath and moved her hand when he nodded. A vocal response was a stronger indication he agreed to follow her instructions, but he wasn't in any shape to be harassed.

"What ... happened?" Rogan wanted to know what she was hiding.

"It looked like she was in a translucent column of a white gaseous substance with red streaks of lightning. She convulsed and stopped breathing for a few seconds." Ben clenched his fingers in Tempest's arms to hold her still.

"Traitor." She hissed at him between clenched teeth. "It's wasn't that bad. Really." She pushed herself up and collapsed at their feet, her knees reacting like limp noodles. "Okay. It hurt a lot." An understatement, she thought. She scrubbed her face with her hands. The men hid their smiles at the dirt left behind.

"The equipment is failing." She mumbled the words into Rogan's chest when he lifted her to her feet, providing the support her legs needed to remain upright. "That's really nothing new ... we've known that all along. The new kink," she wrinkled her nose, "is there was a minor earthquake in the area. The pod evidently is almost on top of a small fault line. The shaking destabilized some of the consoles. The panel controlling Bastian's tube is okay ... for now."

She sighed, cuddling into the comfort of Rogan's arms. A bone-deep weariness drained her composure. Tears leaked from her closed eyes, marking trails in the smudges on her face. There were many decisions to make and an abundance of family members in danger or hurt if she was wrong. So many people to protect. She drew in a hiccupping breath, laughed, choked then withdrew to stand alone ... swaying, but still erect.

"I'm going back to the house to change and wash up. We'll have to go directly to D'eath Towers." She shook her head looking into their faces. "It can't be rescheduled. There's no more time."

The men watched her limp to her Sport Tracker someone had parked nearby and climb in.

Rogan rubbed tired, gritty eyes. Tempest was losing weight and her screaming nightmares in the early morning hours were heartrending. He had thought the nightmares of her time in the Covens were gone. The families and team members had conspired to touch Tempest physically as often as possible and it appeared the remedy was working. Even the most solitary of their group made a point to pat her in some way. And Tempest had started initiating some of the contacts, which was a major breakthrough, but this damn situation with the alien was causing a set-back. Although he had the feeling she was hiding something from them. Once they were at Summerfield, he was sitting her down and having a come-to-Jesus talk. They would discover the catalyst for her anxieties and whatever it was would be ended ... one way or another. "Tulsa, take one of the Turtles. It has the largest medical pack and provides the most protection. I don't like her going off without a doctor looking her over, but like she said there's no time left. No offense, Kodi."

Kodiak flicked his fingers. "None taken. I think we should just dig that damn pod out and to hell with asking permission." He wanted to punch someone or something. He had to run the training course several times ... work off the anger. It had taken too many years to conquer his automatic reaction to hit first and regret later. Self-control was the only way to get out of the military in one piece. He had made his promise to Tempest and he would honor it and her.

"Send Rapier Five for Jake. He called with an update that he's happy with his new recruits. They can take care of Summerfield until we get there. We need him here." Rogan motioned the silent Lorcan to the SUV. His head pounded. "She has to deal with D'eath alone. Why couldn't the damn family change their name to something less sinister?" And why did that have such a portentous ring to it?

"I didn't say anything." Lorcan settled into the driver's seat.

"Shut up." Rogan climbed into the SUV feeling the aches and pains of years of fighting.

# CHAPTER 13

Tulsa steadied Tempest with a hand beneath her arm as she climbed into the Turtle while Judah settled into the back seat checking the locks on the carbines racked in an upright position in front of him. "Are we telling him the truth?"

She rolled her head on the seat cushion to look at Tulsa. "Do you trust D'eath and his people?" She waited for his reply. She trusted Daire based on a feeling in her gut. It wasn't enough to risk the lives and freedom of her family.

"I've never met D'eath or his second, Declan Tath. They have a reputation for being honorable, trustworthy and fair." His eyes focused on the road ahead.

She grunted. "And?"

"What are you going to tell him?"

She stared at his profile. "He doesn't need to know about Sebastian. It's a Duvayne ancient relic. We just discovered its location. It's contained inside a metal container which Daire's scientists may want to study. He can have part of it in exchange for permission to dig on his land. From an initial air scan of the area, a very small amount of vegetation will be disturbed which we will replant with native trees and shrubs."

"Everything you said is the truth … just shaded in nuances. Why are you giving them the pod?"

"A pod. There are two still in reasonable working order. We'll take one and Daire will get the other … and the remains of the transport. He has the facilities and the brightest scientists available to a private enterprise. If it's possible to reverse engineer or develop something new, he'll do it. We'll have the most important part."

He licked his lips, his eyes straying to the rearview mirror to meet Judah's gaze. "Lorcan Called Kin."

She tensed then relaxed. She wanted to pursue the subject, but it was fraught with hidden traps. "Yes, Rogan said he told Lorcan to do it."

"Good. That's good." He shook his head slightly at Judah's questioning glance. Years of caution tied his tongue. He settled deeper into his seat. "Do you want the music on?"

Okaaay. No discussion. Tempest let her breath ease out. "No. If you or Judah want to listen to something …." Her voice trailed away.

A companionable silence filled the interior.

Tempest broke the quiet at the edge of the City. "I want both of you to go in with me."

Tulsa drew a small box from his shirt pocket and showed it to her. "The security on this Turtle was augmented in several areas. This SecComp will send an alert if someone scans or approaches within ten feet and activate a defense mechanism if the vehicle is touched by hand or laser sight. We can leave the vehicle and be sure it's safe when we return."

"Great." Her sense of danger lessened. "We're meeting him in the lower level of the garage in his building. Stay close. I feel itchy. It's likely nothing." She hurried to reassure them noting the exchange of strained looks in the mirror. "And there's no need for more backup." I hope, she thought.

Tulsa stopped at the double bars protecting the private entrance to D'eath Towers. Guards, dressed in body-hugging, black stealth suits and with carbines in their hands, moved to stand at the corners of the Turtle. Three additional guards, one with a sensor, examined the vehicle front to back, scanning inside, outside, and beneath the hood and undercarriage.

Dawkins appeared from the darkness with two men at his back.

Tempest lowered her window. "Mr. Dawkins, it's nice to see you again." She projected thoughts of prey ... soft, fluffy, harmless prey. She didn't want to give up the knives hidden in her boots or the one nestled against her spine. Daire might trust his people, but they were strangers to her. She lightened the wave. Predator adrenaline she could handle, but she didn't want to create suspicion in the men.

Puzzlement slid through Dawkins' eyes then disappeared. "Mr. D'eath asked me to escort you into the garage." He flicked a look around the interior of the vehicle while reaching to open her door. He froze. The surrounding guards stiffened, apprehension notching up several levels. Dawkins raised his hands in acquiescence, looking into eyes holding the quiet confidence of warriors. The men lacked the cold calculation of soulless killers, but their potential for harm to his leader was an overt force.

"Mr. Dawkins, these are my bodyguards, Tulsa Jones and Judah Carrigan. Where I go, they go." She relaxed into her seat.

"Ma'am." Dawkins nodded and stepped away. Using the dotmitter on his collar, he transmitted the information for approval.

Judah raised a hand slowly and wiped the side of his mouth. "What were you doing?" His tongue still salivated from the backwash of Tempest's action.

"Just a little suggestion that I'm harmless," she muttered.

The men hid their smiles and choked back laughter. She was as harmless as a female sabre-tooth tiger protecting her kits. They shifted back into bodyguard persona at Dawkins' approach.

"Interesting." Daire lounged in his chair in the private section of the Blue Myst Restaurant. The spectacular view outside the nearby translucent armor window didn't compare to the scene he watched on the monitor in the middle of the table. He tapped the foldable keyboard sitting on the polished black granite slab disconnecting the CPU from the closed-circuit server. Stroking a finger along a sensor on the arm of his chair lowered the screen below the tabletop. He rolled the keyboard and pushed it into a pocket. Politicians and other top-tier businessmen and women paid a premium to use the table and its built-in accessories, which included an oscillating wave shield for five feet around it to block all forms of recording mechanisms and secure access to any outside computers they desired.

Declan smoothed the linen into place. "The projectors on their vehicle are playing hell with our scanners. She's carrying weapons."

Daire rose in tandem with his second. As they walked toward the entrance to the restaurant, he stopped at the hostess' podium. "We won't be back tonight, Tanya. The table can be cleared."

They continued to the private elevator set into a recess past the podium and Declan pressed the call button. They turned and Daire leaned a shoulder against the wall, his eyes tracking the people exiting the regular elevators, but his mind caught up in the details of their conversation. "Not an auspicious start. This isn't a social appointment so some niceties will go by the wayside, and, yes, I'm positive she's armed. I would be in her position."

"Are you going to require she submit to a body search?"

He entered the elevator, turned and settled against the mirrored steel wall. Disappointment and regret arrowed through him that their meeting was to discuss business. He was still half erect just viewing Tempest on a cold hard machine. His temperature rose, his member stiffening. A vision rose in his head of Tempest naked on a cold metal table. Her feet on the edge, legs bent wide open giving him access to her center. The shivering in her body would change from cold to white-hot heat when he ran his tongue between the protective lips into her core and he suckled and nipped her hidden nub. He dismissed the fantasy and shifted to reposition his now fully aroused sex, tossing Declan a wry smile. Shaking his head at his loss of control, Daire exited the elevator. He halted in the grey demarcation between the shadows beyond the elevator door and the light-filled center of the open space in front of the attendant's booth. He needed a few minutes to let his arousal dissipate.

"No. I want her to feel safe when she's with us and this would be a first step to establishing trust between us." He gave Declan a wry grin. "And her bodyguards would be extremely unhappy for a stranger to have hands on her. Even though I know and trust our guards, I don't want their hands on her either." He pressed the button for his dotmitter. "Let's do this, George."

"Ms. Duvayne, your guards can exit the vehicle, leaving their weapons inside, and escort you as far as the first line of columns. You may proceed forward to Mr. D'eath." Dawkins backed away.

Tempest commiserated with Dawkins' impossible task, walking a tightrope between protecting Daire and avoiding insulting her. As much as she wanted to trust Daire, there were a lot more men in the garage than she had, and it just took one bad apple to pull the trigger to start a war. Tulsa and Judah were Kin; they were faster than the majority of people. They could disarm the closest guards and use those weapons to protect her. If the situation deteriorated, she could give them a few extra seconds with her gun and blades.

Sighing, she nodded to Judah. He stepped out, walked around the vehicle and opened her door, standing between her and Dawkins. The guards stepped back to open a path to Daire and Declan. By the sour and hostile expressions on their faces, it wasn't a normal procedure.

Mini-bolts of lust struck her girlie parts as she walked towards the waiting men. She watched Daire's eyes track her tongue wetting her suddenly dry lips. Her pulse pounded and her nipples ached and puckered when his gaze strolled from her mouth to her breasts. She closed her fingers, one at a time, into fists stifling the urge to thread them through his hair. Every cell in her body vibrated like an engine gone mad. Need pushed her to climb his six-foot plus body and writhe all over him transferring her scent and marking him as hers, establishing warning markers to encroaching females that he was forbidden territory.

She had to dump the electricity crawling through her body. Tulsa and Judah could help her, standing in Rogan or Lorcan's place and acting as dampeners, drawing the charge away from her, helping her regain control. She glanced back at them. They couldn't approach and retreat to them was impossible. She couldn't appear weak. The hem of her T-shirt fluttered like a flag in a light breeze. Deep breath. Smoosh the energy into a ball; stuff the ball behind a reinforced door in her mind.

She had to hurry and definitely no skin-to-skin contact of any kind. The meeting should have been set for another day. Where was her head? Klaxons should have been blaring a warning. The incident with Sebastian so soon after the unusual healing session should have been an omen.

Toughen up, Phillips. Inhale. Exhale.

"Thanks for meeting me, Daire ...," she nodded to the second figure, "... Declan."

Daire watched Tempest's eyes widen, her pupils dilating, as he closed the distance between them. He saw only her. Ignoring the static electricity arcing between them, he reached for her hand clutching the lower edge of her shirt. He wanted to ease the tension in her fingers, spread them out and press her palm against his heart. His breath caught for a few seconds in his chest when she stumbled away from him only to race out of control as her hand twisted, tightening the material, displaying erect nipples which her bra couldn't conceal.

His mouth watered. He wanted to lick the skin beneath the concealing cloth. His heart thudded picturing Tempest braced against a wall, her legs around his hips, her head thrown back and to the side exposing the delicate line of her throat to his teeth and tongue. He inhaled deeply, held it for several seconds then let his breath flow out silently. The scent of her arousal was thick as honey in his nose, in his mouth.

Their first time together should be in a soft bed where he could take his time, search out all her hidden, secret places, watch her lose control and flame in his hands, burning away the last few rational thoughts he might have left and pulling him over the edge with her. But he feared it was going to be hot, fast and out of control … wherever they happened to be when the final threads of his sanity broke. He swallowed then waved a hand at the elevator. "If you're hungry, we can go up to the restaurant."

Tempest shook her head. "No … no … I don't think so." Hungry? She wanted to use her teeth on his skin. The breeze around her ratcheted up a notch. She shifted from foot to foot.

Tulsa stiffened. Something was very wrong. He clicked his tongue catching Judah's attention. Judah looked at Tempest then turned a wide-eyed gaze to Tulsa. Tulsa shrugged.

"While researching Coven Duvayne records, I ran across some references to an ancient family relic, which we would like to recover." She had to go faster. "It's buried deep …," oh, god, she thought, don't even go there, "… on land you own which borders our property in Summerfield. I'd like your permission to excavate it. It's inside a special container, which you can have, although we will be removing a small part for our use. I know your scientists and engineers will want to examine the rest of it. And, of course, we'll replant the area." She prowled the space between Tulsa and Judah behind her, Daire and Declan in front of her, and the surrounding guards.

Daire watched her pace back and forth. "I don't see a problem with that. If you give me the exact coordinates, the date and time you want to start, I'll have people there to help." He was curious about the container, but it took a backseat to whatever was happening to Tempest in the present.

"No. Unh unh. Nope." Momentarily stunned, she stopped. The ends of her hair floated around her face. "The relic is delicate. Needs lots of special handling. You must be very busy. No time for something so trivial. We'll be in and out in a day or two." She marched in a circle around Daire and Declan.

Daire arched an eyebrow at her visibly disturbed guards, motioning them forward, signaling his men to hold their positions. He noted Dawkins' unspoken protest out of the side of his eyes. "What's wrong with her?"

"We have to leave. Keep your guards away from us." Tulsa made a slight movement towards Daire but stopped when Declan stepped between them. "Don't interfere. And whatever you do...DON'T TOUCH HER!" He kept his voice low but filled with authority. "What's your answer about her request?"

"Four of my people will be present. Send Declan a list of equipment you will use, photos of your people, coordinates, date and time."

"Agreed."

"Get her out of here and take care of her." Daire growled. His vision wavered and he saw the garage in two perspectives. A deep rumble flowed from his chest seeing two men closing around his female. A side of himself he had never known before demanded he fight the interlopers, protect his mate. Daire snapped at the hand clutching his shoulder.

Declan dragged Daire into the elevator, shouting into his dotmitter. "Dawkins, clear a path to the vehicle. Stay out of the way. Follow them but give them plenty of space." He disconnected without waiting for a reply shoving Daire into a corner against the back of the elevator. Daire's personality gradually refilled his eyes.

# CHAPTER 14

Tulsa walked beside Tempest circling the floor. "There's clear, clean air outside. You can hear the birds, smell the wind." It was too late to try to draw the energy away from her, it would suck them in, and the power would intensify exponentially as it fed on all their life forces. Spontaneous combustion would be preferable to what they would suffer before death finally granted them relief.

Tempest's beseeching eyes locked on Tulsa's face and voice. "It won't go away, Tulsa. It's got a claw in me and won't let go." She followed him as he slowly backed toward the garage exit.

Tulsa motioned Judah to the driver's side of the Turtle, before leading Tempest to the sidewalk. He scanned the area, noting the positions of the few people in the area. His eyes flicked from place to place searching … always searching. They were in so much trouble. They needed backup.

"Lorcan! Where's Rogan?" Judah stuttered into the dotmitter he reconnected to the Turtle while backing the vehicle into the street. He ignored the screech of brakes and curses filling the air. Stupid drivers! Searching for Tulsa and Tempest, he stopped breathing until he saw them crossing the street. He swerved into the turn lane to the sound of honking horns. "We need help!" Fear crawled into his gut and settled in.

"Tell me what's going on." Rogan's deep calm voice thrummed into Judah's ear.

"Tempest is carrying a load of energy. She needs to dump it. We've got all kinds of outward manifestations."

"Where were you when it started ... never mind." Rogan moved past the unimportant detail. "Where are you now?"

"We're just entering the parking lot at the park near D'eath Towers." He skidded into one of the empty spaces.

"Can she release into the ground in the park?"

"No. I don't think so. There's a cone of wind swirling around her."

"Fuck! Get into a clearing away from people if you can. Ben's technicians just finished the tune-up on Raptor Three. We'll home in on your signal. ETA will be around ten minutes. Can you handle things until we get there?" Rogan galloped out of the house. He slammed into the vehicle at the bottom of the stairs and stomped the accelerator.

"How the hell do I know? Just get here!"

Rogan noted Lorcan racing towards the steel building; gravel spewed from beneath the SUV's tires as he jammed the brakes. Coterie Omega, with three Negotiators and four Protectors, and Coterie Judgment, with nine Tacticals, waited at the hangar entrance. The bird of prey hunkered in the gloom of the structure overwhelming the smaller, more agile Rapiers clustered nearby. The matte black, heavy-duty armored transports carried twenty-five people fully loaded with electronic equipment and supplies. Stripped down, it moved more than triple that number.

Rogan waved the men and women aboard. He climbed inside through the side door and hurried to the cockpit, strapping into the empty seat. "Get us up!"

Tempest was lost. She stood inside herself staring out of her eyes. She could see and hear Judah and Tulsa, but something else was in control. Some part of her she didn't know. Her hands ripped off her T-shirt and the confining strap around her waist. The Feral-spark sneered at the males walking towards her: male predators! She crouched, preparing her attack. Her vision shifted to HyperRealm. Glittering gold and vibrant green permeated the males' auras. She stood, swaying in confusion. Males were red ... alphas who dominate.

Her lips pulled back from her teeth. Her eyeteeth lengthened. She snarled watching the males separate.

Tulsa and Judah stopped.

"We are so fucked!" Judah cursed. "What the hell is happening to her?"

"This is really bad." Tulsa agreed. He was so outside his ability to cope. He winced. Her fingers mimicked claws, the fingernails looked sharp. "We're going to get cut up."

"Get ready." Judah braced for the coming attack.

Feral-spark was distracted. She lifted her head into the breeze and sniffed. Tantalizing mate smell.

She screamed, slashing at the bodies riding her to the ground. She arched, twisted and turned trying to throw off the confining shapes. Blood scent reached her nose. She screeched in triumph renewing her struggles to get free. Hands turned her to her stomach. She bucked, scrambling to get on hands and knees. She had to get free! Her hands tied! Get loose! Get away! Can't move! She lay on the ground panting. Can't ... breathe. Get ... free! Blackness.

Tulsa rolled off Tempest's limp body. He swiped at the sweat and blood rolling down his cheek. His body ached, barely felt scratches in the heat of battle roared to life. He gulped air into his lungs. "We've got to get out of here."

Judah sat beside Tempest, his arms propped on his knees, hands and head dangling between his legs pulled into his chest. "I never want to do that ... ever ... again. Did she at least dump the energy?"

Tulsa struggled to his feet. "I don't think so."

Judah raised stricken eyes to Tulsa. "Fuck!"

"Yeah." Tulsa pulled a bandana from his hip pocket and wiped his face. "She's contained for now. What's happening with transport?" He grimaced when the cloth caught the edges of the scratches on the left side of his face. He stuffed it away and crouched beside Tempest. A finger against her neck read a still faster than normal pulse. He checked her teeth: back to normal. Maybe it was going to be okay.

"Rogan said ten minutes. He's bringing in a Raptor." There would be repercussions from the police, air control and a host of other agencies. Voices and laughter spilled through the shrubs several hundred feet away.

A deep, inaudible to the human ear thrumming roused Feral-spark. She watched the traitorous males standing over her through slitted eyes. The breeze blew the scent of prey into her nose from beyond the mass of green leaves. A shift in the current – acrid, full of strange and caustic odors – irritated her throat. She swallowed the building cough hiding her awareness.

Moving cautiously, she tested the integrity of the bonds on her wrists. An unknown wave flowed from her head to her toes distracting her attention. The body she shared buzzed with energy ... useful, usable energy.

From one second to the next, she was somehow in the meadow near her den in the valley protected by snow-capped mountains! Birds chirped, screeched and honked. Small prey rustled through the grass running for safety. Crunching behind her. The Other! She gulped in the excess force. Her mountain sanctuary disappeared. With an explosion of rage the scale of several atom bombs, she rammed the Tempest-essence into a corner and encased it in a ball of rippling current. How dare it attack!

Fury burned through her and the restraints on her wrists and ankles. Her roar burst outward; she plummeted into the body.

Sebastian's eyes snapped open. Wildfire danced in his mind, along his nerves. Feral-spark! Shock stopped his breath for seconds. How was it possible? Snark! Feral-sparks were the bane of Bloodhawk lineage. Half-bound Reciprocates of human origin were immune – at least as far as he could know.

Get your head out of your ass, Bloodhawk. However it

happened he had to fix it … somehow. And, Bloodhawks didn't kill themselves; they fought to the last bloody second.

He was disgusted with himself. He had no right to give up fighting for life. His men had placed him in a protected place while he was unconscious in the medical pod recovering from injuries he sustained in their last running battle with Skorpus Lair allies. Their decision meant they saw no way to escape and would have sacrificed their lives while leading the vorhols away from him. It would dishonor their sacrifice if he let his long imprisonment affect his reason.

Using the recent influx of energy from Tempest, he stepped outside his body and drifted around the interior of the pod. Control panels for lights, atmosphere, gravity and heating were dead. Scorch marks from fire shadowed the casings and the edge of the transparent cover sealing the upright compartment housing his body.

He studied the board running the systems for the medical chamber. Five minutes later, he sent out tendrils of energy nudging knobs on various gauges. The heavy pressure in his chest vanished leaving him drifting like a feather in a soft breeze. Several careful adjustments reduced the floating feeling. He moved to the power consoles and flipped switches shutting off long dead circuits, watching the gauges inch up several lines. It was the best he could do. With a sigh, he settled into his physical form.

With his personal needs handled for the moment, he looked for a path he could use to slip past the Feral-spark. He had to find Tempest and give her the information she needed to remove it. Her will and resolve would be the determining factor in who would survive the battle for control of the body.

Feral-spark flipped to her feet slamming against the males. Her nose wrinkled at the stench wafting from the huge monster landing on the grass several hundred yards away. She slipped sideways, batting one of the male's hands away, continuing her turn to escape the second enemy. She whirled at the end of his restraining arm using gravity to pull free as she fell to the ground. She scrambled on hands and knees past the men, rising to find her escape shut off by many more bodies.

She screamed her defiance. Gauging the position of the enemy behind her, she stepped back a few feet then ran at the line of bodies in front. With several handsprings and flips, she gained momentum and jumped over two foes aiming a kick at the head of the one on the left. Her feet touched the ground. She dug in and ran.

Her shriek of triumph dampened the sound of feet pounding on the hard ground behind her. She shot around a line of bushes into the midst of more people smelling of sweat and metal. She slashed and cut her way through. Freedom! Her head fell back and her roar seared the air.

"Tempest! Get your head out of your ass and control it!" Sebastian shredded the barrier enclosing Tempest-essence. "Destroy it or swallow it. It's your choice, but there are consequences to ingesting it. Get busy!"

Tempest's rage blasted Sebastian back into his body. She encased Feral-spark in bands of light and squeezed. "Merge with me. I don't want to destroy you. Be one with me."

Feral-spark crouched to spring.

"Don't fight me. We can both survive. Merge with me."

Tempest-essence grappled with Feral-spark. She hugged the doppelganger tighter and tighter. The screech of disbelief echoed for what seemed like years in Tempest's mind before pouring out her open mouth.

Tempest opened her eyes and saw Rogan's worried face against the late afternoon sky. She licked her lips. "It's been ...." She coughed. A hand raised her head, another placed a bottle against her mouth. She gulped the cool liquid. She tried again. "It's been a long week. I don't think I've ever experienced so much chaos in such a short time. Do you think it's over?" She really wanted it to be over. "Is everyone okay?"

"Everyone is mobile. Some cuts and slashes, some

bruising, but it's not bad." Rogan reassured her seeing the horror and self-condemnation on her face.

Sirens cut the air like fingers raking across a blackboard.

Rogan picked her up. He nodded to George Dawkins standing nearby in front of a group of D'eath's men. "Thank D'eath for the assistance." With a nod to the men behind Dawkins, he trotted back across the park. Lorcan, Tulsa and Judah ran in a protective formation around them. He waited for Lorcan to climb into the Raptor, handed Tempest to him, and swung in scrambling out of the way to let the rest of the team inside. "Tulsa, Judah, get to the Turtle and meet us back at base. Don't get caught! If you are stopped and taken to a guardhouse, say nothing and call the attorneys."

Rogan hated to leave the two men behind, but they couldn't abandon the high-tech, expensive vehicle, and it would take too long for them to get to it and drive it to the Raptor, which had the capacity to carry it and the fighters who came with him. He didn't want their technology falling into the wrong hands. Their attorneys were savvy and a specialized team who were part of, and protected, the family.

The Raptor rose silently into the air. Red and blue strobe lights from security force vehicles played across its belly as it disappeared into the evening sky.

# CHAPTER 15

The light flicked into her eye and out. In. Out. Then the other eye. In. Out. Tempest thumped the heels of her boots against the wood table she was sitting on.

"I'm okay, Jake." She watched him reach for another instrument. Her lips trembled, a barely audible growl challenged his approach.

Jake stopped and looked to Rogan and Lorcan propped against the wall.

"You didn't get much sleep last night. You're barely able to sit still. You said Sebastian helped you, but you won't talk to us. And you don't normally growl." Rogan eyed the distance between Tempest and Jake.

She jumped to the floor, sneering at Jake who flinched back. She wanted to grab him by the lapels of his white coat, pull him close and lick his neck just to give him something to be scared about. He smelled like food … prey. She shook her head. That's not right. I don't treat friends this way. What the fuck was going on? She hadn't been right since Daire's benefit.

"I'm sorry, Jake." She turned to Rogan and Lorcan who were within reaching distance. She sucked in a deep breath and let it out noisily, shrugged her shoulders. "I need to run. I need a lot of physical activity. When I swallowed what Bastian called the Feral-spark, she didn't go down easy. He said no one has ever done that before. In every other instance, the person destroyed the spark. It didn't feel right to me. She was real, aware. She felt like another part of me. Bastian doesn't know what will happen. Doctors aren't going to find anything. Let me go."

Jake moved to stand beside Tempest showing her he wasn't afraid. "Her blood pressure and pulse are slightly elevated, but I can't find anything wrong with her. I've taken some blood and will rush the results. A head doctor isn't the answer either." He studied her out of the side of his eyes. "Take her out on the course. Give her the exercise she wants. Maybe it's part of the integration between mind and body." He shrugged and turned to replace the instruments in his bag, struggling to hide his alarm. "I need to finish packing up everything here and getting it on the truck to Summerfield. As soon as the blood results come in, I'll call you. Get out of my lab!"

"All right. The training course is still intact." Rogan blinked at the brilliant smile on Tempest's face. "Are we still going after Sebastian's pod tomorrow? If so, we need to let D'eath know."

It was a good idea as far as he was concerned. Two days of hard physical activity should tire her enough to sleep. Although studies showed the effects of sleep deprivation weren't life threatening, it would affect her ability to make rational decisions. And they needed Tempest focused.

"No! Leave the troublesome male where he is. We don't need him." Alarm filled Tempest as the thoughts floated across her mind. She checked her shields to make sure Bastian wouldn't hear. "Yes." Her voice was almost a hiss. She gritted her teeth and added more force to her tone. "Yes. Make the arrangements." She glanced down at what she was wearing. "I'll need to change before ...." Her sneakers, barely-there top and shorts appeared beneath her nose. "Thanks."

She grabbed the clothes and trotted behind the screen set haphazardly in a corner of the room. "Has anyone fed Gracie and Maggie?"

"They're on the way to Summerfield with Ben. And, yes, they're okay and have been fed, petted and pampered." Rogan nodded at Tempest when her face popped around the side of the screen.

She disappeared. Hands gyrated wildly above the top of the screen. Lorcan cocked an eyebrow at Rogan as the partition shook and wavered. Rogan grinned and shook his head. It wouldn't fall.

"What are you grinning about?" Tempest appeared around the side placing a hand on the partition, halting its downward motion.

# CHAPTER 16

Tempest hung by the tips of her fingers from a net-covered wall. Sweat dripped into her eyes and ran down her back. She had to haul her butt up and over the top before the outline of the netting became permanently imprinted on her cheek. Her arms shook and her body trembled.

Rogan sat on the top of the wall inches from her fingers. "Want a hand?"

"No." Her refusal was flat and emphatic. Other team members had joined them on the course. The first time through – the obstacles had been a breeze. Two hours later and she was flagging on her third loop around the circuit. She wanted to scream her frustration seeing the men lope past her, some turning to run backwards as they yelled encouraging words. She was panting. They were talking back and forth with no hitch in their breathing. She just wanted to smack them. And she wasn't going to give up in front of them.

Samuel Freeth and Strider Condren scampered up the mesh to hang on each side of her.

"I can do this." She puffed, her legs searching for leverage on the next strand. "Touch the foot, Strider, and you'll be on house cleaning duty for the next six months." Her fingers were growing numb. She had to do something.

Strider jerked his hand away and settled against the wall. She meant what she said and she would remember it. He was only going to be cleaning his weapons, not dishes, floors and whatever else she would think of as retribution.

Damnit! She was stuck. Her body didn't have the reserves left to make the final push to the top. "Fine. Help me."

Samuel and Strider moved in to support her as Rogan clasped her wrists. "Let go." He eased her to the top of the wall and held her against his chest while she regained her strength.

Samuel and Strider swarmed up to perch beside them.

"Everyone is aware of what's been happening the last few days. You've lived and fought with them for years. They know your worth. You have nothing to prove." Rogan pushed a bottle of water into her hand. "Drink."

"Rogan!" Massee Koba was the designated Voice for the group on the course.

He lifted a hand in acknowledgment shifting Tempest's weight to Strider. He slipped down the wall and walked to Massee.

With a sideways glance at the trio on top of the structure, she gave her report. "Jindra says there's a Luxury from the Covens at the gate. The dark-tinted windows are concealing the occupants. The driver is asking for Tempest and refuses to identify the passengers until she arrives."

"Fuck. Now is not a good time." He looked up and saw Tempest, Samuel and Strider laughing. "Tell Jindra we'll be back in an hour." He offered a few more instructions then let her go.

Seeing Tempest, Samuel and Strider preparing to slide over the far side of the wall, he whistled and waved an arm. He watched Samuel and Strider joking with Tempest while keeping a close eye on her footing as they climbed down beside her.

The laughter disappeared.

"What's wrong?" Tempest yelled over the noise of the landing Nightwing, its anti-gravity and stealth systems disengaged for the short hop from the hangars.

"A Coven Luxury is waiting at the guardhouse."

The frown burrowed deep into her forehead. "Did someone

forget to mention Father had called to say he was coming?" It didn't make sense. He summoned her to attend him at whatever place he designated; he didn't make social or business calls to the Estate. She sighed. "It must be someone from one of the other Covens wanting me to intercede with The Duvayne. Well, they'll have to wait until we shower and change."

Rogan nodded. "I told Massee to say you are involved in some negotiations and will be available in an hour. Additional guards are stationed around the vehicle to ensure their safety while they wait."

She beamed at Rogan. "I like that! They can't call insult by the extra guards since it's for their protection. Ex-cell-ent! You play the game much better than I do." She hunched her shoulders. "But we'll go into the meeting wearing comfortable clothes."

Seeing the surprised look Samuel and Strider gave her, she scrunched her face at them. "I want them to understand they don't control us and we don't follow Coven rules. At least I'm not appearing before them as I am and I don't plan to put on my leathers. I'm starting out now how I mean to go forward once we're at Summerfield. There's going to be a whole new playing field everyone is going to have to get used to."

She returned the pilot's wave as she stalked past his window to climb into the belly of the beast. Her knuckles turned white from her grip on the arms of the seat. Her anxiety rose with the ascent – why were Coven representatives at their gate?

An hour later, she walked out the front door and down the stairs to the table and chairs positioned beneath an immense oak tree. It had protected the house and grounds for many decades. She would miss the tree. It had sheltered her from many storms: brewed by nature and by humans. She wished she could have it transported to Summerfield.

She curled into the high-backed wicker chair with one leg beneath her. Her pink toenails in open-toed sandals matched the short, wispy skirt wrapped around her waist. With elbow propped on the chair arm and her chin on her hand, a strap of the maroon velvet bustier slipped off her other shoulder. She yawned as she waited, idly swinging her leg encased in burgundy leggings. Her mind offered up alternatives for digging up the tree and transporting it the hundreds of miles to their new compound. Several ideas were so outrageous as to be impossible. She grinned as she examined and discarded them.

A white vehicle swept down the driveway. The escorting matte black Dartbykes peeled away to park in a half circle behind Tempest. The guards dismounted, pulled carbines from sheaths on the sides of the bykes, and moved to their usual positions.

Rogan sauntered down the stairs from the house to lean against the back of Tempest's chair. "You have a weapon?"

Her right hand floated down to the side of the seat cushion; her fingers tapped its edge.

The vehicle's front doors swung open and the driver and a bodyguard exited. They moved in tandem to open the passenger doors.

"What the hell?" Adrenaline poured into Tempest's bloodstream. She hissed at Rogan fighting the urge to jump to her feet. "What is he doing here?"

Disgust tightened Nelson Treadaway's face. He stopped beside one of the chairs set in the informal space and waved for the driver to wipe a cloth over the seats, backs and arms of both chairs. Out of the corner of his eye, he watched Robert Phillips sit down opposite his daughter.

With a quick sideways glance at Treadaway, Robert Phillips cleared his throat. "Really, Tempest, I'm sure you can afford decent clothes. I'll have your Mother send you the clothes you left when Mámá took you if you need them." He didn't know anything about his daughter's financial situation. He really didn't know much about her personal life at all. He and her mother were limited to what they were able to gather from news reports and small amounts of information trickling through Coven society. He cursed silently, hating the circumstances and the man beside him. Betrayal of his youngest child was a weeping sore on his heart and soul.

Anger stirred remnants of Feral-spark, tugging the fragments together like metal filings to a magnet. Tempest swallowed the ball in her throat and metaphorically Feral-spark. The second dose of spark-essence felt like acid surging through her veins.

The years had been unkind to her Father. His dark blonde hair was thinning and stress etched lines into his too-lean face. Her lip wanted to curl in a snarl: he was prey. Her chair vibrated from Rogan's invisible shaking.

"It's always a pleasure to see you, Father." Her voice held the dryness of the desert.

Treadaway relished the antipathy between child and parent. The next few minutes would be sweet indeed. He settled further into the chair. "We have things to discuss, Tempest. Dismiss your guards. While you're changing to something more appropriate, we'll inform Branaugh of our requirements for meals and accommodations for tonight and tomorrow morning."

She blinked, stunned at the man's audacity. Her friends stiffened, several stepped forward a few paces. She relaxed and lounged on the cushions. "I don't keep secrets from my friends." She waved her hand to encompass all the people around her. A flick of her finger drew Morgan Reynolds, a fourth generation descendant of Treadaway's Darksylk coven, to her side. "Morgan, please call Hotel Sanibel and make room, dinner and breakfast reservations for my Father and Mr. Treadaway." She smiled with all her teeth showing. "There. All taken care of."

"I didn't train my daughter to show such contempt for her parents and rulers." Robert Phillips sat upright. He didn't agree with Treadaway's bullying tactics. In fact, there were times when he'd like nothing better than to punch Treadaway like a boxing dummy. But Treadaway was on the Council. Tempest's flaunting of Coven strictures in actions similar to what she had just done had forced him into siding against her. She was so inflexible, refusing to see he had no choice. He had to play the game for the welfare and safety of the entire family. He didn't have the resources The Duvayne did and his mother's attitude had pushed him to the initial alliance with Darksylk. It hadn't been a bad decision ... until Treadaway took control of the Coven. He clasped his fingers around the arms of his chair to hide the tremors.

Tempest straightened and leaned forward. "That's right, Father. You didn't train me. And no one rules me." She slumped. She was physically tired from the training session and emotionally fatigued from dealing with the crap again. "Say what you came here to tell me and get out." She didn't have the stamina for slogging through the minutia of Coven politics.

"There's no need for histrionics." Treadaway so enjoyed the little dramas between father and daughter. His power swelled with the influx of energy. The anger, hurt, and pain tasted so sweet. He could barely restrain showing his delight. "We're here with some sad news. Your Father wanted to tell you himself."

Tempest tensed. Hearing the excitement in Treadaway's voice, she looked at her Father closely. He was sad and unhappy.

Robert Phillips adjusted his coat. "Yes, yes, of course." He smoothed his hands through his hair then settled. "It's my distressful task to tell you that your grandmother was assassinated this morning." He flinched inside at Tempest's cry of shock. He hated breaking the news to her in such a harsh manner. "The police responded to an anonymous tip and found Mikuh Braeden and his men standing over her body. The officers are searching for Braeden and the men who survived the resulting shootout."

Treadaway interrupted. "We'll need to move quickly to reassure all of the stockholders of Coven Duvayne companies that the leadership is intact. There are documents that need to be signed."

Robert Phillips aimed a quelling glance at Treadaway. "I'll be handling the arrangements for Mámá's internment in the family crypt for three days from now. Your old room has been cleaned and your mother and I ... the entire family ... would like for you to stay with us for a few days."

Treadaway broke in. It wouldn't do for the Phillips family to bond now. "You'll attend the Grand Convocation where a decision will be made about dissolution of Coven Duvayne or appointment of a new CEO."

"ENOUGH! Enough." Tempest hugged herself trying to contain the razor-sharp pain like knives stabbing her from every direction. She felt like an old woman as she climbed to her feet. Rogan and her guardians closed around her.

"You've done what you came to do." Rogan's voice froze the air and sent an atavistic thrill along the napes of Phillips' and Treadaway's necks. He looked past them to Morgan Reynolds who nodded his head. "Your reservations are done. Leave."

Without direction, the guards surrounded Phillips and Treadaway and herded them to the vehicle. They stood in a line between the Luxury and Tempest, enclosed in Rogan and Lorcan's arms.

"How can she be gone, Rogan?" She wanted to scream her anguish and pain. Rules, teaching and expectations were the backbone of life with Glory Duvayne, but it was better than the jockeying for position pursued by her parents. Tempest had known The Duvayne would take on heaven and hell to protect her, as long as it fit within the scheme of Glory's criteria. Until Rogan, Lorcan and the other members of her heart family had demonstrated differently, Tempest had been satisfied with Glory's interpretation of family life. She had planned to dissolve her daily connection with her grandmother but losing Glory in such a fashion was surreal. It was outside the scope of her ability to embrace and believe.

Rogan swung Tempest into his arms and carried her into the house. Jake appeared in a doorway, a pressure syringe in his hand.

"No!" Her voice was ragged, tears clogged her throat. She raised her head from Rogan's shoulder and drew in hiccupping breaths. "Put me down, Rogan."

He slid her to her feet, shaking his head at Jake.

Jake frowned and started forward again. He was the doctor, and, in medical decisions, his word was law. Everyone had committed to the idea when he joined the family years ago.

"Really, Jake. I'm okay ... or I'm mostly okay. Let me get my breath." She smiled at all of the men and women crowded inside the entranceway.

"Bronson, Carson and Morgan are following the Luxury to see where they go -- to the hotel or some other lodging." Samuel patted her on the shoulder, his action awkward, in contradiction to his normal elegant grace. "We're sorry for your loss, Tempest."

She hiccupped again and gave him a watery smile, including all of them with her gaze. "Thanks."

She inhaled a deep breath. "Alright, we have a lot to consider. We have to get to Mikuh and his men. Jake, I want you and all our on-hand medical supplies and equipment in the Raptor. And someone get on the security channels, see how close they are to finding Mikuh. You all know the drill. I'll be giving them sanctuary and a permanent home if they want it. Anyone who doesn't agree with my decision should ..."

Their growls caused her to grin. Her strength returned with their confidence and support. She wanted to mourn her grandmother, remember their life together, but there were people she cared for in danger ... and not just the ones in the field.

"Evacuate all of our remaining noncombatants to Summerfield." She wiped her face with the wet cloth Lorcan handed her. The coolness was wonderful and she held the cloth over her eyes for a few seconds. She lowered the rag. "If they went after The Duvayne, we'll be next on the list contrary to what my Father's interest in my well-being might suggest."

Heads nodded, their faces grim.

"Contact Gene and Jack. Grandmother told me several years ago she would be giving them a sealed copy of her Will.

Tell them what happened and get the documents filed with the Courts and World Enclave immediately." Her mind tripped over vignettes of talking, laughing and crying with her grandmother. The pictures whirled through her head, a kaleidoscope of movement, color and emotions. She bent over, her hands around her waist, holding in the pain. It couldn't escape now. There wasn't time.

A warm hand ran up and down her back helping to hold back the ache for now. She stood upright, wiping fresh tears from her face with the cloth in her hand. "Get the extra equipment to the dig site for Bastian's pod." Her voice was dry and hoarse. "Tell Ben he's in charge of the excavation if we're not there. Mikuh takes precedence. What am I forgetting, Rogan?" She turned to her Captain, her friend. They weren't intimate in the Biblical sense and never would be. It wasn't that type of relationship. He was more than friend, more than brother. He was the north in the compass of her life, whether she remained single or married.

"What are your plans for the funeral and Convocation?" He let Lorcan assign people to the various tasks, quickly clearing the room. Leading Tempest into the kitchen, he waved her to a chair, walked to the refrigerator and pulled out a bottle of soda, stepped to the overhead cabinets, removed a glass, filled it with ice at the refrigerator and set both items in front of her. With brisk, economical movements, he fixed sandwiches and soup, casting periodic evaluating glances her way. Placing dishes on the table, he sat across from her, motioning with a spoon to catch her attention, urging her to eat.

"Sorry." She had been lost in memories of the few times her grandmother had pushed everything aside and they had escaped together to one of the distant sanctuaries where her grandmother was safe. They had laughed, talked and played together for several days.

She dug into the hearty soup, her eyes fluttering with pleasure at the explosion of flavor in her mouth. "I didn't handle

Father and Treadaway very well today, but they know which buttons to push and I always seem to respond the same way, every time." She sighed, idly stirring her soup.

"Don't play with your food. Eat it." Rogan handed her a buttered slice of home-baked bread. "Treadaway deliberately made it as difficult as possible for you even though your Father was trying to soften the blow." He shook his head stopping her automatic retort. She was still interpreting her family relationships through the lens of rebellious daughter. He had noticed over the last several years a difference in Robert Phillips' dealings with Treadaway. "It was camouflage for something else. Do you know what's in The Duvayne's Will?"

She chewed the grainy bread and swallowed, then chewed some more. She finally resorted to several sips of the soda to clear her mouth. "She never said and I didn't ask. Even at ninety-two, she was tough. With major discoveries and advancements in the medical community each year, I expected her to live well past two hundred." Her shoulders bowed. "They took her life, Ro! They walked into her home and killed her!" The pain threatened to envelop her. "I don't care about the Will. I'll make sure everything is filed and leave it in the hands of the executors."

"Hmmmm." He suspected there were dangerous secrets in the papers. Secrets which were going to bite them in the ass.

Tempest rose from her chair, walked to the coffeemaker and poured two cups of coffee. Carrying the mugs back to the table gave her a few minutes to clear her head. Setting the mugs down, she turned and went to the refrigerator, removed a pie tin, set it on the counter and, using a knife from the stand on the countertop, cut the fruit and crust into eight slices. Pulling two plates from the cabinets, she used a spatula to lever slices out of the pan and place them on the dishes. She licked her thumb, picked up the plates and set one in front of Rogan before dropping onto the bench across from him.

"I won't be going to the memorial facility. I'm not going to be an easy target. I want five Coteries at the family crypt. I want them noticeable. Full body armor and whatever weapons they want to carry."

He raised an eyebrow. Some of the men and women had unusual tastes in weapons.

"I want our best; the more exotic the better. You, Lorcan, Samuel and Strider will be with me at all times. Make sure everyone understands you are in charge, Ro. You make all the decisions that day. The politics are already starting and on that day, when I'm readily available, family and representatives from the Covens are going to consume me. They'll try to separate us." She sat at the table and fixed her eyes on his. "Don't let them. No matter what they say, or I might say, stay with me. One or more of you must be attached to me like glue."

She rubbed a finger between her eyebrows thinking through the issues. Sadness fogged her mind. She shook her head. "The Convocation isn't important to us. We'll be in Summerfield and Bastian is going to expand our viewpoint to include galaxies, not just one planet." Excitement filtered into her voice followed by trepidation.

The kitchen door slammed open. Tempest grabbed the knife beside her plate, dropped to the floor, and rolled under the table. Legs shrouded to the knees in brown leather halted beside Rogan's chair.

Damn. She settled on the floor cross-legged, her shoulders bowed to keep from hitting her head on the tabletop. The knife dangled from her hand propped on her knee. She had overreacted. "You can laugh if you want."

Rogan's chair scooted back. He sat on the floor. "There's nothing to laugh about. You reacted like a fighter in a combat situation. With the assassination of The Duvayne, they have declared war."

Strider squatted in front of them, his arms hugging his legs. "Good job, Tempest! Your training is working."

They were just trying to keep her from feeling embarrassed. She raised her head and looked them in the eye.

Surprise flittered over her face.

"Yes, we're serious." Rogan accurately interpreted her expression. "I'm glad you reacted the way you did. We don't know what's coming at us in the next days, weeks, months or even years. You have to be ready to defend yourself, particularly when you feel you're in a safe environment." He didn't foresee her being alone, but crap happened. He planned for the unexpected.

"Let's have a group hug." Strider grinned.

A laugh erupted from Tempest's stomach. She hadn't thought she would be able to laugh for a long time. "Thanks, Strider. What sent you barreling in here in the first place?"

"We know where Mikuh might be. The surveillance van is out front with an SUV. We have twenty Darts ready to move. The noncombatants are on the way to Summerfield surrounded by the rest of the Darts and several Rapiers providing air cover. Raptor Three is flying to the standby field."

She scrambled around Strider. Standing, she flipped the knife toward the sink and looked around the room one last time. "Have the cleaners make one more visit. This time we're paying for a major wipe leaving no fingerprints or DNA anywhere. Furnishings, furniture and accessories are part of the house. Ben promised to coordinate transferring all my personal effects." She untied the skirt letting it flutter to the floor and stepped out of her sandals. Walking barefoot to the door, she stopped and turned. "Who has my weapons and boots?"

# CHAPTER 17

"There aren't enough heat signatures, Rogan." Tempest swept the binoculars slowly left to right. The warehouse was sheltered in the middle of a group of eight storage buildings in the abandoned business park. Smoke rose in a fitful stream above groupings of metal containers standing in the center of the small parking areas in front of several of the structures.

"It looks like all of the Wanderers are gone for walkabout." Belly down at her side, Strider used his own binoculars to scan the depression.

The small hill above the square of buildings was a good vantage point for a staging area and surveying the surroundings. The communications satellite they had access to was out of position for their purposes. They didn't have time to wait for it. The antenna attached to the top of the black surveillance van behind them, extended to its highest position and whirling softly, monitored traffic within ten miles of the area. Darts hunkered below the ridgeline of sycamore and oak trees. Bodies lined the crest of the knoll.

"Mikuh had twenty-five men and women in his teams. I count twelve people down there." She squirmed away from the edge, scrambled to her feet and walked to the open door at the side of the van. "Incoming?"

The screens cast a blue glow on Blake's boyish features. A mop of thick sun-bleached blonde hair perched atop his head and onto his forehead like a bowl above the shaved sides. His hand caressed the barrel of a carbine leaning against the counter. "It's clear for now."

With the door against her back, Tempest studied the faces of her friends. It was never easy going into a situation where the possibility existed someone could be hurt or killed. She could let Rogan give the orders and let him carry the responsibility for their lives, but it was part of her commitment to each of them to bear the weight of their trust. To do less would be to dishonor their bond.

"The only place the Raptor can land is five miles from here. The surveillance van has to protect the Raptor and landing site. We don't know how many people are hurt or the extent of their injuries. If we have time, we'll triage and put the seriously injured into the SUV. Everyone else will double up on the Darts. If trouble arrives, split up and get to the Raptor if you can. If it's too risky, head for Summerfield. As soon as you can, call Ben. He'll send a Strike Force, Raptor, or both, to get you. Use your heads. You will all make it to Summerfield alive and well. Understand?" She nodded her head, looking each person in the eye, waiting until their heads joined her affirmative motion. By force of will alone, she would make sure they survived. "Any questions?"

The men and women ran to their Darts. She watched them for a few minutes before grabbing the black T-shirt from the floor of the van and pulling it over her head. Striding to the SUV, she slipped on the custom-made armored vest, checked the gun in its holster on her hip, and touched the knives in her wrist and boot sheaths like lodestones. She settled into the passenger seat. If only there was some way she could wrap their entire bodies in bullet- and laser-proof shields. Hmmm. She slumped deeper into the seat. She needed a power source: the sun.

The energy she had drawn from the sun during her healing session had been overwhelming, almost uncontrollable. What if she created a shield around each person and powered the intensity with …

"What are you thinking about? And just so you know, I talked to Mikuh not long ago. He sent most of his men to a different place which solves the issue of not enough heat signatures down there. I also told him you wanted him at Summerfield as a friend, not potential hireling." Rogan eased the SUV over the rise behind the Darts scattering in different directions.

"What?" Her eyes were unfocused, her expression dazed. No, that wouldn't work. She would need to see each person to hold everything in place and the power had to attach to something. Their metal workers and computer techs could create a lapel pin. No. What if it fell off? She shook her head to clear her thoughts. It wasn't like her to get distracted in a precarious situation.

"I was trying to work out a way to make them completely bullet-proof." A tide of warmth flooded her face and neck. She let the information about Mikuh flow past her. There was enough to concentrate on rather than fussing about something that was within Rogan's bailiwick to handle.

"I know." Rogan kept his eyes trained on the road ahead. "I want to do the same thing every time I give the order placing someone in jeopardy."

"We've got incoming. Ten miles out and closing fast." Blake's voice whispered through their earbuds.

Rogan stomped on the accelerator and skidded around a corner, sliding to a halt at the door of the warehouse.

Tempest threw open her door and raced to the building's entrance. With Rogan at her back, she eased into the darkness. The hair on her neck rising she spun into the body behind her letting her momentum push them into the wall. Rogan appeared from the shadows pulling at the figure.

"It's Tempest." She accompanied the whispered words with a forceful slam of her elbow in the stomach, loosening the arm tightening around her throat. The figure grunted and seconds later slumped against her back. Together, she and Rogan lowered him to the floor.

"Tempest is here." The hoarse voice spoke of extreme bouts of yelling and cursing.

Men limped and stumbled out of the gloom. Two men supported a litter. Blood caked skin and rough bandages.

Tempest did a headcount with Rogan's information in mind and breathed a sigh of relief: twelve people. "We have to get you out now. The security forces know you're here. We need to know how many of you are seriously injured? Be honest with me."

Jordan Cobb staggered from the group. "Mikuh," he waved a hand at the litter, "is hurt real bad. He needs a blood transfusion immediately. We all have injuries in varying degrees, but we can move."

The men stiffened, guns rising. The oversized metal door to the warehouse screeched upward.

"It's okay." Tempest glanced over her shoulder assuring herself as well as them that friendlies were on the other side of the doors.

Darts swarmed into the space, jockeying around with smooth precision. Tempest climbed into the back of the SUV and helped Jordan guide Mikuh's litter into place. Randall Blanchard, one of The Duvayne's newest recruits, climbed into the passenger seat beside Rogan. Tempest arched an eyebrow at Jordan.

Caution, he tapped out on her hand before stepping back and closing the door. She watched him mount the last Dart behind Strider, following them with her eyes as they disappeared around the buildings. She spun on her knees and pulled a bag of blood from a container. Knowing the blood type of the regular members of Mikuh's team had helped Jake prepare the packs in the SUV. There was just enough to stabilize a patient.

Her eyes met Rogan's in the rearview mirror. She checked Blanchard's position noting he was tracking the Darts. She glanced back at Rogan, wiggled her eyebrows and looked sideways at Blanchard.

Knowing he had received her message, she moved quickly, shoving the blood bag between the clamps on the roof. She attached a pressure node on the end of the feeder tube, slapped it over a vein in Mikuh's arm, and nodded her head. Rogan eased forward while she moved around changing soaked bandages.

"Damn, Mikuh," she muttered, "they meant for you to die with Grandmother." His eyes fluttered. She held her breath, hoping he would awaken. His breathing slowed, became shallow.

"Oh, no, you don't!" She scurried around setting oxygen into place and adding medication pads at various places on his arms. Hearing gunfire, sirens and the roar of Dart engines in the distance, she winced. The Darts were equipped with stealth capabilities. The rescuers and their charges were acting as bait so she and Rogan could get Mikuh to the Raptor.

She fell over Mikuh's body, the SUV slewing sideways from the force of a truck colliding with the rear bumper. Bullets rattled against the armored glass. "Fuck!"

She keyed her transmitter and screamed, "Raptor, we're taking fire and coming in hot! ETA is ...," she checked her watch, "five minutes."

"We're on our way." Strider's voice shouted in her ear.

"No! Strider, get to the landing field, transfer Jordan and then leave. Follow the plan." She didn't want too much information going out over the air. "Raptor, get the lasers online. What the hell?"

The men and women in the Raptor and on the Darts were grim-faced when the transmission died. Following the last instructions from Tempest, Darts zoomed into the landing field. Bodies jostled back and forth as rescuers pushed and shoved unresponsive men towards the open door of the aircraft.

Tempest lurched toward the front seat. She shoved her gun against Blanchard's neck. He ignored it, struggling to stab Rogan with the knife in his hand. "Stop!"

She couldn't knock him out with the gun, the seat back

protected his head. Fear ripped through her at Rogan's grunt of pain. "Damn you!" Her choices were gone. She pulled the trigger.

Blood sprayed the windows. Warm liquid splashed her face. Blanchard fell forward.

Rogan shoved Blanchard's body towards the floorboard. His gaze darted between mirrors checking on the location of the ramming truck. It was listing sideways, a concrete column buried in the driver's side. He twisted and zig zagged the SUV around the buildings, eyes scanning and searching constantly. Steering across the intersection of a major thoroughfare and slowing to speed limit, he turned into an alley and several hundred yards later into a byway, halted, pushing the gearshift into park. He slumped against the steering wheel.

Tempest's hand trembled, silent tears streamed down her face. She fumbled with the door handle and fell to the concrete. On hands and knees, in the filth and dirt and noxious smells, she vomited repeatedly.

A cool hand held her forehead. Her stomach and throat burned. The sharp tang of vomit in her mouth caused her to retch. She thrust the arm away and sat back on her heels. With heaving breaths, she let the hand help her to her feet. She turned her head away from the body lying on the ground, focusing on Rogan's arm. "He got you."

Her voice was weak. She walked to the back of the SUV, opened the rear door, drew one of the packs lying scattered across the floor towards her and rummaged through it. With a package of gauze in her hand, she twisted around. Wiping away the blood on her face with the back of her hand, she swallowed back acid rising in her throat. "It may need stitches."

She worked at appearing calm, wrapping the mesh around and around Rogan's forearm. She taped it into place then climbed back into the rear compartment and settled beside Mikuh, checked his bandages, the pressure pads on his arms, and the condition of the blood bag.

Rogan's heart hurt. She had saved his life at the cost of her innocence. It was her first kill. He had never wanted her to have to carry that burden on her soul.

He slammed the rear door shut and walked around the vehicle, climbing into the driver's seat. He ignored the body lying in the garbage where he had dropped it. Traitors didn't deserve anything more.

With a few turns, he was back on the main street. Several blocks later, he switched to a side street. He checked on Tempest every couple of minutes in the rearview mirror and watched for trailing vehicles. When he was satisfied no one was following, he drove to the landing field.

A deep huff left his chest: the Raptor appeared to suck the sunlight into its hull, sitting in the field like a small black rock hill. A frown burrowed into his forehead seeing the line of men and women with guns, prone on the ground. They rose and closed around the SUV. A figure carrying a pack on his back jumped through the open door in the side of the airship and trotted toward the massed vehicles.

Tempest turned her face away from the opening rear door of the SUV. She scooted back letting Jordan inside and watched him place the blood bag beside Mikuh and push the litter out.

She pulled a canister of wipes from a box and scrubbed her face. Her stomach roiled. The tissues were scarlet. She swallowed twice then gagged. With her hand covering her mouth, she pushed past the men congregated at the back of the SUV and stumbled to one side. With a hand braced against the side of the vehicle, she bent over and heaved.

Several people stepped around the side of the SUV, concern clearly reflected on their faces. Rogan walked through the gathered men and women, whispered a few words and gestured them away. He wiped Tempest's face and hands with wet wipes and handed her a bottle of water. He waited as she swished her mouth, spit, and finally sipped. "Okay now?"

She nodded. "How are Mikuh and the others?" Her voice

was gritty and hoarse.

"Jake is with Mikuh inside the Raptor. He's critical, but Jake thinks he's got a good chance. You saved him with the blood, oxygen, and medications. Let's get you on the bird. The sooner Mikuh is at the Summerfield medical facilities the better his chances."

She wobbled forward then regained her balance. Shoulders back, head up, she marched to the waiting group. "Jordan, you and your men get on the Raptor. No arguments." Her tone was adamant, forestalling the protests gathering on their faces. "Is everyone else okay?"

She moved among her team pulling red splattered shirts up or open, checking for wounds. They stood patiently for her inspection saying nothing. Dirt, sweat, and scratches, easily bandaged. Satisfied, she walked back to Rogan's side. "Break up into small groups. How's the traffic, Blake?"

He raised his hand, his fingers in a circle.

"We were lucky." Her voice was hard as the stone in the mountain range in the distance. "I'll see all of you at Summerfield. Stay out of trouble and no side trips." She whipped around and marched to the SUV. "I've got shotgun. Whoever's coming with me, get in." She slammed the door.

The SUV rocked with the influx of bodies. Ugh! I stink, she thought. She powered her seat into a half reclining position ignoring the cursing voice behind her. Whoever it was could crawl into the rear compartment if they needed more legroom. She closed her eyes and kept them closed, her body listed back and forth as the SUV climbed the Raptor's ramp. Blood splattered the windshield and her face behind her closed lids, replaying over and over in a grotesque loop. Tears seeped down her cheeks until she finally drifted into sleep.

# CHAPTER 18

Daire stared in stony silence at the man seated in front of his desk. He had heard through other sources about The Duvayne's assassination. His men were rousting their street contacts for information about what was going on. Taking down a Coven head of such stature meant a purge was in progress and he was afraid Tempest was in the middle of it. He wanted to be with her to offer his condolences and protection, but he would settle for a call, a message, anything to make sure she was all right. He didn't understand his obsession with her after just two meetings.

"Daire, you may have already heard about Glory Duvayne's unfortunate demise at the hands of her security team. It's depressing really. We can't even trust the people we hire to protect us." Nelson Treadaway shook his head. He was dressed in a two thousand dollar black suit he had purchased recently just for this event. His face was set in a practiced, sad expression, but inside he bubbled with anticipation and excitement. Everything he had worked toward for years was now coming to fruition.

"I understand the police department is still investigating." Daire wanted to find out how deep Treadaway was in the conspiracy. "I've always heard Captain Braeden and his people were honest and trustworthy. What would he gain by murdering his employer? An employer he's been with for many years?"

Treadaway waved his hand in dismissal. "Who knows what goes on in the heads of such people? The Council wants the City's leaders to understand that, while the Covens and Council are in transition during this distressing time, business will continue uninterrupted."

Treadaway needed to find out about the relationship between D'eath and the Phillips girl. The dynamics at the Gala would indicate a sexual relationship. Before proceeding with the current plan, he needed to determine how much damage would result from her elimination. Of course, the reformation of Coven Duvayne under Robert Phillips would give the father more control over his daughter. And once she was separated from the barbarians who surrounded and protected her, the long-ago initiation could be completed.

His groin tightened in anticipation of her kneeling bound and naked at his feet, and, until she was trained, her mouth held open with cloth-lined braces, her teeth covered with silicone shields, while his member thrust in and out as fast, hard and deep as he wanted. His eyes glazed for a moment before he recalled where he was and whom he was with.

Daire rose from his chair, walked to the wall of windows and braced his shoulder against the column at the corner. He had to get as far from Treadaway as possible. The avaricious and pitiless look in his eyes sickened Daire. What had Treadaway been thinking about? Daire had to be cautious, appear cooperative, until he identified all of the players. "I appreciate the notice. I'm sure Martin Karbonneau will as well."

Yes, Daire thought, it was one of the reasons for Treadaway's visit – confirmation of the link between Daire and the World President. But what else did Treadaway hope to accomplish?

"We understand the President is in urgent negotiations to settle the recent border disputes in the Asian contingent. The Council will choose a new representative in the next few days to attend the World Enclave's meeting on the matter. Are you attending the services and internment?" He would need to get extra people on the dotcams to specifically track and record D'eath's movements.

Daire slipped a hand into a pocket of his slacks. "I plan to pay my respects to the family." He was deliberately noncommittal about his actions.

"I know you're very busy." Treadaway rose and walked to Daire with his hand extended. "I appreciate the few minutes you were able to give me." And the next time we meet, you will be coming to me. If what he thought was true about D'eath's relationship with Tempest, he relished the thought of greeting the bastard with Tempest bent over a table nearby with a butt plug clearly in place. How delicious! He swallowed a laugh walking out of the office.

Daire wiped his hands on the handkerchief he pulled from his breast pocket and dropped it in the nearest wastebasket. Motioning Declan, who entered the room from a door hidden in the paneling on the wall opposite the windows, to the chairs in front of the desk, he hurried into the adjoining bathroom and scrubbed his hands, rinsing them for several minutes beneath water as hot as he could endure. He shook the liquid off and took his time drying each hand. Tossing the towel in a basket beneath the sink, he strode back into the office.

"A fishing expedition." Declan was propped against the front of the desk, his feet crossed at the ankles.

"Yes. But did the fisherman find the fish he was angling for?" Daire paced the floor. "I think he was trying to find out if I have a relationship with Tempest and how I feel about The Duvayne's 'demise' as he described it. I don't like what's happening, Declan. The ramifications of Treadaway taking control of the Covens are alarming. Start moving our people and operations to Jericho.

"Check the list of companies that want to lease the penthouse. Run deep background checks on all of them. I don't want Coven stoolies in this building. The terms should reflect a move-in as of the first of the month, which gives us three weeks to get out. Have the data techs pull all the comp-plugs and replace them with new connections. It's a short timeframe for everything that'll have to be done, but I have the feeling the crosshairs are turning in our direction." He hurried to the bathroom, stepped inside and again scrubbed his hands at the small sink; he couldn't get the feel of Treadaway off his skin.

"Transfer our datacomps to Jericho on Friday." The echoes in the room amplified his voice. "Tomorrow, notify all the tenants to shut down and insulate their datacomps or move them for one day; we're scrubbing the building on Friday night … and I want it to be a Grade One sweep." Not even the military would be able to hack the building to get to any stray bits that might remain.

"Will you be going to the memorial and burial?"

"I'd like to know what Tempest plans to do and coordinate with her, but yes, we'll be going whether she goes or not. We need to make an appearance to satisfy the politics of the situation. We can't afford any close looks at us right now. You will be with me and you can choose as many guards as you want, without consideration of their backgrounds." Daire gave blank face to Declan's raised eyebrows. "Salty and Pepper might appreciate the opportunity to schmooze with the celebrities and leaders who will make an appearance."

Laughter exploded from Declan. At seven feet each, Salty and Pepper towered over everyone. They honed their bodies in rigorous workouts designed for long and lean rather than bulk and out-of-proportion muscles. Their high-sculpted cheekbones reflected their Celtic and American Indian mixed heritage. Blue tattoos covered the right side of Salty's face and the left side of Pepper's. It was only when they stood side-by-side that the tattoos could be seen as completing a sigil.

The custom-made twin swords they each carried required special permits. They received six-figure fees any time they agreed to perform at exhibitions. They were experts with the swords and with the pistols, carbines, and knives liberally attached by straps to their bodies as well as hidden in various places. And they were completely loyal to Daire.

"I want an additional ten men." Declan wasn't often given carte blanche on the number and choice of men as guards for Daire. "The rest will be needed to oversee the transition to Jericho. And don't forget we have to be there tomorrow for that excavation unless you want Babs to handle it."

Daire stopped in the middle of the floor staring into space. "No, we'll be there. Tempest will be involved with the arrangements for her grandmother. We can take some stress off her by making sure the dig is successful."

"We agreed to four people being present. In the current situation, I don't want you anywhere with only three guards."

"I don't want to break trust with her." He considered the potential for danger. "We agreed to four people at the dig site."

Declan's grin changed to a laugh. "I want a total of twenty of our best, mainly Tacticals. Three will be with you. I'll stay with the main group. We've screened the coordinates they provided and there's something in the ground causing the machines to go wonky. It's located in a small meadow between two mountain ranges. There's a trail from the top of Rocky Ridge. We'll use it as the staging area. You'll be exposed for the five minutes it will take us to get down the path."

Daire considered the plans. "It's an acceptable risk." He stopped in front of Declan. "You agree it's not a relic they're after?"

"Yeah, but whatever they're digging up is important. We'll know more tomorrow. In the meantime ...." Declan slapped his hands on his legs and stood.

The door whumped open. Daire pulled his gun from the shoulder holster and dropped behind the nearest chair. Declan rolled behind a sofa at an angle from Daire, his gun in his hand.

"Mr. D'eath!" Todd Burkens dashed into the office. His

face whitened, the freckles covering his skin standing out in bas relief. His father was going to kill him. He stumbled to a halt. "Sorry, Mr. D'eath ... Mr. Tath." He spoke in a loud, clear voice. "I should have knocked, sir." He looked into Daire's eyes, shoulders back, head held high.

Daire rose and walked to Tech Captain Ray Burkens' son. "It's okay, Todd. Declan and I are a little tense right now. What's happened?" He placed a calming hand on Todd's shoulder.

Todd's enthusiasm and exuberance overwhelmed his control. He babbled. "Mr. D'eath, sir, my Dad and I picked up some chatter on one of the airwaves. Dad is tagging the statcams in the area. The men the 'casts said killed that lady were cornered in Horst Business Park. There was a running battle with Darts and everything. Someone said they saw a Raptor!" An obscure company strictly controlled the sales of the huge aircraft. The military had several older models, but even they didn't have the newest designs. Boy! He would love to see one of those babies in the air. And seeing inside one ... the control panels and datacomps had to rock! "Dad wants you to come to the secure room ... sirs ... if you could."

Daire shielded his grin with the palm of his hand. He turned Todd around pointing him towards the door. Had he ever been that young and eager? Todd's energy and enthusiasm made him feel old and tired.

Daire and Declan trotted behind Todd to Ray Burkens' inner sanctum, opened the door and stepped inside. Five laser monitors, two on each side of an oversized middle screen, dominated the space above waist high metal shelves running the length of the back of the room. The oversized monitor, split in quarters, showed a different angle of the business park. The pictures were static.

Ray heard the patter of his son's voice, smelled the complex intertwining of the scents he associated with his leader and Daire's First. "It's not live feed, Daire." Ray fiddled with the controls without looking around. "I'm still pulling in com chatter and splicing everything together."

Daire and Declan stood behind Ray, sitting at the apex of his horseshoe desk. Equipment littered the desk. Ceramic coffee cups lined one side section in an orderly fashion. Ray had exiled paper cups from the area when an inattentive trainee spilled coffee on one of the tables. Luckily for him, the liquid hadn't reached any sensitive equipment. Little putz.

Todd bustled to the chair near his father, sat down, slipped an earpiece into his ear, and began sorting through the live radio feeds. Ray clapped his son on the shoulder.

Daire glanced to the door, nodding his head at various team leaders and Tacticals entering the room.

"This all happened about an hour ago." Ray tapped some keys moving the images on the main screen to the side monitors. "I'm also sending a feed into the sit-room. And I'm putting everything in motion … now."

Everyone watched the action unfold. Daire's hands knotted into fists, his knuckles turning white, watching Tempest and her team rescue Braeden and his men.

"I tried to capture statcams along the escape route." He pointed to the upper left smaller monitor.

A street map displayed a red line zigging and zagging away from a blue line taking an almost direct course to a large open space.

"I couldn't get any video, but I was able to follow the action using one of the satellites. The blue line is the Darts and the police or whoever the hell else was attacking. The red line is the SUV with Braeden. Here." Ray used a laser pointer to isolate a small section. "The SUV stopped here for about five or six minutes before continuing to the field. There was a Raptor there. I couldn't follow it with the radar, satellite, or the new lasers. The rumors must be true about its stealth modules. Any chance of getting a look into one of those babies?" He looked over his shoulder at Daire. The smile left his face at the grim look on Daire's face and his clenched fists.

Daire inhaled sharply, controlling his fear. He should walk away from Tempest. There were thousands of friends and families depending on him to make the right decisions for their welfare. Leading them into a war with the Covens and whoever was backing them wasn't responsible. He considered the issues for several minutes, his eyes tracking the action. "Can you identify the attackers or the SUV?"

Eyes locked on the monitors, Ray manipulated the data and images, first one way then another. "They're being cute; the ID pulses are turned off."

Todd snickered in his seat beside his father.

Ray shook his head back and forth swiveling in his chair to face Daire and Declan. "Don't let it go to your head, boy!"

Daire arched an eyebrow.

"My son has found a way to hack the modules governing the ID beams. We were able to match the number connected to the beam to the name of a holding company. We followed the trail through numerous partnerships and other companies. It ended at Sylk Transport."

Daire's eyes hardened. "Coven Darksylk."

"We don't know if the attack on the SUV was aimed at Tempest Phillips." Declan played Devil's Advocate. "Braeden was loaded into the back. Someone could have hijacked the cams and inserted new data. And the vehicle could have been stolen so the embedded ID wouldn't mean anything."

"Ray, how easy was it to pull out those images?" Daire ground his teeth.

Ray didn't go into unnecessary details. "On the move like they were, they wouldn't have been able to pull the feed that quick. Everything I got was immediately after the event." He eyed Declan. "No one else hijacked the satellite. I checked."

Daire whirled and stalked out of the room his words trailing over his shoulder. "I know for a fact Treadaway is stalking Tempest. We're not going to help him gain any more power within the Council. Erase the pictures in those cams if you can get to them.  Archive and seal your records."

Declan grimaced.  Daire was already enraged with the Covens.  A pissed off Daire would tear them apart piece-by-piece however long it took.  He had the power and tenacity to make it happen.  It looked like things were going to get exciting for the next few years.

He clapped Ray and Todd on their shoulders.  "Great job! We're moving to Jericho and we have three weeks to get it done. Your group is first on the list.  Daire wants the datacomps moved right away.  Remove the current comp-plugs and install new ones.  And we're doing a Grade One scrub of the building on Friday night."  He grinned at the shocked look on Ray Burken's face.  "Have a nice night."  He walked away whistling to find Daire.

# CHAPTER 19

"How's Mikuh doing?" Tempest chewed her finger as she leaned against the side of the glass observation window studying the still form. It allowed for no patient privacy, but the nurses could easily watch for problems. She winced, the tang of blood flooding her mouth as her teeth dug into skin since the nail had disappeared hours ago.

"He's as best as can be expected for the amount of damage he sustained. The knife wounds were too deep for NuSkin. It took eighty-seven stitches to sew him up. We removed two of the five bullets, which hit him and they all missed vital organs. The other three were pass throughs. Why they're still using bullets is beyond me. What's puzzling are the whip marks on his back." Jake rubbed his nose. Worry lines sliced through his face. He had been in surgery for over eight hours repairing the injuries.

"Do you need more equipment or specialists?" She knew Jake and his teams were among the best in the world, but if he wanted more she would make sure he had it.

"No, we have everything we need. Now it's a matter of time and his will to live." He pulled her finger from her mouth, tore away the paper surrounding the Band-Aid in his hands, situated it on her finger and pressed it into place. He pulled her into a hug then stepped back. "Why don't you go and get some rest?" He had overheard several conversations about what she had had to do. His heart ached. He couldn't do anything to ease her suffering except provide a shoulder to cry on or ear to listen … when she was ready.  He cast apprehensive glances at her disappearing figure.  "She needs to sleep."  He started at the rumbling voice behind him.

"Jake, for what's bothering her, it will take more than sleep.  She'll work through it in time.  I'll talk to her again."  Rogan moved to stand beside the doctor.  "You should get some rest.  Do you need anything more for Braeden?  How are the other injured doing?"

Her shoulders slumped, Tempest walked away.  She needed a shower.  The brief clean up she allowed herself before rushing to the hospital wing wasn't enough to dispel the smell and feel of blood gushing from the dying body.  She jammed a hand over her mouth and ran down the hallway slamming through the door of the women's communal shower and bathroom.  A few nasty moments with the porcelain bowl provided temporary relief.  She flipped the lock on the door of the room then stripped and walked to the large alcove.  Hot water pounded her head and shoulders.  She scrubbed and scoured her skin, sliding down the wall to sit on the tile, letting tears mix with the scalding liquid.

Forty-five minutes later, she wandered through the rooms of the new house.  The colors on the walls were bright and cheerful, the rooms large and open, and with sunshine flowing in through the windows, it would be warm, adding to the welcoming feel.  Its newness was alien, but somehow refreshing.  She felt a sense of freedom: a new start with unlimited opportunities.  She didn't want to think.

Her clothes were in her bedroom closet neatly arranged in rows and her extensive boot collection had its own shelving.  She changed from the scrubs borrowed from the general supplies into worn leggings, a sport bra, and moccasins with a below-the-knee shank.  They would be flying to the excavation site in a short time and then Jake would have another patient to work on.  She didn't want to think.

Ben and his sons were looking after Gracie and Maggie until after Bastian stabilized.  The cats were going to be so pissed at her for staying away for so long. She needed to add their favorite treats to the next grocery run. She didn't want to think! She swiped angrily at the tears inching down her cheeks. She couldn't stop crying. She was so weak.

She needed something to focus on other than herself. Mikuh was grievously hurt. Tempest could tell Jake was very worried about his condition. How could she help Mikuh? She paced back and forth in front of her bed, chewing thoughtfully on another fingernail. It would be cold in his room. She grabbed a long-sleeved hoodie from her closet and headed for the medical building.

The new Summerfield building was nestled in a cluster of giant oak trees. Its outward appearance was a large wood residence with two wings painted white with dark green shutters surrounding white trimmed windows. An oversized porch with cushion-covered chairs, several chaise loungers and a swing with conveniently placed tables added to its innocuous presence. Past the foyer and down the hall, she glanced into an enormous open-space living room with a stone fireplace. She knew the left door led to a gourmet kitchen and a dining room with space for several ten-person tables. Poppa Gammens' architect had designed the rear of the residence on the main floor to contain four master bedrooms with private bathrooms positioned around a shared secluded living room with an additional eight master-sized bedrooms and bathrooms for each on the second floor.

Promising herself a longer, closer look at the different rooms later, Tempest walked to a door in the wall beneath the stairs, opened it and stepped inside. Pressing the edge of the wall, a door slid open revealing a panel with buttons. She pushed the one beside the number two and leaned against the wall as the floor vibrated beneath her feet.

Poppa Gammens and his crews had been very careful when they dug out the three underground sections to leave the oak trees' root system intact. The hidden sections expanded outward for a city-block providing more than enough space for several surgery suites, and one floor totally dedicated to rooms with beds and related medical devices for monitoring patient condition. Steel girders provided the skeleton for the underground section, with a closed air system, if needed, as well as the main house.

A long tunnel connected with an additional underground space at the edge of the forest over a mile from the house. Tunnels branched off the main trunk connecting to more underground rooms, some for stocks of supplies of all types and kinds and many large bedrooms and a shared bathroom with multiple showers and toilets. A patented system of disintegrators handled the disposal of the solid and liquid waste. The below-ground city provided more than enough space for every person at Summerfield, with room to expand when necessary. Tempest had bullied Poppa Gammons into building rooms in the city for himself and all of his family and obtained his promise he would come to them at the first sign of trouble.

Exiting the elevator, Tempest walked down the hallway toward the critical care unit. She stopped at a white wood-encased metal door she remembered from Poppa's plans, opened it and entered the room. Metal shelving units housing a variety of devices lined the walls. A desk and chair occupied a small area at the back of the oversized chamber. She saw what she wanted on the first shelf on the left side, chose a padded bag from the shelf below it and inserted the equipment. She left the room and continued her trek down the hallway stopping at the corner of a juncture of four corridors. Balancing a shoulder against the wall, she stole periodic quick looks around the edge of the wall.

Three on-duty nurses bustled in and around the desks, cabinets and room containing their drug supply near the entrance to Mikuh's room. Others appeared to pop in and out of the walls along the hall attending to their duties with the injured and sick in unseen alcoves. The nurses disappeared into rooms. Tempest shot into and down the hallway, edging through the door of the room at the left side of the nurses' area. Machines beeped and hissed, a metal gathering of local elders discussing the latest gossip. The temperature of the room raised goose pimples along her arms beneath the heavy cotton jacket.

Mikuh's face was as white as the pillowcase behind his head. His breathing barely lifted the sheets covering his chest. Tip-toeing to the bed, Tempest shrugged the bag from her shoulder, setting it on the bed, before ruffling Mikuh's shoulder-length black hair. The dirty unkept look was in direct contrast to his usual shiny, bound at the nape, strands. It was difficult to see him lying so still and inanimate. Awake and aware, he oozed vitality. His umber eyes reminded her of her favorite chocolate treat, until he was angry when she could swear they shined red like the eyes of a demon from hell. He filled the bed even in his unconscious state. He would begin to lose the definition in the corded muscles in his chest, arms and shoulders within days. She couldn't bear to watch him waste away.

She turned away, walked to the corner of the room and steered the screen lounging there into position on the right side of the bed. Lifting the lone chair in the room, she repositioned it at the bed then pulled pillows from the closet and stuffed the barely padded seat. She opened the bag and set a tablet and wires on the bed. Activating the tablet and inserting in the side port the main wire attached to a controller, she selected smaller cords and pushed them into the controller. After attaching connective pads against the skin on her chest and a separate set on her temples, she sat down and leaned forward against the mattress, her hand easing beneath Mikuh's, feeling hard calluses on the palms.

What should she do? How should she do it? Never having done something didn't mean it couldn't be accomplished. Laying her head on the bed beside their clasped hands, she closed her eyes, entered HyperRealm, and checked to make sure her connection with Sebastian was barricaded inside a titanium tower. She drifted around the circumference of the structure examining the shell for cracks. All set.

She conjured a transparent sphere. It hovered before her like a loosey-goosey ball, its edges drooping and fixed in no discernable pattern. Now what? Healing feels "green" and out of the ether, green liquid appeared and poured into the orb. Kool! She floated around it, placing spectral hands on the casing. It felt clean, healthy, but it needed a carrier, something to activate the inherent healing properties. Helmet streamers carried by the solar wind whooshed into HyperRealm trailing a gold filament connection to the sun. The streamers blew through the ball spilling fluorescent green and metallic gold granules. The sphere coalesced into the shape of a glowing green spray gun.

With pistol in hand, she found herself hovering over Mikuh. There were large holes in his aura and black spots on his outer shell. Her spectral self dropped through a hole in the aura. She turned, set the nozzle for gentle shower, and sprayed, closing the ruptures. She moved carefully working her way around its circumference. Satisfied, she streamed into the body. Her breath caught. So much damage. She felt a tug at her inner core—her physical body beginning to assert control on her essence. She had to work faster.

She skimmed through the shell aiming her chimeric gun at ripped, torn, and stabbed muscles, tissues, veins, and broken bone, changing the spray patterns to fit the injury: cone, sharp stream, full flow, gentle shower, jet, flood, or mist. The pulling from her physical body increased. With the major wounds filled and coated with the substance, she allowed her incorporeal self to become granules and floated upward easing out of the husk. In HyperRealm, she gave thanks for the help and released the gun, which vanished.

Tempest blinked blearily at the wall. Transitioning from HyperRealm to her physical shell was more difficult this time. Her head was spinning like she had been turning in circles for a while like she had done as a child on the manicured lawn of her parents' small country place. Using her left hand, she tugged the connective pads off. Mikuh's legs moved just enough to shift the tablet which continued its motion, dropping onto the top of the padded bag on the floor beside her chair before thudding onto the floor dragging the bag onto its side.

The machines attached to Mikuh wailed, sputtered, crackled and popped. Jake, followed by two nurses, banged into the room. The nurses split apart hurrying to check the various apparatus and move the screen.

"Damn it, Tempest!" Jake leaned over, placing fingers against her neck to check her pulse. "Damn it! Barbara! Check Braeden. Somebody get replacement equipment in here stat. And shut those damn alarms off!"

"Water." The voice was low and raspy, but strong.

Jake jerked upright. Without an extensive examination, Tempest appeared to be physically all right. He advised Tempest while walking around the bed to check Mikuh. "No sudden moves."

"How do you feel?" Jake raised the head of the bed and took a glass of water from a nurse's hand while whispering instructions into her ear. He watched her leave then placed the bent straw in the glass against Mikuh's mouth.

Mikuh drank most of the water, his eyes flicking around, noting the people and other details of the room. He licked his lips. "Where am I?" Feeling the softness of hair on his hand, he looked down, seeing Tempest, her upper body lying on the mattress beside him, her head cradled on folded arms.

"You're safe at Summerfield." Her voice was barely a whisper. She cleared her throat and raised her tone. "We found you and eleven of your people. They're all down the hall except Blanchard who died after we picked you up." She didn't provide any details about his death. She cocked an eyebrow at Jake but continued when he tipped his head sideways. "There are a lot of injuries, but everyone is in good shape. You were hurt the worst. They meant for you to die with Grandmother, Mikuh. Where are the rest of your teams? We'll go after them right away."

"I feel bruised, sore and achy, but I'm not critically injured." He raised an eyebrow at Jake who had a scowl on his face before turning his head to Tempest. "The teams are waiting for a call from you, Tempest. Casper is the contact. We set it up that way so no one could contact any of them and say they were calling on my behalf."

"What's going on?" Rogan entered and stopped in front of the door. The room was crowded with people. He looked at Jake standing beside the bed with arms crossed glaring at Tempest.

"What?" Tempest sat up. Her head felt like it was going to stay attached to her body, but she wasn't up to standing or moving around. She raised a shaking hand to push the hair out of her face.

The door slammed against Rogan's back pushing him further into the room. An orderly entered the room carrying a tray with a glass of milk and an assortment of nuts, raisins, a banana, oats, and bran flakes. Following Jake's pointing finger, he set the tray on the side of the bed, backed away and left accompanied by the nurses.

"I was testing a theory." Tempest hated the whiny quality in her voice. She examined the food wrinkling her nose. She wanted bacon, eggs, and toast with lots and lots of butter.

"Without proper supervision." Jake caught Tempest's gaze and imitated eating.

"What … is … going … on?" Rogan gritted his teeth. He knew he was going to need a dentist by the time they made it through the current crisis.

"Well, I didn't know if anything would happen. And nothing went wrong. I'm just a little shaky." She munched a handful of raisins and nuts as she ripped the skin off the banana.

"You're not supposed to talk with your mouth full." Jake extracted the clipboard from the bottom of the bed and made notes on the pages.

Tempest huffed and nibbled more food. The oats and bran were dry and boring. She needed to prepare her usual granola mix and get it out to all the facilities. "I tried to heal Mikuh. And

I did ... mostly ... I think." The food was helping her recovery. She'd need to remember to have her granola mix nearby the next time she experimented.

Rogan looked at Mikuh leaning against the half-raised head of the bed. He definitely appeared stronger. His skin tone was normal, the grey cast gone.

"Next time you have some hare-brained idea, talk to me first." Jake returned the clipboard to the hook attached to the bottom of the bed. "We could have monitored you and recorded what was happening. If you had gotten into trouble, you would have had backup. We've also lost the opportunity to find out what's happening to you."

She looked at him through the fringes of her eyelashes and gave him a half-smile. Bending to the side, she pushed the padded bag away, picked up the tablet with cords dangling and waved it at him. "If my vitals had fallen to dangerous levels, an emergency code would have been sent to your phone. I don't know if the recorded readings will be of any use, but here you go." She handed him the tablet.

"Brat!"

Rogan wasn't satisfied with the ambiguous answer to his question, but Jake would follow up later with Tempest after analyzing whatever was on the tablet. He would also talk with Jake so he would be better prepared when Tempest did it again because she would since it apparently was successful this time. In the meantime, Mikuh needed to answer some questions. "How are you feeling, Mikuh? What happened?"

"The Duvayne received a phone call." Mikuh shook his head. "It made her angry. She told me to give her some space." He shrugged. "That's not all that unusual. Sometimes she wanted to be alone to ... 'meditate' was her word for it. I left, but only as far as the window at the end of the hall. Maybe fifteen minutes later, I heard noises, sounds of a struggle. I called for backup and ran to the door. It was locked." He looked confused. "I used my master key in the lock. When I got in, she was on the floor, blood pooling around her." He blinked away the moisture in his eyes.

"How did the police get the drop on you?" Rogan balanced against the foot of the bed, a frown wrinkling his forehead.

"It wasn't just the police." He looked at Tempest before continuing. "A combined Darksylk/Phillips force was standing over The Duvayne. Your Father wasn't there, Tempest, nor any of his personal guards." He rushed to reassure her. He looked puzzled. "Blanchard was there on his knees, hands behind his head and he wasn't in there when I left. There was no damn way for anyone to get into that room except from the hallway. And I was there. I didn't leave for any reason. I would never leave her unprotected."

Tempest sucked in a breath becoming the focus of all three men. "Actually ... I thought she had shown you, Mikuh."

"What, Tempest? Shown me what?"

She didn't want to cause him more pain but that was what was going to happen. Damn her grandmother! "It's a little-known family secret, limited to only a few people."

"Damn it, Tempest, what secret?" Mikuh sensed he was about to be hit with a major splat of shit.

"I don't mean to drag this out. It's just that I don't ...," she placed the tray on the floor and sat on the side of the bed with a hand on Mikuh's chest. "I don't want to hurt you, Mikuh."

Her fingers drew together into a fist. "There's a hidden passage into the room. Grandmother showed it to me when I was around ten years old, I think, and ...," she shrugged, "I just forgot about it." She chewed on a third fingernail since the other two were gone. "You know, she only showed me the door and the mechanism to open it then told me if anything bad ever happened to go through it and follow it. I don't know where it ends."

Pain etched lines in Mikuh's face, aging him in seconds. He turned his face to the wall. He thought of the years he had spent beside Glory, the laughter, the tears, the anger and pain. He now saw their relationship in a different way: she hadn't trusted him; he was just a hired gun.

"Don't, Mikuh! Grandmother cared for you to the best of her ability." Tempest's heart ached. "I loved her, Mikuh, but I didn't have any illusions about her: she was a hard, cold, ambitious and ruthless old bat. Everything to her was for the good of 'our people' and, in the beginning, she did a lot of great things." Tempest sighed. "She lost focus on people and crushed on power."

Mikuh had to face the reality of his time with Glorianna Duvayne. He forced himself to acknowledge out loud the actuality of that time. "I was just a bodyguard."

Tempest swallowed the lump in her throat. Tears gathered, but she refused to let them fall. Mikuh needed time to come to terms with his new perspective of The Duvayne. He deserved the same consideration Tempest took for herself to deal with her changed view of her grandmother.

Rogan cleared his throat. "Did they say anything?"

"No, they just started shooting. I managed to get back through the door and down the hallway. I took a couple of hits before the team found me. We fought our way out of the estate." The frown between his eyes was as deep as a chasm. "We didn't hear any sirens until we were a couple of miles from the estate. We were under continuous fire." He continued to think through the action. "We didn't have any time to think. They stayed on top of us, driving us. We finally slipped free and made it to the Horst Business Park. Kolder knew it was empty. Why did you ask about the police?"

"The broadcasts on the security channels said the police found you and some of your team standing over The Duvayne's body. Said there were dotcam vids as proof." Rogan studied Mikuh's body language, his eyes, for tells that would indicate he was lying.

"No. The Duvayne didn't allow dotcams in that area. It's too close to her private sanctum and vids were never authorized there."

"I'll have Smythe sneak into the police computers and grab a copy of the vids. He'll be able to tell us how it was put together."

Tempest checked her watch. "We've got to get going. I'll call Casper as soon as I leave this room. Mikuh, you and your teams are a part of our family." She stood beside his bed. "Let me make this simple. I offer sanctuary and alliance for you and those of your teams who want to stay and whom you trust. You can retire and have your own space here at Summerfield or you can continue as a Captain and work with us. But you have to accept Rogan as overall commander of security for Summerfield and me."

Mikuh nodded. "Thanks. I'll discuss it with the group." Since the phone call with Branaugh, Mikuh had considered the potential ramifications of joining with Tempest. He would accept the offer without any hesitation, and he had no problem working under Rogan Branaugh. The men in his teams had to decide what was best for each of them. He wasn't going to influence or coerce them in any way. The decision was theirs. He was tired to the bone. Let someone else make the life-and-death decisions. "Are you sure you want to take us on with the authorities looking for us? You would be an accessory to whatever we're charged with."

"You're going to be cleared and exonerated, Mikuh, and whoever murdered Grandmother will be found – the real culprits, Mikuh, not just the triggermen. Rest now. Recover. Take all the time you need to make a decision. There isn't any time limit on the offer." She touched Mikuh's shoulder then walked to the door. "Jake, do you need to stay with Mikuh and the other injured?"

"No. Dr. Crabtree is on duty and she is more than capable of handling emergencies. I think you should get some sleep. That pod has been buried for over two hundred years and it can wait a few more days."

She shook her head. "No. We have to get this done

before the memorial and internment the day after tomorrow. Who knows what's going to happen after that. Get what you need. It's time to get dirty. I'll meet you at the hangar bay. Is everything ready for Bastian?"

"As ready as it can be without knowledge of his physiology and needs."

"What the hell is going on?" Mikuh shifted restlessly. His hand automatically searched for a weapon, his touchstone in times of uncertainty.

"We don't have time to go into it now, but we'll let you know when we come back." She peered around the jamb of the door. "Rogan, don't forget to give Mikuh his gun before we leave."

# CHAPTER 20

After placing the call to Casper, assuring him Mikuh and the rest of the group were recovering, advising him of her offer and giving him directions to Summerfield, Tempest grabbed her denim jacket from the hall tree, stepped out the door and walked down the gravel path to the SUV where Rogan and Lorcan waited. She climbed in the front passenger seat and slammed the door. When Rogan opened his mouth, she hit the front of the jacket several times. "Armored."

"Good." He started the engine and shot down the driveway. "The equipment is already in place at the site. Smythe hijacked the satellite again and reported there's a group of men on the rim above the dig. Massee did a walkabout and got close enough to identify a group of around twenty of D'eath's men. She left when one of the men seemed to sense her presence."

Tempest grinned in appreciation. "Daire's good. We did agree to four people at the site and, technically, they aren't at the site. We can't continue seizing control of that satellite. When will our orbital transmitter be ready to launch?"

Rogan nodded toward the thin shelf in the dashboard. "Check the tablet. Smythe uploaded the current information this morning. I haven't had a chance to read it yet."

Tempest pulled the thin computer from its nest and turned it on. She pressed her thumb against the screen when the security prompt appeared and selected the document in the middle of the screen. A few minutes of silent perusal of the synopsis pages and she nodded. "Okay. The components are starting to arrive from the subcontractors. Even if someone traces all the businesses and copies the plans, all they'll have is a shell. Our tech gurus are almost finished with the ...," she set the tablet in her lap and crooked her fingers, "'guts'. We should be able to get it assembled on time in a couple of months." She rubbed her forehead between her brows. "Getting it into orbit is going to take a little longer than expected ... maybe six months."

Rogan grunted. He parked in the space closest to the runway. "Was there anything about the vids of Mikuh and his team?"

She opened her door and stepped down. "He pulled copies from the police servers and followed the links to the other places with copies, grabbing those versions as well. Smythe tossed the vids to his best techs. The techs are going to rip the data apart, find out how the vids were created and try to identify and trace the people who assembled and distributed them."

Tempest walked between Rogan and Lorcan around the side of the hangar. Men and women bustled around the bird of prey basking in the sun on the tarmac. The Raptor's design was reminiscent of the VTOL, vertical take off and land, jets of the early 2000s. The engineers started with the base design and upgraded the systems, shell, and engines. There were models produced by other companies, but none of them had the speed, maneuverability, and stealth capabilities of the Raptor and she strictly monitored the production and sale of the machines. The huge crafts were exciting in appearance and performance. Chills fought for room on her skin whenever she was around them. The new Predators they were constructing were bigger, badder and had longer range ... including space travel to not only planets in their solar system but other more distant worlds. Her body vibrated with awe and excitement when she stood beside one and standing beside more than one ... it was orgasmic.

She climbed the ramp and walked to her seat, sat down and buckled in. The subsonic throb of the engines wove into her bones intensifying the bubbles of anticipation in the pit of her stomach. For less than a second, she was weightless then the G-force pushed her into her seat. It was almost redundant to use the Raptor for the short flight to the dig site, but its cargo space was essential for transporting the rescue sled and its speed critical to returning Sebastian to the safety of Summerfield.

Less than two minutes later, Keegan Lohar edged the craft into the hilltop meadow and within a short walking distance of the dig. He lowered the cargo ramp. Tempest stood at the lip of the ramp, hands on hips, enjoying the faint breeze against her face. The morning sky promised a cloud-free day and a broiling sun. She removed and tossed the denim jacket to Strider who was her bodyguard for the first part of the day. Nearby, an erector set of pipes stood in stark contrast to the light grey horizon.

Tempest stepped onto the ground and strode to meet Daire and his companions. "Daire, I didn't expect to see you here today."

Daire controlled the torrent of hunger he felt whenever he saw Tempest. He picked up her hand and raised it to his lips. "And I didn't expect to see you here. Tempest, you have my deepest sympathy. We," the wave of his hand included his men, "were very sorry to hear about The Duvayne's death. Is there anything we can do to help you other than this?"

The warmth of his concern helped to placate some of her pain. She placed her hand on his cheek. "Thank you. The shock is still wearing off."

He turned to walk beside her. "I don't want to add to your pain, but there are some things we need to discuss. The Captain of my tech crew was able to synthesize a recording of your rescue of Braeden and his men. We pulled in a lot of extra footage from statcams and relay chatter in the area. I think you'll find the information interesting." He placed the SSD drive Ray had made into her hand and pulled her to a stop.

Strider closed on the couple then swung away at Tempest's slight gesture.

Daire drew in a deep breath. Just lay it out, he thought. "I know it was an assassination. They're going to come after you. If they can't break you and use you, they're going to kill you. I'm moving my people and headquarters to Jericho, just across the hills from your Summerfield. We should combine forces."

"I agree. We should talk. Being allies sounds like a good thing, but you may not want to take on all my enemies. Let's get through this and get into all that later." She stepped away and looked back over her shoulder giving him a grin, discretely handing off the drive to Strider. "Invite your men down from the mountain top. They'll have a better view if they're closer to the activity."

Daire returned her grin with a smile as he followed her. He hesitated before saying, "I'm attending the memorial and burial for The Duvayne. Because of the situation, I'm taking additional fighters."

She stopped beside the laser drillers positioned above the coordinates Jesse Ranier had plotted and gave Daire her full attention. "I won't be going to the spectacle the Covens' CEOs are preparing, which is strictly for political and business interests. The real ceremony for Grandmother will happen tomorrow night." Grief caused a hitch in her breathing before she collected her control. She shifted away from his unconscious movement to console her. She didn't want to hurt him, but she would fall apart if he enclosed her in his arms and offered any kind of comfort. "I won't be there either."

She debated providing more information. But if they were to become allies, honesty…as much as she could reasonably provide…was important. "I'll be at the family crypt with five teams when she's laid to rest in the mausoleum. The CEOs aren't going to like the show of force. You should keep your distance until we know more about the people behind Grandmother's murder."

He thought about what she said. The two of them were responsible for too many lives to make decisions based solely on personal want and desire. He nodded. "Thanks for the warning, but we'll stand with you." He anticipated her response. "Yes, I can make the decision for everyone in my organization. If this situation goes as deep as I think it does, it will only be a matter of time before 'they' come for us. We can't afford to stand on the sidelines."

She reached out to touch his arm but drew back before making contact. He regretted her hesitation. "My friend, Martin Krafft, will be at the memorial and he's requested my presence at his side. World Security Forces will be protecting him, but his behest means he doesn't trust them. I have to be there for him."

"Do what you feel is necessary, Daire. And thanks ...," she was going to say more but a shout from one of the drillers interrupted.

"We're ready, Tempest! Whenever you are!"

She waved in response and hesitated, then, with an audible huff, she grabbed Daire's hand and pulled him into motion beside her. Together, they strode into the open-sided tent shading computers and monitors on portable tables.

"Turn'em loose, Bearin." Tempest stood behind the blue-haired technician. He had returned to the Estate the night before after cruising several writers' conventions and hadn't had time to return his hair to its usual glossy mahogany. She hadn't had time to take the tour with him this time. Mingling with authors, readers and role players at the conventions often stimulated her creativity. When she reached an impasse on a new design, the colors, excitement and eccentricity of the people attending gave her a fresh perspective, oftentimes driving her down a different tangent, resolving the problem. It was also her connection to the underground truth-seekers, people who collected secrets like they were rare and valuable paintings.

It had been a long, hard-fought battle to become one of them, protected by them. She never played any of the small inner core five-person group, answering their questions honestly if not with many details. The relationship had paid off, with huge benefits, many times.

Bearin murmured into the dotmitter. On the screen, dirt spewed into the air.

"Here's the pod, ma'am."

Tempest punched his shoulder. "I told you the last time. 'Ma'am' me again and I'll punch you. So here's your punch!"

Bearin grinned and touched the simulation. The images consumed the screen. Green, red and white lines and blotches illustrated the inside of the simulacrum. "Here, here and here are dead spaces." He tapped a blinking red section. "This one's got me worried. An overload is inevitable in that circuit. Best I can tell ... when it goes ... boom!" He clapped his hands and waved his arms. "That thing is gone. I'm surprised it's run as long as it has. Be real careful when you go in. Shut down everything you see."

Tempest gripped his shoulder in acknowledgment, watching the lasers shut down and the heavy-duty diggers move in.

People walked in and out of the tent. Shifts changed every two hours. Tempest stayed at the computers absently drinking the water and nibbling the food periodically pushed into her hand. Daire had whispered something to her and left some time ago. Her eyes narrowed and she leaned over the new technician for a closer look at the screen. She hit the dotmitter. "Stop!"

Silence filled the air, except for the sound of low-pitched voices. "I think that's as close as we can go with the heavy stuff. Looks like handwork to me. Rogan?"

He moved around her and scanned the monitor. "Yeah. Break out the shovels!"

Bodies flowed en masse for the side of the hole. Repurposed diggers raised and lowered two cages.

Tempest jerked to a halt, her foot in the air, and one step from the floor of the first cage to go down.

"Not so fast." Rogan tugged her away from the platform. He pulled the shovel from her hand and passed it to the nearest person. "No." He shook his head in emphasis when she opened her mouth. "You'll be needed later. Go get some sleep or at least lie down and rest until we reach the top of the lifeboat."

She crossed her arms and glared mutinously into his face. She wasn't pouting and she wasn't tired ... well, at least not stumbling over her feet tired. She blew her hair out of her eyes.

"Jake! You've got a patient." Rogan grinned, all his teeth showing, and crossed his arms returning her scowl.

She broke first, laughing. "You're right. I'll lay down for a short time." She dropped her arms then raised them to rumple her hair with her hands. "It's too damn hot to argue."

Daire walked to Rogan's side watching Tempest amble here and there, stopping beside people to say a few words and moving on. "She's a handful."

"You play with her, you hurt her, and you're dead." Rogan's voice didn't change from his normal tone. He dipped his head, spun around and trotted to the tent.

"Protective, but not possessive. It's not a sexual relationship." Declan tapped his sunglasses up his nose.

Daire shrugged one shoulder. "There may not be sex involved now." He bit his tongue. "No, I shouldn't have said that. The two of them have a tight bond based on love between family and years of fighting together. Take one, you get the other. More complications." He turned to stare at the rock outcropping looming over the meadow. "See anything from up there?"

"It's quiet. Maybe too quiet." Declan followed Daire, walking around the gouge in the ground. "Ray sent his son for jammers. He's monitoring the background noise for signs of interest in this area." He tilted his head toward the action behind them. "Any ideas how long it's going to take?"

Daire pinched the bridge of his nose. A headache was building at his temples. One more pain to add to the ferocious ache in his lower body. Relief for that area wasn't likely to come soon. "Several more hours at least."

Tempest backed out of the shadows cast by one of the

diggers parked at the back of the tent. She followed Daire and Declan with her eyes as they paced to the far side of the excavation. Daire wasn't fully cognizant of all the risks involved with allying with her. She didn't even know or understand all of the forces against her. He was such an alpha male, and her body wanted him. It was hot and achy. She wasn't innocent. She had experimented with a couple of men and the liaisons had been pleasant. Her battery-operated toys relieved most of the sexual tension now. She didn't have the time, energy or inclination to work on a relationship and one-night stands were not in her repertoire. But Daire was different. Her body and emotions tangoed whenever she thought about him. Even from a distance, he had the power to disarm her defenses and stir up things she had packed away. He was a puzzle.

She needed some alone time away from bodyguards, friends, strangers, family, and potential sex partner. Pulling several light blankets and a few pillows from the stacks near some cots, she wedged into a dark corner of one of the tents on the ground under a table protected on one side by the tire of a digger. She closed her eyes and her mind relaxed. Her Grandmother was dead! A close friend had almost died! Strange things were happening to her – mind, spirit and body. She was responsible for the welfare of hundreds of people. She had killed a man! The litany of recent events stomped through her psyche.

She wanted to scream, yell and pound on something. She wanted to let loose all her control and cry, sob and wail. Tears seeped from beneath her eyelids, her nose clogged up, her chest hurt holding back the pain, grief and guilt. The thunder, lightning and downpour passed into sleep.

The knife against Rogan's throat flashed in the sunlight. A thin line appeared on the tanned skin; red seeped around the edges.

Her bones identified vibrations moving toward her. The knife slipped into her hand. She rolled out of the cocoon of blankets and flipped, her body in motion before she was conscious. She landed in a crouch, the blade braced against her forearm turned outward.

"Everyone stop." Rogan's voice was soft but commanding. He tracked Tempest's eyes, the tension of her body. "Don't move." He cautioned the people behind him.

Daire stumbled into the tent pushed by an overeager Todd Burkens. "They've reached the top of the container." Todd's grin died.

Feral-spark swung toward the movement. The shell flowed forward at her urging. The weapon in her hand was unknown but well balanced. Another male imposed itself between her and her target.

"Tempest! No." Rogan's voice was firm.

Feral-spark sank beneath the Tempest personality without a struggle. Later.

Tempest straightened, stretched her arms over her head, and yawned. She looked around the enclosure at the motionless men and women. "What's happening?" She frowned, eyeing the knife in her hand. When had she drawn it? A shiver raced through her. She had lost time. What was happening to her? She hid her fear with a smile that shook at the edges and tucked the weapon away.

And just like that ... everything was okay. Motion resumed. Men and women walked to the tables, their hands loaded with food and beverages. Some grabbed containers of water, walked outside the canvas, bent over and dumped the liquid over their heads. Dust and dirt coated hair, faces, hands, and clothes.

"Is everything okay?" Tempest could almost recall her dream just before waking, but it was a dim memory.

"Todd just arrived to let us know the top of the pod has been reached." Rogan hid his concern. For a few seconds, it had seemed the feral-spark was back and in control.

"Great!" Tempest just wanted to ignore whatever had just happened. She didn't normally bury her head in the sand, but this time she didn't want to have a post-discussion of her actions. "Let's go."

Following Tempest, Rogan shook his head at Daire's questioning gaze. He didn't know what to say.

Tempest ignored the men several steps behind her.

Todd rushed up beside her like an overenthusiastic puppy. He spun the cap off the top of a bottle of water, put the bottle in her hand then opened the paper around a sandwich, folded it over making a pocket and put it in her other hand. "Dad always forgets to eat when he's caught up on a project, Ms. Phillips, so I figured you might do the same. Ma told us to be aware in stressful situations and make sure those around us are being careful. I hope I haven't overstepped my boundaries, ma'am." He looked at her through the fringe of hair flopping in his eyes.

Her stomach growled. She laughed. "No, Todd, you haven't transgressed, and you know to call me Tempest or Tempe." She raised the bottle and took a drink then chomped on the sandwich, swallowed. "Thanks."

Tempest sauntered across the dusty grass with Todd, listening to him prattle about the activities that had occurred while she slept. He fed her information like he had given her food. She glanced at him from the side of her eye. He looked at her and grinned. Yeah. He knew what he was doing. "I think it's time to give you more responsibility. Samuel has an opening in his team. You'll be a dogsbody for them for a while, but they need an electronics expert. I'll follow up with him later if it's what you want to do."

"Oh, Ms. Phillips ... Tempest. That would be really great, but I ..."

Tempest laid a hand on his arm and looked up into his eyes. "I do not believe you were trying to take advantage. When I find someone with talent, intelligence and can step outside the box to get things done, I want him or her to have the opportunity to go as far as possible. I won't forget our conversation, Todd. Let's focus on our undertaking for now."

At his nod, she pushed through the crowd surrounding the dig site and entered the lone cage hovering at the edge of the hole. The platform rocked with her movements. Excitement and terror swamped her, the emotions fighting a duel in her stomach. It was exciting to finally connect a physical form with the voice in her mind and terrifying to think about the changes his presence would create. And there would be one more alpha male in her life telling her what to do. She sighed.

When had her life become so complicated? So filled with people? She seemed to stumble over them all the time. She had been a 'surprise' baby for her parents, arriving twelve years after the youngest born son. A long succession of nannies and housekeepers and being alone in her room comprised her earliest memories. By the time her parents considered her important enough to include in their activities, she was beyond their influence.

She bent her knees and swayed with the motion as Rogan, Daire, Declan, Lorcan and Dougal McKain surrounded her. The descent was slow but ended sooner than she wanted. When the movement halted, Rogan and Lorcan raised the panel in the center of the floor and latched it open.

Dougal dropped to the metal surface and mumbled under his breath while examining it with various tools and scanners. He scooted to the edge, wiped debris out of the way and drew an 'x'. "Here's the best place to cut. It'll take a couple of diamond bits, but I think we can get through ... maybe." He returned his equipment to various drawers and slots in his case and swung back onto the platform.

Tempest jumped down and stepped gingerly to the mark. "Bastian, can we cut through the roof at this point?" She opened a receptor in her mind allowing him access to her sight. A bolt of excitement shot from him through her. "Can you tone it down a couple of notches?"

It was difficult. It had been so long since he felt anything other than despair and hopelessness. What would this new world be like? He cleared his thoughts and embraced the calmness of Shu-Tai-Ree. "Yes. The area doesn't have any essential systems or conduits. Get me out of here, Tempest!"

"Calm your jets! This metal is out of this world." She smiled, visualized a mouth with a grin, and sent the image to him. "It's going to take some time." She sobered. "I'm going to agree to alliance with Daire D'eath. He's a good man and I trust him."

She stopped to consider her statement. She did trust Daire on many levels, but there was still a small child inside who refused to totally trust anyone ... even Rogan. "Do you want to remain hidden? I can ask him to pull back with his men when we're ready to extract you. I'm giving him the ship and one of the medical pods. He has the best people and facilities to develop new technology from studying it and the ethics to use the results for all the people of this world, not just a few. Your pod is still in reasonable condition and our research team will be getting it."

"I will follow your lead on this matter." Sebastian sensed D'eath's spirit connected to Tempest's heart by a long golden thread. The strand was fragile, but it contained the potential for more. He didn't interfere in his Reciprocates' personal lives unless their decisions created immediate life or death consequences. "These are the systems you must shut down as soon as you enter." He transmitted detailed images of walking to various machines and flipping switches, turning dials. "The medtube will require some time to cycle down. I don't know the equivalents based on your system."

She chewed one of her few remaining fingernails, focusing on nothing while pictures danced in her mind. Her head ached from the force he used to push the pictures inside. Giving Bastian a final assurance, she scrambled back onto the cage floor. "Dougal, it's up to you. What do you need?"

"I need my men down here and everyone else up there." He pointed to the rim of the hole. "Don't need excess bodies cluttering up my space and getting in the way."

She moved to the center and signaled the operator of the digger, unconsciously leaning against Rogan for support. It was a reflex built up over years of camaraderie.

Daire gritted his teeth and swallowed anger and jealousy. Tempest's familiarity with her Captain was a natural extension of their relationship. He didn't like the instinctive need to challenge other males about a woman. It had never happened before. The women he had sex with knew going into the situation that it was a short-term affair. He hadn't wanted anything more – until now, with this particular woman. At the top, he followed Tempest and her men to the tent.

The heat of Tempest's hand on Daire's arm burned away his resolve to view things more rationally. He heard voices but all he could process was the blaze shooting downward and the swelling against his zipper.

"Daire?"

Tempest dropped her hand and stepped away a few feet. The mix of emotions she saw in his face for several seconds was easy to read. He had good reason to be angry about her initial half-truth. Alright, it had been a lie. But the pod was over two hundred years old and that definitely qualified it as a relic. She tossed her head. He could think what he wanted. So, he had a hot body. So what? There were a lot of men around with hard abs, killer butts, large hands and bedroom eyes. She refused to feel guilty for her actions.

She turned to face Daire acknowledging Declan standing at his shoulder. "The pod was part of an alien spacecraft which landed here a couple of centuries ago. Inside is an inhabitant from another galaxy. He's the reason we're here. We're taking him to Summerfield. The ship and one medtube are yours; the other undamaged one is ours and our techs will remove it after we remove the extraterrestrial." Her voice was low and urgent. "Whatever you can reverse engineer from the technology? Use it for the benefit of everyone."

"Dougal broke through quicker than expected. He and his people are returning to the surface." The young technician was excited to be included in the mission. Even if it was monitoring systems or going for coffee, he was working with the first team and the Lady herself.

Striding past the computers, Tempest clapped the young warrior-in-training on the shoulder. Had she ever been that young, watching the pink tide wash up his neck to his eager face? She wasn't much older than him, recognizing Tora and Blaine's oldest son, but experience-wise, at times she was older than Sebastian. She quickly sketched the different boards in the pod from memory onto several sheets of paper. She caught Jake's eye. "Are you ready?"

She glanced at Daire and Declan as she passed them. The stunned and disbelieving looks on their faces were predictable. Processing the reality of aliens would take some time.

She walked beside Jake to the dig site. They stood to one side letting the four medtechs carry the transfer sled onto the platform. She scanned the faces at the rim of the hole and was surprised to see Daire. "Daire, do you have any scientists with you? As soon as we enter, we'll be shutting everything down. You and two people are welcome to come down with us, watch what we're doing and we'll provide you with a copy of these diagrams."

Daire nodded. A few words in his dotmitter and two people stepped out of the crowd.

Declan's mouth tightened. Letting Daire go into an unknown situation without backup went against every instinct. Daire trusted the woman and her people. All the reports indicated they were honest and trustworthy. But he couldn't base Daire's safety on words written on paper. The short amount of contact with the group wasn't long enough to have a solid fix on its ideology and the woman's warriors' first instinct and creed would be to protect her, leaving Daire vulnerable.

Daire waved away one of the men. "We'll go down

together, Declan. We need eyes looking at the same things but seeing them from a different perspective." And he knew the way his First's mind worked. Declan would be worried about Daire's safety. Together, they stepped onto the floor taking positions to balance the load.

The cage lowered, settling softly against the metal hull. A rope ladder rolled into the opening and Tempest climbed down. She hurried to the medtube.

More bodies descended and moved quickly to various panels comparing the diagrams in their hands to the boards around the space. Tempest's people waited to close down systems until Daire and his men recorded the readings on each console on their dotcams. Jake and two medtechs guided the gurney through the hole and carried it across the floor to the column.

Tempest drew in a deep breath. "Ready?"

At Jake's nod, she swiftly flicked switches and turned knobs in cadence with the other people around the room. "It'll take a few minutes to cycle down."

The die was cast and in the next few minutes the world changed forever ... for her, the people who depended on her, and everyone on the planet.

The door on the tube clicked open and stopped. They waited. When nothing happened, Tempest and Jake rushed forward, gripped the edge with their fingers and pulled. It was stuck. They jerked harder, stumbling backwards as it swung open and the table slid down and out, the lid rising sluggishly. Jake and the medtechs lifted the body, placed it gently on the sled, strapped it down, and locked the top into place. Jake fiddled with the oxygen controls, nodded, and stepped back. The medtechs lifted the transport and carried it to the entrance where ropes dangled. They secured it and the sled disappeared through the hole, quickly followed by the assistants.

Tempest stepped to Daire's side. "We're going now. As soon as our group has removed and loaded the tube, they can help with extracting the ship."

He shook his head. "We're installing jammers above and down here. As soon as things are set, I'll send to Jericho for reinforcements. Thanks."

"No. Thank you. I'll see you at the crypt." She hesitated then stood on tiptoe to brush a kiss across his mouth.

He reached out to clasp her waist, but she was gone ... her legs disappearing through the roof. "Declan, get the techs and more Tacticals out here. We're got a very valuable resource to protect."

Minutes later, the chamber shuddered with the vibrations of the Raptor lifting off.

# CHAPTER 21

And she was back in the medical facilities. Again. Tempest groaned. She had to get some painters in with more imagination. White or grey walls were so depressing. While Jake worked to stabilize Sebastian in the critical care unit, she stood under a hot shower for half an hour, changed into clean clothes and had time to check on Mikuh.

"He's in surprisingly good shape for a several thousand years old corpse." Jake shrugged away the glowers at his attempt at humor. "He's in decent condition as far as I can tell since I don't know what his base measurements should be."

Tempest put her back against the wall and slid down to sit on the floor. Space was at a premium with equipment surrounding the bed against the far wall and technicians bustling around it and in and out of the room. Specialists hovered in the background or outside in the hallway watching through the gallery window, their quiet voices a low distracting hum.

Rogan broke the silence. "Well. He's out of the ground."

Jake asked the question hanging like a specter in the air. "What now? His physiology is humanoid. He's comatose." He lifted one shoulder. "I don't know if that's good or bad. It's all guesswork."

"He needs blood transfusions. We talked about it when he was sure we would get him out. I'll donate blood now, wait long enough to recover some then donate again. The process works differently in his culture, but resurrection after two hundred plus years has never happened as far as he knows. The initial contribution should be enough to start the revivification process. It could take a couple of weeks following this procedure, but he believes it's the safest way." She glanced at Jake. "It's all guesswork."

"Alright. We can extract the first supply here or move to another room." He cocked an eyebrow.

"Do it here." She scrambled to her feet.

Jake pulled containers, gauze and pressure nodes from a cabinet. "Someone bring in some orange juice and energy bars."

The door to the room opened and footsteps whispered away.

"Stop!" Rogan ordered.

Tempest walked across the room and stood in front of him. She laid her hand against his chest. "It's okay, Ro. You knew this was coming."

"Yeah, in an abstract way, but now it's time. It's real. We know whoever gives blood becomes the alien's slave."

"No, Ro. Not a slave. A connection is formed, but I'll have free will."

"You'll be bound to him!" Rogan jerked away from her. He paced to the wall, turned and marched back. The tension and anger inside forced him to move since there wasn't a convenient heavy bag nearby to pummel out his fear.

"It won't be a slave/master relationship ... not like it is with most of the Covens, not like it is with others of his race." Project calm – release the dread and apprehension. Focus on the positive aspects of the Joining. She didn't want to lose her freedom and independence! Peace and serenity.

"We don't have to do this, Tempest. Let me die."

She whirled and rushed to the bed picking up a hand and clasping it in hers. "No, Bastian! I'm sorry. It's..."

"I have lived longer than I ever expected. I should have died with my men. Our binding is not close enough yet that you will die with me. Let me go, Tempest."

"No." She denied his request in a loud, firm voice, projecting it into his mind as well. "I'm ready. I'm not going to let you be a coward." A faint laugh wafted through her mind. "Yeah, I just gave myself a pep talk. Let's do this, Jake."

She gently returned the hand to the sheets then stalked to the second bed shoved against the side wall. She climbed onto it, turned over and gave them a resolute smile. It was a good thing Bastian was still unconscious and couldn't see her face. "Get over here, Jake."

"While you were mind melding with Dracula, we came up with an alternative." Rogan moved to her side.

She frowned at his epithet for Sebastian, but let it pass without comment. "What's your solution?"

"From what I gather, he needs a lot of blood. And the preferred treatment would be all of the blood now and not over several weeks. Correct?" He saw her nod but continued to work through his thoughts aloud. "It doesn't matter what the blood type is, right? They don't pick and choose?"

"Bastian? Do you have to have a particular blood type?"

"It must be fresh, whole blood. Our history includes instances where one of my kind was drawn to a specific person, but it was not considered important enough to investigate. I doubt blood type was the reason. What is happening?"

"Do you have enough strength to listen to our discussion?"

"Yes."

She redirected her attention outward to find all eyes on her. "I'm creating a connection like a speaker phone which will allow Bastian to hear what's being said. If he has any comments, I'll relay them to you. He said type isn't a factor, just fresh, whole blood."

Rogan paced across the room to lean against the end of her bed. He addressed his comments to the body lying still as death across the room even though the man wasn't physically conscious. "This is the way it is, Bloodhawk. More than two hundred men, women and children here … in Summerfield

... depend on Tempest to keep them safe by making the right decisions. And that doesn't include the thousands more scattered across this country and around the world. Without her, many of them would have died or be in serious jeopardy now." He raised a hand as Tempest opened her mouth to interrupt. "No, Tempest, you need to hear this, too."

She closed her mouth and resettled to sit cross-legged in the middle of the bed.

"We're family. We protect our own. Trust has grown between us over years. We are already facing several critically dangerous situations. You're a stranger and an alien to our world. We know nothing about you, your ethics, your family, your enemies, or your world. Yet you expect us to give you our most precious treasure. I speak for all of us here and elsewhere." He glanced around the room receiving nods of agreement from everyone, including the physicians and nurses huddled near the door, ending with a direct stare into Tempest's eyes. "That is not ... going ... to ... happen."

Tears sparkled in Tempest's eyes and spilled down her cheeks. She sniffed and laughed when three different hands offered her a tissue. She hiccupped, randomly chose a tissue, and wiped her face. Love, pride and fear of doing or saying the wrong thing swept through her. She was at a loss for words.

Rogan pushed away from Tempest's bed and drifted to the middle of the room. "Here's our proposal. We volunteer to donate the blood you need for an immediate recovery."

The offer surprised Tempest and stirred anxiety low down in her stomach. She frowned, nibbling the same fingernail she was using at the dig site, and listened to the voice in her head. "He says it's possible everyone who gives blood will be connected to him. I will still need to complete the Reciprocate binding with him, particularly because of the feral-spark." She ignored the grimaces on the faces of the men who had been involved with subduing her when the feral-spark had been in control. "He understands and agrees with your concerns and would be honored by your gift of life. He looks forward to the opportunity to earn your trust and hopefully eventually become a part of the family."

The door swung open shoving one of the nurses further into the room.

"Tempest, me darlin', what are you attemptin' to do without me?" Ben's brogue often deepened when he was under the influence of strong emotions.

"Ben!" His arrival confused her.

Strider pushed through the door and held it ajar. She saw more people congregated in the hallway. How did they always know what was happening? It was like having hundreds of mothers, all intent on keeping her on the straight and narrow.

Strider winked at her questioning look. "I know what you're thinking. No woo woo powers, or extrasensory perception: we bugged the room."

"I love each and every one of you." She smiled at the groans from the hallway. "I think you are all the greatest, but you don't need to do this. Take a few hours and think about what it would mean for you and your families."

"Enough of the gushy stuff." Jake swallowed hard. "Dr. Crabtree, set up in the other rooms. He said fresh blood?" At Tempest's nod, he ran some calculations in his mind. "We only need five donors to start, but I want a couple of extra people on hand in case something comes up."

"I'll donate first." Ben escorted Dr. Crabtree out of the room with a hand beneath her elbow. Rogan, Lorcan, Tulsa and Strider followed. The room emptied and the rumble of voices in the hallway cut off as the door swung shut.

"Promise they'll be okay, Bastian, and mean it." Fear added bite to her words.

"I will protect you and your people to my death and beyond." Tempest really didn't understand what he was promising. He was pledging his life and soul and the lives of his Lair to back up his pledge. He normally wouldn't jeopardize his Lair's souls without their willing and conscious consent. He didn't trade in bodies and souls like most Lair Masters in the Worlds League. But he was hundreds of light years from his home world and without doubt considered twice dead by his Lair. He was risking only himself.

"You do you know what you're doing, don't you?"

"Yes, I do." He made the tenor of his voice strong and sure.

"Oh my god! You are such a liar! You're winging it!"

"What does 'winging it' mean?"

"It means you have no idea what's going to happen." Her voice seemed to echo in the suddenly cold room. Her chin dropped to her chest. "That's why you're willing to try a cocktail from everyone." She crawled off the second bed. Her thoughts flowed better when she moved. Following Rogan's path to the wall and back, she projected her thoughts while she talked. "Our DNA is different from what you're used to. Is this dangerous for you, Bastian?"

"There are advantages to being buried for so long, Tempest. My body hasn't metabolized blood for a substantial time. Our physiology allows for sustenance from many genomes. I believe your species' blood will be compatible, but I cannot know for sure until it is in my body."

"Has someone from your species ever consumed incompatible blood?"

Jake re-entered the room before Bastian answered. "You can talk later."

"We really need to finish this conversation, Jake."

"There's fresh blood on the way." He stood at the end of the bed. "I'm going to use a low-feed pressure node. We'll reintroduce blood into his system slowly."

"Tell him to leave when he's done, Tempest."

"He should stay, Bastian, especially since you don't know what's going to happen."

"He will be unable to do anything once the blood is in my

body. I'll either live or I'll die."

"Damnit, Bastian!" She hated not having control. She forced her words through clenched teeth. "After you've set everything up, he wants you to leave."

"I should be here to monitor …. Right." Emotions swirled around him. He studied Tempest's face and then Sebastian's. "Fine. It's against my better judgment, but five minutes, Tempest. Then I'm coming back in."

The door swayed open and a nurse backed in with a tray overflowing with blood bags. She handed one to Jake who inserted it into the first shelf of the metal stand at the head of the bed. He positioned four more bags in the remaining shelves, fiddled with various controls, and closed and sealed the doors.

"It's on automatic monitoring. When the appropriate levels are reached in his body, it shuts off." He checked the pressure pad on the flaccid arm and reluctantly backed away, turned and stalked out.

Sebastian jerked. The bed rattled with the force of his shaking body. "Now, Tempest."

She hesitated. With a deep breath, she walked to the bed, leaned against the mattress and placed her wrist against his mouth. She bit her lip and gagged, the taste of her own blood on her tongue stirring memories of Blanchard's death.

HyperRealm exploded around her.

"I AM ALIVE!"

The words reverberated around her in the black, grey and red landscape. A figure dressed in close-fitting carnelian shirt and pants strode toward her. His braided auburn hair swung back and forth at the middle of his back.

In all his centuries of life, he had never felt so full of strength, energy and well being. His control snapped. He picked Tempest up swinging her in a circle. Laughter spilled out of his mouth. Her chest touched his at the end of the swirl.

"No!" He tried to push her away.

Brilliant white lightning bolts stabbed through their heart

charkas tearing out the symbols of their connection, dragging them into form above their heads. The symbols revolved in replication of the spinning of their respective worlds ... Bastian's whirling at a slightly faster pace.

In various rooms of the medical facility, men and women crumpled to the floor or slumped in chairs. Doctors, nurses and orderlies rushed around checking vitals and easing figures into more comfortable positions.

On the upper plain, spectral figures appeared behind Tempest. Tiny glittering blue and gold Celtic knots poured from the symbol above her head flying to each person and slamming into their chests.

Three pulsing red orbs burst from the center of the flaring hawk emblem above Sebastian, bobbing up and down lazily. Their appearance shocked him. Sebastian snatched at the balls. Re-establishing contact with his people was his decision. The orbs darted away from his hands, transformed into sleek triangular pellets, and blasted out of sight. Borrowing from the Earthers' vocabulary, he cursed. "Fuck!"

Gold and white ribbons descended from the grey-blue sky entwining in the curves of the Celtic knot, binding it against the hawk's breast, sealing them together. An energy wave pulsed across the landscape in all directions. A solitary blue and gold ball bobbed at the end of a yellow thread, trailing the new rotation of the combined signs.

# CHAPTER 22

In the Karnesta galaxy, thousands of light years from the Milky Way, Consul Charge Ren Boden swayed at the podium in the FolKin Assembly Chambers, a huge amphitheater with well-defined sections, each marked with the sigils of the currently viable FolKin Lairs. The leaders, bodyguards and a few members of the ten First Lairs occupied the top tier of room-sized units. Five lower tiers with smaller units housed the remaining Lairs.

A wave of energy rolled through the room and past Ren. He raised a shaking hand catching drops of blood beading at his temple. The murmuring voices of the assembly members died. All eyes focused on the Consul's face as Genus Acolytes rushed to his side.

"Sebastian. Impossible!" Drawing a deep breath, he waved the Acolytes away. Standing straight, he raised his voice. "You are Seen at this meeting of the Assembly. Calling of the Lairs will begin at the hour of Trey later today."

His eyes swept the faces of the Tribunes and, with a small nod, he walked to the door at the back of the raised platform leading to the High Chamber at the rear of the arena. He collapsed into the nearest chair with no concern for the crest at the apex of the high back. Even with his eyes closed, he knew who entered the room – first to last. The men ranged around the chamber deferring to Second Consul Len Syrus.

"Ren ...," Syrus' voice trailed off.

"Did you feel it?" Ren's voice wavered softly. Their

negative responses didn't surprise him. He was one of the last Lair Brothers remaining from the Splintered Time when the leader of the most ancient noble Lair was lost. Ren suspected a rival Lair assassinated Bloodhawk, but evidence supporting the theory was impossible to find. A shudder rolled through him. He pointed to the nearest acolyte. "Inform the Sentry Protectors to expect Blood Lair to arrive in force. Escort the Lair Mistress to me as soon as she arrives."

"Blood Lair is preparing for the move to Debenture." Twinges of anger undercoated Syrus' statement.

A weary sigh escaped Ren's mouth. What an unmitigated disaster. The current circumstances negated the just-finished negotiations among the Lairs.

"It was agreed Blood Lair is moved to third tier and relocated to the bond world where they will stay for three centuries at a minimum." Skorpus Lair Patriarch Jims Geddes sat in his newly assigned Council chair. He had lobbied for splintering Blood Lair and scattering its members forever. It was a shame the Chronicles were amended centuries ago outlawing genocide of entire Lairs. "The Sentry Protectors will be enforcing the Assembly's decision, Consul Charge Boden ... right?"

Jims smoothed his hands down the front of the purple robe. Skorpus Lair was finally where it should have been from the beginning: in First Tier. Skorpus could now influence policy. He had formed alliances and established trade agreements with First and Second Tier Lairs. His maneuvers placed Skorpus in a very advantageous position, and in a few years ... well, it was past time for a new Consul Charge. Len Syrus was a strong ally and an Elder. When Syrus assumed control of the Council, Jims would remind him often of his obligations to Skorpus Lair ... and Jims personally. He tapped his fingers together. Replacing Boden was the essential element in his plans for the Council.

Ren cleared his throat. And so it begins. "First Chair is in dispute. Blood Lair's penalty is suspended."

"NO!" Boiling waves of enmity blasted from Jims.

"Control yourself!" Ren rose and edged left to stand in front of his Lair's chair. He stifled a sigh as comforting energy swirled around him from the family collective infused in the metal and crystal crest.

A wave of embarrassment cooled Jims. A First Tier Council member maintained mastery over himself at all times. He gritted his teeth. "Defend your declaration."

"Wait with the Sentry Protectors and show Blood Lair to the Sanctuary. Go ... now." Ren waved the Acolytes to the door.

Several Councilors opened their mouths only to close them, their unasked questions hanging in the emotion-laden room. Ren raised a shaking hand to his head. "If Blood Lair doesn't arrive within two counts of the hour as written in our Laws, the treaties will be enforced. We wait." He eased down into his chair allowing the family energy to sooth the headache caused by reactivation of the dormant Bloodhawk node. It was propitious the Disengagement had not taken place. The energies needed to reverse Disengagement would have left all the Lairs dangerously weak at a time they needed to show unity and strength of arms and will to the Worlds League.

Ren's fingers closed into a fist on his leg beneath the massive sculpted white quartz table. It gleamed in the subdued lights of the meeting chamber chiseled into the side of one of the rock caverns inside Mount RoHart. His fingers inched toward the controls for the Tru-Arc imager embedded in the smooth surface in front of him. He restrained the urge to touch the keys. Was the Blood Lair Mistress' lineage strong enough to sense the revival of Bloodhawk, the originator of her royal line? He avoided eye contact with the other Councilors – even those sympathetic to Blood Lair and his own Draco Lair.

The murmuring among the Councilors stopped. The distant sound of steel clanging against steel grew closer accompanied by deep grunts and guttural groans. Ren's fingers relaxed. He concealed his shudder of relief by standing and striding quickly to the chamber's entrance. Acolytes scrambled to push open the twelve-foot double wood doors.

"Enough!" His voice boomed the length of the corridor swirling with figures fighting hand-to-hand and with swords. All motion halted. Highly polished blades glittered in the air, appearing to overwhelm the grey-coated opponents which seemed to inhale shadows from the ceiling and corners.

He captured the Master Protector's gaze allowing mild reproof to show briefly in his eyes. With a minute dip of his head, the Master Protector eased his sword into the casing strapped to his waist. The sharp clattering of swords sliding into metal coverings mingled with the soft susurration of blades returning to flinx-hide sheaths. The figures separated into two groups.

A slender woman, her red hair restrained in a braid reaching below her ass, strode down the corridor. Her well-proportioned figure was sheathed in a midnight-blue shape-hugging vest and pants with a rampant hawk stitched on the left shoulder in crimson threads. Flinx-leather boots dyed to match climbed her legs to her knees.

Two men flanked her, their over six foot bodies making her appear delicate, breakable. Sleeveless vests the color of fresh blood covered broad chests. Intricate designs in gold and silver threads sparkled in the light drawing attention, camouflaging the female. Their ear-length hair ... one blonde and silver and the other burgundy and gold ... framed deep-set eyes, high cheekbones and determined square jaws. They were often mistaken for brothers, but Ren knew they were the offspring of twin sisters mated with Patriarchs of different Lairs allied to Blood Lair for centuries. Powers flowed between and from the trio creating eddies of current playing run and seek with hair and loose material on bodies and hangings on walls.

Ren bowed his head slightly as the trio halted several feet away. "Mistress."

Lavender eyes briefly flashed elation before fading to dark amethyst. Tucking her excitement into a transparent globe in her head, Kalia Sanborne made a quick bow to the Consul

Charge, ignoring the angry mutterings of the Councilmen at his back. Kenton Bloodstar and Braman "Ram" Wolfanger stood so close against her back she felt the heat of their bodies. She let them enclose her in their personal shielding making it easier for her to draw on their solid restraint if she needed in order to present calm composure in the presence of their enemies. Tonal Mates considered it an imperative and duty to ensure the health and welfare of their Key.

"Consul Charge Boden." She had prayed for a way out of the trap entangling Blood Lair. Never in her wildest imagination had she dreamed she would be able to slip the death grip in this manner. Her voice was firm, steady, with a lilt she couldn't hide. "Blood Lair becomes Seeker. The Royal Patriarch Bloodhawk has Commanded."

Ren nodded. He had the response he had hoped for. "Seek your destiny, Blood Lair. Do you Seek in toto or…"

"Blood Lair Seeks as one, retaining Right of Commerce with allies."

Jims Geddes pulled free of Councilman Poncius Maclin's restraining hands marching to Ren's side. "No. I don't know what trick you're trying to pull but it won't work. Sebastian Bloodhawk met his final death long ago. The Master Protector will assemble a Warrior Regiment which will escort Blood Lair to the spacefield. They will board their ships and lift immediately to Debenture escorted by the Guardianships. Right of Commerce has no meaning in this situation."

Kenton and Ram edged sideways, with one step they would be a shield for Kalia. Blood Lair fighters glided into defensive positions as tension rose in the hallway. Many Lair Mistresses and Patriarchs viewed Kalia as an adolescent at one hundred six turns and looked down on Blood Lair for selecting such a young leader. They refused to see she held more power and talent in one little finger than they would ever hope to attain in their many centuries of existence.

Kalia focused only on Ren. "Blood Lair renounces First

Chair. As Seeker, Blood Lair claims all lands, territories, worlds, solar systems, and Lightgates servicing the area within five Lightgates of the place of residence of Sebastian Bloodhawk, retaining Right of Commerce with allies."

She waited for the bargaining to begin, swallowing the riptides of excitement from Kenton, Ram and the fighters behind them to maintain the façade of indifference. She blinked at a small tendril of satisfaction mixed with the explosion of shock from the Councilors in the corridor. Quick taps against her back from Kenton and Ram let her know they couldn't pinpoint the anomalous reaction.

"Agreed and confirmed." Jims mentally rubbed his hands together, ignoring the dismay and disgust on the faces of the other Councilors. As Patriarch of the affected Lair, his word bound all Lairs, the Worlds League and all worlds chartered to the Worlds League. If they wanted to follow an unbelievable and unsubstantiated energy wave, let them. He had effectively exiled Blood Lair forever.

Kalia casually swung her arms behind her, grabbing her mates' hands. Unbridled triumph thundered into her through the Blood Lair node in her mind. "Confirmed and accepted." She squeezed Kenton and Bram's fingers drawing on their control when her Uncle Boden winked at her.

An Acolyte hurried from the Council chambers clutching a datagram in his hands. Jims pressed his thumb against the screen presented to him and waited impatiently for Ren and Kalia to do the same. Exquisite joy filled him as he watched the document disappear from view speeding its way to the Lairs' Archive of Laws and the Official Library Chronicles of the Worlds League on Charon.

Kalia, Kenton and Ram bowed to Ren, spun around and strode down the hallway, the leather-clad Blood Lair fighters enfolding them in their midst.

Outside the Assembly Citadel, Kalia laughed and laughed. Kenton picked her up and twirled her around and around. Ram watched them, chuckling … rubbing his hands across his tearing eyes. Grins burst from the solemn faces of the still alert fighters, eyes tracking ground level and overhead.

Ram's datacom buzzed twice and stopped. He stepped into the arc of Kenton's next swing, caught Kalia and tucked her into his arms. "Celebration will need to wait for a time. All ships have left the planet and are holding at the edge of the system for us." He gathered the fighters together with a glance. "No, Kalia." He countered the feminine push against his shoulder. "We're going to Hunter speed. I'm carrying you."

Kalia whispered into Ram's ear. "He didn't think, Ram. He didn't hesitate to consider the ramifications. We got FIVE Lightgates, and the territories, trade routes, mining, everything!" Her voice rose. "And we keep our connection with our allies!" She concentrated and shifted her molecules to lighten her weight. "I've cut the Tru-Arc connection, Ram. His consciousness is very faint, but together we'll be able to find him."

Held securely in Ram's arms, she balanced on the edge of HyperRealm and wove a link-web. In the gestalt of HyperRealm, tiny dots in a variety of colors pulsed against the grey background. She cast her net over the specks massed around a large blob – the people surrounding her and her Tonal Mates. Noticing one dot outside the web, she tweaked the edge of the grid to encompass it. Yellow light flared around the spot shoving the thread away. Who? No time to investigate. She turned her attention to the web and with a gentle push began feeding the accumulated energy from the confrontation with the Councilors to Kenton, Ram and the men and women surrounding them in a defensive circle. Hunter mode ate energy quickly. Distributing the energy in this manner was good practice and utilized the abundance.

A quarter turn later, a silver ship displaying a red rampant hawk on its skin blasted from the spaceport. At the outer atmosphere, its surface shimmered for a few seconds then became as black as the space surrounding it.

"You fool!" Councilor Maclin shook his head as he turned

and stalked into the Council Chambers. "Five Lightgates!"

Jims wanted to crow. Excitement charged through him stimulating an erection the likes of which he hadn't felt in many Turns. Dreena. He had to get to the Pleasure Manor. He had to contact Mistress Plemia. She would make sure Dreena was reserved for his use. His eyes glowed for a few seconds before focusing on his fellow Council members.

"What's the problem? The databurst the Temparens picked up was garbled and they weren't able to pinpoint its location, but it was audible. Bloodhawk was seriously injured. Searchers would have found his ship if it crashed within known quadrants. Besides, it was over two hundred Turns ago. His pod is failing by now. By the time anyone locates it, if they can even track him, he'll be dead. The agreement will be void. Blood Lair's move to Debenture is just delayed for a short time if they survive the Seeking." He waved a dismissive hand.

"How strong was the pulse, Ren?" Syrus leaned against the table, his arms crossed.

"The initial contact was strong and the connection is still active but I don't sense his consciousness at all now."

"There are enough Elder Council members here to activate the Tru-Arc to trace him to the planet using your node." Syrus hesitated. "I don't understand why Blood Lair didn't demand their right to the Tru-Arc. Bloodstar and Wolfanger know the Laws even if Sanborne doesn't."

Ren ignored the arrogant dropping of Kalia's title. He found it interesting the Council had forgotten Sanborne was a first generation expansion from the Boden line. When they insulted Kalia, they insulted him.

Braga and Liama Sanborne had asked him to stay away from Kalia when she was born. His fear for their safety had dissipated when Sebastian Bloodhawk offered Sanctuary to the small Lair. Then Sebastian was lost during a routine escort mission to Delphia. And within Turns, the Malkonian world launched an attack on Carpria. Some Elders died in the battles, but the initial assaults during sleep cycles killed many. It was bloody. It failed. A quarter of the invading Malkonians escaped to spread horrific tales of vengeance and retribution.

Several Lairs, including Skorpus, escaped the brunt of the assault. He couldn't prove those Lairs were involved, but he knew they were guilty. He had a long memory. He had survived assassination attempts in the past. Justice would prevail eventually.

"It was the Mistress' decision. Bloodstar and Wolfanger would have briefed her on her rights before they arrived here if she didn't already know them." Braga and Liama would have taught Kalia the rights, responsibilities and duties of a Mistress. Ren motioned the four Elders to their Chairs and settled into the Draco Chair. Using the keys in front of him, he initiated the power source. Drawing in several deep breaths, he looked at each Elder and in unison they touched the gold strip around the circumference of the table.

The surface rippled. A black fog coalesced above the table to form a three dimensional map of the known space. Lair worlds glowed green. The Worlds League home world winked red at the center. Allied worlds glimmered white and enemy worlds glowed strident hot blue. Neutral territories glittered rich gold.

The Elders braced for the transition to a different galaxy.

They waited.

And waited.

Syrus raised furious eyes to Ren's face. "The connection was deliberately cut. Consul Charge Boden, you have overstepped your authority. Charges will be filed for your misconduct and penalties will be levied on Draco Lair." His voice grew more strident at the small smile on Ren's face.

"Look deeper, Second Consul … if you can." It was a deliberate insult. Ren didn't care. Draco had expanded more than the Council or Assembly knew by offering Sanctuary to the smaller, younger Lairs … those that didn't join with Blood Lair.

The Lairs and allied worlds routinely transmitted Alliances, trade agreements and matings to the Worlds League, allowing the League to usurp more and more control. But it wasn't a law ... yet. Draco entire had voted to only transmit innocuous reports at regular intervals and file the important ... the dangerous ... information in the Archive of Laws only. The Archive ministered by Draco allies.

Shock tightened the lines in Syrus' face. "It's impossible. Sanborne doesn't have the power." He nodded to himself. "Right. Her Lair helped her ... someone helped her." He looked accusingly at Ren again.

"Shut up, Syrus." Elder Legba withdrew his fingers from the table and leaned back in his chair. "Mistress Sanborne severed the connection ... as is her right. She negotiated very well for her Lair. She followed all protocols including bearing only swords as weapons. If Bloodhawk is dead and Blood Lair returns, all penalties are void. The Lair can establish new territory on any Class A Lair world they select. So is my Word to which All are Bound." He aimed a stern look at the bellicose Jims. "Now would be a propitious time for you to go celebrate whatever victory you can pull from this debacle."

His eyes swerved to the Consul Charge. "Ren, you have the apologies of this Council." Legba rose from his Chair. "Messages will be sent to the Assembly that Calling of the Lairs will occur in two Turns. Housing will be provided in the Citadel for all representatives." He turned and walked out the door.

Acolytes scurried behind the Elder. Outside the door, they ran at full speed down branching corridors. Fear and excitement were twin emotions inside them. It had been an historic day and they had been a part of it. It was a race to see who would be the first to tell the tale. The money for retelling the events would be immense but the prestige of being a participant ... even as a bystander ... was worth much more than mere money. They had Status!

"We come, Life-Giver. Do your duty and keep the

Patriarch alive." The forceful voice whispered through Tempest's mind.

HyperRealm dissolved. Sebastian opened his eyes for the first time in hundreds of Turns reveling in the ball and chain of gravity. He lapped the skin against his mouth sealing the small pinpricks created by his incisors. He released the arm. Only a few swallows of her blood and the richness and purity, with an unusual undertone of spice, appeased his hunger like nothing before. The cocktail insinuated in his veins from the others had acted as an activator for the catalyst of Tempest's blood. He sat up in the bed.

"You might want to take your time there, Bloodhawk." Jake moved away from the blood dispenser, stopping beside Tempest. "Your system has had some hard knocks in a short amount of time, Tempest." He checked her pulse and placed a glass of fluid, rich in electrolytes, in her hand. "I'm ordering you to bed until Friday morning. We can fix up a space for you here or you can go home. I'll check on you every couple of hours." The threat was clear in his tone.

Sebastian stroked the soft curls, guilt overwhelming his thrill of physicality. "I'm sorry, little warrior. I did not plan bonding with you this day and time. It was most unexpected." He remembered the three orbs. It would be best to wait until later to discuss the ramifications of those spheres. But not too much later.

# CHAPTER 23

Strident yowling and tentative patting on her nose woke Tempest from the embrace of a lucid dream. She gripped her pillow tighter against her chest. She was in that one position where a slight movement in any direction would become uncomfortable. Her lids drooped; the dream threatened to drag her back under. The patting became harder with a hint of sharp pricking. Her eyes crossed as she opened them from the closeness of two lime green circles with black slits at the centers. "Hey, Maggie, where's Gracie?"

Feet padded up her leg and along her hip. Fur sank onto her waist. She looked down and saw Gracie, paws tucked into her chest, eyes half-closed. She stroked Maggie's head and down her back. Maggie butted her face against the return caress pushing it to the place she wanted.

Tempest let her thoughts float while absently smoothing the soft pelt. Her hand slowed and stopped. She dropped back into sleep.

Fingers circled her wrist. She jerked, slammed her other hand against a hard chest, rolled away from the presence and off the side of the bed. Maggie and Gracie shot off the mattress like shells launched from a cannon. She twisted left, swept an arm beneath the pillows and drew out a sheath. A tumble forwards away from the bed, she crouched, one arm in defensive position with scabbard in hand, and the other arm low, blade clutched in her fingers ready for a quick slash. Time slowed. "Damn."

An ocean of pink swept over her face. Ignoring Rogan standing in the doorway, she rose and stepped back to the side of the bed shoving the knife into the casing and then beneath the pillows. She accepted the robe from Jake, wrapped it around her nude body and tied the belt. The fog over her mind was lifting. "I'm just a little anxious. There's nothing to worry about."

Her fingers trembled minutely as she pushed her hair behind her ears. She was reassuring herself as much as Rogan and Jake. This was the second time in two days she had been ready to attack for nothing more than a physical touch.

The men made a conscious effort not to exchange looks. Tempest didn't need the additional pressure of knowing how concerned they were about the erosion of her control.

"How are the patients this morning? Is there any coffee?" She lifted a leg and put it down. One step at a time. She just had to keep moving forward. One hand pushed the bathroom door open. A few more paces and she passed the privacy wall, pulled the handle on the faucet in the shower starting the water, removed the robe and stepped inside the tiled sanctuary. God! the hot water against the knots in her shoulders was wonderful. She turned and propped her hands on the shower wall letting the liquid cascade over her face and hair.

Jake and Rogan followed Tempest leaning against the bathroom wall near the door. Jake raised his voice. "Braeden and Bloodhawk are driving my nurses crazy wandering in and out of the rooms on that floor. Braeden's group is recovering and their wounds are healing well. His second group arrived and everyone has been cleared. They've added to the number of people checking in on Braden and the other injured. Ben said there are a couple of group houses ready so I'm sending Braeden and his people there.

"Bloodhawk has already tested his tolerance for Earth's daylight. He has an allergy to our sun, but the side effects aren't as debilitating as it is on many worlds ... or so he tells us. Since he plans to attend the ceremony, I'm loading him up on sun blockers. And someone brought back some of his clothes from the shuttle. There's a full-length cloak he can wear."

Tempest flicked the switches to activate the jets in the surrounding walls. Her groan echoed against the tiles.

Rogan and Jake exchanged grins.

"Need some help in there, Tempest?" Jake rapped the wall with his knuckles.

"Go bother someone else. I'm having a religious experience here. Someone get me some coffee! And don't I have to be somewhere?"

"You have two hours to get ready for the internment at the crypt." Rogan raised his voice above the noise of the water.

"What!" Her head popped around the side of the partition then disappeared again.

Jake pulled a towel from the warmer. "You've been asleep for almost twenty-four hours." He held the cloth around the side of the wall. The water shut off and a hand yanked it away.

"That's impossible." Her words came out muffled and jittered. "Is everyone ready?"

"We're taking in Raptors One and Three and six of the Rapiers for protection. Everyone is suited up. We're just waiting on you."

"Well, give me some room. I'll be ready in half an hour." She walked around the partition with the towel covering all the essential parts. "And get me some coffee!" she shouted at Rogan's and Jake's disappearing figures.

Maggie stropped Tempest's leg meowing. Tempest wiped the moisturizer from her hands and lifted Maggie to her chest. She counted beneath her breath while stroking Maggie's body: one ... two ... three ... and the furry body squirmed. Laughing, she stroked Maggie's head twice then set her on the floor caressing her sides. Maggie darted away from the approaching Gracie. Gracie's legs buckled and she flopped onto her side stretching her body tight then releasing. Tempest giggled and ran her hand back and forth on Gracie's stomach. She placed a hand at Gracie's chest and butt to pick her up, but Gracie jumped up and ran into the bedroom.

Tempest slapped on eye makeup, drew a brush filled with powder around her face, and bent over at the waist to dry her hair. She dropped her towel into the laundry basket and walked into the bedroom. Someone had made the bed and the clothes she planned to wear, along with a rolled cloth bundle, rested on the covering.

Starting with matching black bra and panties, she began to dress. She pulled black leggings up her legs and over her hips and sat on the edge of the bed to drag on austere black boots, with a cap covering the knee and tapering at the sides to the back. Her hand grabbed the black top from the bed as she stood and flicked it over her head. She turned to check her appearance in the floor mirror running a hand down the front of her stomach to settle the folds of material below the empire top of the black bustier. Her daily runs on the obstacle course and workouts with Rogan and other men and women using various martial arts and methods of attacking and defending herself helped control the accumulation of body fat. Cocking her head to the side, she considered the silky material below the bra top deciding to let it hang free over the waistband of the leggings.

Turning to the bed, she unrolled the cloth bundle and slipped black handled matte-finished knives into special holders on the inside of each side of her boots. Eyeing the short sword in its leather scabbard and her wrist sheathes, she shook her head and rerolled them into the pack, picked it up and strolled into the walk-in closet at the back of the room. She thrust the pack onto a shelf, turned and walked down a few feet.

A tug at a drawer exposed several rolled belts. Her fingers picked through the selection and withdrew a wide fabric band with pockets attached along its sides. From another drawer, she took out a holster which she snapped onto the belt then clasped it around her waist beneath the flowing bottom of the top. She returned to the front of the space, counted the bins in the floor-to-ceiling storage shelves, withdrew one box, opened it, reached inside, and removed five thousand dollars, folding and pushing the bills into the pockets on the belt. She randomly selected another box and moved it to the empty space inserting the one in her hand into the vacated place. A purse wasn't necessary and would only get in the way. The money was for emergency purposes ... just in case. Turning, she pulled a heel-length, long-sleeved cobalt blue microfiber duster decorated with black swirls and circles from a hangar and swirled it on.

The majority of the people attending the ceremonies for Glory would be dressed in slick, expensive, formal clothes. The bodyguards and security teams would be wearing official gear. Tempest chose her outfit to reflect her personal style. There was nothing about her clothes disrespectful to Glory. But the Council would seek to punish her for violating the apparel guidelines listed in the Charter for such occasions and would likely start the process with a toady appearing at her door with an envelope sealed with wax enclosing one sheet of exclusive paper detailing in handwritten prose the amount of money she would pay and the number of hours she would serve as an attendant in the High Circle. She walked down the hallway from her bedroom to the entry chuckling. Boy, were they in for a shock.

Rogan offered Tempest a gun, waited for her to put it in the holster at the small of her back, and then gave her a coffee mug and her sunglasses. With a hand at her back, he directed her towards the front door. "You look exotic and like a young man's wet dream come true."

She sputtered. "I know it's over the top for a Coven function, and the Council will attempt to censure me for not following the rules, but that wasn't exactly what I was going for." She sobered. "This is a very dangerous game, Rogan."

He opened the door and stepped back. "We can always cancel if that's what you want, but I think it's important we make a show of force. The Coteries in Raptor Three are at the cemetery.

Reports are coming through on a regular basis and so far there's been no movement on the grounds. The two-person detail at the memorial site says there's a lot of activity. The Covens have several strike forces in various locations." He handed her into the front of the SUV and closed the door.

Tempest turned sideways in her seat. "Are you sure you want to be part of this, Sebastian?"

He pushed the material of the hood off his head. Black sunglasses hid his eyes and added an extra fillip to his guise. "I wish to see more of this world and its people and I want to assess the dangers we are facing. We are ... family ... now." He used the weaker euphemism to define the real relationship between him, Tempest and her beholden. He turned his face to the warmth of the rising sun. "I also desire to walk in the light, feel the breeze against my skin. I have been a very long time in darkness, Tempest."

Rogan slid into the driver's seat and slammed the door. "Lorcan is at the hangar." He started the engine and drove the short distance to the airfield. He had entered the vehicle in time to hear the alien's last few words. He didn't pity the being; he understood the desire for fresh air and sunshine. Anyone with experience of shadows treasured freedom and light.

Arriving at the airfield, he backed the SUV up the ramp into the belly of the first Raptor stopping a few inches from the front of another vehicle. He withdrew a white envelope from his pocket and handed it to Tempest. "This was dropped by the front gate during the shift change. It was passed on following the procedures for hand deliveries."

The vehicle vibrated slightly as engines revved. Lorcan slipped into the second row of seats as the Raptor rumbled and leaped into the air.

Tempest accepted the packet. Coven stationery: the groups all used the same supplier. She broke the seal on the flap – the Ruling Council's crest studded the wax – and tugged the paper. She cleared her throat. "The CEOs have called a

Convocation for after the internment for reading Grandmother's
Will. Grandmother's attorneys agreed to comply with the
Council's request. It says here, '...an appropriate place for
transfer of leadership.' I think they're making assumptions
without the benefit of knowledge." She jerked a shoulder in a
dismissive shrug. "I haven't a clue what Grandmother put in
her Will. She kept her secrets close to her breast. I'm just glad
Mikuh can't go."

Rogan frowned. "We don't have enough fighters at the
graveyard. I don't like this, Tempest." Bloody hell! He grasped
the steering wheel tightly, his hands turning white. With effort,
he released his grip flexing his fingers to loosen the tension.

"I don't like it either, Rogan, but I don't think we have
much choice in the matter. This is a Council Directive. We have
at least two choices. The first one is we turn around and get
the remaining people headed to Summerfield tonight. Hmm. I
think the last part of that thought is a good one. Lorcan, contact
all of the leaders at all of the outlying properties to get out now.
No more waiting. Tell them to move in small groups, no large
convoys."

She nodded then waved the paper in the air. "Our second
choice is continuing to the gravesite and attending the meeting,
although the Recordkeeper should have informed the Council of
my current status. One, I'm no longer a dependent of Father's.
Two, I haven't participated in Coven Ritual for enough years that
I am now considered an outsider. And, three, with Glory's death,
I'm no longer one of her retainers. I don't know what they gain
by calling a Convocation and insisting on the reading of her Will
at the same time."

The Raptor landed with a slight bump. The ramp slowly
lowered. Sunlight burst into the gloomy interior. The SUVs
rolled down the incline onto the runway pavement. Rapiers
dropped from the sky to perch around the Raptor. A liquid
mirage danced in the distance above the hot concrete.

"Keep the Rapiers grounded for now. We don't want

to stir up the military brass attending the memorial." Tempest tapped the envelope against her chin watching the scenery passing by the side window.

Rogan tapped the transmit button once on his dotmitter to indicate receipt of an incoming message. "Two 'giants' have arrived at the tomb saying D'eath sent them as additional guards for you." He gave her a quick glance before returning his attention to the road. He checked the side mirrors, hit the turn signal, and drove through the entrance of the cemetery. He tapped the brakes twice and rolled to a stop. "Proceed or contact D'eath and confirm they were sent from him? Bayzee wasn't anxious; he sounded impressed."

"We go. Right now, we likely have enough fighters to handle them if they aren't who they say they are." She checked her watch. "We need to get into position. The schedule I was given shows the memorial ending in the next ten minutes. We should have an additional thirty minutes for the building to empty, the vehicles to be sorted out, and the body transported here."

She returned to staring out the side window, surreptitiously flicking a tear from the corner of one eye. Her throat hurt from holding back her tears. "You should make the decisions starting now, Rogan." She tried to remain calm and collected in order to make the right decisions for the welfare of all, but memories of her Grandmother were getting in the way.

She bent her head and sniffed. Sensing movement beside her, she edged closer to the door. "Don't hug me, Ro."

With a deep sigh, Rogan dropped his arm and drove to a parking lot at the back of the grounds, backing the vehicle into a shaded space. The second SUV settled into a space at the front of the lot. Doors opened and bodies exited hurrying to defensive positions.

Bayzee Tenor trotted into view. "Hoo, boy, ma'am, you're sure lookin' fine. We've got a place all picked out for you. You'll have the best view of the people as they arrive and we'll still be able to cover you when you go into the crypt. Once inside, all bets are off."

Tempest shook her head as she followed Bayzee across the grass. "I'll pay my respects to Grandmother another time. I'm not going into that enclosed place with Coven CEOs, their entourage, and whoever else was invited." She looked up into Rogan's eyes. "I won't be intimidated by the family or CEOs into using bad judgment."

Relief made Rogan shudder. The only way to ensure Tempest's safety was to surround her with bodies while in the burial chamber and that wouldn't have been possible. He circled her waist with an arm.

Sebastian analyzed the interaction between his Reciprocate and the loyal Captain and her beholden following them across the grass. She was the center stone of an intricate and resilient necklace of courageous, dedicated warriors and families. The Lady and Her Consort had blessed him this time with their Choice. His skin tingled and he tucked his hands beneath his cape. It was exhilarating to actually feel the rays of the sun, but he wasn't foolhardy about the damage exposure could produce.

He tried to understand their custom of burying the dead instead of the cleansing flames of fire. Many of the Interworlds at one time shared the same ritual. As the population expanded, land became a valuable commodity and fire became the norm rather than the exception. The Lairs' Ruling Houses always moved swiftly to recover bodies of the same lineage. Fire made Resurrection impossible. Mages who resurrected a body before three days passed, the time period during which the 'soul' of the person detached from the physical shell and moved on, could bind the personality and force it to do whatever the Mage or the Mage's benefactor wanted.

He staggered, falling against a stone marker for support. His head swam. He tightened his shields and doubled the protection around Tempest's symbol in his mind. A FolKin was trying to drag him into HyperRealm. Before his incarceration in the MedTube, no one would have dared such an act knowing he would retaliate a hundred fold against the perpetrator.

"Are you all right, Sebastian?" Tempest moved in beside him. She restrained her automatic reaction to touch him since she didn't know what would happen. Someone from his world was trying to force contact. The wrenching on Sebastian's crest in her mind had been like a hand reaching into her chest and squeezing her heart. To be at the center of that force must have been like actually having one's heart ripped out.

Relief jolted through her seeing his eyes open. At his nod, she took the handkerchief from Lorcan's hand and blotted the beads of blood from Sebastian's forehead. "We can spare some people to get you to the Raptor and back to Summerfield."

"That is not necessary. I am fine now." He straightened, making unnecessary adjustments to his clothes to regain his bearings. He hesitated before commenting. "My people are aware of my Rising. We will need to discuss the consequences of this knowledge soon. For now, I believe we have other more urgent matters to attend to."

Tempest knew by the tone of his voice it was not going to be a cheerful discussion. Add it to the future things list. She turned and found her nose buried in Lorcan's back. She stepped back onto Sebastian's foot. Rogan filled the space beside Lorcan.

"Whoa, people." Bayzee rocketed between his comrades, with suddenly bristling weapons, and the approaching duo. He waved a hand at the seven-foot tall men. "That's Salty and Pepper. These are the guys Mr. D'eath sent over."

Blue tattoos on the opposite sides of each man's face drew the eye and dyed wings of bright blue hair led the focus to thick black hair cut to just above the ears. Hip-length sleeveless cobalt blue vests with plaited inserts along the ribs covered broad muscular chests. Tips of silver glinted from small pockets along wide belts at waists, twin swords poked above their shoulders and black-coated handles of throwing knives jutted from the tops of boots the same bright blue as the trousers and vests.

Salty backed away and turned sideways. The waist-length braid sparkled in the light at irregular intervals.

Tempest pushed around Rogan and Lorcan to get a closer look: small razor sharp metal hooks dotted the twisted hair. If she decided to let her hair grow long, she would remember the clever trick. With a nod, she walked between the twins. They were on duty and conversation wasn't invited.

The group, with Tempest at the center, crossed graveled paths. Mature shade trees towered over family plots. The feathery limbs of willows caressed grassy mounds and concrete markers.

"Here you go, ma'am." Bayzee halted two hundred feet from the Duvayne family crypt jutting from the ground, a grey and white intruder at the center of seven oak trees. Shrubs at one side of the behemoth oaks provided a discrete hiding place. They settled in to wait.

# CHAPTER 24

"The hearse has arrived, ma'am, and there's a crowd headed this way. We've got government strike force soldiers making a perimeter around the guests. Do we pull back or hold our ground?"

Rogan scanned the immediate area before replying. "Pull back. Squad Dover, move all vehicles to the west lot and prepare for a quick departure. Everyone else form up on our position at the oak trees west of the Duvayne crypt."

"Excuse me." Tempest stepped around Salty. A sound of pure exasperation escaped when the man mountain moved in front of her again. The tumultuous emotions seething in her wanted an outlet and tackling the fighter would relieve some of the pressure. But he was an innocent standing between her and the real culprits. She wanted justice for her grandmother. She wanted to break the control the Covens held on the welfare of others. She was sick to her soul of the political maneuverings by Covens, military, governments, and corporations. A small smile briefly turned up her lips: several of her companies were heavily involved with the world system. She would be fighting herself.

Robert Duvayne herded his wife and children into the mausoleum. He stood for a moment on the stairs and searched the crowd for his wayward daughter. He glimpsed Branaugh standing beside a black-cloaked figure at the edge of the Seven Sisters. If he was here, Tempest was close. His brow furrowed at the spectacle of men armed with barbaric and outdated weapons as well as rifles prominently displayed.

The Coven Archivist's 'link call last night was worrisome. Someone accessed the amended Coven Charters from a blocked account and tracing the unauthorized intrusion was like catching sparks from a fire, the specks disappearing on drifting air currents. As head of data retrieval and collection, he initiated security protocols and clamped down on the reporting of the trespass. Walking into the cold, dark vault, his neck tingled and a shudder ran up his spine.

Tempest smiled at Daire threading through the people. When he reached her, she flipped her hand toward the twins. "Thanks for Salty and Pepper." She lowered her voice. "Were you able to move the object?" She didn't want to say more. Hovercams had been darting around the area since the arrival of the memorial guests.

He nodded, silently answering her question. "Will you be going inside?"

"No." She watched the CEOs enter the crypt. "It's a politically suicidal decision among the Covens, but I don't have any aspirations to become involved in the leadership so it doesn't really matter to me." One shoulder shrugged dismissively.

She used her chin to point to one side of the circle of trees. Men scurried around erecting a white tent with side panels. "The CEOs called a Convocation ... a meeting of the leaders of all the Covens ... to start after this final ceremony. I received a Directive to attend. The attorneys for Glory's estate contacted me advising me that the reading of her Will is to occur at the meeting. The Council was able to force the time and place because Glory was Ryniah and the Council has a vested interest in her bequests. Having the reading of grandmother's Will now isn't exactly a breach of protocol and the courts generally stay out of Coven business unless it's a radical violation of rights. This just toes the line. I agreed since I'm one of the beneficiaries, but I sent word to the attorneys that for security purposes I wouldn't enter the crypt with all those people. The tents are their solution."

A shadow at the corner of her eye caught her attention. She continued to stare toward the crowd gathered outside the vault watching the proceedings on temporary plasma screens attached to the stone walls. Minutes passed. A commotion beyond the chamber drew all eyes. Soldiers closed in around the mourners and several moved inside the crypt.

Tempest leaned into Rogan and lowered her voice to barely audible. "A man behind us to your left wants my attention. I'm going to take a look. It looks like the games are about to start. Can you handle this?"

Voices spilled from his dotmitter. He tapped the fingers of his right hand against her hip in a pattern indicating agreement and caution. Tempest edged backwards as Rogan stepped closer to Bloodhawk hiding her movements.

Hovercams zoomed by. The soldiers pressed the crowd together causing small female shrieks to waft into the air.

Daire strode to Rogan, said something and flicked his fingers to Salty and Pepper. He threw a smile at Tempest and ran towards the vault followed by his men. The World President would be looking to him for protection.

She worked her way to the edge of the ring of trees flicking subtle finger signals at the guards assigned to her protection. A scream in the distance gave her the opening she needed, and she slipped through the shrubs. The Coteries formed at the front of the space creating a wedge of protection as soldiers herded part of the crowd around the mausoleum towards their shelter. The distraction should keep them occupied for the time she needed. She ducked below the top of the hedge and ran.

A figure stepped to the edge of the shadows cast by a giant concrete angel, wings outstretched, protector of the sanctity and silence of a family plot a few hundred yards from the Seven Sisters.

"Ms. Phillips." The voice was raspy, deep, congested. The clothes hanging on the tall, thin man were patched and spotless. A salt and pepper close-cropped beard couldn't hide the deep grooves around his mouth. Pain and disillusionment filled smoke grey, weary eyes. He leaned on a wood cane, fingers clenched around the padded handle. "I'm alone."

Tempest halted in front of a waist-high marker: close enough to hear what he had to say but with room to fight or run. Keeping him at the edge of her eye, she scanned the area. She considered using HyperRealm to search for body heat. She would only be vulnerable for the seconds it required to get in and out. No. Anything could happen in even that short amount of time. She cocked her head toward the commotion. "Your work?"

A barely there smile momentarily relieved the strain in his face. "A necessary distraction so we can talk."

"I'm willing to listen."

He nodded, began to speak, coughed, choked, bent over and coughed harder. His body shook with the effort. He raised his left hand to stop Tempest's automatic reaction to help and struggled to stand upright. His body wove back and forth slightly then steadied. "Sorry, ma'am." He drew a flask from a back pocket and sipped the contents. "It's an herbal mixture." He didn't want her thinking he was drinking alcohol. He cleared his throat, felt a tickle in his throat and drank again. He returned the container to his pocket. "I heard about the call you put out for men. I represent a group who would like to apply."

She leaned against the side of the gravestone. "Okay. We're running background checks. I'll need names, personal identification numbers, and photographs."

He ducked his head and thought for a minute before looking into her eyes. "Thank you for your time. We wouldn't pass a security check. You should go back now." His shoulders slumped from months of fatigue and deprivation then straightened.

"Wait!" She walked to his side placing a hand on the arm holding the walking stick to halt his withdrawal. "I'll give you and your men a fair hearing. I'm in a precarious ..."

"Yes, ma'am, we know."

She made a split-second decision. "Are your friends close by?"

He shook his head and twisted to point behind him. "I didn't want the men to get too close to the activity. Our camp is just beyond that far structure."

She opened her shields for a quick check. Roiling predatory emotions filled with insatiable appetites for pain and suffering smoldered in a pocket on the left. Her personal guards were giving her the room she needed, hiding in a staggered formation on her right. Green, white and red heat signatures were approaching in a semi-circle from the direction of the Seven Sisters: Rogan was coming. It would look suspicious to the man in front of her and his people if Rogan didn't make the appearance of searching for her. She had to move the meeting along fast. "I'd like to meet your people if only for a quick introduction." She was confident she would be able to discern their basic natures.

The limping figure led her past long rows of old and new headstones in all shapes and sizes. Family mausoleums sprang from encroaching graves like grey blocks of ice. He guided her through the section of the cemetery reserved for the less fortunate. Overgrown grass, dead and dying flowers lying on or in front of markers, and weeds creeping at the edges of concrete instilled a sense of exhausted neglect. The headstones were smaller and a few tumbled on the ground in pieces. A cluster of old Weeping Willow trees huddled at the boundary of the grounds; long fronds lazily flicking grass tucked into thick roots.

"Please wait here, Ms. Phillips." He tightened his grip on the handle of his cane as he picked his way through the rubble. He turned and leaned against the side of a weathered angel, its head turned to the heavens as if importuning the gods to free it from its cold vigil. Figures rose around him like zombies pulled from dirt-encased homes.

"I'm sorry I didn't introduce myself earlier." He made a slight bow. "I'm Nathan Collier and most of my companions here," he swept his arm around the half-circle at his back, "served with me in the military."

She inhaled deeply. She recognized the name. The news stories had crucified and vilified the man and remaining members of his teams. Reading between the lines, she had asked Jack and Gene to make some discrete inquiries in the military and mercenary communities. An ambitious career politician with security clearance and access to battle plans had betrayed the men, handing them to the enemy like pot roast on a plate. She knew at least one or maybe more military brass was involved, but they had scurried into bolt holes like rats, sealing their identities and actions behind the mantle of the Global Security and Suppression Act.

"Captain Collier, I understand why you might not pass a background check if you were applying for a job with a regular company. I'd like to give you unequivocal acceptance, but not all of the people here were in your teams." It was difficult meeting the eyes of the men and a few women scattered among the barren grave site. Their spare forms radiated their need for a safe place to sleep and nutritious food to fill empty bellies.

Staring at the twenty-five people, forewarning crept along her spine like a thief in a house, raising the hair on her neck and arms. She crossed her arms, rubbing up and down. She sensed it was vital that she give them sanctuary. "Alright, all of you are hired. I'll need to arrange transportation to my compound in Summerfield."

There was a release of pent up breaths. Collier's eyes shimmered. He limped to her side and tucked her hand into his elbow. His fingers flicked a message to the group who melted into the terrain.

"Thank you, Ms. Phillips. I didn't expect an immediate answer nor did I believe it would be in the affirmative. I appreciate you being willing to follow your intuition." He acknowledged her sudden forewarning. His voice broke then strengthened. "I didn't know how I was going to continue to protect them. You need to get back. I do apologize for making you come to us."

She followed his lead matching her steps to his. "How badly are you injured, sir? We need to set a rendezvous site where I can have vehicles pick you up."

He shook his head slightly. "We know where your new estate is located. We'll get there on our own unless you have immediate need of our services." His eyes flicked to a shadowed place and with a slight pressure steered Tempest down a different path. "I should be fit and ready for duty by the time we arrive in ten days if that's satisfactory to you."

She palmed money from the pockets on her belt and slid it into Collier's jacket pocket. "An advance for you and your people." She patted his hand seeing his automatic rejection and rethreaded her arm through his, urging him forward. "Ten days is acceptable. We'll set up schedules once we have a chance to get to know each other." She whispered near his ear. "Rogan is close. We can help you if there's a problem."

"That's not necessary. Just a few young wolves testing the fitness of the head of the pack. The leader won't wait long to follow and try to intimidate a young woman." He gave her a winsome smile, released her arm and edged away. "He doesn't see you as an alpha bitch." He shook his head sadly and with resignation. "No, they are like fleas. Unless the medication is potent, they'll just hang on. I'd prefer not to use lethal force, but … go," he gave her a push. "Return quickly to your captain. If we're not there in ten days, forget about us."

Tempest grabbed his arm. "You are mine now. You will get to Summerfield." She stooped to catch his eyes hidden by a suddenly bent head. "You get in trouble, you call for help." She shook the arm she held. "Understand?"

Raising his head, he gave her a crooked smile. "Yes, ma'am. I hear you."

She squeezed his arm then turned and ran across the graves, apologizing to the occupants beneath her breath. She flew around a corner and slammed into a fleshy wall. She would have fallen if hot hands hadn't gripped her arms and pulled her against a hard chest.

The earthy smell of musk, sweat and the unique scent of a particular male body wrapped Tempest in a cocoon of want and need. Liquid flowed from inside her cramping channel dampening her panties. How did he do that, she wondered, before all reason fled.

Daire drew in a deep breath inhaling the aroma of feminine flesh: a slight tang of sweat over the scent of body lotion and beneath that the spicy addictive scent of this particular female. The silky coat she wore had fallen away from one shoulder exposing the tender slope of her neck. He sniffed delicately at the white skin then tasted it with the tip of his tongue. Her essence exploded in his mouth sending the craving for more shuddering through his body. He drew back, his eyes closed savoring the flavor.

The quaking in Daire's body infected Tempest with tiny tremors, which quickly intensified until she vibrated with hunger. His scent enveloped her on a wave of heat from his throat when her fingers flipped open the buttons at the top of his shirt. Her hands smoothed down his cloth-covered chest, her thumbs pulling back the edges of the shirt. Tanned flesh entreated a more detailed examination. She gripped the cloth more firmly and jerked it open.

Testosterone laden male bodies surged around them. She released the material, swallowed hard and reluctantly and with great difficulty took a step back from the six-foot temptation.

"Did you get what you needed?" Rogan's voice held a twinge of amusement at his inadvertent double entendre.

A laugh sputtering out, Tempest jammed her fingers through her hair. Pins from the curly mass popped against chests before falling to the ground. "We had an unexpected opportunity which I grabbed."

"Damn it, Tempest! This was just supposed to be a quick assessment!"

She huffed a deep breath. "I know, but I had to make a quick decision or we would have lost them ... and I couldn't let that happen. I ... I just couldn't." Her fists slammed onto her hips, her stance widened. Aggression poured off her. "And as I was just reminded, I'm the alpha bitch of this group so I get to make decisions."

"Alpha bitch?" The laugh snorted out before Rogan could contain it. A smile trimmed his lips.

Sebastian wasn't ready to back down. Rules were the cornerstone of an organization. "You have responsibilities to your people, Tempest. You should have talked with one of us and together we could have decided if the risk was worthwhile."

Rogan, Lorcan and Daire inched out of the line of fire.

"Get buried! Decisions by committee in a fluid situation aren't possible." She pushed against his chest then stalked around him when he didn't budge. Damned know-it-all males. They got on every single goddamn nerve and then demanded more to trample on. She stomped towards the Seven Sisters. "The call for fighters netted us an unexpected coup. Nathan Collier, the remainder of his teams, and some others he trusts will be heading for Summerfield. He has some rogues to get off his back, but he promised to call if he needs help."

She glared at the hand on her arm stopping her march to the mausoleum. The fingers opened and the arm drew back slowly.

"He didn't want help?" Rogan's voice was soft. Collier's contact was surprising, but Tempest had made the right call. And if he had been in Collier's situation, he wouldn't accept assistance either, which was a dumb choice from both of them.

Tempest rested against Rogan's side. "He's hurt, Ro, but he won't accept help or transport. I was only able to get him to promise to call if the situation becomes untenable." She was tired. Lethargy weighed her down and she still had to get through the Convocation.

Sebastian sighed watching the interplay between his

Reciprocate and the loyal warrior. He had fallen too easily into the role he had played as a FolKin Lair leader. This was a new world and he had a fresh start, unfettered by restrictions and expectations based on a millennia-old society. The deep breath he took deposited an overwhelming abundance of unknown scents inside his body stirring unfamiliar emotions. He started at the feminine hand absently patting his chest.

Rogan squeezed her shoulders. "We'll watch for contact and be ready to send immediate help. In the meantime," he nudged her forward, "we have a Convocation to attend."

# CHAPTER 25

Tempest's rage burned as hot and incandescent as the sun at its core. Sweat dripped from her red face. She planted her feet and rained blows against the dummy hanging from a grille work of beams below the vaulted ceiling of the spacious room. The black sport bra and cotton shorts she wore were soaked.

Weight machines, free weights, treadmills, and other strength and cardiovascular building equipment grouped in the adjoining space were idle. Several thick pads occupied the floor of the other half of the room. Men and women gathered around one padded area watching Lorcan and Davina Custer demonstrate the pros and cons of the martial arts disciplines each used against the other.

With a last punch, Tempest collapsed against the black bag, dragging ragged breaths in and out. Ignoring Rogan and Sebastian watching her from a water bar situated near a side door, she pulled open the Velcro band on the boxing glove covering one hand with her teeth, jerked it off, opened the band on the other hand and slammed both of them into the bin in the corner. She grabbed her towel off a bench, swiped her face and upper body, and tossed it into a laundry cart. They were certainly chummy after such a short time. She stood for a few moments studying Lorcan and Davina. A hot sweaty bout with both of them drew her like a bee to nectar, but she wasn't in control of her temper. She turned away, slid an oversized cotton T-shirt over her head, and snapped up her bag. She wrenched open the door at the main entrance and stalked down the hallway.

Men and women lounged on sofas and chairs in the reception area. Food and bottles of wine, beer and water overflowed low tables in front of the seats. Her shoulder blades itched with the weight of their gazes as she strode past, head down, her fingers rummaging through the pack. She dropped her sunglasses on her nose, tossed the backpack onto her back threading her arms through the straps, nodded to the guards behind the counter, walked to the exit and jerked open the door. Outside, she paused. The sun was bright, but the air was chilly matching the ice in her belly. Knowing the guards were watching her on the cameras tucked below the top of the counter, she began a slow trot down the hard-packed dirt path.

At the intersection, she stopped and bent over, her hands on her knees. With a glance through the curve of her arm toward the building, she saw one of the guards from the counter and several of the people from the lounge huddled at the door talking. The guard turned his head to respond to a hand on his arm. Quick as a striking cobra, she darted sideways and out of their line of sight. A few seconds later and she was on the trail to the obstacle course. At the first stretching station, she dropped the bag in a secure bin and eyed the bottled water cabinet. A memory intruded sending her hurtling through the first barrier.

✱✱✱✱✱

"I understand one of the beneficiaries is not able to be here … Mr. Mikuh Braeden." Preston Granville, of Granville, Stoner & Regis, the leading law firm in the world, raised a hand. "Please, Mr. Treadaway, until he is convicted of Ryniah Duvayne's murder, Mr. Braeden is still a beneficiary under the terms of this Will."

"I have his power of attorney, Mr. Granville, in the event he happened to be mentioned. It's dated over a year ago." Tempest handed a folded paper to the attorney.

"I dispute this child's right to represent a murderer in

these proceedings." Treadaway's temper simmered beneath his glacial control.

"That is sufficient, Ms. Phillips. If you please, Mr. Treadaway," a long sigh escaped Granville's frowning mouth, "don't interrupt the proceedings again. I've allowed your presence because you're a member of the Ruling Council, but I will have you removed if you persist. Now, shut up!" Sending a stern look over the top of his reading glasses at the people congregated beneath the canvas tent, he continued, "Everything will go much faster if all questions and comments are held until after the reading."

$$*****$$

Tempest tripped over a log across the trail sending her sprawling. She fought the urge to bang the ground with her fists and feet in a temper tantrum. Regression to childhood wasn't an option. She planted her hands in the dirt, counted twenty-five pushups, and jumped up. Pulling her T-shirt up, she swabbed her face then reached for the water bottle at her waist. She hissed through her teeth. No bottle. She had allowed the memory to distract her.

With hands on hips, she stared down the trail debating a return to the clearing, shook her head, flinging beads of sweat, and jogged forward. There was another station a couple of miles ahead.

Strider sat motionless beneath the trees. He watched Tempest work her way through the line of tires on the ground. She was so absorbed she didn't see him in the flickering shade from the wind-tossed limbs above him. He waited until she was back on the path then stood and picked up his pack from the ground. His fingers searched in the side pocket, pulled the dotmitter free and slid it into place.

"Rogan, it's Strider." He stretched his arms over his head, fingers interlocked, twisted left then right, and released. He bent over touching his toes stretching his back and legs. He bounced in place a few times then walked to the water station.

Rogan raised a finger halting the conversation with Bloodhawk and Lorcan. "Go, Strider." At his acknowledgment, the men with him engaged their receptors.

"Do you know where Tempest is?"

Rogan's eyes narrowed. "She had a long bout with Charley." His mouth pulled into a brief smile at the name Tempest had bestowed on the boxing dummy. "The security post said she left the building and headed toward the house."

"I'm out on the training course at the first station." He guzzled half the bottle of water he chose from the locker replenished at regular intervals during the day, poured the remainder over his head, and pitched the empty container in the recycle bin. He shoved two fresh bottles into the slots on the pack he strapped around his waist.

Rogan aimed a puzzled look at the group across the room. "Thanks for reporting in. What does this have to do with Tempest?"

"She just passed me headed toward the expert course." Strider bypassed the tires and trotted down the trail.

The words buzzed through Rogan's head. He wadded the towel in his hands and heaved it against the wall. She was angry and hurting but it was no excuse for abandoning common sense. A long weary sigh escaped his mouth.

"Yeah," Strider huffed, "I'm right there with you. I'm tracking her. I don't want to assume she's on the course and miss her. FUCK!" He skidded to a halt and backtracked. Tempest's footprints veered into the trees. "She's off track. Repeat. Tempest is off course." He checked the compass on his watch. "Has the north sector been cleared?"

Rogan strode towards the door, Lorcan and Bloodhawk trailing in his wake. "No, it has not been cleared. Our Trackers have reported seeing prints of ghost cats in that area. I'm calling in a Cote. Get her in sight. How are you armed?"

"I'd like my Dectonics and a pulse carbine. I'm only

carrying a couple of knives." He dodged a low hanging tree branch. "Do we really want to push up on her en masse right now? She is entitled to some privacy." He agreed with Rogan's decision, but felt the need to protect Tempest in some way.

"Yes, she deserves privacy, but that area is one of the wildest and it hasn't been completely mapped. Aerial views show ancient man-made trails – some connecting with back roads off the main highway which is wide enough for Rough Roadsters. We can't get drones in for a better look because of the density of the trees." He switched to an open frequency. "Coteries Five and Six go to alert status."

A covey of birds darted into the western sky. Strider stopped and dropped to one knee. Silence descended. "You're right." He lowered his voice to a whisper. "There's activity west of my position. I'm off air." He shut down his dotmitter, rose and faded into the trees.

Heat seeped into Tempest's body from the rock beneath her. Puffy white grey clouds dotted the bright turquoise sky stimulating the imagination into seeing animals and objects. Fragments of the confrontation at the family crypt swirled in.

*****

"Gloriana Duvayne cedes her Coven title and forty-acre Duvayne Estate, including all possessions currently within it, located outside New York proper, to Robert Phillips, his wife, and children, excluding Tempest Duvayne Phillips, to do with as they wish. A separate bank account exists under the Duvayne Estate name to cover the costs and expenses of maintaining the property as well as care of the inhabitants, including all personnel hired for security, housekeeping and landscaping and other incidentals. All other cash, bank accounts, jewelry, and real estate owned by Gloriana Duvayne are bequeathed to her granddaughter, Tempest Duvayne Phillips, as her sole and separate property."

Granville cleared his throat. "Ryniah Duvayne provided

instructions to this law firm to say the following. She paid for all of the assets gifted to Tempest from sources originating outside the purview of the Covens and its Ruling Council. If any member of the Covens and Ruling Council, or any member of the Phillips' family, contests her Will, we are instructed to immediately give each such person ten dollars in full and complete settlement of any claims.

"The language regarding this qualification was written and approved by Supreme Court Justice Nigel Demeter." He nodded to his partner, John Stoner, who handed a piece of paper to everyone except the men surrounding Tempest. "This document is signed by all the Supreme Court Justices affirming that no lawsuit will be accepted seeking to overturn Ryniah Duvayne's Will."

$$*****$$

Tempest blinked, eyeing the pale raven overhead chasing small cloud creatures. Another fragment appeared.

$$*****$$

Robert Phillips drew in a deep breath but otherwise stood in silence staring straight ahead. Anna Phillips placed a hand on her husband's arm and squeezed. Her calm, serene mask dissolving briefly, allowing triumph to spill into her eyes. Tension flowed from her body. Finally. Her husband was finally receiving the status he deserved. He would be an excellent CEO and provide a more reasonable voice on the Ruling Council. She looked at Treadaway and his cohorts from the corner of her eyes. Their machinations would no longer involve her family. At last, they had protection.

Treadaway swallowed his fury. That bitch! Her son may think he and his family was safe, cloaked behind a CEO's status, but Phillips was in a new arena now ... one Phillips didn't have the experience to navigate. Nothing would change for Phillips and his family. Phillips would quickly learn his true position, but first the daughter.

Treadaway stalked towards the attorney stopping a few feet away. His ire swelled when Nigel Granville stood his ground with ease. "I believe Challenge is outside the scope of Glory Duvayne's instructions and the legal system." He spat his words into Granville's face. Duvayne hadn't deserved the Ryniah title. "I Challenge Tempest Phillips." He turned to inspect the girl. When he won, all her holdings would cede to him and she would become his possession ... if she survived. He didn't care one way or another. He would rise within the hierarchy of the Ruling Council to stand second to Grande Marshall Delia Peloquin and be in position years early to take over the Council when she retired early ... with a little help.

Granville's heart stuttered. He had to negotiate the minefield before him with extra care. "Challenge is an old practice and hasn't been called in hundreds of years. It's unnecessary. The Ryniah's wishes are clearly and simply written."

Treadaway pivoted to Grande Marshall Peloquin. "Grande Marshall, Challenge was issued. What say you?"

Delia Peloquin drew her cloak around her shoulders. She sensed Zook Fessler stepping forward to stand directly behind her, close enough to absorb the shudders of fear arching through her. Treadaway would come for her after he decimated the Phillips girl and her family. Zook and his men were Tacticals. It would require an enormous expenditure of money and bodies to overwhelm them in a direct assault. It was more likely an assassin would come for her and Treadaway could assume a mask of innocence, but Zook would still be in the line of fire. Her soul screamed at the thought of losing him, her lover and mate, who took his job as bodyguard seriously. There had to be a way to curb Treadaway and his cronies for the protection of the Phillips family, the Prime Covens, and her own people.

She cleared her throat. "Challenge is offered. What is your response?"

The roil of emotions in the tent made Tempest sick to

her stomach. Epiphanies often occurred at the most inopportune times. Watching her mother and father, a torrent of incidents rolled through her mind's eye. Where they had seemed to submissively follow Treadaway's commands, she could now see how they had tried to protect her in the only way left to them. Her father stepping in to enforce punishments decreed by the Council to mitigate the results as best he could. The sacrifice of one to save all the other members of the family must have been a difficult choice to make. Her new perspective allowed for healing and forgiveness ... in time. And maybe, in the far distant future, trust could develop again.

Finding herself the cynosure of all eyes, she inhaled deeply, grateful for Rogan's solid wall of confidence and Sebastian's steel will seeping through her shields. "I accept Challenge."

Treadaway laughed wildly. Victory was in his hands. "The disposition of Glory Duvayne's estate ceases until Challenge is resolved, and, as a Council member, I claim the right to a Champion." He needed time to search the Duvayne Estate. He knew the old bat had secret projects in progress and confidential records on many corporate and world leaders. He needed those files.

"No!" Robert Phillips stepped between Treadaway and Tempest. "This has gone far enough. You played the game and lost." He strode forward until he was in Treadaway's face. "Rescind the Challenge! You've gotten enough blood from my daughter and this family. It ends here. It ends now."

"Fool!" Treadaway spat. "The young bitch will follow her granddam's path. Challenge is to the death."

"Enough!" Grande Marshall Peloquin stepped between the men and pushed them apart. She stumbled slightly as Zook gripped her arm and yanked her away, holding her with her back against his chest. "Ryniah Duvayne's estate will be distributed now in accordance with the instructions in her Will. No! You will be quiet, Councilman Treadaway. You have taken many liberties during this meeting and I agree with new CEO Phillips: it ends now." In the blink of an eye, she inhaled the energy overflowing the space, molded it then attached it to the auras of Treadaway and his cohorts.

"What are you doing? No! Damn you, witch!" Treadaway fought to turn the spell away but he was too late. "What have you done?"

"Until Challenge is ended, any magic you perform will also affect each of you." Zook inched closer, the heat of his body calming the minute shivers coursing over her skin. He always provided whatever she needed before she even knew what it was. She turned her head. "I'm sorry, Ms. Phillips. There's nothing more I can do for now."

✳✳✳✳✳

Tempest kicked out at the hand around her ankle drawing her along the face of the stone.

"Stop it, Tempest! Get down here. We're in trouble."

She stopped struggling and slid over the edge dropping to crouch beside Strider. Her eyes followed his pointed finger to the birds swirling above the treetops in the distance. She nodded her understanding.

He bent his head placing his mouth against her ear. "Rogan and two Coteries are on the way."

Together, they headed to the southern tree line, stopping just inside the demarcation between sun and shadow. Strider pressed her against the bark of a lofty oak, protecting her back. She held her breath. A doe and two fawns bounded out of the forest and raced toward them. Sensing their presence, the threesome veered to the east.

A figure in green and tan camouflage fatigues stepped from between the trees and stopped in the shade of the towering rock formation at the edge of the meadow. He squatted, unmoving except for his head slowly turning side to side.

Minutes passed.

Birds sang. Insects buzzed.

Silence descended again. More men entered the sunshine.

Tempest tilted her head back gradually until she was looking into Strider's face. His body was like metal against hers. His blue eyes filled with cold-tempered rage. She returned her gaze to the figures continuing to erupt from the woods. Two men stopped several hundred feet from the main unit. She zeroed in on a man holding a paper between his hands. Her eyes followed his head as he looked up and turned toward three more men emerging from between the tree trunks.

She gripped Strider's arm, her fingernails digging into his skin. The man's styled blonde hair glowed in the sunshine. His shadows, one step back and on each side, loomed over his slender frame. William Busch. Commander William Busch, leader of the World Enclave's military contingent: the notorious butcher and rapist of innocent women, villages, and countries – the killer of babies and children. A growl rumbled in her throat. He was responsible for the massacre of Rogan's military team and Rogan's torture. She strained against the rigid cage of Strider's arms and body.

"No, Tempest. Quiet! We need to back out of here. We have to get to Rogan and the others. We can't face them alone." He slid his hands down her arms and clasped her wrist drawing her away.

They backed from the meadow: one step; stop. Another small step … halt. Out of sight, they sped up making sure each foot landed without noise. Urgency spilled around them. Three hundred yards from Tempest's perch, they turned to run.

A five-man squad rose out of the brush, their weapons up and ready. Strider pushed Tempest toward a rock wall cutting off their retreat.

"Stop! Put your hands behind your heads and lock your fingers together." The leader gestured with the barrel of his pulse carbine.

With the stone protecting their backs, Tempest hissed

at Strider taking a position ahead and partially in front of her. She lassoed her frustration. His automatic gesture of protection wasn't a mark against her skills as a fighter. Capturing her would tie his hands more effectively than any physical binding. "You're trespassing on private property. I'm Tempest Phillips, the owner."

The stranger ignored her, speaking briefly into his dotmitter. He added more force to his words. "Put your hands behind your heads and lock your fingers together ... now!" He motioned one of the men forward.

Tempest's eyes locked on the molded fiber restraints dangling from the man's fingers. A flashback gripped her. The altar was rough and hard against her back. Her arms and legs ached from her struggles with the ropes holding her down. Shudders rippled the muscles along her spine as unconscionable men surrounded her. She shook her head back and forth in refusal. Her stance loosened. A growl rumbled from her chest and out between clenched teeth.

Strider glanced at Tempest from the edge of his eye. He moved directly in front of her. A tingle shot down his spine. Which was the more dangerous opponent: the men he was facing or the woman at his unprotected back? "Back off. You're trespassing."

"You're surrounded. I'm not going to say this again. Put your hands up. Do it now!" The leader turned cold eyes on the man holding the bindings. "Cuff them."

Strider heard pebbles rolling behind him, the feminine growling rumbled inside him like a ball slamming against metal rods in an arcade game. The situation was out of control and the assholes he was watching didn't even know it. "You don't know what you're doing!" Fear for Tempest coated his words.

Feral-spark rose like a leviathan from the depths of the sea. For a split second, Tempest calculated the opposing threats ... Busch's men or the Feral-spark ... and chose. Tempest-spark twisted around and leaped to the top of the boulder. She crouched, fists against the sun-baked granite. Her head fell back: a guttural roar tore from her throat echoing throughout the forest.

Alarm jolted through Sebastian. "Lady and Consort, no!" He sprinted towards the sound reverberating through the valley. Rogan and the Coteries raced after him.

# CHAPTER 26

Lips drawn back in a snarl, Tempest-spark crouched on the hot stone. Fury battled fear and lingering helplessness, a deadly brew for the males below. She inhaled deeply, drawing in the pallid scents the body's olfactory senses allowed. The heat from one male roused unfamiliar sensations. Not mate, but the need to protect. A breeze brought the stink of many bodies from two directions: one close, the other farther away.

Low growls were a constant rumble in her chest and throat. She rocked back and forth. She wanted to leave, had to be free. The green foliage enveloping the meadow promised shelter, food and water. Healthy prey scampered away from the invading unit. A slender thread bound her to the solitary figure below her perch.

Men stepped past the ragged border and marched across the grass and rock-covered expanse halting in front of the captives.

"Well, well, well ... Condren. What a pleasant surprise. It's been a while since we last met." William Busch stood ahead of his men, feet apart, shoulders back, his mocking smile a fitting accessory to hard, granite grey eyes. An imperceptible flinching at the corners of his eyes was his only concession to the feral roar ricocheting in the air. "Get your pet down and control it, Condren, before I have my men shoot it."

Tempest-spark took two leaps forward and flipped into the air landing in a squat in front of Strider. She rose in slow motion, grunts of pleasure flowing from her mouth as most of the men stepped backwards.

"Hold your ground, you spineless fools! It's only one man and some mindless beast." His muscles tensed as the unflinching stare of the creature locked on him. For a few seconds, he had the impression it comprehended what he said, but he quickly dismissed the thought. Impossible. "Contain it! We'll take it back with us. Dr. Neuterman will enjoy having a new research subject."

"Sir!" Bindings clutched in his hand, the soldier checked the movements of his compatriots and sidled forward. He froze, terror shooting like light strobes into his guts.

The panther was a monster of its kind standing at least five feet at its shoulders. Its face wrinkled in a snarl; the eyeteeth more reminiscent of a saber-tooth tiger of prehistoric times. It loomed against the sky on the promontory. Two smaller pumas settled into reclining positions on either side of him like Egyptian sculptures. The tan-colored hides of the cats blended with the dirt-covered rock.

Tempest-spark paced five steps left then whipped back five steps right, her eyes never breaking contact with the fighters. On each pass, she edged Strider backwards until he pressed against the stone wall.

"Kill the beasts and secure the prisoners!" Busch shouted his orders.

"Not a wise decision, Busch." Rogan eased into the situation, the Coteries moving smoothly around him, weapons raised and ready. "Have your people lower their weapons … slowly. Keep your fingers off the triggers."

"Branaugh." Busch laughed, turning to face the new arrivals. Several soldiers moved into place protecting his back. "Delightful! I was wondering when you would appear. What have you created for the Phillips bitch?" He flipped his hand at Tempest-spark.

Rogan focused on Busch. A part of his mind unconsciously

evaluated the Commander's and his men's body movements, watching for the decision to engage. His voice lowered an octave, soft, but the command cut through the air like the prow of a ship through the leading edge of an ice flow. "I'd prefer weapons on the ground, but the movement and sound may set off what I want to stop. Get your weapons pointed at the ground ... now."

The soldiers exchanged glances, the weapons in their hands spontaneously lowering. Busch's personal guards at his back remained alert, concentrating only on Tempest and the cougars on the rock.

Seeing the movement, Busch barked, "No! You answer to me. Raise your weapons and fire on the beasts." He began to turn, his carbine lifting. And stopped. Fear made him furious and the knife pressing against his throat was more than a warning. Determination poured out of the man holding the steel ... resolve and a guarantee of action. Where had he come from? Busch's breath sissed through his teeth slowly. "I don't know who you are, but you will regret your actions." The answering grin incensed him and his fingers tightened on his weapon. His neck muscles tensed. A sharp pain and the trickle of blood down his neck loosened his grip on the carbine. He gritted his teeth as he flipped his hand ordering the stand down.

Rogan craved allowing the confrontation to continue to a bloody conclusion. He sank into the free space where the decision to act was made and emotions suppressed. Like a movie on a viewer, his mind played out the skirmish. The sane part of him rose to the surface. An infinitesimal shudder along his spine settled him. He reached out and pulled the Folkin Elder away from his quarry, backing far enough to talk privately, and waving the Coteries forward.

"What's happening, Bloodhawk? I thought the spark was gone."

Sebastian held the naked blade along the side of his leg as he studied Tempest crouching on one knee, her fingers digging into the dirt. A snarl deformed her features making her face almost unrecognizable. "She's hiding inside the Feral-spark. This shouldn't be happening, Branaugh. With the bonding, the Feral-spark should be gone, and Tempest is resisting my efforts to pull her out of the link. Why is she refusing to cut loose?"

A click in Rogan's ear signaled an incoming message. He raised a finger then tapped the dotmitter. "Contact acknowledged. Go."

A calm, feminine voice spilled from the earpiece. "Company approaching from the east."

Tempest-spark sniffed the air. The reek of bodies in her meadow was overwhelming, coating the air with a myriad of scents. A tentative breeze ghosted across her nose bringing the odor of more men ... and females! Invaders ... Challengers! She shot to her feet and coughed her defiance, the shriek filling the valley.

"Can you identify?" Rogan wanted to follow Tempest's example and bellow his frustration. More people were only going to add to the volatility of the situation.

"Daire D'eath."

"Stop him!" Rogan's jaw ached from clenching his teeth.

"Too late."

Daire stopped at the edge of the tree line, his people spreading out behind him. The ghost cats snared his attention. Wonder and awe filled him. Cougars were an endangered species and protected under the laws of the World Enclave. They were solitary creatures and were more likely to steal away than confront. Three at once was unheard of. And a male, much larger than normal, in full view and confronting the intruders was astounding.

"What do you want to do?" Declan moved into place at Daire's shoulder.

The additional people were too much for the male cougar. With a booming scream, he jumped to the ground and butted Tempest-spark with his shoulder. He yowled and rammed her again when she turned on him with a snarl. He jerked away from her swiping arm but held his ground, low rumbles flowing continuously from his chest.

Daire and his fighters entered the meadow. Spooked, Tempest-spark made a last swing at the protective cat, turned and ran. The feline swung his head to stare at Strider plastered against the granite. With a last defiant screech, he bounded in Tempest-spark's wake, the two smaller female panthers behind him.

For a few moments, everyone froze in place. Strider pushed away from the rock, his movement breaking the tableau.

Rogan felt pulled in different directions. He needed to follow Tempest and get her back, but first he had to get rid of the intruders. "Why are you on our lands, Busch?"

Knowledge and authority gave control and Busch had both. He relaxed. "Braeden and his men have been classified as terrorists and the hunt for them now falls under my purview. Given his close connection to Phillips, I have the World Enclave's authorization to search anywhere I deem appropriate. When the Director of the Planetary Guidance Institute found out I would be in this area, he asked me to check out an anomaly the PGI detected near here." He smiled, pleasure and anticipation rolling off him in waves. He so enjoyed his job. "I'm arresting all of you and confiscating Phillips' lands and assets because of your experiments on humans."

"Get off these lands, Busch. Check with your boss. Earlier this morning, the authorities cleared Braeden and his men of all charges. The forensics lab proved the recordings on the DVDs are fabrications and DNA and other trace evidence from the scene dispute the stories of the witnesses. As I understand it, the so-called witnesses are being looked at closely for perjury and possible other charges." Rogan's teeth flashed in a grin, shining like the polished grillwork on a car.

Busch's eyes narrowed. "Check it!" he barked at his second-in-command. He stood with legs apart, his hands clasped behind his back studying his nemesis. "There're still the issues of human experimentation and the anomaly." He was on shaky ground. The hunt for Braeden and his men was an indisputable objective. His real commanders, the Tribunal, had seized the opportunity and given orders for listening posts to be set up on Phillips' lands.

"The SAT Act doesn't cover 'anomalies.' And you can search private property only with owner permission ... and neither Tempest nor I gave our consent to anyone. As for human experimentation," Rogan shrugged a shoulder, "we deny the charges. You have to have proof of illegal testing. Whatever you and your men may think you saw is an anomaly." He tasted the word in his mouth. His body buzzed with pleasure and he allowed his satisfaction to show on his face. Turning Busch's word against him was gratifying.

Rogan turned his back on the Commander and his soldiers. "Escort these people to the nearest main highway."

Busch vibrated with anger. His finger tightened on the trigger of his carbine. He yanked away from the calming hand and whispered voice of his second confirming the dropping of charges against Braeden. "Next time, Branaugh."

Busch strode away ignoring the Coteries, leaving it to his second to gather the soldiers. The Tribunal had gambled and lost. He wouldn't have any black marks against him for not being able to accomplish their directive, but it was galling to yield ground to an adversary, particularly Rogan Branaugh.

# CHAPTER 27

Strider squatted to study the tracks in the grass. Finding Tempest's prints, he stood and walked to his partner, Samuel Freeth, standing at the edge of the circle of fighters surrounding Rogan and Bloodhawk. He took his shoulder holster from Samuel and slipped it on, strapping it down then exchanged the pack at his waist for the backpack dangling from Samuel's fingers. With Samuel at his side, he paced to the edge of the rock.

Rogan bent sideways, looking past Daire D'eath. "Where are you going, Strider?"

Strider paused at Samuel's tug on his arm and flung a look over his shoulder. Turning back to the trail, he submitted, "I'm going after Tempest."

Rogan stepped away from the knot of warriors, moving closer to Strider. "We need to know what happened to Tempest, Strider, before we go after her."

Strider hesitated, scuffing a foot in the dirt. He opened his mouth and closed it, shook his head. "She was sunning on the rocks over there." Samuel ducked away from Strider's arm. "I pulled her off. Told her we had to go. We got here and ran into a trap. They gave us the usual crap instructions. That's it. Nothing unusual happened." He scrubbed his hands through his hair leaving dust in the strands.

"There had to be something." Sebastian halted a few feet away.

Strider closed his eyes and ran the sequence of events through his mind. "She was sunning on the rock. I pulled her down. We ran and were stopped by Busch's men." He opened his eyes and glared around. "We raised our hands. One of Busch's men started towards us with those molded fiber restraints in his hand and it all went to shit after that. That's it. Nothing else happened."

"Fuck!" Rogan spun away from the small huddle and kicked a stone conveniently in his sight, spewing out several more curses in different languages. He noted the confused looks when he turned back. It wasn't his story to share, but he felt he had to offer a short response. "I only know the bare bones of what happened. It was a long time ago. The Duvayne and Braeden were participants in the action, but Braeden's never filled in the back story. All I know is Tempest has major issues with being tied up and surrounded by a group of men." He frowned at the ground. "I have no idea how to help her."

Daire was confused. His groin had surrendered without protest, hardening at the unknown female's lithe, graceful movements. The lack of control was embarrassing and baffling. A quickly scanned report from his security team filtered into the forefront of his mind. "That was Tempest?" He bared his teeth at the snarls from Tempest's men.

"Will she become herself once she calms down?" Strider directed his comment to Bloodhawk.

"I don't know." He resettled his cloak on his shoulders like a bird settling its feathers and stared at the granite wall, ignoring the questions in the others' eyes. "In all my Turns, I've never heard of this happening after a bonding." He repeated his previous remarks. "She's hiding inside the feral-spark and I can't force a separation." Frustration and fear shone in his eyes.

"If we follow and contain her, will it make the situation worse?" Daire wanted to know. His gut roiled. The people who should know how to help Tempest didn't have a clue. It was irrational, but he wanted to pound on someone until he got a solution. "What about the panthers? They're solitary creatures. They don't run in groups and they don't protect people."

Strider ran out of patience. "You stay here and work out a plan. I'm tracking." He stuffed the dotmitter into his ear. "I'll call when I find her."

Rogan laid a restraining hand on Strider's arm. "A small group will go." He pointed to Sebastian, Samuel, Strider and himself. "The rest of you search the area and make sure Busch didn't leave any strays. Each of you check the ground, trees and rocks for any devices that might have been left behind. D'eath, you're welcome to come with us, but your people either stay here or return to your place."

Daire nodded and stepped away to talk with Declan. Their voices were low, but Declan's tone was firm and uncompromising. At Daire's quick dip of his head, Declan pointed to two men. He slapped Daire's shoulder and with a sweep of his hand aimed the remainder of the teams at the tree line.

Daire rejoined the small group. "Declan doesn't want me off by myself without personal guards. He and the rest will stay here. If things go wrong, they can get to us quicker from here than at Jericho."

Rogan nodded. "I understand his concern. Tulsa, Lorcan, you coordinate with the teams remaining behind. With D'eath's guards, we'll still be small enough not to push too hard at Tempest."

Strider was several hundred yards away and moving quickly, stopping periodically to pick over the ground before rising and gliding forward.

"How are we going to handle the ghost cats?" Samuel kept one eye on Strider as he fell into place beside Rogan.

"If they were somehow linked to Tempest, hopefully the connection will have dissolved when she left," Sebastian offered.

"And if the link is still in place?" Tulsa settled his carbine beneath his arm and across his forearm.

"I don't know," Sebastian snapped. He was tired of saying those three words.

Sensing the FolKin had reached the end of his control,

Rogan interrupted. "Fire in front of them to scare them off. As a last resort, if they attack, shoot to kill." He shook his head. "I understand they are a protected species, but it can't be helped. I'll deal with the authorities and Tempest's remorse later if it's necessary."

# CHAPTER 28

Feral-spark lolled on the thick limb of the tree peering through the leaves. She had eased onto the branch slowly, holding motionless for minutes at a time when the perimeter guards looked in her direction. The clothes on her body irritated her, the colors inhibiting her ability to blend with the environment. Her lips pulled back in a smirk watching the men following her trail. Wait. Wait.

The group disappeared around the rock. She lowered her gaze to the fighters in the shade of the trees. One male was dividing them into small teams. A lone female strolled toward her hiding place. The woman's audacity provoked Feral-spark and she rolled off the wood ditching her plan to wait.

Tempest-spark froze her hand at the upswing for the few critical seconds the woman needed to see her. Fabric tore and scratches with beads of blood appeared across the woman's abdomen rather than the disemboweling gouges Feral-spark had intended. The woman yelled, swinging her weapon in an upward motion to deflect the second strike.

A grin spread across Feral-spark's face. Her blood churned with excitement. Saliva flooded her mouth at the coppery smell of fresh blood. Her body froze. A scream of frustration tore from her throat. Not now ... in the middle of battle.

Tempest-spark struggled against the walls restraining her core personality. Fighters were running in their direction. In the distance, Rogan and his small band were racing toward her. She couldn't allow the Feral-spark to do any more damage. Neon red bolts pierced the column surrounding her. She convulsed. Blackness.

With a triumphant yowl, Feral-spark used her doppelganger's memories and offered to the oncoming figures. "Let's play!" She jumped, grabbed the branch above her and swung into the concealing foliage.

Tempest-spark jolted awake to an inferno of pain like fire ants skittering through every muscle, tendon and vein. The outer reality wavered like a mirage in the desert. Relief coated her like syrup on pancakes. Great. Just great. Just what she needed: another personality in her mind even if it seemed friendly.

"Fight it, Life-Giver!" Kalia swayed, her equilibrium shifting before she was able to shield against the distant feral-spark trying to seize energy from her. She turned away from the viewport, ignoring the quick looks from Kenton and Ram. Ships winked at the edges of the screen, floating in formation in front of the Lightgate. Additional ships were checking in with ComTech Chicopee Bloodmoon as they transitioned from the second Lightgate.

It had been her decision to transfer through the gates in five waves with the Colonizers shifting last. The arrival of the four gigantic ships housing their hopes and dreams – the last remaining members of Blood Lair – briefly ignited the unstable tides of energy which formed around Lightgates creating a gestalt effect. She had felt the impact of bolts thrown by a Feral-spark and backtracked the pathway to Sebastian's possible Reciprocate.

She shook her head at Kenton and Ram staring intently at her from different sections of the bridge. She turned her back on them and ambled to the rear consoles. These were female issues; male intervention would only exacerbate the problem. "Don't fall for its tricks. The image in your mind is a ruse. It has embedded hooks in your soul. Fight it. You must dominate it."

Kalia gritted her teeth. She sympathized with the Bloodhawk female ... so many challenges to meet; so many decisions to accept responsibility for – good, bad and mediocre. She wanted to reach out and help the woman, but whoever inherited a feral-spark had to find the balance between their dominant and submissive character traits. The feral-spark would win if the woman remained submissive. A dominant feral-spark only had three goals: death, destruction and procreation. And the only resolution was hunting down and killing the rogue body.

There had to be something more she could do. Until she was sure the female wasn't the Patriarch's Reciprocate, she had to keep her alive. She glanced over her shoulder at Kenton and Ram leaning against the consoles, arms and legs crossed watching her. They sheltered her in weak moments. She wondered if the distant woman had someone who provided the same care. Kenton and Ram's emotions sped through her. Passion suffused her, rampant flashes of hot, hot lust moistened her, readying her. She hadn't felt their members breaching her vagina and ass for many long weeks. She faced the wall, staring into the mirror finish of the metal.

Heat warmed her back. Her nipples stood erect in anticipation of the hand sliding surreptitiously along her side and up to cup the fullness of her breast, fingers lightly squeezing the buds at the apex. Ram's large body surrounded her concealing his actions.

"What are you thinking about, Kee?" His voice whispered next to her ear, the tip of his tongue skimmed her neck. "Kenton and I were just discussing how soon we could take a break together … all three of us. You've been away from us too long."

She gave in to her desire, pushing back against his hardness, her feminine lubricant overflowing into her panties. With a hiss, she elbowed him in his side and twisted away slamming into Kenton. How had he managed to sneak up on her? "Give me some room." She pushed the words out of gritted teeth, thrusting an elbow in Kenton's side for good measure. They could be complete zabuks.

Rubbing his ribs, Kenton drawled in her ear. "No one can

see what we're doing." He shrugged. "They know to keep their eyes on what they're doing." He slid a hand between her legs and his tongue teased the sweet spot at the curve of her neck. "We have a quarteTurn while the area stabilizes for another shift," he cajoled.

"Keep your body parts to yourselves." Her legs quivered and lower abdomen ached as fingers tantalized her nub. Her breathing doubled, her mind supplying details of one of their lovemaking sessions. She stifled a deep groan. Ram's hand smoothed over her butt heading for the crack between her cheeks. She knew better. Commands stimulated their alpha centers.

Love and the need for sex powered Tempest-spark. She tapped the link and reached for the sunspot she sensed erupting from the sun. She ate the energy speeding towards earth.

Kenton and Ram jerked to either side of Kalia. With arms spread wide and palms facing, they raised a shield, containing the phantom flames enveloping Kalia's body. They inched forward. Skin met skin, their fingers notched together. Ram pressed against Kalia's back and Kenton her front. Lines etched their faces. Together, they pulled the energy away from Kee and funneled it into storage cubes at the ship's core. They braced Kalia between them as her muscles loosened and she went limp. Kenton brushed the damp hair from Kee's face. His fingers slid downward to check her pulse, his heart thudding triple-time in his chest. What seemed like many Turns had only been sectims.

"Crap! Sorry!" Tempest-spark flung the apology into the bond, poured mint coolness down the line, then sliced the cord. Her bloated HyperRealm body pulsed. Well ... it was time to get it done. Taking several deep breaths, she slammed against the wall, blasting her will in all directions.

Tempest fell from the tree, unconscious, her limp body rolling several feet. Tempest-spark backhanded Feral-spark in HyperRealm. Feral-spark spun, crouched and leaped.

Now or never, Tempest-spark thought. She sent all the accumulated power to her right hand and shoved it into Feral-spark's chest, grabbed its heart and yanked. Rage flashed across its face, the figure glowed then dissolved into rainbow colored specks. With her left hand, Tempest-spark directed the fragments into the earth with a prayer.

She contemplated the pulsing heart. Grant mercy and integrate it with her own spirit? How would she change? Would it be a good choice or a bad one? She shook her head. Twice it overwhelmed her in a dangerous situation. It couldn't be trusted. Cupping her hands around the red shape, she formed a tie with the sun. A second prayer and she sent the Feral-spark into the volatile vortex of a developing sunspot. It was a fitting playground for the Feral-spark's untamable spirit.

Tempest opened her eyes, worried faces blocking her view of the sky. "Hi." She tried to smile but every muscle in her body throbbed. "I'm going to lay here for a while if you don't mind." Details of the outer reality seeped into her mind. A long, guttural groan escaped her lips as she tried to push up. She managed a few inches before crumpling backwards. "Where's Strider? Where's Busch?" Her voice was close to a scream.

Strider pushed through the people surrounding Tempest, falling to one knee at her side. "I'm fine, Tempe. Busch is gone. How are you?"

Tempest managed a weak grin. "We showed that bastard a thing or two, didn't we?" She clasped his forearm and let him pull her upright. "I gave the Feral-spark a new playground ... a place that's more in keeping with its character. It's definitely gone for good."

Seeing Sebastian in the circle, she tilted her head. "Who's Kalia?"

Rogan blinked but focused on the immediate threat. "Are you sure it's gone?"

# CHAPTER 29

Tempest braced both hands against the shower wall and dropped her head to her chest. The almost-too-hot water blasted her neck and back, loosening tight muscles and relieving aches and pains – at least for a short time. She sent a silent "thanks" to Poppa Gammons and his sons for early completion of the water system Keegan and Bearin designed, utilizing massive buried reservoirs fed by underground hot springs and filtered recycled water from their homes. Hot water tanks were unnecessary and extra-long showers were a blessing.

She pushed away and sank to the floor of the stall. Steam rose, forming a wafting cloud at the ceiling. Her head thunked back against the wall. Just a few more minutes. She could pull herself together and go out to the impromptu food fest with Daire and his people. They had to pool their information about Busch and jointly decide how to handle his intrusion. And she still needed an answer from Sebastian.

Her eyes drooped and closed. She slid sideways. "Ow!" Her eyes shot open, lashes blinking like a hummingbird's wings. She staggered upright, rubbing the side of her head where it had connected with the tiled floor. Quick twists of knobs cut the flow of water. With a towel wrapped around her body and another blinding her as she dried her hair, she walked out of the bathroom and bounced backwards. Hands grabbed her arms, halting her fall.

"Damn it!" She pulled the cloth off her head and looked

up into concerned grey eyes. Words, language, knowledge vanished from her mind. Flames of heat erupted on her skin beneath the supportive hands.

"Are you okay? Rogan let me use the shower in his room and I was just going outside when I heard your yell." Daire willed his fingers to release his grip, but they refused to obey. Hazel eyes turned a rich apple green inviting him closer. Honey mingled with her natural scent, an exotic feast drawing his nose to the bend of her neck. The tip of his tongue tasted the sweet spot before moving up. His lips caught the lobe of her ear and he suckled it lightly adding a hint of teeth when she moaned.

Tempest dropped the towel she was using to dry her hair. Her fingers opened, the towel wrapped around her body loosened and the cloth slid down her body, the nubby material scraping along over sensitized skin. Her breath caught as the towel rubbed across her nipples on its descent to the floor. "You should leave." She sighed, tilting her head, giving him more access to the side of her neck.

He accepted the invitation, pressing small kisses along the tendons following with laps of his tongue. "Can you tell me what happened out there? What happened to you?" He nosed into the damp loosened curls covering her ear.

His breath chased the path of his tongue, stoking the heat surging through her belly and below. Her thoughts cleared at his question. "It's complicated. The short version is that the problem has been resolved and won't recur." Her eyes crossed and fire radiated inward from the nipple he drew into his mouth. God! she loved having her breasts sucked on.

His teeth grazed her other nipple. His hands roamed across the sides of her hips to cup the fullness of her ass, fingers clenching in the taut globes. He lifted his head. "Rogan was worried 'it' wasn't gone."

"It's...." Words fled as his mouth settled on hers, his tongue foraging into the depths of her mouth. He had used the toothpaste she preferred, but beneath its astringent quality was a spice no manufacturer could ever duplicate. Did he taste like that everywhere? A cavernous ache grew between her legs. A tsunami of anger, frustration and hunger flooded her body fed by a hidden ocean of carnal feelings stuffed away for years.

She pushed Daire ... one step, two. She followed his body down as his legs met the side of the bed and he fell backwards. She straddled his hips melding her wet center with the bulge beneath his zipper. Her hands grabbed the edges of his shirt and yanked it open. Buttons flew everywhere, one popped against her cheek. She ran her tongue from his belly button to the dip beneath his Adam's apple. She shoved the material away from his chest and nibbled first one nipple then the other. Rocking, always rocking against the thick shaft hidden in his pants.

Daire shoved against the softness of the mattress and twisted unseating Tempest and rolling her beneath him. He kneeled between her legs. Her skin glowed against the backdrop of the dark blue bedspread. He flung the remains of his shirt away. His hands met Tempest's at the waistband of his pants. He wanted to take his time, hours made up of minutes and seconds he could use to find and savor Tempest's secret places. He should slow down the pace. "Let me." He gasped when Tempest's fingers tugged the tag of the zipper on his pants. His hands shook as he eased the metal over his engorged member.

Tempest pushed the cloth down Daire's hips. Her breath caught as he sprang free. She twisted until she was free of Daire's body, growling as he slid off the bed. She slinked like a cat across the mattress, over the edge and onto the floor. She clasped his shaft and ran her tongue across the head, capturing the liquid oozing from its center. Mmmmm, mmmmmm, good!

Daire's fingers clenched in Tempest's hair as she licked and mouthed his shaft. He bent quickly ending her teasing, his control gone. He had to get inside her. He pitched her onto the bed, her legs dangling off the end, and pushed her legs open. The lure of her naked mound acted as an accelerant on his self-control.

The orgasm came from nowhere and it hurt. The intensity blew through Tempest's mind, heart and soul. Years of taking care of her personal needs with B.O.S.S.es—battery-operated substitutes – got the job done but lacked the emotional connection she needed for truly fulfilling completion.

HyperRealm wavered. The inner plane was only as solid as the creator visioned it. Her usual visits filled with color, sound, and solid objects. She was ethereal as was Daire and Sebastian when he abruptly appeared. A myriad of Celtic Crosses twinkled against the blackness surrounding them, her family joined to Bastian through her blood.

A cross on a tether burst from Daire's chest and hung in space in front of his projection. His mouth opened in a scream, but no sound came out. Twin blue lightning bolts exploded from the cross slamming into Tempest and Sebastian. Three united forms materialized in the distance surrounded in a white aura. A third bolt streaked across the distance penetrating the field.

A brief wave of sound rolled across the space: sharp splats of hands on bare skin ... husky female moans ... guttural growls in different timbres. The female, sandwiched between the male bodies, turned her head giving Tempest a sharp look. The bolt split striking her and her companions. She stiffened, her eyes glazed, and the exquisite relief of orgasm flooded HyperRealm.

Tempest thudded into her physical body with a shriek, hearing Daire's shout, her body pulling away from Daire's thrust. She was too tight and he was too big. She felt his attempt to stop and draw back, but the bonding dragged them together. Her breath stopped as he hit the end of her channel. Now it wasn't enough. Her hips lifted and her breathing returned. "Move, Daire. You have to move! Aghhhhhhhhhh!" Her body bowed with her second release.

They pounded together, reaching for a plateau neither had ever felt before. Their bodies convulsed.

Tempest licked Daire's shoulder. She shuddered as the taste sent an aftershock through her system, her vagina clenching on his shaft and he pulsed inside her again.

"Stop. Don't do that again, please, Tempest. At least not now." He pressed his forehead against Tempest's, laughing with her at the simultaneous shudders coiling through them as he withdrew from her. "Gods!" He rolled to his back pulling her against his side. "I wanted our first time to be special. Flowers, dinner, and long, slow lovemaking." He shook his head, a rueful smile covering his mouth. "I barely made sure you found your pleasure."

Tempest rose, bracing on her bent arm. Filtered sunlight from the gauze-covered French doors sketched interesting shadows on the smooth chest inviting exploration. She tried to resist but failed, pressing a kiss on the tanned skin above his heart. Raising her head, she gave him a tender smile. "I'm allergic to flowers. Dinner is waiting for us outside, and long and slow is highly overrated. You only have to look at me and my body creams for you." She laughed as a smug expression crossed his face, but it was the gentleness in his eyes which made her turn away. She disguised her withdrawal with a kiss to his shoulder before dropping to her back and continuing the motion to the edge of the bed. Rising, she walked into the bathroom.

Daire turned to his side lying half-propped on one arm, the other draped across his waist. She was retreating from him. He cocked his head to one side thoughtfully; his hand rising to rub a deep-seated ache in his chest. He raised his voice so she could hear him. "Did you see a brilliant blue light just before our mutual explosion?" He wasn't going to let her close him out.

Tempest stiffened as she wrung water out of the cloth in her hand. With a deep breath and a reassuring look at herself in the mirrors above the counter, she strolled out the door and across the carpet. "Let me." She protested the tugging away of the rag.

Daire clenched his teeth as he swiped the warm, wet cloth over his groin, the feeling reminiscent of Tempest's moist channel. "If I let you anywhere near my cock right now, you're going to be on your hands and knees and it's going to be buried deep inside." He swung his legs over the side of the bed, stood and ran a hand over the curve of her butt as he passed. He tossed the washcloth into the hamper and spent the few minutes in the bathroom taking care of his needs and bolstering his self-control. The silence from the bedroom made him uneasy.

Leaning against the doorframe, he watched Tempest fighting through excess material of an oversized T-shirt, her arms waving wildly in the folds. Navy blue panties covered her mound and hips. His cock hardened as he watched her breasts bobbing and swaying. Hunger blinded him and he was across the room, his hands cupping the cream white globes, raising them to his mouth. His tongue curled around one small bud, teeth sinking in, sucking as he pulled his head back stretching her taut. He released it and did the same to the other side. The unexpected pain of her fingers clenching in the strands of his hair returned his sanity. He seized it and clutched it tightly, raising his head and releasing her reluctantly. "Damn, but you go to my head like sweet chocolate."

The throbbing between her legs and the knowledge it wouldn't be satisfied made Tempest edgy, firing her temper. She opened her fingers and released Daire's hair. She turned away grabbing the bottom of the shirt and pulling it over her breasts. Her fingers trembled as she fought the urge to tweak her damp nipples. She should have put on a bra while he was in the bathroom. She swallowed several times trying to release the spontaneous antagonism. It wasn't his fault they couldn't crawl back onto the bed … or use the carpet and all that floor space … and the potential involved while bending over the back of the chaise lounge. Sweat broke out on her forehead, her eyes glazed. Her pulse pounded like she wanted Daire's body to do in hers. They had to get out of the bedroom … out of the house and in the company of people … lots of people.

But first she had to respond to his question. She didn't understand what had happened much less what the ramifications would be. She walked to the French doors and leaned against the frame seeking answers from the oasis of greenery in the enclosed courtyard. The burbling water on the rocks in the fountain in its center soothed the irritations.

She turned to face Daire who had approached silently and was sitting on the back of the chaise, legs outstretched and crossed at the ankles. "Yes, I saw the blue light." And Sebastian. And a woman and two men. And the icons representing all of her people. She jammed her fingers through the hair at the sides of her face, smoothed the strands back, and pulled them into a ponytail at the top of her head. With a huff, she released the plait, the curls tumbling into disarray, enhancing the effect of just having had sex.

"I don't know what you believe is real." She stuck out her tongue when he cocked an eyebrow. "I wish I had control of my facial muscles to be able to do that." She held up her hands as both eyebrows inched upward. "Okay, okay. I'm dithering. Sebastian Bloodhawk is an alien." Her eyes rose checking Daire's expression.

Daire crossed his arms on his chest. Thinking his position might lead her to think he was closing down, he dropped his arms and placed his hands on either side of his hips on the back of the chair. "Okay. I know that."

"I'm going to give you the short version. Hell, I don't know what the long version is at this point. Anyway, Bastian is a FolKin Elder. His people live for thousands of years." She moved to sit cross-legged on the end of the bed. She continued irritably. "It seems like the humanoid species can't get along wherever they happen to live. There was a holocaust of some sort and the resulting effect was a dependence on blood for food." She hurried faster when he held his hand up and twirled it around. "They have powers." She shrugged helplessly. "He's only been with us a very short time and we don't know what he can or will do and neither does he.

"On his world, the people developed an allergy to their

sun and they needed helpers during daylight hours to handle ... stuff. Reciprocates ... that's what they're called ... were bound psychically to their ...," she shrugged again with a twist to her mouth, "... masters. Sometimes, but it's a very rare occurrence, people the Reciprocate cares about also become bound to the FolKin Elder. That's what the blue light was about. You're bound to Bastian through me."

Astonishment flashed across his face. He breathed deeply, uncrossed his ankles and walked into the sunshine. He leaned a shoulder against the doorframe and stared blindly outside. He didn't have any psychic abilities nor did he have any skills which would draw him to the attention of the Covens. He was bound to the FolKin through Tempest. He let it sink in for a few minutes then concern for Tempest flared. He spun around. "You said you are bound to him. What exactly does that mean?" He took the few steps between them and pulled her up and against him.

The warmth of his body touching hers and his clean sage smell eased the panic his initial alienation created. "I don't know." She repeated herself when he shook her slightly. "Even Sebastian doesn't know what's going to happen. He could tell us what happens with Reciprocates on his world, but this is a new galaxy, a new planet, a species with possibly dissimilar DNA, and differences are already showing up. The Feral-spark shouldn't have happened." At his questioning look, she fluttered her hand towards the window. "The thing that happened out there." She lifted a shoulder and stated in a flat tone, "That's a story for another time."

She stepped back and gravitated to the small shaft of light from the windows. "Sebastian can be in the sun. He needs sunglasses and sunscreen, but it's something he's never experienced before and he's over five thousand years old by our reckoning. The rest of it: we just ... don't ... know."

Daire closed the distance, wrapped one arm around her waist, and placed the other hand on the back of her head tucking it into his neck. Her breath on his skin calmed the ragged edges of his nerves. "It's alright." His hands coasted up and down her back. "We'll figure it out together."

She bent back, shaking her head. "I believe I can cut you off from the connection. We still have an alliance between our people, but you shouldn't get too close. You don't know the other forces we have to deal with. I don't know the other forces we'll be dealing with. And the business with Sebastian … who the hell knows what's going to come out of that? Your first obligation is to the welfare of your people since your well-being affects them. You know that." Tears gathered in her eyes as she tried to make him understand and give him the freedom he deserved.

"Shhhh. It's alright, Tempest." He let her go and clasped her hands, bringing one after the other to his mouth and placing a kiss on the knuckles. "I'll discuss it with Declan and my people and take the time to evaluate the consequences. We'll talk again. But I expect you to keep me informed about what's going on. As allies, we need to discuss things together and develop our plans accordingly."

He gave up too easily. She knew he was placating her, but she didn't want to fight with him. Rogan, Lorcan and Strider were her foundation, but she needed Daire in a different way. She didn't want to take away his choices. That had happened to her too many times in the past to ever want to do it to another person, particularly someone she loved. Her mind froze, but her body continued to move beside Daire's to the bedroom door. Love. She loved Daire. No. She shook her hair back and at the same time shoved the neo-feeling behind a door in her mind. It wouldn't close completely.

# CHAPTER 30

Tempest rested in the lounge chair, replete from sex and excellent food. She ignored the glances out of the side of eyes from most of the people. At least they were polite. Sebastian, Rogan, Lorcan and Declan grinned at her and Daire every chance they got. Even Ben wasn't hiding his delight at her discomfiture. Among so many people, she didn't have a hope of having a private life.

She and Daire had been sucked into the food line as soon as they arrived at the outdoor kitchen and dining area. She had carried her overfull plate to a lounger beneath a shade tree Sebastian had claimed. She had started to ask her questions again, but the smell of the barbequed meat, baked beans, and several salads had snared her, giving her tunnel vision. She surfaced when she licked the last crumb from the plate.

Knitting her fingers together across her achingly full stomach, she contemplated the clouds streaming across the early evening sky. Rain for sure tomorrow. A yawn caught her unaware and she raised a hand, hiding her mouth. Her eyelids wavered. She blinked rapidly forcing her eyes wide, giving the group around her, some in chairs and others lounging on the ground, a dazzling smile. Cicadas' strident calls, combined with the occasional deep burp of bullfrogs and the low voices around her, formed a symphony lulling her eyes closed; her head rolled to the side.

A sound roused Tempest from a dream. She felt drugged

and it was a struggle to wake. Her lashes edged up. A tall young man with chocolate brown hair trotted away from a dusty Tracker parked on the grassy verge near the covered pit. Smoke and fragrant odors floated in the air above the open fire.

The man waved a hand in response to various calls, but he remained fixed on Rogan. The paleness beneath tanned skin deepened the dark circles under his eyes. Stress lines at the edges of his eyes and around his mouth aged him beyond his twenty-six years. He squatted on his soles beside Rogan's chair his arms wrapped around his legs. His chest slowed from pumping bellows to natural breaths. "Gods! Thanks!" His head tilted back, his Adam's apple bobbing, as he drained the bottle of water placed in his hand.

Morgan Reynolds tried to follow polite manners, taking the plate of food from Bayzee. His stomach rumbled and he sat hurriedly on the ground as his vision wavered. He tore bites of meat from the bone, licking sauce from his fingers. Unasked questions hung in the air. With the first pangs satisfied, he wiped his hands on a napkin and picked up a fork.

"Treadaway's representative is at the gate. The security screen was on so he didn't know it was me when I came through." Morgan shook his head refusing the bottle of beer but accepting the second container filled with iced tea.

Tempest sat up swinging her legs to the ground.

Morgan gave her a sidelong glance but returned his gaze to his plate. "I still have friends within Coven Darksylk. Treadaway hired mercenaries to look for me. I got out of Bessmer International's corporate headquarters just ahead of them. Carter and Bronson were in place to protect the president of the company so the contract is safe." He raised a laden fork to his mouth.

Tempest leaned forward on the end of the lounger, one hand reaching out to touch Morgan's knee. "The important thing is you're safe." She lifted a shoulder. "If Bessmer cancels the contract, it's their loss. It's okay, Morgan, really." She reassured him when he made to protest. "The main source of our revenue doesn't come from the security business although it does bring in a nice chunk of change." She slanted a look at Rogan.

Morgan nodded, but kept his face carefully neutral. He stared at the remaining food on the plate, his stomach roiling, making him wish he hadn't eaten. "I want you to bind me ... like you did the others." His voice was low, but steady, firm.

"No." Tempest stood up shaking her head. "No." She walked to Rogan and laid her hand on his shoulder. "We should greet our guest, Ro."

"Damnit, Tempest! Stop!" Morgan jumped up, ignoring the admonishing looks from the older men. "Protocols have to be followed. You didn't have a strict upbringing in Coven rituals. I did. You can't let Treadaway gain the advantage." He took the few steps to Tempest, grabbed her shoulders and shook her.

"That's enough, Reynolds." Rogan jumped to his feet, waving everyone else down. Daire ignored the gesture, striding forward to stand behind Tempest, his lip curled back in a snarl.

Morgan released her and twisted away kicking the bottle at his feet. He stabbed his fingers through his hair grimacing at the oily texture. All he wanted was a hot shower and a clean bed now that he had eaten. He turned around. "You don't understand. None of you do." Frustration caused his voice to rise. "Treadaway Called Challenge. He gets to select whomever he wants as his Champion. And that's me! He chooses the date. You select the time and place. He chose first level which is death Challenge.

"You have to put me beyond his reach! Bind me! Do it before Rogan meets with the representative at the gate. It'll be too late if you don't. He means to use me to hurt you. To make you bend to his will." He spun away, paced back and forth.

Leaning against Daire's chest, Tempest bit her lip watching Morgan's growing agitation. "You don't know what you're asking." Hadn't she just gone through this with Daire? She wanted to join Morgan in his pacing. How many more friends and family were going to be yanked into jeopardy?

"If I had been here instead of at Bessmer, we wouldn't be having this conversation. I would be part of the binding along with everyone else since my blood would have been used as part of the cocktail." He waved a hand at the men and women standing silently around them. "Treadaway will force me to forsake my honor and kill you or we're both dead because you won't kill me and I won't kill you. And then all of this," he swung his arm around to include the entire area, "will be gone. He doesn't care. He wins. He gets rid of you, cripples what you've built so he can pick off what he wants at his leisure, and he destroys what's left of my family's small Coven. I'm still the eldest son of the Patriarch even though I renounced my position. If I'm forsworn, my family is killed ... all of them!"

He loved Tempest, as a young warrior for his leader. She had given him opportunities far beyond anything he could have dreamed of had he stayed subordinate to Coven Darksylk. He still had hopes of providing new lives for two of his sisters if he could just free them of their life-long brainwashing before their initiations.

He strode past Tempest halting in front of Sebastian sitting beneath the shade tree, black lenses in dark frames hiding half his face. "Bind me! I freely submit to your will." He dropped to his knees bowing his head. He could only bend that far; abasement on the grass was beyond his control. His spirit refused ... even for the protection of his leader.

Sebastian pulled the sunglasses from his face. He shot a helpless look at Tempest, who shrugged. "Your offer is commendable." He scooted to the edge of the chair, his arms braced on his thighs, hands dangling between his legs. "Look at me." He waited for the eye contact. "I could bind you here and now but it would be a tight blending ... maybe more than you can handle. I need to receive your blood like the others ... through a transfusion while Tempest gives me a little of hers. The connection will exist through her." He paused. "It's a better solution."

Morgan beat his hands against his thighs. "You aren't listening to me."

With a pat on his arm, Tempest pulled away from Daire's arm around her waist and took the few steps to crouch at Morgan's side. "We understand. I understand. We'll do what you want, but it will take a little time to set up." She looked over her shoulder. "Jake will take you to the medical facilities."

Morgan rested his hand on her arm. "You can't be at the meeting with the representative."

She didn't want to give in but nodded, reluctantly agreeing when he squeezed her arm. "Fine. I'll go to the clinic with you while Rogan deals with this person." She sniffed and urged him to stand. "There're showers you can use. Maybe you'll have time for a nap."

He shook his head. "It has to be done now ... tonight." He stumbled.

Sebastian placed a supporting hand beneath Morgan's arm. "So shall it be done."

Tempest stopped in front of Daire and lifted a hand to his cheek. "Thank you for your help today. You and your people are welcome to spend the night. We have plenty of room to accommodate all of you."

Daire dropped his head and bussed her lips in a light caress. "I'll talk it over with Rogan and Declan. Go do what you have to."

She slid her hand down his arm as she walked away. She turned her hand to catch his briefly before letting go. A buzzing datacomp broke the tableau, scattering men and women in all directions.

Tugging Morgan in her wake, she remembered the question she had meant to ask. "Sebastian, who the hell is Kalia?"

# CHAPTER 31

"Damn! This day has got to end!" Anger shattered inside Tempest, creating mounds in her neck muscles. The dull ache stretching from the back of her head to her temples changed to ice picks slamming into the middle of her forehead. Her hand rose, fingers rubbing the skin at the middle of her brow. She tracked the converging Coteries through squinted eyes.

Sebastian's hand tightened on her arm, halting her sideways tilt. She pushed the juice bottle into Morgan's chest and released it, uncaring if he caught it, and twisted her arm from beneath Sebastian's hand. She stumbled, exacerbating her irritation at him. He still hadn't answered her question.

"What?"

The men and women surrounded Tempest, stopping a safe distance from her. Their faces were blank, silence hovering over the group with a coverlet of calm and nonviolence.

She pushed the air from her lungs in a huge gust. "I'm not going to explode like a bad batch of nitroglycerin. Someone get over here and tell me what's going on."

Strider galloped through the line of warriors, skidding to a halt in front of Tempest. He waved the fighters closer. "You're needed at the gate."

Her fingers rubbed harder at the pain between her eyes. "I thought I couldn't be within kissing distance of that Coven rep."

"Lorcan is pushing him along. This other thing has

precedence. If the Covens want to fight about the rules and regulations later, Rogan said he'll set them on a righteous path." Strider's hand was warm against the small of Tempest's back, shoving her forward.

The irritation in the feminine voice added a rhythmic backdrop to the crunching gravel growing louder. It was a minute sliding of the eyes, a slight curve to Peter Twilley's lips. Rogan slammed him into Riley and Stonebreaker and turned to run.

The black dartbyke blasted into the open space in front of the gate. Dirt swirled into the air as the rider shifted sideways throwing the rear wheel in an arc around his stationary leg.

Tempest twisted and dropped to one knee on the ground feeling a tug at her sleeve. The distant boom of a rifle echoed through the lane. She slammed into Sebastian inside a circular barricade of guards. Excited voices rose as dust settled to the ground. She waited several minutes then rose and elbowed a path between hard muscled bodies.

Strider bobbed in front of her. "Rogan hasn't given the all clear."

Puffing her hair off her forehead, Tempest narrowed her eyes.

Strider batted his eyes at her. "Procedures are in place for a reason, Tempe. Until Rogan says otherwise, you've got a wall between you and the big bad."

"I happen to be the head of this organization." She slammed her hands on her hips, her usual posture when attempting to exert her authority, her chin thrust forward. A shrill whistle floated overhead. "This isn't over." She hid the smile threatening to spill onto her face and ignored the subdued grins on the faces of the men and women moving away but still close enough to surround her. She walked the short distance to the entrance. The tableau stopped her.

One of three guards was shoving a man into the driver's seat of a Coven sedan beside a two-toned three wheeled offroader tilted on two wheels at the side of the security building. The remaining two guards held the arms of a struggling young man while Kodiak bound his wrists together.

But it was the man facing a bristling Rogan and Lorcan who was the most dangerous of all the combatants. Her eyes tracked two thin braids lining a patrician profile and a black mane with hints of gold pulled back and caught at the nape of his neck with a holder, the long thick tail ending at the middle of his back. The patched grey-on-grey shirt and pants beneath the synth-leather coat retained the stamp of expensive, well made. The shape of the side of his face was familiar and when he raised his head and looked around her breath stuttered. Her gaze shifted to Rogan, noting the striking similarity in eyes, nose and mouth when they stood so close together. Brother, cousin, or kissin' kin they were related in some way.

Apprehension and anxiety fought for supremacy inside her. Was he here to take Rogan away? Would Rogan go with him? What would she do if Rogan left? The relationship with Daire was still too new, even considering the binding with Sebastian. Would Daire stay or would the events hitting them fast and furiously drive him away if only to protect his people? Her familiar world shifted like stepping off a stone path into quicksand. The bulwark between her and standing alone was shattering. She stuffed trembling fingers into the pockets of her jacket.

The tires on the Coven sedan spun, littering the air with small rocks. In the distance, from the direction of the outer training field, five men trotted toward the gate. They stopped, raising their weapons at the vehicle barreling towards them. The sedan hesitated then swerved away, picking up speed as it raced down the road. Their weapons remained up approaching the group massed in front of the stone guardhouse.

The stranger's gold-flecked, navy blue eyes lasered across Tempest's skin. She dug her nails into the seams of the jacket pockets. The urge to scratch the unmarred handsome face was breathtakingly hard to control. And it wasn't the Feral-spark leaping out of an unknown hiding place. It was truly gone forever. This man roused her deepest terror, stirring her fight-or-flight reflex and flight wasn't a choice.

At the edge of her left eye, Strider's gun rose, his frame shifting into a more open stance. Sebastian was suddenly half a pace in front of her, protecting her right side. She wanted to reassure them, tell them everything was all right, but those words were stuck in the pit of her stomach.

"Captain Collier is in the same condition he was in when you met with him at the cemetery." The deep voice poured over her like syrup on pancakes, the compulsion to trust hidden in the tone like the calories in the sweet liquid.

"Who are you and what do you want?" Her gaze locked on his face. Animosity coated each word.

He settled deeper into the saddle of the Dartbyke. His hands open on his legs. He projected calmness. "The cub," he pointed his chin towards the youth Kodiak was guarding, "is working with your enemies. He was sent here as a distraction. Captain Collier overheard a few words of a conversation between his 'fleas' and two men he couldn't see. He sent me ahead to warn you."

"He's lying! Captain Collier sent me ahead to warn you about him." He punched a shoulder at the man on the Dartbyke. "And to ask for help. The Captain and some of the others are hurt bad and need transportation to get here." He twisted in the restraining hands. "Get these goons off me. I'm just trying to help."

Tempest read contempt and dismissal in the stranger's eyes before he turned back to Rogan and Lorcan. Anger erupted inside her, threatening to overwhelm her good sense. She wanted to walk up and punch the man a few times. She hated when the male species stood in judgment and then reached a conclusion based on the faulty wiring in their brains. And why the hell was Rogan just standing there like a stone statue?

She lifted her chin in the air and shoved past Strider and

Sebastian. "Kodi, put the young man in one of the secure rooms in the gatehouse and call the Sheriff for this area. He can haul the kid's butt away." She started walking down the lane into the compound. "Rogan, extend our thanks to Captain Collier for sending a warning. Provide transport for him and any of his people if he wants it. Tell him I'm looking forward to seeing and talking with him when he gets here. If there's anything I need to know about the Challenge, I'll deal with it later."

She stopped in front of Daire laying her palm against his chest. "You and your people are welcome to stay as long as you want. There's a bedroom available in the house for you." She answered the question lurking in the depths of his eyes with a sad smile. "I need some time to myself tonight. Please understand."

Daire pressed Tempest's hand. His voice softened. "I need to get back to my place and take care of some things. Let me know the details about the Challenge. I want to be with you." He tipped her face up with a finger and waited.

Conscious of being the focus of many gazes, she controlled her impulse to suck his finger inside her mouth. "I'll make sure you get the information." She didn't promise she would personally call him. She wanted to be the one to talk to him, but circumstances often got in the way. Ignoring everyone else, she marched several yards along the lane before cutting through the trees, trailing three guards.

"She's young for such a position of authority. I would have thought you would have better control of her. I'm Lazarus Watters."

Rogan seethed beneath the surface, but he projected calm outward weaving the stream of energy from Lorcan into the expanding wave. The men and women holstered weapons and slung rifles over shoulders. Small groups formed and the buzz of conversation rose like bees returning to a hive. He released Lorcan's support and pulled back on the projection. Damn! Only a short time within the stranger's influence and a trine formed pushing him into old habits. Watters had to be kin or tied by blood to his family Tribe.

"Is Captain Collier all right?" Rogan's low voice chilled the air.

Watters stiffened, his hand edging to the top of his boot. He froze.

"Let's keep this friendly." Strider nudged Watters's back with his gun. Keeping the weapon firmly against the rigid spine, a newbie move since the man could … possibly … turn the tables on Strider, he leaned forward and removed the knives from the tops of both boots. "You want a thorough search, Rogan?" He handed the blades to Lorcan and moved to the side, weapon steady and aimed at Watters, maintaining a view of the trio around the Dart.

"That's not necessary. Right, Watters?"

"I didn't expect to be treated as a threat. I am here at Collier's request. The wounds he sustained while in the military are giving him problems, but there are no new injuries. He and his people are bone weary. Transport of some kind would be a blessing although he didn't ask for it."

Rogan nodded to Lorcan who trotted away. "You'll lead the team to the group?"

Watters raised his right arm into the air and moved his left one slowly to a small square attachment on the handlebars of the byke. His index finger tapped the metal. "Your man can relax. This is a Lo-pin. It will take your people directly to Collier."

Rogan flicked his fingers. Morgan sidled along the cycle on the side away from Strider. He detached the cube, backed away and strode to the gate. Rogan aimed a look at Strider who refused eye contact keeping his weapon aimed at the insolent outsider. His finger pressed gently against the trigger. A little crease wouldn't be harmful and would teach the interloper some manners.

Rogan shook his head at Lorcan moving up on Strider. "Strider. Go with Morgan and the others. Bring the Captain and his people back." He waited.

Strider leaned forward, his weapon once again pressing against the stranger's back. He wanted to impress upon the man his extreme displeasure. "I really don't like you. Don't ever disrespect or hurt Tempest again. I don't care what your connection is to Rogan. Do it again and you'll hurt for the rest of your life ... if I decide to let you have one."

After a few seconds' hesitation, Strider made a slight bow to Rogan and took a step back, then another. His arm inched down as he retreated. Several hundred yards away, he tucked his gun in the holster on his hip and jumped backwards onto the bed of the last vehicle in the convoy. He sat on the end, his legs kicking back and forth watching the group.

"Don't relax yet, Watters," Rogan warned.

"You Called. I Answer." Watters dismounted from the Dartbyke. He bent backwards, hands on the small of his back, then side to side to relieve the kinks caused by sitting too long. His modified Dart was very smooth on the road, but the tension from the run to arrive in time and the unexpected face down of potential allies had caused his body to stiffen.

"Tempest Phillips is family and our leader. Your contempt was uncalled for. What the hell do you want?" There wasn't any give in Rogan's voice or stance.

Watters sighed, pinching the bridge of his nose with his fingers. "Damnit, Branaugh! You have a duty to the Tribes and their allies." He shook his head. "I've gotten off to the wrong start ... with you and the woman." Frustration deepened his voice. "There's just no time to ease into the situation. You don't know what's at stake."

With a deep breath, he started again. "You must assume your responsibilities as Hereditary-Regent and provide sanctuary for seven Tribes and their allies and the demi-Folk Flairs who crossed with us. We're camped near the Farlight dimensional gate. It's still active and someone on the other side can find a way to reopen it. We have guards watching it so we'll know when or if that happens." He rubbed his eyes seeking relief, but the sensation of grit coating them intensified. "Something happened ... here ... in this world ... several weeks ago. Several youngers were playing near the...," he waved his hand. "That's not important now. What is critical is we discovered a solution to our long-time problems, and we grabbed it. You are the Key. You have to deactivate the gate."

"No! I don't know what you're talking about." Steel formed in Rogan's eyes, his back stiffened. "My father had three sons; he chose the middle and youngest as his heirs. I was disowned and exiled. I'm of this world now," he waved his arm in a circle, "these are my family, and" he tipped his head towards the grove of trees, "she is my family, my friend and my leader. I have no ties to Karatouche."

Watters stomped towards Rogan his arms rising. Maybe he could shake some sense into Branaugh's head. His foot slipped on a rock and he almost staggered into the rifle pointed at his chest as Lorcan ghosted in front of Rogan. He backed away, his hands out to his sides, halting in front of the guards who had moved up behind him.

His feeling of urgency was making him clumsy and this son had the sire's pride and stubbornness in full measure. He hoped Branaugh took after his mother's family and wasn't a vicious and self-centered bastard like his father and brothers. "You are the last of the Calindra line and your family's blood is keyed to the gates. Farlight is open and unbound and you have to close it, before the King sends an army through to ravage this world." Watters struggled with the overwhelming feeling of losing the battle to save his people. "You have to listen. You have to help. The Seers foresaw if we stayed on Karatouche in six generations there would be no more children. Very few of our women bear children to full-term now and less than one-fourth of the premature babies live. We need new bloodlines. We need you, Lorcan, Tulsa and Judah. And we need her." He tipped his head towards the unseen buildings.

"Fuck!" Rogan let his rifle drop to hang by its strap on

his shoulder. He jammed his fingers through his hair and turned to take ten paces right, spin and stride back ten steps. He cursed, his native language coming easily to his tongue as well as the dialects of other countries he picked up from his stint in the military. His mind whirled. The buzzing of the com in his ear halted his tirade and his movement. "Get some rest, Tempest. I'm okay. We can talk in the morning." He waited to hear her murmuring agreement before clicking off. His fingers curled into the palms of his hands before slowly relaxing. He whipped around. "The magic in this world is raw and buried deep. The demi-Folk will die."

"No. The Light dances through this Universe just as it does through ours. Thought-forms about magic are abundant. The Seers say in a few months the energies will realign and there will be more physicality to the magic. This system is on the brink of change. We're just giving it a small push."

The lines in Rogan's forehead deepened. "How the hell did you hook up with Collier?" He flicked the question away with his fingers. "Lorcan will show you to the visitors' quarters for now. You'll share space with Captain Collier and his people until we can arrange something different. I can't make any decisions or promises now. I have to discuss it with Tempest. It's her decision in the end." Weariness clothed his body like a shroud. He threw up a hand. "No. No arguments, no more information. I don't want to hear anything else. Just … go." He signaled the surrounding guards away, and watched Watters push his byke to the small covered parking area beside the gatehouse.

The trio of searchers approached, gave a brief report and separated, taking different directions back into the trees away from the fence. With Stoney in tow, Rogan lurched into motion treading the lane towards the house he shared with Tempest, his legs feeling weighed down in concrete.

"They find anything?" Stonebreaker's voice rumbled like heavy trucks barreling down a paved highway.

"Very little. The shooter was a professional. We were

very lucky he missed. Professionals don't miss. Watters' arrival was good for something." His mind shut down then stuttered forward. "We should have been better prepared for an attack against Tempest. Boyd and his team are going back to expand the search area. If there's anything to find, they'll uncover it." Rogan jerked his rifle up tracking right, dropping to one knee. A quick laugh sputtered out as three squirrels scrabbled across the grass and up an oak tree. He stood, shaking his head. "I understand why Tempest is so jumpy. What happened to the quiet days when we trained, decided what jobs we wanted to take, and used the downtime to enjoy things?"

Stoney's laugh boomed, scattering birds into the sky. "What reality are you remembering?" He chuckled. "Downtime? I've been with you for over fifteen years. Yeah, we have some good times. Tempest makes sure of that. But vacations? What the hell would we want with those? Most of us kicked around the world fighting for various factions or following orders of the so-called military to fight in their dirty little wars. We have a home and family with Tempest. Only the young pups don't understand the value of what she's given every one of us. If I go down keeping her alive ... well, it's not something I want to happen, but if it does ... I'll be a satisfied man." He slapped Rogan's back. "Come on, my man. Get some rest." He pushed Rogan up the steps of the house. Checking the watch on his wrist, he turned away with a flap of his hand. "Things will look better after four hours of sleep ... which is all that's remaining of tonight."

Rogan stood on the edge of the porch, gazing at the retreating back. He was surprised by the depth of caring Stoney had shared. He started at the soft voice from the darkness behind him.

"Ro? Stoney's right. You need to sleep."

He turned and walked into the house. "What are you still doing up?" He turned the bolt on the door and set the alarm. The panel above the keyboard lit up showing green dots along the perimeter of the diagram. With a press on another button, the diagram for the second floor appeared with rows of green specks.

Tempest hugged her favorite oversized plush bathrobe. The hem dragged along the floor and brushed against her toes. "The house was empty." She had to get Maggie and Gracie back from Ben. She missed them. It was the first time they had been away from her for longer than a day or two since she adopted them. But with the uncertainty of the outcome of the Challenge, she knew they needed to become familiar with someone else ... just in case. And, without Rogan nearby, she felt threatened, exposed.

Rogan placed a hand against Tempest's back and urged her up the stairs. "What's wrong?"

Tears clogged her suddenly tight throat. "Are you leaving, Ro?"

He grunted. "Not right now. I'm going to get some sleep ... and so are you. We can talk about the problems later."

She nodded. "Okay." The word was soft but laden with unspoken emotion. She held her breath when Rogan tugged her to a stop and turned her.

"What's going on?"

She bit her lip. "Are you going with him, Ro?" The nightlight in the hallway provided enough illumination to see the puzzlement in his eyes. "Your kinsman. Is he taking you away?"

"Oh, honey." He sighed, clasping her against his chest. He kissed the top of her head, laid his cheek against it. "No one can take me away from you. You're my family. This is my home. And when you move on with Daire, I'll still be around."

Tempest shoved him away. "I'm not moving anywhere with Daire." That was one subject she definitely didn't want to discuss.

"And I'm not going anywhere with Watters. We'll talk in the morning." He pushed her into her bedroom and hauled the door closed. Moving down the corridor to his bedroom, he briefly considered taking a shower, but the bed consumed his vision, towing his body to its side like a calf at the end of a rope. He fell across the mattress and sleep yanked him under.

# CHAPTER 32

Tempest rolled away from the sunbeam prodding her through the open curtains. Blast! She had forgotten to close the drapes before she went to bed. She flopped onto her back and tugged the blankets around her shoulders. Crap! Could she have sounded needier last night talking to Rogan? Bollocks. And what had Rogan meant when he said 'when she went off with Daire'? She didn't have any plans for tying herself to a man and letting him take over. Oh ... yeah ... the FolKin bond tied her to not one but many men. She sat upright in bed as the sun stabbed her again. But that didn't mean they could take over and ruin ... no, run her life.

She flipped over and tumbled to her knees beside the bed. With a tug here and there, she straightened the blankets and bedspread, grabbed fresh panties and bra from the dresser, and pattered into the bathroom. A hearty groan escaped her mouth as jets of hot water massaged her from every direction. She tilted her head back letting the liquid soak her hair. Goose bumps erupted on her skin. She turned away from the spray aimed at her suddenly taut nipples. Gods! A little buzz from the B.O.S.S. in her drawer in just the right place and relief by battery would make the day glisten. An eye cracked open. She spread her legs and propped a foot on the edge of the tub. She slanted her lower body to just the right angle for the surging water. ZING! She staggered. The orgasm crashed into her like a car hitting a wall at a hundred miles an hour. Wowza!

Bubbles of laughter zoomed around inside her. Staggering away from the shower, she stepped to the floor, grabbed a towel and delicately patted her mound. No sense resurrecting the demon from below. She threw the cloth into the hamper and dragged the hair dryer from beneath the sink. Ordinarily she let her hair air dry, but she wanted to take her time. Sometimes solutions materialized when she wasn't thinking about anything in particular.

A knock on wood and the smell of coffee were twin assaults on her attention. Leaving her hair damp, she shoved the hair dryer and makeup into drawers and rushed out of the bathroom, across the bedroom and into the closet as the hallway door eased open.

"Want some coffee?"

"I'll be there in a minute, Ro." Her hand faltered hearing the second voice.

"May I enter as well?" Sebastian stood in the doorframe and scanned the room. He hoped to satisfy some of his curiosity about his Reciprocate. He squinted from the sunshine pouring into the room until Branaugh slid coverings across the glass. Books littered the floor, overflowed from packed storage cabinets, and were stacked on all the surfaces except the round table with four chairs pushed into one corner. He fingered the sleeve of a white robe sprawled on the dark red and green squares concealing the bed. Her essence permeated the room and he inhaled the musky scent with a touch of spice at its core.

Tempest poked her head around the doorjamb. "Hey, Sebastian." Heat melted over her seeing his fingers rubbing her fuzzy robe. "Uh, I'll be with you in a minute." She pulled back, all thoughts temporarily erased from her mind including what clothes to wear. Sebastian was a very handsome man; some might even say he was a stud muffin. Jeans clung to his legs and tight ass and the black long-sleeved shirt molded the muscles in his arms and emphasized the fact there wasn't a hint of fat on his abs. She licked her lips, her eyes glazing. She was attracted to Daire and she was monogamous … at least she had always thought she was a one-man woman. One deep breath. Two deep breaths. Okay, she wasn't dead. She could admire a very attractive body. She nodded her head twice. Right. That was her story and she was sticking to it.

"Are you all right, Tempest?" Rogan poured coffee into his cup. He filled Tempest's cup and mixed in the cream and sugar she preferred. Holding the carafe over a third cup, he raised an eyebrow at the man sitting down at the table.

"I would like to try this brew. All who drink it appear to like it very much. It has a pleasing mellow smell."

"It's an acquired taste," Tempest yelled, "but Rogan knows I only allow flavored coffees in this house so it will be less bitter than other types. Was Jake able to find out if you have any allergies?" She squatted, testing the stretch of her pants. Satisfied with its flexibility, she rose and fingered the handles of several knives tucked into the pockets of the protective cloth hanging on one wall. Since she didn't know the agenda for the day, she chose two sleek knives and eased them into the reinforced lining at the inner side of each of her knee-high boots. She edged smaller blades into pleats sewn on her bra, bent over, adjusted the fit of the cups of the bra and swung upright, swaying back and forth for a few seconds with dizziness from a head rush.

"He pricked my skin with needles. There was no reaction and the tiny holes disappeared almost immediately. He said, 'be careful.' I must re-introduce food and drink to my stomach in small amounts to see what my body can now tolerate."

Tempest pulled a semi form fitting hip-length emerald top over her head. She smoothed it into place, her head down, as she walked into the bedroom. She accepted the cup Rogan pushed into her hands, blew on the hot brew and took a quick sip. It was just the right temperature and the mixture was perfect. She closed her eyes and gulped several swallows, her system waking up and shouting hallelujah. Out loud, she cooed, "Ahhhhhhhhhh."

Feeling alert and capable, she opened her eyes and

laughed at the grin on Rogan's face. She was really going to have to teach Sebastian the intricacies of a great cup of coffee. Plopping into her special oversized padded chair, she drew her legs beneath her. With a piece of fruit in her left hand, she used her right to drag a leather binder from the pocket attached to the side of the chair and laid it on the table. She leaned back. "We have three immediate problems to deal with." She raised a finger. "The Challenge." A second finger joined the first one. "Finding out what Busch is after." A third finger jutted up. "And settling Grandmother's estate."

She hesitated when Rogan cleared his throat, dropping her hand. At his nod towards the fruit bowl, she chose another cantaloupe cube and nibbled at the edges.

"Treadaway's rep chose tomorrow for the Challenge. And Morgan was right. Twilley selected him as Treadaway's Champion and he was impassive when I said no. He recited that a provision in the Charters allowed one rejection, but then the Challenger could withhold the alternate's name until the time of the gathering. I fell into their trap. Damnit, Tempest, you know Treadaway was behind last night's assassination attempt even if there's no evidence to prove it."

"That's not a surprise, Ro. We knew he would try something. Is the Challenge still on for tomorrow?"

"Yes. The gathering will begin at four in the afternoon. Challenge will occur an hour later. I chose blades or a quick duel with the Coven ritual pistols. We make the final choice of weapon when we see the Challenger-Elect." Rogan scrubbed his face with his hands. "I don't like this, Tempest. Even withholding our decision about the weapon gives them too much room to maneuver."

"Did our choice of location stand?"

Rogan laughed. "Yeah. Twilley was offended we chose Barnabus' circus pavilion, but since Treadaway confronted you, it's your right to select the location of the showdown even to his disadvantage."

She let out her breath. Good. She trusted Barnabus Kale. He was a fair man, an excellent choice as a neutral party. She had fought with his bladesmaster on the turf Barnabus had specially created for solid footing inside his rings. "We'll use blades."

Without any urging, she selected another cube of fruit. Her spirits rose. A thought occurred to her, halting the fruit midway to her mouth. "Treadaway can't demand that we strip or change clothes, can he?" The thought had her hand lowering. The cantaloupe dropped onto the small plate.

"No. You'll wear padded shirt and pants. I want to take your armor with us. If I can get it on you, I want it available. We'll take all of your blades, including your sword and katana."

"This Challenge thing is foolish. Her death will affect many. I will do what I can to protect as many as possible before I die with her, but there are no guarantees." The ball of foreboding grew in Sebastian's stomach. It wasn't for himself. He had lived a long life. This Reciprocate and her protectors were different. They awakened long-forgotten protective emotions.

Tempest laid a hand on Sebastian's arm. "We don't expect you to sacrifice yourself, Bastian. I can't back away. If I did, the results would be a hundred times worse than death. I'm not exaggerating." She leaned back, opened the portfolio beside her plate, pulled a stylus pen from its holder, and made notes in the document she pulled up on the tablet. "Is there anything else I should know about the Challenge?"

"I want to take some time with Lorcan and Strider to set up the rest of the details. Tempest … ." Rogan closed his eyes to shut out her trusting gaze.

Tempest sighed, rubbing her eyes and then her neck. One of them had to initiate the conversation about the elephant in the room. "What does Watters want?"

Lorcan sidled into the room carrying a tray with several covered dishes. "Ben knew you would be up and he sent you a special present."

Tempest sniffed. Avarice demolished her concentration.

A quick shove and the binder thudded onto the carpeted floor. She gave the bowl of fruit a disparaging look, lifted her arms and crooked her fingers. "Gimme, gimme."

The men's laughter made her feel happy. She hummed when the plate clicked down in front of her. Lifting the metal cover, steam rose from the packed omelet, the aroma twining around her like a vine growing on a tree. The first bite melted in her mouth. She flapped her left hand at the empty chair, patting Lorcan's arm when he settled into place. For a short time, silence ruled while she, Lorcan and Rogan savored the food and Sebastian sipped from the mug in his hand. Tempest shook her head at the offer of part of the omelet Sebastian had declined, wiped her mouth with a napkin, and sat back. Reaching over the side of the chair, she picked up the portfolio and rested it on her knee.

Lorcan stood and stacked empty dishes back onto the tray. He waved her offer of help away, taking the debris to the hallway and sitting the platter on the floor. He closed the door and returned to his seat. "Ben said he would send someone to pick it up later. He told me to be firm with you that you are not to touch it.

"Ben said Maggie and Gracie are doing fine although they stalk around his house looking for you. He understands your reasoning, but he said if you don't drop by in the next few days he'll come and get you. And Captain Collier and his people are in the medical building. He didn't want to disturb you when we arrived early this morning." Lorcan folded and refolded the napkin in front of him.

Rolling her eyes towards the ceiling, Tempest propped her elbow on the arm of the chair and her chin on her hand. The elephant was smelling extremely bad. "What does Watters want?" And to keep everyone on their toes, she eyeballed Sebastian. "Who is Kalia?"

The men were silent, each enveloped in their own pocket of apparent meditation. She cleared her throat and waited. "You can reflect on the navel of the Universe at another time. Oh, for god's sake." She huffed when the men jumped at the sound of her voice.

Lorcan took the lead. "It's complicated."

"Isn't that always the way it is." Tempest fluttered her eyelashes and smiled, thrumming her fingers against her cheek.

Rogan took control. "He's Kin. He's asking for sanctuary for a lot of people, maybe more than we can handle. And there's a potential threat involved which could impact our safety."

"Poppa Gammens is going to be thrilled with the extra work to build more houses. Margreet and Thomas need to know about the influx of people as soon as possible. She needs to purchase extra supplies and Thomas can start setting up temporary shelters and add the new homes to our master design." She picked up the pen, reopened the document and began a list. "I think our stash of cash," a grin winged across her mouth, "is low so get Jack and Gene to drop ship five of the two by four containers to us." She erased a line, absently raised the end of the pen to her mouth and teethed the end. "No, make that twelve containers. And tell them to start liquidating stocks and purchasing gold, silver, diamonds and the like, increase the purchase of property in this area, and take the last step on the Project. And close your mouths."

"Tempest, you need to think about this before you decide." Relief made Rogan's head light, and apprehension settled on his shoulders like a ten-ton concrete block.

"He's Kin. We Called. I just need to know when they'll arrive." Her voice became almost a whisper. "Should something go wrong tomorrow, Jack and Gene have my power of attorney and will follow through on these instructions. You have my power of attorney, Rogan, for everything else until it goes into trust. You'll be able to take care of everyone as trustee and executor of the trust."

"Tempest." Rogan's voice wavered. His eyes burned and he blinked rapidly to clear them.

"And that's enough of that." She managed a bright smile. "How much time do we have before Kin arrive?"

Lorcan cleared his throat. "Watters said …," his voice died for a moment as he swallowed his sadness. "We need to provide transportation which is going to be an issue since the camp's location is over two hundred miles from here. Isn't there any way to stop the Challenge?"

"Jack and Gene are searching the archives and consulting with Granville, Stoner & Regis, the law firm handling Grandmother's estate. They found a reference to the First Book of the Coven charters. The electronic form the Covens have been using is a revised version from 2000. Granville's private investigation firm is searching for the original."

"What good would it do since the rules have been changed?"

She inserted the pen in its pocket in the portfolio on the table, shut down the tablet and closed the cover. "Ah, but were the new rules ratified and approved by a majority of the Covens' members? Because of the Challenge, the attorneys have access to the Coven library. Their assistants have searched extensively online and book-by-book in the library. It has been determined every document creating a change in how the Covens work ends with the provision that, in any dispute, the First Book always takes precedence and all the Covens agreed the provision could never be deleted or amended in any way. We just have to find the damn thing, but we still have to keep moving forward as if it doesn't exist." She shrugged. "It may not exist. It could have been destroyed years ago."

"Or more recently." Lorcan's voice was hard and inflexible as steel.

She nodded in agreement. "Or more recently. Zook Fessler is checking around with some compatriots to see if they remember anything about it and where it might be."

Rogan's eyebrows lifted in surprise. "The Grande Marshall's mate? Is Peloquin involved with the hunt?"

"No. She doesn't know we're hunting it. Zook ran across one of our searches and offered his assistance. If Delia asks him about it, he said he'll stop all his own inquiries. He won't jeopardize her standing in the Covens." Tempest pushed out of her chair, stood to let the tingles in her legs dissipate, and walked toward the bed. She turned and paced back. "And that's the way it should be. I don't want anyone else dragged into the shooting box." She spun and headed back toward the bed.

Smiles flitted across Lorcan's and Rogan's faces. When Tempest was thinking, she had to move.

"I agree to provide Sanctuary to Kin." She stopped behind her chair and leaned on the back, her arms crossed along the top. "I know I said Thomas could add them to the master design here, but they can have another option. If they only want a place of safety, Poppa Gammens can build on that property we have in the southern part of the state. It's isolated enough where they can create their own community and integrate with this world at their own pace. Or they can bind themselves to our fate, integrate with our families, and work in our businesses, including fighting whatever battles that might come up, and they'll live here."

Lorcan glanced at Rogan, his eyes wide with amusement.

Rogan gave Lorcan an annoyed glance. "That seems to be the complication Lorcan was referring to earlier. You see … ." He didn't know what to say. He didn't know how he felt about the situation other than aggravation.

"It's not that complicated, Rogan." Lorcan meant to make a point. "I pledged my life and loyalty to you years ago when we made the transition to this world. You were and still are my Prince. You'll just be assuming the role you were born for: Hereditary-Regent, only on Terra-Nol."

Tempest's mouth fell open. Royalty. Well, if that wasn't a pile of horse pucky.

"He's right." Lazarus Watters leaned against the doorway, his arms crossed on his chest. "I knocked downstairs and the door swung open. I followed the voices. Please accept my apology for entering without permission. And the Second is correct. Branaugh is the Hereditary-Regent of the Tribes and its allies. He can bind us to whatever arrangements he wants."

Rogan jumped up. "Why would all those people follow what I say? A person they've never met. Brother to the men who have been committing atrocities against them and their families for years?" His voice rose until he was shouting.

"Half-brother." Watters firmly made the distinction. "Lineal descent comes through your mother's blood. The Calindras were the royal line, not your father and not his sons from his second wife. Bind us, Branaugh."

Rogan's laugh cut through the air. "Bind you to her?" He pointed at Tempest. "Earlier you showed contempt and disgust for her leadership. Now you want us to trust you with her life? That's a rather abrupt turnaround."

Watters straightened and paced across the floor. He dropped to one knee in front of Tempest and bowed his head. "I beg your pardon." He pulled a blade from a placket on the side of his synth-leather pants. Holding it in his right hand, point of the blade turned toward his chest, he laid it on the palm of his left and lifted it to Tempest. "I sacrifice my life as reparation and for sanctuary for my people."

Tempest stiffened, her face emotionless. Following a compulsion she tried to resist, she drew the blade across the palm of Watters hand as she accepted the knife. Blood flowed freely from the scratch. Her next words flowed from her mouth without her choosing. "Your debt is paid. Your Hereditary-Regent will choose for you." She took two steps back, drops of blood falling from the tip of the knife onto the carpet. "Your warrior has honor. I willingly accept him as one of mine if that's what you decide. What say you, Regent?" She agreed with the statements, but the loss of control worried her. She didn't need more strangeness in her life.

Rogan's mouth opened and closed like a fish in an

aquarium. He collected his scattered thoughts. "Initially, the people will be housed in temporary structures here. When they've had time to settle down and feel secure, they can decide for themselves what they want to do." Yes, it was the fair and equitable solution. They deserved freedom and the choices involved with that way of life.

"And what of the people who don't want what you call 'freedom'? What will you do about them? Will you abandon them?" Watters twisted as he rose until he faced Branaugh. He had to make Branaugh face the truth ... and his duties and responsibilities.

Tempest stepped into the breach. "Gentlemen, we have two weeks to decide who makes what decision. In the meantime, we have more immediate concerns. I suggest we dissolve this confab and move on. Rogan, please call Daire and fill him in on the arrangements for the Challenge." At her bedroom door, she turned and stabbed Sebastian with a look. "Who is Ren Boden?" She whirled and her footsteps echoed into the quiet room.

"Who!?!" Sebastian shouted.

# CHAPTER 33

Tempest reached the last movement in the first part of the kata, turned and brought the sword in her hands around, over her shoulder and pointed in front of her. She focused on the air, the scents around her, the turf beneath her boots, everything but the blade in her hands. Her movements had to be automatic; the metal had to become a part of her, an extension of her body and will. Slow ... slow movements, but here ... make it fast, effortless. Sweat dripped past the band around her forehead holding back her hair, sponging away most of the water escaping her body.

"Let me show you." The female voice whispered into Tempest's mind. "No." A firm push anchored Tempest in her body. "Watch me and follow my movements."

"Kalia." Tempest held her breath until the feeling of assent brushed her like a moth's wing. "Who the hell are you and how do you know Sebastian?" She murmured her thoughts aloud.

"We don't have time for that now. Here." Kalia planted the image of a stuffed parchment envelope in Tempest's head. "Let it open and seep into your consciousness. You'll learn what you need to know. But now you need my help. Let go of your control. I promise no harm will come to you."

Her gut instinct was to agree; she needed help from someone with practical experience, but trusting a stranger was difficult particularly after the feral-spark debacle. Slowly she relaxed. With a small sigh, she let go.

Kalia became a mirage superimposed over Tempest's body. Tempest staggered a few steps on the floor before moving with Kalia around the ring, slipping in and out of a fragile balance with the sword.

"You're trying too hard."

Tempest huffed with exasperation. "Sword play in a session with a teacher or friend is completely different than using one in a real fight. I much prefer blades to guns, but this is my first actual fight. There's no dodging a bullet. However, with sufficient skill, I can increase the odds of my winning."

Her eyes rolled up in her head. Layers of metallic flavors rolled across her tongue; fire consumed her aura; hammers pounded her into a new shape; and goose bumps erupted from her skin as cold water set her form. An infinitesimal bit of her soul broke off, trailed by a tiny rainbow-colored mote, and took up residence in the metal. A slender thread stretched taut between the blade and Tempest. It flickered then became solid and resilient. She staggered before catching her balance. "What the hell did you just do?"

"Nothing. I did nothing. The Goddess and Consort have blessed you. Name it." Kalia moved her fingers in benediction. "To make it yours and control it, you have to name it. Stay alive. Keep the Patriarch alive. We're coming." She withdrew.

"Timebender." The name whirled into her mind. Tempest blew the word into the shiny alloy. She flowed around the ring, one movement following the next ... only Tempest and the steel – its outward projection stiff, straight, sharp; the inward reality: fiery, molten, flowing into hidden cracks and potentialities.

A sharp beep impinged on her awareness. She felt energized, refreshed. She boogied to the bleacher and snatched a towel from the padded seat. Swiping at dripping sweat, she flicked a button and read the datacomp screen. Goth and his Cote had arrived.

Rogan had agreed with her decision to leave half the

Coteries behind to protect their home. The remainder had already filtered into Transylvania, the permanent home of Kale & Keasley Circus. The three enclosed perma-crete rings fronted a wild animal sanctuary. It was unlikely any snipers would set up inside the refuge, but Goth and his team would hunt them out. As the best in the world, Goth and his men would search out the optimal locations and remove any pests from their hidey-holes.

"Tempest." The voice boomed across the expanse followed by a short, slender figure dressed in a grey Armani suit with a burgundy shirt peeking from between the lapels. As he approached, small lions, tigers and bears embroidered in gold appeared on the maroon tie between thin black stripes.

A delighted smile bloomed on Tempest's face. "Barnabus! It's so good to see you." She raised her hand in front of her body shaking her head and laughing. "Don't come any closer. I'm pouring sweat and that's a designer suit." The bubbles inside her wanted to overrule her head and hug the dapper man. "Thanks, Barnabus, for letting us use your home."

"It is my pleasure, Tempest. I wish there was more that I can do. Nemesis is traveling with the summer show this year. He will be devastated to learn he was not here for you."

"I'm sorry, too. Tell him I'll see him when he's back. Are things going well?" She let her gaze slide past the infinitesimal tremor in his hands to look into his blank happy eyes.

"Yes, of course." He shook his head, the gay façade fading. "I never could lie well. It is a hindrance in many situations." The sigh gusted out like the gale force winds of a hurricane. "Keasley is retiring. He has triggered the withdrawal clause in our partnership agreement." He waved a hand. "It is nothing. We are ready to assist you however you need in this dishonorable charade."

Tempest rubbed a finger along her nose. "How long did Keasley give you to come up with the money? That's why Nemesis is on the road tour, isn't it?"

"Tempest, really, it is not your concern. We can talk of

this another day."

She turned to the seats and began stuffing her things into the carryall while a litany of assets raced through her mind: the wildlife sanctuary, the performing animals as well as those rescued from intolerable situations, the artistes and their families, and the one hundred acres of prime real estate. "Who's offering to be an Angel?" She stabbed him with her insight.

"No Angels, Tempest. A European coalition has offered Keasley many millions for his forty-nine percent interest and a substantial bonus if he can persuade me to sell them at least two percent of my share."

"Ah. They would have control of the circus. Are they aware that the partnership doesn't include the sanctuary and real estate?"

"It does not matter. My people are part of the partnership agreement. The land is unimportant compared to their health and welfare. But I have a backup plan for the animals. It's not optimal, but they will be safe and I can provide resources for their care. One of the high wire acts made a last minute check of their equipment before a performance. The flyers discovered the lines and nets loosened. Someone could have been seriously injured or killed. I cannot play Russian roulette with my family. I cannot." Tears glimmered in his eyes.

"What does Keasley say?" She rubbed a small towel across her face, down her arms and wiped her hands.

He shrugged and turned sideways to lean against the railing beside the seats. "He sees dollar signs; more dollar signs than he could ever have imagined. He must look after himself and his family. Who am I to judge his actions?"

She breathed out. "How long do you have left?"

"Six weeks to raise five million dollars. But the Coalition will offer more. I will not be able to outbid them."

She took his shoulders in her hands. She had done her best to clean up as much as she could. Whatever residue remained, well, he could dry clean his suit. "You have a written agreement,

Barnabus. Keasley has to follow the terms of the agreement."

"But ..." Hope flickered then died in his face.

"There is no 'but.' Don't do anything." She shook him. "Can I use your office for a few minutes?"

A resigned look settled on his features. "Yes, of course. Walk with me."

Tempest looped an arm in his, tossed the strap of her bag over her shoulder and tenderly grasped Timebender in her hand. She pulled Barnabus into motion. "I'm going to contact Jack and Gene. Have you been doing all the negotiations yourself?" At his nod, she continued, "You have a new partner and Jack and Gene can finish the transaction with Keasley. And if Nemesis doesn't want to be on tour, bring him home." She jerked to a stop, a blush washed over her face. "I'm sorry, Barnabus. I didn't mean to just take over. If you want to handle this differently ...," her voice trailed off.

Barnabus gently patted the hand on his arm. "I accept the help, but it is not necessary for you to give us more money. Your support of the sanctuary through the years is more than enough. I want to return the funds wired to the business account for use of the ring."

"We can structure it like a loan, Barnabus, if you want, but I really want to be your partner." She squinted in the morning sunshine. A catalog of recent events flipped by in her mind. "No. You're right. It's better your name isn't linked to mine in a major way. I'll let Jack and Gene work out the details."

He turned her to face him. This time his hands were on her shoulders. "What is this? Why are you backpedaling?"

"It's the better way." Her voice stuttered as he shook her.

"Tell me the truth." He tightened his fingers.

Her eyes fell to the grass. "There's a lot going on, Barnabus. There are adversaries popping up everywhere, unexpected powerful immigrants, and some really out there strangers." Her laugh was caustic. "You need to keep your distance to protect yourself and your family. But I will help you."

His laugh was bitter. "You help me, but you won't let me help you. If Nemesis were here, he would box your ears. So I will do it for him ... metaphorically speaking, of course." He felt her body stiffen beneath his hands. "If you truly desire to become a partner, my family and I wish it. There will be much relief and calls for a great celebration. We'll begin the preparations. And when you are done with the foolish business that brought you here, we will sing, dance and drink tomorrow into being."

Since he was only an inch taller than she was, it was easy to slip from beneath his hands and plant a quick kiss on his mouth. "To seal the bargain." She stepped back ... into a flesh wall.

"And what are we arranging?"

Tempest jumped at Rogan's voice beside her ear.

"Whoa, my lady! What the hell is that thing?" Rogan moved his hand back and forth above the sword clutched in Tempest's hand. Power surged outward pushing his hand away forming an aggressive ring around her figure.

She whirled around facing both men. Sebastian, Lorcan and Strider were several paces away. "Uh. Keasley wants out so we're buying his part of the circus. Wanna' become a performer? I bet Barnabus could create an act for us." Her teeth gleamed white in the filtered light.

He frowned but let her omission about the blade pass. She would tell him when she was ready. "You need to eat. Thomas has arrived with a couple of assistants and a truck full of supplies in tow. He's setting up in the Tent to cook for us. You're welcome to join us, Barnabus." The Tent was actually a solid structure, the exterior carved, shaped and painted to resemble a circus tent.

"Thank you, Rogan, but I have already eaten, and I must send some documents to my new advisors and talk with Tallman about preparing a feast for our celebrations tonight." He threw a general wave at the group and walked away, head up and whistling a low tune.

"You're using the commingled accounts for the buy-in, aren't you?" Rogan felt a little sting of energy and glanced at the sword at her side from the edge of his eye.

Tempest scuffed her foot across the grass. "I was going to use my accounts. Everyone doesn't have to be involved."

He pushed against the limits of the field around her and used a finger to lift her chin. "Use the combined funds." Rogan put an arm around Tempest's shoulders and tugged her beneath his arm. The unusual force from the sword disappeared. "How are you feeling today?"

"I'd like it better if I could clean up and change before eating."

Rogan looked over his shoulder. "Anyone want to wait to eat while Tempest showers and redresses?"

A boisterous laugh burst from Tempest at the loud, emphatic chorus of "noes".

# CHAPTER 34

"Coven Offensive Protectors are arriving. The Primes are here in full force and there are a few Omegas checking in. Delia Peloquin and her Tacticals came through ten minutes ago."

"Has Daire or my father arrived yet?" Tempest lounged on the sofa. The soft Egyptian cotton robe covered her from neck to past her toes. An occasional spike of bristling energy from Timebender resting on the cushions beside her bounced her hand up and down like the flow of air against her hand held outside the window of a moving vehicle.

Feeds from cameras – hand-held, hovercams, and mounted at various places throughout the compound – cycled through in ten second intervals on the six, thirty-two inch laser screens on the wall across the room. Additional cameras linked to monitors in special areas in other rooms allowed two people to watch assigned pictures. Every hour, the observers rotated out to keep fresh eyes scanning the incoming images for anomalies.

Tempest jerked upright and rolled off the sofa. She scrambled to her feet, rubbing her hip where she had rolled across the sword. "That's Nemesis! Ro, move the camera back! It's Nemesis!" The robe tangled around her feet and she stumbled several feet towards the monitor before catching her balance.

"Dorrie said Nemesis is with the summer tour, but you said you told Barnabus to bring him home early. He's just here sooner than expected." Moving away from the table where a three dimensional grid of the entire complex had been created, a wave of green and blue dots flickered at the edge of Rogan's view. He murmured instructions into the dotmitter hidden beneath the skin of his shoulder. It was their first live test for the grid with the bioscanner component and the transmitter implanted in his body. The hardware was stable, but the software was still buggy as evidenced by the gold blob hanging at the corner of the model.

"No, Ro. It wasn't right; he wasn't right. It was all wrong somehow."

"Where did you see him?"

"The site just cycled through again and he's gone. But I know it was him, Ro. I know it."

"Calm down. I believe you. Did you catch the camera number on the screen?"

"No." She drew in deep breaths. Her eyes riveted to the flashing pictures.

"You're hyperventilating. You're going to pass out if you don't stop." He stood behind her, massaging the muscles in her shoulders.

"That one. It's that one: 229749."

"All right." He stopped the rotation and studied the image. "Nothing appears out of place. Maisie, step back on camera 229749 about five minutes, loop it to Station One, and play forward."

Tempest jittered around on her toes. "There … stop there. Who are those men with him?" She raised her voice. "Maizie, zoom in on the faces of the men and run them through our databases."

"Tell the others you have priority access." Rogan smoothed a calming hand over Tempest's hair. "The line to Summerfield has been tied up periodically."

"I want to talk to Barnabus." She looked around the room searching for the communicators.

Rogan grabbed her arm, halting her headlong rush to the bureau beside the door. "Thanks, Maizie. Release the camera for normal operation." He pulled Tempest to a desktop monitor.

"Those men popped up quickly because we have them on our 'watch' list. They have ties to Valmont. Why would Coven guards be escorting one of Barnabus' performers? What exactly did you and Barnabus discuss about Keasley's buy-out?"

"He said there was a European coalition with unlimited funds who wanted controlling interest in the circus. The only thing I could think of is they believe the land is covered by the partnership agreement."

"Did he give you a name?"

"No." She pushed her hair behind her ears. The alarm on the clock sitting on the desk chirped like an angry bird startling Tempest. "Barnabus and Nemesis will have to wait. I have to get ready."

She scooped up Timebender as she walked past the sofa and slipped behind the screen positioned in the corner of the room, laying the sword across the arms of the chair sharing the small space. She caught up a bandeau from the seat of a bench, bent over and wound it around her hair. Swinging upright, she faced the mirror tucking stray curls beneath the wrap. She wouldn't win any pageants, but the special material would keep an opponent from using her hair against her.

"Are you sure I need this much padding?" She pulled the trousers on, squatted several times, and made some lunges.

"Yes."

"Okay." The daring, blue, long-sleeved top molded every bump and curve on her torso. She clasped her hands at her waist and twisted. "I love this outfit, Ro. Order me some more."

Her teeth caught her lip as she realized what she had said. It was good to be positive as long as it didn't become overconfidence. A spark of dread rose on tiny wings like a firefly in a summer's night sky. She squashed it down. One spark could become a conflagration and she needed her focus on winning. She bowed her head and prayed to the Goddess and Consort for protection of all her family and friends. A warm feeling like a hand caressing her heart passed through her.

She looked into her eyes in the mirror and with a brisk nod of her head she turned, picked up the blade and strode around the side of the screen. "Let's do this."

Tempest waited for Rogan's signal before leaving the room. Maizie and Carson were waiting outside. "Hey, Carson, did you complete the Bessmer contract already?"

"I told the president of the company people were being rotated so he was covered by individuals who were rested. Blake and I wanted to be here when this went down."

She patted his chest and touched Maizie's arm. "Thanks. You'll be protected no matter what happens." She walked away quickly before they could say anything.

Turning the corner at the end of the hallway, she looked back. Carson and Maizie were standing in the doorway, solemn expressions on their faces. She waved and with a resolute set to her shoulders marched out of sight.

"Jake is here with the mobile surgery and his main surgical team. Bloodhawk will be moving around outside the boundaries of the smaller ring staying as close to you as possible. He says his saliva contains a coagulant. As long as it's not a heart blow, he believes he will be able to control any bleeding." Rogan opened a door midway down the corridor nodding to Jeffers and Cree standing on either side. "We're taking the underground passage. Jake got a blood sample from Bloodhawk and our researchers are looking into finding a way to duplicate the results with a topical binding agent."

Tempest frowned. "I don't want Sebastian used ..."

"It's all right, Tempest. I mentioned the same thing and Bloodhawk said he thought it was a reasonable request. He wants to be helpful. Donating body fluids is a small matter." He pulled her back as Cree ghosted past them onto the landing and down the flight of stairs. "His words, Tempest, not mine."

Cree appeared at the bottom of the stairs and nodded. Tempest led the way through the door with Rogan close behind. Jeffers closed, locked the door and resumed his stance at the entrance.

"Everyone is being searched before entering the pavilion." Rogan nodded to the men and women standing at intervals along the corridor. "Since we chose swords, we can confiscate everything that isn't a blade. There are some very unhappy people and many protests, but those stopped when they were given a copy of the rules of conduct for a Challenge direct from the revised Charters." He cleared his throat. "Your father arrived a few minutes ago. He was alone. D'eath brought a small contingent and they're near Delia. He said he sent his Tacticals to protect the access roads to Summerfield. I alerted Ben."

"He needs those fighters to protect his lands and people." She closed her eyes for a second. "Okay. You told him the same thing and he said everything was covered." She gave him a sideways look. "Where's Watters?"

A flurry of emotions flashed across Rogan's face. "Haven't seen or heard from him. He took off on his Dart without a word." He laid a hand on her arm. "Wait."

Cree moved past them. He dropped back, his carbine raised to his shoulder, watching the exit open. Lorcan stepped through, holding it open, bracing his back against the metal. Judah was just beyond, facing forward, his weapon cradled in his arms scrutinizing a well-lit tunnel between concrete walls painted in multi-hues of orange like a sunrise on a spring morning.

"Goth cleared this area. He and his group are staying close. He said his spine prickles." The lines between Lorcan's brows were deep slashes. "All access to the grounds is now closed. It's been around ten minutes since the last person came through." He shook his head slightly at Rogan. Like Rogan, he had hoped Watters and some of their Kin would arrive as backup.

The men formed a barrier around Tempest and moved her swiftly through the passage. Her breath caught at the sight of the people in the stands, filling the seats to capacity. She glanced around and her heart stuttered. Her father was standing in the area reserved for her fighters. She blushed when he sent her a fleeting smile, a proud look. A movement in the stands on the far side of the building distracted her. She stopped abruptly and stumbled into Lorcan's back when Judah, who was looking up and around, ran into her.

Rogan's hand steadied her. She reversed her motion stepping on Judah's boots and pushing him backwards. "There're children out there, Ro! Why would parents bring their children into a situation where there's danger, blood and possible death?"

The men tossed a grimace back and forth. Rogan glowered at his companions then smoothed his face. "Did you see any females?"

"Yeah. I did. Delia and the other Beldames and ... some of the Coven Thralls and ...." She threw her hands on her hips. "No. There weren't any young girls or wives. I'm a lesson? Those bigots are using the Challenge as entertainment? Fine. Well, just fine then. Let's get this damn show started." She shoved through the tall bodies and strode into the ring.

The circus' riggers had repositioned the floodlights for the center ring to illuminate the inside of the small arena on the left side. Tempest stomped to the middle of the space, stopped beneath a spotlight, planting her feet, legs braced apart. She glistened in her cobalt blue top and pants like the sea along Mediterranean beaches. Timebender thrummed hungrily when Tempest removed the sheath from its face. She rested the tip of the blade in the turf in front of her, hands clasped at top of the hilt.

Rogan and Lorcan joined her beneath the lights taking positions on either side. Rogan removed the sheath from her hand. "Focus solely on your opponent. Bloodhawk will make sure he's in the right place at the right time to help you." His voice was just loud enough for Tempest to hear.

Delia Peloquin walked to the center of the floor and raised a hand. The low rumbling of many voices dwindled away. "Challenge was issued and accepted. Challenged has appeared at the time and place agreed upon. Challenger must come forth now or forever renounce his claim."

Minutes passed. Displeasure covered Delia's face. Her skin itched with vague warnings floating in the air currents. "Challenger has failed to show. I declare ..."

"Not so fast, Grande Marshall." Treadaway strolled forward. He was in his element, the center of attention.

Tempest relaxed deeper into earth and metal. She lifted an inquiring brow at the flash of white behind Treadaway's smarmy smile. Satisfaction filled her seeing the smirk replaced by clenched jaws at her apparent lack of concern. She held her breath as a mean pleased expression settled on his features.

"Challenger is here." Treadaway motioned towards the darkness with his hand. "And this is my Champion." He lightened his shields ... and swallowed the shock and rage flooding the atmosphere, savoring the heady brew.

"No!" Tempest surged forward raising Timebender to shoulder height, but hands on her arms stopped her. She gritted her teeth watching Nemesis being escorted into the space by three guards: one on either side and the last trailing behind him. His gaze was impassive, no hint of recognition in his eyes, when he was turned to confront her. Rogan blocked her sight as he moved around her. She wanted to resist Lorcan's attempt to drag her back, but she followed his cues. She wanted to turn and walk away from this farce, but with so many lives involved that was impossible ... or was it? How the hell had the bladesmaster been coerced into representing Treadaway?

She listened to Rogan arguing. She couldn't hear the words, only his tone which lowered and deepened to a rough growl. The shadows outside the arena shifted and spewed forth the members of the Ruling Council. They gathered around the opponents. The volume rose close to shouting, but the words remained garbled. Rogan broke away from the assembly with clenched fists, his knuckles turning white.

He stood in front of her, hiding her reaction from the enemies behind, knowing Lorcan protected his back. "The majority of the Council voted Treadaway is within his rights. Since you haven't lived with your parents for years, Treadaway is basing his choice on the fact your father has met Barnabus at some point." He responded to the puzzlement in her eyes. "Because Robert Phillips knows Barnabus and Nemesis is a subordinate of Barnabus, they decided Nemesis is distantly linked to the Covens. It's enough of a connection to satisfy the rules of the Charter. Delia disagrees, but she was overruled as being biased in your favor."

She hissed. "I'm not fighting Nemesis, Ro."

He got in her face. "You don't have a choice."

"Everyone's got a choice. The Council has declared me rogue many times. We don't need Grandmother's estate."

Rogan wanted to shake her, but loss of control in the current situation would only lead to serious repercussions. "Think past the obvious, Tempest. Your grandmother had something Treadaway wants. Yes, he wants to destroy you if he can, but there's a larger agenda. I wouldn't press this if I wasn't sure it's something we need."

She stuffed Timebender into Lorcan's hand ignoring his panicked inhalation. She shook out her hands dissipating the buildup of energy. Ignoring everything and everyone but Rogan, she took four steps right, turned and retraced her route stomping her feet. The fizz and sparkles were scattering. "You're right. Okay. Mikuh would know. And since the revelation about the secret passage in her office, he's been replaying all their conversations so he'll be able to tell us if she was hiding something even from him. Be sure Sebastian and Jake are close, Ro. If ..."

Rogan gripped her shoulder hard. "Stay alive. Keep moving. You've fought against each other. You know his strengths and weaknesses just as he knows yours. It should be a standoff in terms of advantages. He has a longer reach, but you're smaller, quicker. Use it. And use that thing in Locan's hands to exploit every vulnerability." He leaned in. "You have to trust Nemesis to keep himself from harm. He knows the stakes in this game we're playing."

Delia's voice rang out. "Time. Challenger-Elect and Challenged, take your places in the middle of the ring."

Tempest gathered the blade from a white-faced Lorcan. She gave him a sympathetic look. "Sorry, Lorcan. I didn't know it would hurt you."

"What is that ... thing?" Lorcan snarled at Rogan watching Tempest step toward her opponent.

Shouts from the head of the tunnel distracted Rogan, causing him to miss the first feint. The clanging of steel against steel seized his attention drawing his gaze to the two fighters. Tempest dropped and rolled past the arc of the descending sword. The blue sleeve along her right forearm bloomed red.

Curses and the splats of fists against skin echoed across the floor from the darkness of the passageway. A solitary figure burst from the mouth. "Grande Marshall! Stop the Challenge! I have proof!" Morgan Reynolds waved a thin book above his head.

Rogan slapped Lorcan on the shoulder, nodded to the entrance then turned, took two running steps toward Tempest, and found himself on the ground. Shaking his dazed head, he saw Tempest and Nemesis, back to back, twisting and turning, their swords flashing as they wove a steel barrier around themselves holding back five strangers. He pushed to his knees, and finally to his feet.

Four men surrounded him, evenly spaced five feet apart, in the shape of a diamond. Each man aimed his left palm toward the right palm of the next man. Bound. They had enclosed him in an Elemental Diamond. Only Kin could do that. His head snaked around searching for Watters.

Bloodhawk was at the point where two stands came together, facing out, fighting three men. Daire and his people were with Zook Fessler protecting Delia Peloquin and Robert Phillips; a large contingent of fighters slowed their progress to an exit. But no sign of Watters. His eyes jerked to Tempest at her cry of pain. A stranger pulled a sword from her shoulder and raised it overhead in preparation for a killing blow.

# CHAPTER 35

A three dimensional hologram hovered in front of the portal in the ship's outer shell in the command center. The blast doors were open giving the officers and crew members a view of the new stars. Four squads of fighters were investigating three worlds the boards indicated were capable of supporting life. The system was one Lightgate from their destination.

"Countdown to Colonizers in three ... two ... one. Colonizers shifting now."

Kalia sauntered past the captain's chair and braced her legs apart in front of the image. "Chicopee, please ask Captain Drakken to watch his drift." She studied the picture and nodded.

"Incoming, sir!"

The replica ships in the holograph bobbed up and down like a float at the end of a fishing line. Massive vessels popped through the Lightgate, their positions blooming on the imager. The battle cruiser's stabilizers hummed and dischargers crackled. A surge overwhelmed the capacitors. The energy whipped out catching Kalia in its grip. The hologram buzzed and swelled to encompass the bridge; the picture fuzzed then cleared. Figures replaced the black and white canvass of the star system.

Kalia reached for the sword at her side, ducking away from the snarling fighter sprinting toward her, but her fingers found empty space. She rushed to the command seat and grabbed the first blade from the special holder on the right side. She turned and gasped when he ran through her. Her eyes flew to a cluster of three. A sharp pain struck her heart. He looked so much like her parents – the same bone structure, the curve of the mouth. Sebastian Bloodhawk, the originator of their Lair. He was taller than she expected, heavier in the chest, and his arms and legs were more muscular, but the hair color was the same. She wondered if his eyes were the piercing blue of the canid breed of the northern mountains – the color that had branded their Lair as mavericks.

She crouched, snarling as a third man crept along the side wall. The two warriors shifted and Bloodhawk turned with them.

"Captain?" ComTech Chicopee Bloodmoon twirled her seat. She half-rose to her feet but resettled on the edge of the cushion when Kalia drew the sword from the side of her chair. Chicopee gestured the other command officers against their consoles. Keeping Kalia in sight, her fingers automatically found the call sequence on her control board. "Commander Wolfanger, report back to Rampart Prime immediately. Please respond."

She shook her head and mouthed "no" at the young CenTac inching along the metal panels. Urgency to stop the oncoming wrackage added fervor to her voice. "Wolfanger, respond now. Commander Bloodstar, report to Rampart Prime."

"Wolfanger receiving. I'm twenty sectims out. Kenton, where are you?"

"Eighteen sectims out. Bloodmoon, what's happening?"

"When the Colonizers shifted, we had the usual disturbances. The capacitors and stabilizers kicked in. There was an overload." Chicopee could hear her voice rising.

She shook her head at the CenTac again, scanning the bridge for help from one of the other officers. The hologram was expanding, eating up the open space. No one was close enough to outrun the machine and they couldn't enter the image without causing worse problems for their Captain.

"There was a breach in the imager's protocols." She licked her lips. "There's something weird going on. We've got visuals from some type of battle. It must be from that new world. The backlash has trapped the Captain in the action. She's reacting to the images as if she's part of the fighting. Tac Graelan, don't interfere. She'll slice you to shreds."

"Ram, I can't get through to Kee. Her shields are up and my pathway to her mind is barricaded."

"It's the same for me. Fifteen sectims out." Ram reported to the bridge.

"Ready bays eight and twelve. We're coming in hot. Ram, take bay eight. I'm using bay twelve. I'm a few sectims ahead and we should arrive at the bridge at the same time. Bloodmoon, whoever is trying to interfere, tell them to back off and that's an order." He heard her voice echoing his command. Kenton tightened the harness across his chest and activated the force field on his seat. "Ten sectims out."

"Commander Wolfanger, you are rerouted to bay fifteen; the deck on bay eight is fouled. Repeat. The deck on bay eight is fouled."

"How long until it's clear?" There must have been an unscheduled shift change; it wasn't Decks Master Garitt Stoneracer's voice. Kenton would likely be able to handle the situation, but Ram was wary. The closer they came to Bloodhawk and his Reciprocate the more unpredictable Kee's actions were becoming. He and Kenton had to resolve the situation soon. He would find some way to break whatever bond was developing between Kee and the Patriarch and his Reciprocate.

"Reroute to bay fifteen, Wolfanger. The debris is too large to allow access."

"Rerouting." He trusted the Decks Master whether it was Stoneracer or a replacement. "Now ten sectims out."

Ryley Bloodmoon strolled across the metal floor behind Bristan Merkayle, the Decks Master's third in command. In an offhand move, the bar in his hand thunked the door of the waste removal room.

Garitt Stoneracer shouldered opened the hatch, head down, fingers buckling the belt at his waist. His eyebrows lifted when he looked up but saw no one nearby. He dismissed the incident and reconnected to the network catching a word or two as the burbles from all the inflowing channels passed by.

"Uh, Desks Master Stoneracer, sir." Ryley edged away from the side of the parts cabinet where he had been out of Merkayle's view. He was taking a risk going outside the chain of command. His Aunt Chicopee had drilled into him the right way to address officers and instructed him to keep his head down and stay out of the widespread politics which were a part of any organization. And he had. He volunteered for extra duty so he could improve his station but when he sensed even a hint of dissension he found another place to be. But this time he couldn't walk away. The Captain and Commanders were legends. Not that he wanted any of that kind of action, but they were the Lair's leaders and good ones.

Garitt smiled at the youngster. Bloodmoon was from a well-placed family, but he was coming along fine. He'd make a good deck officer if only Garitt could keep the boy out of the fighters. "Bloodmoon."

Ryley threw his shoulders back. "Sir. Commanders Wolfanger and Bloodstar have been called back and are at full throttle."

A puzzled frown pleated Garitt's forehead. "Merkayle is on the deck. I'll get his report in a few sectims."

"There's a problem on the bridge with the Captain, Sir. Aunt Chicopee needs the Commanders' help. The Decks Master has redirected Commander Wolfanger to bay fifteen. Damnit, sir, the Captain's in trouble."

Garitt stopped the rotating channels and listened to the chatter in the command center. He ran towards his flight console eyeballing the end of the shaft as he raced past. Caden Nightshade's fighter balanced at the edge of the entrance to the bay. Garitt planned to investigate why an experienced fighter pilot missed the runway. It wasn't impossible, just improbable. He noted the force shields still in place and a group of men huddled at the damaged bird's side.

He scanned the information flowing across the screens on the console in front of him. He snapped out a hand and pressed an icon slowing the stream of data. A frown etched his brow when he saw half the communications system shut down. Garitt searched out Merkayle, noting a satisfied smile hanging on the man's mouth.

Garitt caught the eyes of two SecTacs and with a few flicks of his fingers sent them to stand close to Merkayle. He activated his override, locking the systems to his commands only and opened a system wide channel. "Gentlemen, we have fighters coming in on an emergency. Clear the shaft. Tractor Eleven, push the fighter over the side." He nodded with appreciation, watching Nightshade shove the men into motion and directing the tractor towards his aircraft. "All ships give us a twenty point radius. Salvager Sorrel, get pinters out and surround the bird we're releasing with emitters; handle it Priority One. Commander Wolfanger, you are cleared for bay eight. Confirm your approach."

Relief caused Ram to shudder. "Two sectims to touchdown."

Good, Garitt thought, there was just enough time.

"Ram, I'm down and headed for the lifts. Good landing." Kenton slammed through the closing doors. "Bridge."

"Bloodmoon," Garitt said in a calm voice, "get the main lift down and hold it ready for the Commander." He clasped his right wrist with the fingers of his left hand, grunting approval when the SecTacs closed on Merkayle. The struggling men staggered to the maintenance lift and disappeared.

Ram hit the deck running. He threw up a hand to Decks Master Stoneracer, clapped Bloodmoon on the shoulder, and slammed into the transport. He stepped out sectims later to find Kenton cycling open the door to the bridge. Ram followed Kenton, his eyes sweeping around. He noted the crew's positions through the barely there forms in the light wave consuming the room.

\*\*\*\*\*

Rogan reached inside himself and yanked energy from a silver ocean, throwing it against the invisible walls around him. The barricade wavered. Watters appeared in the ring shoving men into an opposing diamond pattern outside the first group. The barrier strengthened. Rogan crouched. A blur of wings materialized around him. In a surge of energy, the men tumbled backward and the shield fell.

\*\*\*\*\*

"Damn you, you frizbragins!" Kalia's knees buckled. Golden bolts struck the floor around her. Ram and Kenton charged the shimmering veil their faces grimacing with pain as they broke through. Kenton fell to his knees in front of Kalia and pulled her up into his arms. Ram knelt behind her pressing his chest against her back, clasping Kenton's upper arms, feeling Kenton's hands squeezing above his elbows.

The imager crackled, popped and the hologram disintegrated. The field around them began to spin, faster and faster, rising above their heads, a thin tail growing below a wide mouth. It spun and dropped down over them flooding their bodies. The trio collapsed to the floor.

"The aliens are trying to kill Sebastian's Reciprocate." Kalia managed a whisper. "If she dies, he dies. And with him, the Lair dies." Her voice strengthened, became hard as stone. "I will not allow it to happen. We all appear to be bound to one fate and I choose life. Sebastian must be protected." She laid a trembling finger on Kenton's pulse, heard him grunt then clasped Ram's wrist draped over her waist. His hand turned and threaded fingers with hers.

"Captain."

Kalia looked up into Chicopee's worried eyes. "We

appear to be okay." She moistened her lips. "How is the ship?" "We're in one piece, sir. The systems are functioning within parameters." She stepped back withdrawing her helping hand, watching Kenton and Ram push to their feet and lift Kalia to hers.

"Contact the Colonizers. Get the tech teams to work reassembling the fighters mothballed in their holds. Have half the supply ships move their goods into the empty holds and refit for receipt of the new fighters." She leaned against Ram with Kenton at her back.

*****

The basso roar of enraged beasts reverberated around the theater from several directions. The fighting stopped abruptly. Barnabus appeared in one exit with two orange and black tigers straining against the leashes in his hands. At another exit, a female figure followed growling, hissing black leopards. White tigers emerged from the shadows at the end of the building towing another shape.

Morgan pushed through the huddle around him, using his left hand to wipe the blood from his mouth. His look of disgust and threat stopped Treadaway who moved out of his way. He shouted toward the stands. "It's a lie. All these years and you've forced us to live a lie! Submission, Thralls ... all of it."

Morgan stood in front of the Ruling Council. "You knew!" he accused. He glowered at each one, identifying the knowledgeable ones by the arrogance of their stance, the guilt in their eyes. "This is the real Charter." He shook it in the air. "And Challenge isn't allowed ... EVER! That rule is immutable. All the Covens agreed ... to protect the bloodlines. You are foresworn!"

"Peace, young one." Delia leaned against Zook, ignoring his second who was bandaging her arm. "Let me see the book."

Morgan backed away. He darted a glance around, a shaky breath escaping when Lorcan and Strider appeared at his shoulders. He allowed them to guide his steps to Tempest. The book fell from his fingers. "Oh, gods, Tempest." He dropped to his knees at her side. Tears rolled down his cheeks.

Sebastian leaned back, red smeared across his chin. Daire supported her head and shoulders. Her eyelashes were long fringes on the white skin of her face. Blood swirled black across the blue lace covering her breast.

"Get out of my way! That tunnel is big enough for a truck. Someone get the mobile in here stat!" Jake shoved Sebastian away. "Lay her down, D'eath." He went through the motions quickly, his jitters settling. "She's going to be okay, Morgan. Let Dana take a look at those cuts." He looked around for his assistants. "Call the rest of the team in here and get started mopping up the blood."

"I've got it, Morgan."

He heard Strider, felt the pat on his arm, but his fingers continued to scrabble over the floor. His breathing settled, his focus came back when Strider tucked the book into his hand. He shifted as the female doctor settled beside him and shrugged her away. "I'm okay." He didn't feel the blood dripping down his face, arms and side.

With the physical fighting stopped, Barnabus handed the leashes for his tigers to their guardian and signaled the others away. He watched their exit to make sure there were no problems before turning and rushing to Nemesis sitting on the rim forming the boundary of the small ring. He placed his shoulder beneath the towering bulk and hauled Nemesis to his feet. "Thank you, but our doctor will handle this." He waved away the young woman hurrying towards them with a medical bag in her hand. "You must go and attend to the other wounded. I will be back later to check on Tempest." Uptight fighters with raised weapons barred all approaches to the huddle around Tempest. There was nothing he could do to help right now.

The sharp splat of a fist against skin and the thud of a body hitting the ground jerked heads around. "What the fuck were you doing?" Rogan bellowed. He was so furious he shook. "Get up!"

Watters rubbed his jaw and stayed on the ground where he had landed. If it was the King or the brothers, he would have rolled away and come up in a fighting stance. Weak combatants faced kicking and pummeling until the King decided otherwise even if they submitted. But Branaugh. He was a different kind of man. "If you die, the gate remains open. Our people die. The King and his sons invade this world, millions die and anyone remaining is subjugated to the vagaries of madmen. Is that what you want?"

"Lazarus is right." A light whirring and the rising of a two-foot tall female body in front of Rogan accompanied the soft feminine voice. "We aided you because it was wrong of Lazarus to imprison you in dual Diamonds." She turned accusing eyes on Watters who refused her gaze. The leather-clad, small figure shoved a glowing blade into a hide-like sheath belted around her waist. Her scorching look included Rogan. "But you are also wrong for risking your life and all our lives and the lives of our people in this manner." She waved her arms around, ignoring the ducking heads of several of her guards, to encompass a circle of twenty Kin and an equal number of demi-Folk.

Rogan's anger had faded, but it blazed higher, hotter. "That woman bleeding on the floor over there is my family."

"We are your family." The delicate but inflexible voice retaliated.

"Where were you ...." Rogan stopped. He shook his head. With a growl, he turned away.

"Do NOT turn your back on me." The susurration of metal on leather drifted over the sounds of continuous movement in the ring.

The small female fluttered back from Rogan who spun around and stalked toward her. Buzzing saturated the air as a dozen demi-Folk charged forward circling the petite woman. Watters rose like a puppet on a string. He bowed to the woman then turned to Rogan. "You haven't been properly introduced."

Rogan sissed through his teeth. "I don't have time for this."

Watters closed on Rogan, grasping and squeezing his forearm. "Let me present you to Nateesha Rosamund Dumont, Queen of the Nobelling Flair." He pulled Rogan into a bow with him then released his stubborn Regent.

"Queen Dumont, long life to you and your Flair. If you will excuse me, my friend, my leader, my family, lies bleeding on the floor. I must also find out how many of our fighters are hurt or dead. And we have a controversy to settle. Queen Dumont … ma'am." Irony plastered his final words. He backed away with a nod, skimmed around on the ball of one foot and strode away cursing under his breath with every stride.

"Our Regent is quite unruly, but there's very good material to work with." The Queen scattered her warriors with a toss of her head. "Very good material indeed. We return to the camp. The gate must close before the dark of the moon of this world. You know what you have to do." Faster than a hummingbird, she swept away, her bodyguards quickly surrounding her.

# CHAPTER 36

Treadaway lounged against the side of the stands at the east exit of the stadium eyeing the activity. He folded his arms across his chest. "We don't have much time." He informed the figure lurking in the shadow-filled tunnel behind him. "The security around the Duvayne Estate should be negligible. Use tranquilizers on any guards and get into The Duvayne's private office. Tear it apart. Pull the computer, all the disks. She had that backdoor so look for secret drawers or hidden safes. Tear up the floors if you have to. Grab everything and take it to my nightclub, the Demon Spawn. Contact Rorie when your people have what I want. He has the access codes to the Spawn's backroom. Go!" He didn't care if the guards died, as long as he didn't know who held their reins. He had to be very careful at this juncture.

He straightened and intercepted Valmont and Parkes hurrying in his direction. "I thought that damn book had been destroyed."

Shock widened Parkes' eyes. "It is the First. The illuminated pages are priceless, and it contains the genealogy of the First Families."

"Keep it down." Treadaway looked around. "It's not the original." He gave them a hard stare.

"But, but … it is." Parkes stammered.

Treadaway rolled his eyes. "Just keep your mouth shut and don't say anything to anyone. I'll do the talking." He swaggered to the knot of people at the opening of the ring. "Since Challenge was interrupted by Phillips' men, I assert penalty and claim the Duvayne Estate as immediate restitution, with Challenge to recommence in two days' time and all of Phillips' holdings to stand in place of the Duvayne Estate as recompense."

Rogan, Sebastian and Daire rose, their backs to the Coven leader, stances rigid. Since the mobile unit had been a little too large to fit within the tunnel, it was necessary to bring in the portable litter. The clatter of the gurney rolling across the flooring plugged the sudden silence. Jake ignored the implied threat hanging in the air and urged the portable bed to his side.

"Lift me real careful, guys. You drop me, you pay the price and it won't be pretty. Shoot me full of drugs, Jake, just this once." Tempest added an extra fillip of shrillness to her tone. It was a little too easy to let the moan escape her compressed lips as hands gently lifted her to the padded surface. "I know this thing has an upright position and that's where I want to be." She allowed her muscles to relax in slow increments. The wad of bandages on her shoulder was a knot against the back.

She lifted cold eyes to the Council and Treadaway. "Why did your fighters attack us? It appears I'm the one who has the right to call foul. I guess you didn't expect someone would find the Book. Or did you pay to have it destroyed?"

"How do we know that book is real and it's the original?" Treadaway bluffed. "This is a hoax. I demand the Council affirm my right to the Duvayne Estate, the Phillips' holdings will stand in place of the Duvayne Estate as recompense and the rescheduling of Challenge."

Charles Edgeworth advanced into the fray. "As Council Paladin, I'll take the book into custody now. I guarantee its protection. The Archivists will schedule an appointment with Art Alliances for authentication and evaluation. If it is affirmed as the First, it will be stored in the Archives."

Tempest laughed until tears rolled down her cheeks. She shrugged away the soothing hands. "I'm not interested in being calm. That damn book isn't going anywhere near the Covens or the Archives. The Council can have a copy of it, but the original will be placed with people I know and trust who will protect as well as preserve it."

A deep-seated rumbling vibrated the ground. Several poles swayed; the wires between them emitting a high-pitched resonance.

The Paladin shared glances with the Councilors, ignoring outside noises and remaining focused on the immediate issue. "It is not your property to do with as you want."

"I'm born and bred Coven. I have as much right to it as anyone here. I wouldn't store a piece of toilet tissue in the Archives much less the Chronicles. Besides, why would you want to claim it? One of your Councilors has denounced it as fake."

"If you don't allow us to authenticate it, the Challenge will resume in two days as CEO Treadaway has requested."

"Blackmail! How quaint."

"I suggest you rethink your position, Paladin Edgeworth." Preston Granville, impeccably dressed in a grey pinstriped custom-made Jiwani suit, negotiated the obstacle course of men and women like he did a contract in high-stakes transactions, with assurance and control. "As of now, you talk only with me. First, the Challenge brought against Ms. Phillips is illegal and it is over. I will discuss with her whether she wants to bring suit in the World Court against the Covens, the Coven Council and each individual CEO for the unlawful and malicious attempt on her life and the lives of her friends and family."

"You go, Mr. Granville." Tempest murmured beneath her breath, relaxing against the raised back of the portable bed.

"Second, the Glory Duvayne Estate has been confirmed by the World Court, with no dissenting votes, to be the sole property of Robert Phillips and all liquid assets and other properties to be the sole property of Tempest Duvayne Phillips." He held up a hand to halt the hot words spewing from the Councilors.

"Third, this is a representative of Global Restoration & Art Protection, Inc." He continued, knowing the man would be where he was supposed to be. "He will take possession of the History and Chronicles of the Natural Faith." His voice softened. "Mr. Reynolds, please place the book in the briefcase." His agents had compiled a quick dossier for all the people surrounding Tempest Phillips once The Duvayne was murdered. He always obtained background checks on potential clients.

"It's okay, Morgan." Tempest inched into a more comfortable position on the gurney, stifling the moans of pain she wanted to release. "I trust Mr. Granville, and Global Restoration always protects the art first and then considers ownership."

A tall man, with raven's wing black hair caught in a queue at the nape of his neck, dressed in black jeans and grey long-sleeved shirt, dropped to one knee beside Morgan, laid a silver case on the ground and flipped open the top. He gave Morgan a reassuring smile and allowed the young man to nestle the codex in the padding inside the attaché case. He closed the top and twirled the combination lock on the front. With a metallic click, a handcuff connected the case to his wrist.

Rising, he nodded to Preston Granville. "I'll wait for you in the Corsair."

Two steps and he lifted Tempest's hand to his lips, placing a kiss on the back. "Ma'am, it's a pleasure to finally meet you although I truly regret the circumstances." He covertly slipped a piece of paper into her hand. "Global Restoration will take your call at any time." He placed her hand carefully on the sheet covering her lower body, spun and left the building.

"Global Restoration has world renowned historians and specialists on staff who will authenticate the book. They will provide a report on its condition, provide an estimate to repair it if it's needed, and store it in environmentally controlled vaults if desired." Granville stuffed his hands into his pockets. It wasn't something he normally did, but he needed to in order to control the unexpected and uncharacteristic urge to plant his fist in several faces. The blood on Tempest Phillips offended him. "Does anyone question the reputation and integrity of Global?"

Members of the Council looked away or at the ground. Delia braced herself on Zook's supporting arm as she moved slowly to the front of the group. "Mr. Granville, I would appreciate a copy of the Chronicles as soon as possible. Please make sure it is delivered only into my hands or the hands of my Security Captain, Zook Fessler."

She glanced over her shoulder and dared the others to comment. She frowned at Edgewater who subsided before any words escaped. "Challenge is revoked. Mr. Granville, we will hold ourselves ready to answer any charges Ms. Phillips decides to initiate." If it was within her power, she would give Tempest Phillips the justice she deserved, but Treadaway had a slim majority control of the Council. She could do nothing for now, except instigate an intensive, secret investigation into his activities.

The voice in his ear said one word … "done" … bringing a smile to Treadaway's mouth. "Of course, Grande Marshall. As you will. I assumed in good faith like all the Covens that the charters in the Archives were true. I would like a copy of the Chronicles as well so I can catalog the differences between the versions. For something so integral to the center of our canon, you do plan to provide copies to all the CEOs, right, Grande Marshall? I'll expect one at my office in a week." He turned and left, snagging the majority of the fighters away.

Tempest pursed her lips, considering the nuances of the conversation. Treadaway had given up a little too quickly and quietly. The small amount of drugs Jake had pumped into her arm was creating a haze around her thoughts. She needed to clear her mind and focus closely on Treadaway's actions. She needed to remember something. She bumped her head against the pillow on the back of the gurney. The idea was gone … for now. She wet her lips and held out a hand to Preston Granville. "Mr. Granville, thank you so much for leaving your office on short notice and coming to our aid."

Granville clasped her hand in his with gentle care. "Believe me, Ms. Phillips, it was my pleasure, but I am distraught to find you in this condition. I'm sorry it took so long for us to arrive. Is there anything else I can do?"

"I want to have Jack Karlyle send you a substantial retainer if that's all right. I have the feeling we'll be needing your services for some time ... of course, if you still want us as clients."

"My dear," he patted her hand, "we certainly wish to be your counselors." He handed a business card to Rogan standing at her side. "My direct and home com numbers are on there. Call me whenever you need to. If you're sure everything is secure, I need to return to the courthouse."

"Of course, we're fine. And thanks for hiring the Global Restoration rep. His presence was a bonus. Just send the bill for their fees to me."

Granville frowned at her. "I didn't hire them, Ms. Phillips. He turned up at the office just as we were preparing to leave. I thought you had contacted them. Do you wish for me to check into the matter for you?"

The loss of blood, the drugs, the fight and the harangue afterwards had taken a toll. She couldn't concentrate. Her body was shutting down. "No, no, that's okay. He's with Global Restoration. No one in his or her right mind would consider impersonating a GR rep. Not with their reputation for protecting their name and position in whatever way they consider necessary."

"Very well, Ms. Phillips. Please take better care of yourself." With a courtly bow of his neck, he turned and left.

"I don't want to piss on everyone's feel good parade, but ...." Strider knelt beside the bed, his weapon slung on a strap on his right shoulder where he could easily swing the barrel up. Everyone had cleared out; privacy wouldn't be an issue.

"It can wait until another time, Strider." Rogan grasped the edge of the gurney. "We need to get Tempest and the rest of our wounded to Summerfield."

"I don't think we have time."

"Jake, stop." She saw attendants moving in to wheel her away. "I want to hear what he has to say." She gave Strider an encouraging smile. It was always in their best interest to pay attention when Strider was persistent.

"I don't know who the little people were, but between them and Watters they put on a better show than you did, Tempest. Treadaway is going to be hunting down information from everyplace. He thinks he knows D'eath's status with you, but curiosity has got to be killing him about Rogan and Watters. And as for Bloodhawk? Treadaway's going to be searching hard. And in the end, what is he going to find? You, Tempest. You're at the center of a triad with access to power the likes of which Treadaway only has wet dreams about."

Tempest frowned.

"Through Rogan, you have access to a dimensional gate and unknown allies."

She laughed, stopping abruptly when pain coursed through her past the numbing effects of the light drug dosage. "Yeah ... but Treadaway doesn't know about gates ... and those allies – they're the type that want to kill everyone and everything in sight and force domination over whoever remains. Besides, we're closing it as soon as we can."

"Through D'eath, you have the ears of the World Government and the wealthiest leaders around the globe. And through Bloodhawk, you have off-world connections and the accompanying alien technology in weapons and ships, medical, who knows what else ... even if it's not known yet."

She got the point. "Treadaway, even Busch, will go after them ... Rogan, Daire and Sebastian. But we've known that all along, Strider."

Strider gripped her wrist. "No, Tempest, they'll go after you. You're the center. If they have you, they control the men and the people who depend on them." He cursed, seeing her deny her worth. He had to wake her up. If they were to survive, she had to come to terms with her importance. He released Tempest and rose. "Rogan, if someone came to you and said they had Tempest and her life was in your hands, what would you do?"

Rogan blinked and stared steadily at Tempest.

Strider nodded. He swung left. "D'eath, what would you do? Would you introduce them to special people? If there were no deaths involved – immediate, readily apparent deaths –would you provide introductions and information to save Tempest's life?" He didn't wait for a response. The look on D'eath's face said it all.

"Bloodhawk, what about you?"

Sebastian wasn't so reticent about his feelings. "She is literally my life. She dies. I die. I would do whatever I had to do to save her. I've done terrible things in my long life. If it took just one more thing to keep her safe, yes, I'd do it. But the alien technology is only available through D'eath."

Tempest winced, from pain and because of what she had to say. "Uh, Sebastian. The Kalia I've been asking about?" She kept her eyes on the blanket her fingers were plucking. "She connected with me before the Challenge began and left a kind of package to unfurl in my mind. She's Ren Boden's granddaughter. I know you remember him. You were … uh," she sorted through a few of the pseudo-papers, "Lair Brothers? Kalia is on her way here with the entire Blood Lair and most of its allies. She's one … Lightgate? ... away. I felt her while we were fighting. I think she could somehow see what was happening and she's really pissed. I don't think she's going to be in a very good mood when she gets here."

Rogan collapsed onto the barrier outlining the arena. He braced his elbows on his legs and dropped his head into his hands threading his fingers through his hair, gripping the strands. "Drek, what a bloody mess." His laugh grated the air like a knuckle on a shredder.

Tempest rubbed her forehead. "I'm tired. Has anyone

seen Barnabus and Nemesis? I need to talk to Barnabus."

"Barnabus stopped by a short time ago. Nemesis required many stitches, but he'll be all right. Barnabus said he'll be in touch in a couple of weeks and you should go home." Judah saw Tempest flinch at his choice of words. "He didn't mean anything … those weren't his exact words …, damn it, Tempest, you know he wasn't complaining about what's happened around here today. He just wants you to get medical help and be someplace safe where you can heal."

A small laugh escaped. "It's okay, Judah, I know what you were trying to say. I just … can we just go home? I'm tired."

Her complaint was enough to initiate a general exodus to the exits. The gurney bumped over the floor finding every rough spot on the otherwise even surface. Quips streamed out her mouth rather than the groans of pain she wanted to release. She drew a shuddering breath of relief when the group surrounding her stopped outside the building. It gave her a chance to catch her breath and prepare for the jostling to the Corsair taking her to Summerfield.

Oh, for the love of Pete. An argument among the bodyguards and medical personnel continued longer than her nerves could contain. Moving carefully, she swung her legs off the side of the padded rolling bed and sagged over the edge.

Phhhht, phhhht, phhhht.

Three holes appeared in the white cover on the raised back of the gurney. She fell to the ground and rolled. Within seconds, bodies dropped on top of her. Angry shouts inflamed the air and the ground vibrated with the thudding steps of people charging in different directions. Hands clamped onto her and carried her behind a concrete barricade.

"Let me through, people." Jake dropped beside Tempest and ran expert hands and eyes over her before checking the bandage on her shoulder. "No seepage of new blood. She's okay except for more dirt on her clothes and skin and likely bruises from being at the bottom of a pile of bodies." His voice rose to a shout at the end.

It was the final indignity. Beads of sweat popped out on her forehead as she forced her body perpendicular with her right hand. She plucked a gun from the holster at the waist of the closest guard and whipped around the half-wall ignoring the dismayed shouts behind her. She skipped sideways from the hands reaching for her. All movement stopped except for the two bodies with weapons that fell from the trees in the distance. The sharp report of gunfire rebounded against the walls of the buildings. Tempest stumbled into Sebastian as Rogan swirled her into the center of the crowd of fighters.

Goth strolled across the parking area. "Thanks, Tempest, for drawing them out. We knew there was someone out there and had just pinpointed the location when you MADE YOURSELF VULNERABLE! What the hell were you thinking?"

Tempest cringed inside, but she didn't let her discomfort show. Even if she was wrong, she couldn't show any weakness. The first time she did she would find herself in the background wrapped in so much cotton she wouldn't be able to breathe. She handed the weapon to its owner and placed her freed right hand on her hip. Hiding the lightheadedness was tricky. She wasn't aware she was tottering slightly. "Thanks for your help, Goth. I was just about to take care of the problem myself."

Goth's eyes narrowed and she swore she could see steam coming out of his ears and maybe a little fire from his mouth. She eyed him with suspicion when his face relaxed and a tiny smile flitted across his lips.

"The team is scouting the area, but the assholes are gone." Goth informed Rogan. "Stay alert until you're on the Corsair. I received notice of a weapons bazaar I want to check out. We'll be back to Summerfield in a few days." He turned, whistled through his teeth, and galloped past the parked vehicles. Four men trotted out of the tree line at various points and fell into step behind him. They quickly disappeared from sight.

Rogan scooped Tempest into his arms and fast stepped forward. He tensed seeing her eyes close, feeling her body become limp. He stopped long enough for Jake to give her a quick scrutiny. "It will be interesting to see what toys he brings back for us to use. I believe this recent event throws your theory off, Strider."

Strider shook his head, falling into step beside Rogan as he resumed his jog. "No, it doesn't. It just means the people behind this attack set it up before the Challenge. Once a sniper goes on a job, he's out of touch. And if he managed to kill Tempest, well, they would likely see it as a second case scenario. They wouldn't give any serious consideration to reprisals since they would likely believe we'd fall apart as a force."

"Not very smart thinking on their part if that's true." Hearing sirens approaching in the distance, Rogan increased his speed. "Get everyone headed to Summerfield, Lorcan. We'll see you in a few hours. D'eath, do you and your men need transport?"

"I'd like to be with Tempest, but there are people I need to talk to." He was gratified none of the men questioned his commitment to Tempest and dedication to protecting the many and varied secrets. He planned to talk discretely and only theoretically with scientists he knew and trusted and, of course, with Marty Krafft, the World President. As World President, Marty's first priority was global welfare, but Marty knew wealthy companies and individuals hid beneficial technologies from the public under the umbrella of world stabilization. The President could follow their example and would if the incentive was strong enough. But Daire wouldn't give the scientists any details. Details could kill too many people.

"We'll see you at Summerfield when you can." Rogan climbed aboard the Corsair.

# CHAPTER 37

Tempest adjusted the sling around her shoulder again. It was uncomfortable and the skin beneath the bandages on her shoulder itched. Feel good fuzzies burbled inside her sending a smile across her face as Daire's hands lifted the strap and smoothed it around her neck. She acknowledged his care with a smile and tapped the map spread on the conference table. "It's a cave."

"Yes." Watters sat on one hip on the end of the table, one arm braced against his raised leg. "Caves are transitions between realities. In this case, between this world and Karatouche."

She waved her hand at his statement. "One of my teachers said the same thing a long time ago. He said it's a myth, or only esoteric crap proselytized by people who want to make their lives more exciting by believing in "woo-woo" bullshit. I'd like to show him the real thing. He made my life hell for the year I had to be in his class because he considered me a Coven brat." She smoothed a detailed topographical diagram printed on clear transparency over the map. "It's a government protected system. How on earth ... no pun intended ... did you get all those people here and out without anyone seeing you?"

"It's one of the largest natural formations on this continent." Rogan traced several highlighted areas. "There are a lot of unexplored areas."

Watters rose and moved to stand beside Rogan. "Yes. When we found this world, a few of us came through first to see if it would support life." His eyes gleamed. "We sensed the presence of a Key. We reported to our Tribal Leaders and they sent us back to observe any civilization that may be present and locate you.

"We found sets of three crystal formations on each side of the entrance of the cavern we were in. It's one of the larger offshoots and this map," he ticked the diagram in one area, "doesn't come close to estimating its real size. Someone embedded strong 'fear' and 'stay away' commands in the crystals at some time in the very distant past, but they were starting to fail. We sent for a mage and that's when one of the demi-Folk guards slipped through and Queen Dumont became involved."

"While this is all very interesting and I'd love to hear the full story at a future time, we're not going to be able to go in there and blow up any portion of that cave." Tempest's hand rose, but Daire's hands beat hers to the strap.

"It wouldn't bother you so much if you'd stop playing with it." His breath on her neck following his murmur beside her ear sent goose bumps skidding along her skin and curls of heat sifting down to the center of her core.

"Cree and two teams have gone in to reconnoiter the actual site." Rogan ignored the subtle loveplay between Tempest and Daire. "Cree should be back soon and he'll be able to tell us if there's an easy way to close the portal. I have the feeling we're dealing with double jeopardy here. If I'm right, it's not only government-protected ground, but a tourist attraction."

"Well, you're going to have to move quickly before the decision is taken out of your hands. Queen Nateesha has a low threshold for patience. She has decreed it must be closed before the dark of the moon and she'll do what she believes to be necessary to protect her Flair."

Tempest hissed at Rogan as he moved past her and smoothed down the Velcro tab she had just jerked loose on the sling. Daire's silent laugh rumbled against her back. She elbowed Daire. "It would be easier if you and Jake would just back off and let me heal myself."

"I agree with Jake when he said you're too run down. You've lost fifteen pounds in the last few weeks."

"What're a few pounds? It's not like I didn't have some pounds I needed to lose."

"No, you didn't." Daire shook his head.

Rogan nodded. "Daire's right. Let the wound heal naturally this time. I'd say get some rest, but it looks like we're going to have to do something about this damn gate. You could sit this one out. It's a Kin problem." Rogan sensed the men backing away from him and moving to stand behind Tempest.

Tempest tamped down the hurt. "Why didn't you stand back from the Challenge? It was a Coven issue."

"It's not the same thing." His eyes closed, hearing his voice in the still air. He opened them and looked at Daire who shook his head and snugged closer against Tempest's back. "I can't believe I said that." He placed his hands on her shoulders. "You're hurt and barely starting to heal. As Strider pointed out, you're the center of a lot of people. This isn't safe."

She placed her healthy hand on top of one of his. "There isn't any safe place, don't you know that? I can't stand aside and let evil things happen without doing something. What affects one, affects all. We are stronger together than we are apart. Don't weaken us, Rogan. Don't make us less."

He scanned the faces of the men and women in the room seeing their acceptance. "All right. We move to intercept Cree now ... all of us." He swung to face Watters. "What exactly is a Key supposed to do? We're talking about blowing things up but is there a more subtle way to shut down the gate?"

Watters scratched his head. "This is more a mage thing, or one of the Elders might have an Origin story giving us more information. The last gate was found so long ago all the Elders with direct knowledge about them have been killed or died in accidents or of natural causes."

Tempest looked around pointedly. "I don't see either of

those advisors here. Maybe someone should go get one?"

"Tempest, you need to tone down your impatience. It is the pain working on your nerves. Jake has offered some medication I believe you should take." Sebastian eyed the men backing away from him. He gritted his teeth. He always seemed to be sticking an appendage inside his mouth, borrowing one of the colorful colloquialisms from his new family's vocabulary.

"Thanks, Bastian, I'd appreciate your getting the pills for me." She hid her grin. The others thought she was going to follow up with some snarky remark, but she would gratefully swallow drugs to get some relief from the constant aching. And, of course, it would keep the others on their toes. She settled her butt more firmly in the cradle of Daire's groin enjoying the felt-more-than-heard groan in his chest.

"I agree with Rogan. We move now to meet Cree and his team. Strider can take Watters …," she stopped and backtracked when she saw the stony look on Strider's face, "uh, Judah can take Watters to the camp and retrieve a mage or someone who can give us more information." She nudged Daire in the ribs to move his hands which were becoming too familiar with her lower stomach. They were getting a little too close to sensitive areas and it was distracting. "How soon before the final groups are at Summerfield?"

"I believe I am the last and we thank you for sanctuary. We have many skills and much knowledge we can share as equals." The man had the skin and wrinkles of a senior, but the strength of personality shining from the pale green eyes and the erect, proud carriage spurned the trappings of age.

"Damn, Tempest," Strider muttered close to her ear from his perch on the side of the conference table. "Be careful what you ask for. This is just too spooky even for you."

She pulled free of Daire's light clasp and moved forward, watching the group behind the elder's shoulders. Four of the six men were definitely bodyguards. "I agree we have much to share. Be welcome in our home. Please have a seat." She swept her arm towards the chairs along the circumference of the table.

He shook his head at the offer and Watters who approached from the side. "We haven't time. I am Padyn Oldaker. Lazarus said our Regent follows you."

"That's not exactly correct, sir." Tempest held the eagle sharp gaze. "We're business partners, friends, family. We share responsibilities for decisions."

"Ah ... but who makes the final choice?" He waved a hand. "No, it is not necessary to answer. This is a pivot point. There are many realities which branch off what is decided here today."

"No pressure." Tempest shoved her irritation down, pasted a smile on her mouth.

Padyn's green eyes glimmered like the cool depths of aquamarine in sunlight. Years of witnessing friends and families dying, and the stress of months of running and hiding until the gate was discovered crashed into him, overwhelming and draining him. He swayed.

The two men standing behind Padyn pulled his arms across their shoulders, guided him to a nearby chair, and lowered him to the seat. One of the men knelt beside Padyn, drew a flask from his side, popped the top and pressed it against the maven's mouth. Padyn turned his head away, but the man was insistent, forcing the liquid into Padyn's mouth. After a few swallows, Padyn pushed the hand away, dabbed his mouth on a cloth pressed into his palm, and leaned against the back of the chair with his eyes closed.

"We've been running a long time. I am Tolar Rainsmitter. Three," he pointed to himself, the man beside him and Padyn, "are one. Our synergy can best be described as mage to disciples." He settled onto the floor cross-legged. "A millennium ago, the gate system was built, one reality at a time. Some realities crossed and merged because one person in each world made similar decisions. Powerbrokers seized people susceptible to gate energy. The battle for control is too long to detail now, but the end result was independent Gatekeepers who decided which realities to include in the network. It was a few hundred years before the Gatekeepers realized the unbound gates of the excluded realities were dangerous. During our wars, several viable realities were destroyed by warring factions using them as battlegrounds then returning to their own worlds."

The second disciple squatted beside Padyn's chair. "I am Kavin." He took up the explanation. "To combat the unfurled use of the doorways, the Grand Mother, so it is written, in secret even from her family, sacrificed her life, giving her blood and tissue for implantation in the foundation of all the portals. For generations, volunteers in her bloodline became Keys and were bound to specific doorways." He hurriedly continued, seeing glacial expressions solidifying on the many faces surrounding them. "The Grand Mother died by her own hand against the wishes of her most trusted friends and advisors; it is imperative that Keys remain alive and functioning as productive moral beings."

Padyn opened his eyes and patted Kavin's shoulder. He picked up the thread. "The bloodline thinned, mostly through assassination. Gates closed or became Rogue, uncontrollable by anyone, when Keys … died. There have been many Searchers, but this is the first gate in two centuries to awaken. It's come at a grave time in our peoples' lives, bringing much needed hope."

"The history lesson is riveting but can you get to the end. As everyone keeps saying, we don't have a lot of time. Just tell us how we close the damn thing." Tempest swallowed most of her exasperation, but some managed to emerge.

"Yes, of course." Tolar stood slowly, placed his hands at the small of his back and stretched.

"Oh, Great Ancient One! Bleed on the damn thing." The exasperation in Padyn's voice swept through the room. "Branaugh, you're a Key because you're a direct descendant of the Grand Mother's bloodline. Prick your finger, puncture some part of your body, but just get your blood someplace on the crystalline structure surrounding the opening!"

Tempest blinked slowly, assimilating the information, half listening to the whispering around her. It seemed simple. She focused on the mages. "You say it takes Ro's blood to close it. How dangerous is it for him?"

"We would never harm our Regent, much less a Key." Outrage reflected outward in Kavin's voice and body language.

"Yeah, well, let's just say I haven't been in a real trusting situation lately. Why should we believe you? You may be Kin and we've heard your side of the story, but what about the other side? It takes two sides to make a conflict." She didn't doubt they were the good guys, but she was annoyed and her damn shoulder itched. It wasn't fair to pick on the guests. But they were such large marks and she could use a little target practice. Besides, Ro, Lorcan and Judah had reasons for separating and staying away from Kin. Until she knew the cause of the distancing, trust was going to be in very short supply.

Watters bared his teeth. Tolar and Kavin stiffened. The guards inched hands to the butts of weapons.

Padyn's eyes twinkled, his mouth stretched into a grin. "It is good you are thinking. Yes, there is another side to our conflict. If you listened to the King and the half-brothers, they could pretty their side up to match ours. It's a matter of trust like you've said. How do we prove ourselves?"

Tempest aimed an air kiss at the guards and Padyn's disciples. "An impossible task I'm sure you'll agree. We'll just have to take it one very small step at a time."

Padyn guffawed, ignoring the frowns on his men's faces. "I like your doyen, Rogan Branaugh. I look forward to our continuing relationship." He wiped his eyes, and the smile remained in place. "For now, we should start towards our objective, yes?"

The quartet of bodyguards drew their weapons and swarmed the trio forming a living shield. Sebastian sauntered through the door and across the room handing several pills to Tempest.

"Stand down!" Tempest barked in answer to the reciprocal movement behind her. A headache blossomed to match the ache in her shoulder. She transferred the water bottle stuffed into her right hand to the hand supported by the sling, accepted the pain pills in her right hand and tossed the pills into her mouth. Clasping the bottle with her freed healthy hand, she gulped the refreshing liquid, washing the pills into her stomach. Gods, let the medicine work quickly. Setting the bottle on the table, she leaned against Daire who once again spooned against her back. Her head dropped onto his shoulder. "This is Sebastian Bloodhawk." She opened her mouth to add more but didn't know how to describe their relationship to outsiders. And it was none of their business anyway.

A stray thought clicked together with the recent revelations in her mind. She elbowed Daire in his ribs as she pushed upright. "Oh, god! It's blood activated. What happens? How is Ro affected?"

Padyn considered her panic with caution. "I understand it can create a pull on the senses once it is locked by the Key, but it evens out over a short time."

"What are you thinking, Tempest?" Rogan saw the trepidation in her eyes, the anxiety stiffening her body.

"Ro, you contributed to the cocktail of blood Bastian drank. Will what happens to you cross the barrier of blood and affect everyone who was part of the initiation? If you are incapacitated by the binding, will everyone be disabled ... in the midst of what is sure to be a battle of some kind?"

Padyn frowned. "What is this thing you are talking about? Who is this Bastian?"

"Oh, lord! If it pulls us in, will it affect Kalia? Shit! We need some time to think this through."

Watters broke in. "There is no time! I have said this several times."

Tempest shook her head. "Well, stop saying it. This isn't Nateesha's world so she can just get a tight grip on her panties. We have to be careful."

"Explain yourself." Padyn pushed his hands against the top of the table and stood. "What madness have you participated in, Rogan Branaugh? We need to know. We can break any tie."

Weapons ratcheted around and behind Tempest, filling the air.

Padyn cleared his throat. "Perhaps I was too hasty and forceful in my statement." He pushed his way past his guards, ignoring their hushed orders, his arms spread wide. "We mean you no harm."

Tempest ignored him for now. "Kalia needs to know she may be incapacitated, but I don't know how to reach her. Bastian, you're Lair Patriarch. You should be able to connect with her. Can you shield her from any effects?"

"I have missed part of what was said, Tempest. What has caused this panic?" Sebastian's voice was low. He stood in front of her, his back to the intruders as he rubbed his hand up and down her arm. His skin prickled with apprehension at positioning his body with his back to unknowns, but he trusted the men and women surrounding them and in his gut knew they would protect him.

"To close the dimensional gate, Ro has to use his blood on it. When we bonded, the hookup pulled in everyone who gave their blood and through you it's captured Kalia Sanborne, the Blood Lair Mistress, and who knows how many of her people. This mage said it could affect Ro's senses before evening out. But what if it does more? What happens to all of us," her hand and arm waved wildly in the air, "if we have to fight?" Absently noting the buzz of a dotmitter, she broke free of Daire's hold and charged away from Sebastian. Five steps away, she spun and darted back. Her hair floated upward on an invisible wind.

Padyn and his disciples gaped in amazement, unconsciously allowing their guards to tug them to the doorway.

"Tempest!" Rogan stepped into her path and settled into his stance, rocking slightly when she slammed into his chest on her return course. He shielded her left shoulder while grasping her right arm. "Calm down. Oldaker said he thought the effects would be minor."

She stared up at him in disbelief. "You trust him that much?"

Rogan didn't want to offend the guests, but he had to be honest in his appraisal of the circumstances. "No, I don't trust them. I think they are here only because it suits their purpose. That's not necessarily a bad thing for us; it's just the way things are. Some of what they've said rings true to me. It draws out pieces of images in my mind. Yes, I believe it will take blood to close the portal." He leaned over placing his mouth close to her ear. "We can bind the gate to us. I've given blood for transfusions for you before and you've done the same for me. You and Sebastian have been teaching us about shielding. Together, Tempest. You and I can do this together and protect the others."

"There's trouble at the cave." Strider interrupted the tableau with a calm voice. "That was Goth. Cree has sent for him and his team. I suggest we pull ourselves together and get moving."

# CHAPTER 38

Tempest strolled among the swarms of tourists. Dust floated in the air from the arrival of another bus. She dodged a small covey of children chasing each other around standing adults. Hundreds of voices created a buzz like bees in a hive. The sun loomed over the trees lining the edge of the quadrangle adding to the heat of her black denim pants tucked into black knee high, low-heeled boots. She had changed into a cobalt blue shell top which emphasized the whiteness of her skin. She carried a pack in her right hand with a rolled black denim jacket inserted in the loops at the top. The extra covering would be needed while inside the much cooler sanctuary of the cave.

Declan had refused to let Daire walk at her side and she had spurned the escort of her friends and family. Even with her arm in a sling, she would be less noticeable alone than she would be even with one person beside her. Their enemies would be looking for a group; they wouldn't expect her to be anywhere alone. Alone in a close net of many fighters formed by her people and Kin. She had only to turn her head and she could see Daire and Declan sauntering in line with her ten feet away.

She glanced down where Timebender reposed on her right forearm. Shocked wasn't sufficiently descriptive of how she felt about its metamorphosis. Even stunned didn't accurately reflect the men's reaction to seeing it melt and reform into the pliant armguard covering her skin from wrist to elbow. It was strangely comfortable and comforting. They had been walking down the sidewalk from the house to the vehicles when she hit an invisible brick wall. "I can't move forward," she told Sebastian and Rogan. Daire and his people, and Watters with the mages and their bodyguards, had already left to find their own way to the cave.

"Can you move in another direction?" Rogan studied her face.

She backed several steps and let out a gusty breath then walked forward only to again run into the unseen barricade. She clasped her stomach as a burning sensation erupted inside.

"What the hell?" Rogan caught her up and carried her back into the house.

"It's the bedroom, Ro. I'm drawn to the bedroom."

Timebender reposed in brackets on the wall above her headboard. With Sebastian and Rogan standing slightly behind her, they watched it jitter, turn liquid and ooze down the wall. When it reached the bed, it was a pulsing, shining silver blob. There was no reasonable explanation for what it was doing. She couldn't move, only watch it flow over the side of the bed and along the floor. Her breathing stopped when it slid up around her leg to her arm resting in the sling. It crawled onto her forearm transforming into the armguard she now wore. It took all her control to keep from screaming and attempting to yank it off.

She stood in line behind a tall man at the ticket kiosk. Over his shoulder, the young girl in his arms sucked her thumb giving Tempest a wide-eyed look out of chocolate brown eyes. They moved away and she was at the booth. She purchased a ticket and ambled behind the father making faces at the little girl who only stared at Tempest.

She continued her ruminating. There was metaphysical magic and then there was this physical shit. She dropped her pack on the ground in the shade of several mammoth oak trees, knelt and dug in the front pocket for a snack. Using her teeth, she tore the end off the wrapper, dropped the paper in the bag and stood up. Slowly easing the strap of the bag over the sling supporting her left arm and onto her left shoulder, she walked to the booth at the main cave entrance nibbling the chocolate and peanut candy bar. She had thought dealing with what the Covens handed out was the scariest thing she had ever had to do but seeing metal melt and reform on its own was beyond chilling, it was just plain creepy.

She handed over the ticket and entered the gloomy interior trailing behind a boisterous, large group of teenagers and stressed teachers. Five hundred yards inside the passageway, it diverged into two trails.

"Ma'am, that tunnel is closed. Please follow the others to the main cavern. You don't want to miss the guide's stories about the formation and discovery of this system. He's very good."

Tempest gave the earnest young woman a warm smile. "I got a little ahead of my group who should be coming along any time now. It's cooler inside so I thought I'd wait for them here."

The girl shifted foot to foot, clearly anxious to catch up to the people meandering around the bend just ahead. "I can wait with you, ma'am. Our prefect doesn't want anyone left alone."

"It's all right." Daire sauntered to Tempest's side and brushed a kiss across her mouth. He leaned against the wall behind her. "We're part of the larger group and we'll wait with her. Why don't you catch up with your friend?"

She frowned. "The prefect said a guide must stay with the groups at all times."

"Our leader is right behind us. He was stopped by a family to answer a couple of questions, but he said he'd catch up." Rogan flashed a smile.

The young woman backed up a few feet intimidated by the small group of muscled men gathering behind the new arrival. "Oo … oo … okay," she stuttered. She turned and hurried down the path glancing over her shoulder periodically.

Tempest and the others smiled and waved until she disappeared around the corner. "Good save, Ro. Do we really have a guide headed our way?"

"No. We didn't group together until we got inside out of sight. Who's got the map? Has anyone seen Watters?"

"We need to move into the tunnel. We've got people headed this way." Strider tromped by and into the grey light emanating from the hole in the rock wall.

Tempest swept forward with the tide of bodies. "Keep your scrawny butt out of that cave!" Kalia's voice was loud, clear as if she were standing at Tempest's side.

"Scrawny butt?" Her feet stuttered when she twisted at her waist to look at her ass. "I don't think it's particularly small." She projected the words through her mind as she spoke aloud.

The men exchanged puzzled looks. Several followed Tempest's example and scanned her backside. Rogan mouthed "scrawny butt" to Daire who shrugged and shook his head.

"Uh, Tempest. You have a great ass." Strider shot an apologetic gaze to a frowning Daire.

"We have to close the gate now, Kalia." These little tete-a-tetes were getting on Tempest's nerves, particularly since she didn't initiate any of them. It was convenient this time since she hadn't been sure how to make contact with Kalia. "When the portal closes, you may be affected through the bond you have with Sebastian and me."

The ebb and flow of energies fundamental to Lightgates buzzed the imager providing sporadic quick glimpses of visuals in Kalia's mind. "Don't place yourself and Sebastian in a dangerous situation. Let your people handle it."

"Is that what you would do?" Tempest stopped. She continued to carry on the conversation in her mind as well as out loud. It made walking easier. She sensed Sebastian closing on her and she stepped into his arms. Cradled against his chest, she felt a questing tendril ease into her thoughts.

Kalia lied through her teeth. "Yes." She gave up the deception. "No, I wouldn't, but if he dies, you kill all our Lairs.

And it's not just fighting men and women. We have fathers, mothers, children, grandparents, sisters and brothers."

"Mistress, you are a more than worthy leader for the Lair. I thank you for watching over our people and doing what is necessary to keep them safe. But what you ask now is impossible. I want to know you and your mates. I want to be among my brethren again. But we must do this thing. This world with all its fathers, mothers, children, grandparents, sisters and brothers ... and friends ... they would all perish or be slaves to evil men like the ones in our world. Continue to live and protect the Lair, Mistress. I'm going to cut you off now. Be well, Kalia Sanborne, granddaughter of Ren Boden."

"Patriarch! Sebastian! No!" Kalia swayed between Ram and Kenton who held her within their clasped arms. She stumbled forward out of their arms to the control panel. Ram and Kenton followed her, wearing concerned looks on their faces, taking up positions at the boards on each side of her.

Kalia flicked a button. "Pilots, we don't have time for regular passage. All Tier One and Tier Two pilots to berthing. Decks Masters, stack and rack. Senior Pilots, half of you can settle in the Rampart Prime tunnels, but it'll be a rough ride."

Mobilizing the ships was imperative, but the slightest miscalculation and precious fighters could be lost. Cleaning any resulting mess in the tubes would slow down any rescue time. She tuned out the chatter among the pilots and fed numbers to Ram and Kenton. She contemplated the imager, which had steadied, and called out more figures.

"Captain, there's space for all of us in a bubble."

Her eyebrows winged up. It was a quick solution, and if it worked there wouldn't be any recovery time. But it was very dangerous. Was the situation worth the risk? The men and women were the premier pilots among all the Lairs. She looked to Kenton and Ram for guidance and saw confidence and assurance. "Very well. Take your places."

She studied the patterns, watching each ship slide into

place. In a soft voice, she directed, "Korina, Romack, and Andrus, correct your positions by thirty-two point nine decs."

The dots bobbed into a new configuration. "Hold." She counted through two sectims letting the wave complete its formation. "Release controls to the bridge. Ram, lock them in place."

Chicopee stood two feet to the left of Commander Wolfanger's position, eagerly noting every movement of his fingers, checking actions against the end result in the imager. She didn't have the experience to manage the maneuver and had willingly given up her seat. She shivered with nerves and the usual cold of the bridge. It was very perilous. All or part of the pilots and ships could be lost and Rampart Prime could be caught in the Lightgate eddies and pulled into the Afterverse. They would all be lost forever.

"Transition occurring … now." Kalia's voice was calm and steady instilling courage and determination.

# CHAPTER 39

Tempest jumped when Cree materialized at her side. "I hate when you do that."

Usually he smiled, but this time his features were grim. "There's something you need to see." He whipped around and moved away from the route to the gate.

Worried, Tempest changed direction. Around bends and through two small passageways, she found Cree kneeling on one knee beside a dark object on the stone. His team was on guard in strategic places. Goth popped up momentarily on a tall flat stalagmite then disappeared. She slowed. Blood pooled beneath the body and rivulets ran along natural channels in the rock.

"She's here." Cree offered the affirmation in a solemn, comforting tone.

The man was three feet tall if he had been standing. Blood-filled hair stringed around his shoulders. It was a handsome face, etched with pain lines. She gazed in wonder into the suddenly opened turquoise eyes: the clear green shade, not the blue seen most often in high-priced jewelry. Green was her favorite color.

"Captain Targus LaFlamme." Cree's voice was gruff.

Tempest flicked her eyes to him. There was more emotion in those few words than she had heard from Cree since Rogan had hired him. Taking her cue from him, she dropped to her knees beside the tortured man. "Captain LaFlamme, we have our doctor with us." She looked over her shoulder for Jake. Rogan, Sebastian, Daire and a few others were taking defensive positions around her and the injured man; the rest of the men were moving further away to provide additional protection.

"You must promise to take care of them." His voice was hoarse, his words cracking on the ends. He ignored Jake who pushed around Cree, dropped his medical bag and began a quick examination.

"Queen Nateesha and her Flairs will be safe. She has Kin and demi-Folk guards."

"No. Not her. Not them." He coughed. He pushed Jake's hands away and clutched his chest. Cree shouldered Jake back and gently lifted LaFlamme's head. Targus gratefully sipped from the bottle Cree held to his lips, a sigh escaping his lips as Cree eased him to the jacket pillow. "Thank ... you."

"Who did this to you?" His pain and the extent of his wounds made her tremble.

He flicked his fingers. "That is unimportant." He turned his head to Cree and shook it slightly before returning the strength of his gaze to Tempest. "Promise me you will protect them."

"Protect who?"

"You can trust her." Cree urged for confidences.

"The youngers and select breeders ... from the other Flairs. Dumont's sister, Queen Dahlia Rosamunde DuFrayne, sent them here. The King and his sons don't know. The Flairs protect the secret." His body shook.

Tempest questioned Jake with her eyes. Her gaze filled with sorrow when he shook his head. "I promise to protect them." She sensed a sudden shifting among the men behind her. "I will protect them." She sent a stern glance over her shoulder.

Targus' body relaxed. For a moment, Tempest thought he was gone. But his chest rose once, twice, before settling into an uneven rhythm. "Good. Good. Dumont will need their bloodlines to keep from inbreeding. But she will cage them and use them for her purposes. She will force them to mate with who she wants. They will have no freedom, no choices."

Tempest's forehead wrinkled noting Targus' failure to use

the Queen's title and first name, the vitriolic tint to his words.

"She gave her sister to the King in her place. She was the first born and the hereditary leader of all Flairs. The King wanted her. But she forced my Lia to take her place in the blood bond ceremony." Voice trailing off, his eyes filled with resolution, his fingers dug into the skin of Tempest's arm. "Don't trust her. She'll deny everything."

He released her and scrabbled in his pouch. Light streamed from between his fingers. He raised his hand to his mouth and kissed the talisman in his palm, swiped it across the blood on his chest. "Take this. Lia sent it for you. She and the remaining Queens and their Consorts infused it with life energy … for preservation … as a gift." There wasn't time to ease the Dimension Straddler into all her potential powers. He had to rely on the Ancient One and the prophecies that what he was doing wouldn't kill her.

Tempest didn't want another unknown element in her life, particularly since she didn't know how Timebender would react. There was a rueful twist to her mouth as she considered the reactions of inanimate objects. She accepted the object he pressed into her hand and swallowed the scream erupting from her throat. The item burned, but she couldn't drop it. Targus jammed it against her palm and held it in place. The light faded and the item cooled. Against her will, she jammed it into a pocket. She wanted to throw it as far away as possible but couldn't bring herself to reject it. She opened her hand, expecting raw red meat. Her skin was smooth and clear. Put it away, think about it another time. "Do you have children? You and Lia? Are your children here?"

"Yessssss. Dumont will particularly want them."

"Don't worry, Targus. Your children, their mates, and all the generations to come from them will have sanctuary with me and my family. They will be as my children." She was compelled to make the assurance. Her honor forbade anything less.

A faint smile was on his lips. "Thank … you." His arms

rose, fingers flickering in a complex signal. His body convulsed and collapsed inward.

Tears streamed down Tempest's face. Cree knelt at the soldier's side, water sparkling in his eyes. He smoothed his hand across LaFlamme's face closing his eyes.

The air filled with the whooshing of hundreds of wings. Small bodies rose from everywhere, tiny figures clutched against many chests. Six figures broke from the crowd and flung themselves onto LaFlamme's body. A male youth followed them slowly, landing at Targus' feet. His hand gripped the hilt of a sword strapped around his waist. He leaned over and gently touched one leg before rising and turning to Tempest.

"I am LaFlamme." Tears sparkled in his eyelashes, but his face remained dry. "My father trusted your word would be true. If you fail in your pledge, I will find a place of safety for my Flair and exact retribution on everyone for harm to those I safeguard."

Her heart ached listening to the sobs of anguish from the children covering the dead body, watching the innocence fall from the courageous youth who became a man in seconds. "It will take time to develop trust between us. I will keep my promise to your father and to all of you. We need to get you out of here and back to our compound and we have to close that damn gate."

LaFlamme brushed a traitorous drop from below one eye. "I can take you to it and help. The King sent through some soldiers. He and one of his sons plan to come here with a legion at the dawn's rise tomorrow. The other son will remain behind to hold the throne. But you should bind the gate, not close it." With a bound gate, he could hope to someday rescue his mother, even from a blood bond with the King.

"Have you seen Queen Nateesha and Kin?"

"Dumont." He spat on the ground away from his father's body. "She did this." He pointed to his father.

Tempest inhaled deeply. She had feared as much. "Did

Kin help her?"

The black curls around his face bounced as he shook his head. "She sent them on a brubear chase. Told them she saw soldiers. She had one of her guards lead them into one of the more dangerous tunnels." Fury vibrated in waves from his body. "She tortured my dad." A long angry hiss filled the air. "He told them nothing." Sorrow and sadness pulled his shoulders down. "He wouldn't let us help him. He forced us to promise to hide until you came. All his hopes and mom's," his voice choked, "are on you. Why? Why are you so special?"

Tempest wanted to give him a hug but kept her distance. The weeping was diminishing. The figures drew back, wiped faces. An older female handed a tiny baby to another and unfolded a blanket Cree handed her. She tenderly and carefully covered the body, patting the cloth a last time before reclaiming the baby. She gathered the others, and with a tear drenched look at the youth, she herded them back to the main band.

"I don't know why he considered me special, LaFlamme. Cree, would you and Goth make sure they get to Summerfield? Please take the Captain's body as well." Some of the tiredness left her when Cree went to the boy and laid a protective hand on LaFlamme's shoulder. "Do you have a first name I can use?"

"Targus. I am Targus LaFlamme." His shoulders firmed, his chin rose.

She nodded. "Targus, Cree needs you to help him get the others to safety. We'll track down Kin, bind the gate ... not close it ... and meet you at home." If the elder Targus' wife was still alive, a bound gate provided more options than a closed one. Rogan might question her decision, but he would follow her lead. And, if any Kin warriors attempted to dispute her decision, she would set them straight.

She turned and let Daire give her a quick hug. No looking back. Tears were too close to the surface. "We have some bad guys to take care of." She drew the men closer with a glance. "We keep this between us. We'll handle Nateesha as we have been for now. We're going to have to split up. Lorcan, can you find Watters and whoever is with him and bring them to the gate? Judah, head for the entrance. Call in Strike Force teams. We're definitely going to need more help. Have them bring in the Predators. Once the noise starts, people are going to be stampeding out of here and the authorities are going to get involved. I want us out of here before they arrive, and we'll need the transport space the Predators provide. Get three Renegades in first to get the youngers and the Captain's body out." She listened to the light scrapes and scuffs fading away as the men moved to complete their assignments, unconsciously rubbing the material hiding the talisman in her pocket.

A small group remained; not enough for a pitched battle. "Our only goal is to bind the gate. We have to get Rogan close enough to bleed on it." Her teeth gleamed in the dim light. "If we can force some of the soldiers back through the portal, do it. But we stay together. I think Nateesha has an agenda of her own."

✵✵✵✵✵

Light bloomed a few hundred light years beyond the dwarf planet Pluto.

"Transition complete." Kalia sent a quick prayer of thanks to the Shining Gods: the bubble was intact; all the fighters were in their pre-conversion positions. "Starling, move us away from the Lightgate."

Sectims later, a brilliant flash of white breached the blackness, then another and finally the last. Rampart Prime's sister ships angled into formation.

"Good job, pilots! Decks Masters, split our Ryders between all of you and settle them in the tunnels. Lock and load. All pilots, get some food and hit the refreshers. We'll be going in hot."

Kalia turned a sparkling smile on Ram and Kenton. She toned down her vivacity and included the bridge crew in her regard. "All of you did a great job. We made it through only because each of you knows your job and you remained calm. Start monitoring electronics, any type of communications. Karr, you have the bridge. Rotate around so everyone gets an opportunity for food and refresher." With a finger flick, she strode across the floor and through the door which whooshed closed behind her. She spun and jumped onto Kenton wrapping her legs around his waist. She leaned back against Ram who closed in behind her, turning her face to give him a quick kiss.

"We are the greatest!" she crooned.

# CHAPTER 40

Tempest gritted her teeth against the throbbing pain in her shoulder. "Jake, stop messing with it before I shoot you myself."

"Half the stitches are broken and you're bleeding again. I have to pack this tight enough to keep some of the red stuff in your body. God, Tempest, our lives used to be …"

"Dull and boring?"

"Normal. I was thinking normal." Jake didn't appreciate her humor. He added another pad to the seeping bandage and wound more strips around her shoulder. Finally satisfied, he eased her arm back into the sling.

"I've got plenty of fresh blood showing, Rogan." She had to be flippant or she'd be screaming. She leaned back against the rock with a heavy exhalation. "Can we get to the gate from here? Is everyone still alive?"

"Yeah." Rogan braced his gun on top of the stone providing cover for them. "Everyone is moving. Stay down!" Damn that Watters. He was like a jumping jack, popping up long enough to draw fire then finding another hiding place. "So far only three fighters have been tossed through the opening. I believe they prefer to die here rather than on the other side."

She leaned sideways around the boulder for a brief look and pulled back quickly. "Yeah, that would be my guess. Where's that fighter I wrestled with in the first wave?"

"Watters pitched him through with the other two."

"Kool. Remind me to give Watters a raise. Any word

from Judah about reinforcements?"

"He's got his own troubles. The Renegades came and got the little ones and the Captain out, but the authorities were faster than expected. When the Predators touched down, the cops were all over them like jam on peanut butter. The teams are stuck on board since we don't want to scare the locals." Rogan wanted to use more earthy terms, but he was following Tempest's lead trying to keep things on a lighter level.

"Anyone see Nateesha?"

"Nateesha and her merry band are supposedly helping check the side tunnels for stray fighters. Jeffers said it's been a while since she left."

Tempest's breath caught. "She's looking for the kids."

Rogan fired off three rounds, dumped the empty clip and slapped a new one in, firing several more times. "Yep. That would be my guess. She knows LaFlamme was doing something important for her sister. She's just trying to figure out what. I don't think she knows about them for sure ... yet. We've got to move, Tempest. If the King is coming with reinforcements at dawn, we need to get this done now. Sebastian, get Tempest to the entrance. Lorcan and I will get the portal closed. We don't have time to figure out how to just bind it, unless the procedure is the same." He had to deviate from the plan to close it together. The number of warriors from the other side was more than he expected.

"No." Tempest refused in a decisive tone.

Rogan swung his head around and aimed an order at Daire. "Get her out of here."

"Rogan. No. Daire, I'll put a bullet in an unimportant place if you make a move toward me." She dared the other men crouched nearby to counter her command. "Rogan, remember what you said to me earlier. We can do this together."

He locked eyes with her then shifted them to her left hand sliding down her leg to the side of her boot. He flicked a look back to her eyes and nodded. She darted around the boulder knowing Rogan was at her back and they zigged zagged across the central cavern. Men on both sides of the conflict rose from hiding places. Weapons blazed. Tiny pieces of rock bit into Tempest's arms and legs as projectiles hit all around her. She leaped, Rogan only seconds behind her, and they slapped bloody hands on the rim of the opening. Her body flew backward crashing into Rogan. Bolt after bolt of blue, green and red energy struck the floor, ceiling and walls.

Her awareness returned, jigging up and down across someone's shoulder, upsetting an already shaky stomach. She gagged and swallowed hard. Shouts and screams mixed with the booming roar of falling rock. A moan escaped.

"It's done, Tempest."

Relief shuddered through her intensifying the urge to hurl. She planted her hands on Rogan's lower back and pushed up. Her stomach might be bubbling, but the pain in her shoulder had subsided. Somewhere along the way, the sling had disappeared.

Her gaze roved the tunnel. Sebastian and Declan supported Daire. Strider and the rest of their fighters provided rearguard, but the only sound was crashing stone, the only movement from the gate cave was clouds of dust barreling toward them.

"The gate closed?"

"Yes and yes." He acknowledged her unspoken question that it was bound, not destroyed. "The King's fighters threw down their weapons as soon as the connection from the other side shut down. As long as it appeared the King was coming through, they had to continue to fight. They're asking for asylum. They are in Watters' custody for now … at least until we decide what we want to do."

"You can put me down now. Jostling around on your shoulder is making my stomach very unsteady."

"We can move faster if I carry you. Get a grip and don't throw up!"

"Can I ask one last question?" She didn't wait for his consent. "Are there more fighters hiding in the other tunnels?"

"I don't know. Nateesha says it's all clear. Do we believe her or not?" His fast jog slowed; the light was increasing. "In our last communication, Jeffers said the authorities are still here."

"Where is Nateesha?" She saw Watters and his men on their right. She felt an imperceptible thrumming in her bones and waited for Rogan to mention he felt something. She kept quiet when he bumped her off his shoulder and into his arms. The 'present' from the Flair Queens throbbed in time with her pulse.

"She left. They have wings. She told Watters she would see him at Summerfield. She'd get there quicker on one of our ships, but she says she doesn't like all that metal around her." He sliced a glance at Watters then back to her. "We talked to Cree. He knows she's on the way. Everything is safe."

Rogan stopped inside the entrance, staying well within the shadows. Police cars, emergency vehicles and ambulances littered the parking area and concourse. Three Predators, black and menacing, crouched in the overflow car park, locked up tight. Figures dressed in black with large white letters on the jackets formed a line in front of the crafts. The Predators were three times the size of the Raptors, their largest plane on the market. The craft were their most covert experiment. Bringing them into the open before their drives were finished was a calculated risk. Military, businesses and all types of riff raff would be searching hard for their blueprints and offering to throw obscene amounts of money at them for one or two of the ships. And the Space Authority would be salivating once they discovered their real purpose – space flight.

"This is so not good," Tempest remarked. "Put me down, Ro."

He lowered her legs and set her with gentle care on her feet. "Once we go out, the cops are going to mob us. The teams aren't going to stay on the Predators."

"We still have communication with them …"

"Tempest, the only reason they're still on board is Jeffers

told them we are on our way out and we weren't under fire. When we step into the open, they see you're hurt, they'll swarm out. And the locals are going to get a scare. Things are going to FUBAR quickly."

Thunder rattled the heavens in the distance. She turned her face up to catch the wind, but the air was still. "Is my pack still around?" She took two unsteady steps and rested against the granite, closing her eyes and leaning her head back. She heard shuffling and the murmuring of voices. The rock vibrated against her spine. She blocked it out and sent her attention into her body. A red slash covered her right shoulder. Spatters of green permeated the center and edges. She stiffened with horror … was it gangrene already? She sent a tendril of smell and a second one of sight to the center blob. She sobbed in relief: healing granules, not an indicator of rotting flesh. She gave the green areas a boost of energy then withdrew.

"Tempest!"

She blinked, lazily puzzled to find herself sitting on the floor. She raised a hand to her burning cheek. "Did someone hit me?"

"I said no healing," Jake barked. "You faded out and collapsed. Are you trying to kill yourself?"

"No, Jake," she spat. "I wanted to see what my reserves were like; if I had any internal injuries. I saw something that looked like gangrene and it scared me." She hurried on at the trepidation on the surrounding faces. "Everything is healing. I just sent a little energy boost to help them along."

"Here's your pack." Rogan shook the bag beside her.

She released the loops holding the denim jacket. "Help me up and get this on me." She let them lift her. Jake held the short coat and she slipped her right arm in. He draped the left side over her shoulder hiding the extra padding. She swayed. "I'm okay. I can do this … we can do this. How're Daire and the others?"

"Daire followed you and Rogan when you went for the

gate. When the damn thing went nuts and you and Rogan went flying, Daire and a couple of others were close enough to catch you. Spreading the resulting tumble among several bodies kept everyone from critical or serious wounds. He has some cuts, massive bruising and maybe a couple of cracked ribs. I won't know that until we can scan him. He'll be fine and so will everyone else in a few weeks with rest."

It felt like her energy poured down her body and out the bottoms of her feet. She sagged against Jake. "Keep me on my feet, Jake," she whispered.

"The authorities are going to question everyone, and it'll take time. I don't have anything in my pouch that'll keep you going that long."

She searched for Sebastian with her eyes. She really didn't want to alarm the men, but she needed to know if he could help. "I'm fading. Jake doesn't have any chemicals to give me. Is there any way you can give me a boost, Bastian?"

"I can try." He waited until one of the other men took his place supporting Daire then edged to her side.

"No, wait." Rogan searched the skies for lightning. The thunder was closer. All he could see were billowy, puffy clouds blanketing the pale blue sky. He settled his shoulders and ignored the prickling along his spine. "Jake, can't you use the injuries as a medical emergency? You can say we'll give a statement once everyone receives treatment."

"What about those of you who aren't showing injuries? Do you want to separate? I can probably get the injured out, but the rest will have to stay and answer questions."

"No." Tempest rested back against Bastian's chest. "No. I don't want to leave anyone behind. We stay together no matter what. As soon as we're out, get someone to call Granville, Stoner & Regis. I didn't expect to need their help so soon. Send a Corsair to pick up the representative.

"I need everyone's attention," she called. "Here's the story. We heard about the caves when we decided to move to this area. We wanted an informal setting to get to know each other and decided to take a tour. We gathered in the main corridor waiting for our guide when we thought we heard a call for help. We rushed into the tunnel to locate whoever it was and offer assistance. We didn't find anyone and were returning to the main tunnel when we heard roaring behind us, and we ran to get out. Parts of the roof collapsed around us, causing the injuries. One of the people in my group had a datacomp and rushed ahead to call for assistance. He didn't know what caused the issue with the cave so, with an abundance of caution, he requested our security personnel bring their weapons. With time being of the essence, our personnel used the big birds to ride to the rescue. That's it. Simple, clean and mostly true. Everyone got it? No embellishments."

"We know that, Tempe," Strider chided. "Let's hope the cops accept our version."

"Since it appears we were the only ones left inside, there won't be anyone to dispute it; as long as everyone sticks to the story … and no embellishments. Don't give up your weapons. We all have permits to carry and also for concealed. I don't care if they have sniffers which would alert them the weapons have been used."

Heads bobbed and grins covered everyone's faces at the additional admonishment.

"Who gets to support me? Where the hell is that thunder coming from? Those aren't rain clouds." She wound an arm around Bastian's waist and let him lead her across the pavement taking her time and putting on a show of being hurt worse than she was.

"Stop where you are." The law officer was short, probably no more than five feet six inches tall. He didn't have much of a waist, but he was solid. No fat hung over the sides of his belt and his tan uniform was crisp with only a slight circle of sweat ringing his armpits.

"Please, Lieutenant. You're acting like we're criminals.

Do we look like we've been having a wonderful time? I don't appreciate your tone of voice."

"What are those things? Why are they here? Who do they belong to?" He tilted his head to the Predators, his gun stance steady, his eyes focused on Tempest and the people at her back.

She shifted forward to keep the cop's attention and stopped. He was close enough she could see his finger tightening on the trigger. At the side of her eye, she saw Jeffers fade behind Lorcan, Strider and Blazer, and turn sideways to conceal his conversation on the datacomp.

The ramps of the Predators lowered. Tension escalated. The line of police raised their weapons; a few dropped to one knee.

She flipped her story into oblivion with the accelerated hostility. "Those are my ships, Lieutenant, and those are my people who came to help extricate us from the cave in. Do not fire on innocents, Lieutenant." If she kept reminding him he was an officer of the law maybe he would take the hint and cool things down.

"What the hell happened? We've got hysterical and wounded civilians."

"We may not be hysterical, Lieutenant, but we also have injuries." She wanted to point out he seemed a little overwrought himself. "Why are you picking on us? We're innocents."

He jumped as thunder rippled across the sky. "What the fuck is going on?"

A brown sedan slid in the gravel stopping fifty feet from the confrontation. A tall, handsome athletic man with a black goatee stepped out of the cruiser. He took a few moments to survey the situation, slammed the door of his car, and sauntered to Tempest's group. "Riley, what are you doing?"

"These people came out of the cave."

"Some of them have injuries, Riley. Why are you holding a gun on them and why does the SWAT team have their weapons on those planes?"

"We got a call of weapons fire and civilians and park employees hurt. We got here and those things swooped in and landed." His gaze didn't move from Tempest and her group nor did his gun waver. There was something suspicious going on and they were at the center of it.

His explanation was concise and short. Tempest appreciated that. She wished sometimes the reports she received were so simple yet full of information.

"I see. Put the gun down, Riley." He raised a hand and called one of the deputies to him. "Have the SWAT teams stand down," he said in an undertone. He shook his head and rubbed the fingers of his left hand down the sides of his goatee. "Riley, holster your weapon and back away. Go to the highway and direct the military to this area. Now, Riley." He waited for his officer to ease his gun into the holster and step backwards to his car, always maintaining a view of Tempest and the men surrounding her.

"Now, Ms. Phillips. I'm Sheriff Tobias Walker." A smile replaced the stern look on his face. "Yes, I know who you are. You're in my county and I make it my business to know all the big dogs in the area. I'm sure you've explained this situation to my lieutenant, but why don't you repeat it to me."

A young deputy inched close to the Sheriff with a portable com system in his hands. "Sheriff, you need to hear this."

"Not now, Ketch."

Tempest leaned more heavily against Bastian smiling wanly at Walker. She quickly ran through the details of the operation in her mind. With careful omissions, she gave the Sheriff the truth.

He listened with intent and care. At the end of her recitation, he nodded. "That's a good story and should hold up even to the military honchos headin' this way." His head tilted at the grumbling sky. "Strange weather. I should hold you here while the investigators take a look around. But I won't. I trust you to come in and give me formal statements in the next few days. In the meantime," he swept his hat off and smoothed a hand across his hair, "you might want to get on those fancy birds of yours and get out." He settled his hat on his head, nodding once.

Jets screamed across the sky at close range.

"Really, Sheriff, you need to listen." Ketch disconnected his earpiece. Static burst from the handheld then settled.

"We've got bogies all around us. Fuck, I have one right above me and one on each side. They're playing with us." Engines roared as they revved. "I can't shake'em."

A harsh voice interrupted. "You are ordered to fire."

"Fire! You want us to fire on these bastards? We can't even get close to them. They'll shoot us out of the sky like fish in a barrel if we start flinging our arsenal at them. Are you trying to kill all of us, General?" The squadron leader was a patriot and was willing to lay down his life for his country, even the world, but not for a general with his eyes on a post with the World Enclave. Politics were at the bottom of the death of too many warriors and he wasn't going to offer his men up as willing sacrifices on the altar of the officer's ambition.

"We have a secondary plan in process. Do as you're ordered, soldier, or you'll be grounded and face courts martial when you land!"

The pilot's radar lit up with streaks from the ground. "Holy fuckin' heaven! Who the hell do you think you're going to hit? Those missiles are going to get us, you fool! These guys are going to flit out of here and leave us hangin' in the wind for you to kill. And what about the people we're supposed to be protecting? Pieces of us are going to rain all over them!"

Sheriff Walker flicked a button on the pod. "Well, it seems we've got an even bigger situation." He raised his voice. "All right, people, we need to get back to town and calm our citizenry." He tapped the brim of his hat. "Ma'am." The young deputy and SWAT team leader converged on the Sheriff, listened, then ran to the filling vehicles.

A parade of vans and cars charged the road. Dust clouds swelled above the screech of brakes. The brown air parted and camouflage painted vehicles rolled into the car park.

"Damn," Tempest cursed. "Everyone start towards the Predators. Anyone close enough get on board." Before she could continue, the Strike Force teams ran down the ramps, some taking up defensive positions and the remainder forming a half-circle around Tempest and her group.

Whitman Busch exited the passenger side of the front military vehicle. He placed his hands against the lower part of his back and stretched. "Isn't this delightful? Phillips, Branaugh and even D'eath. All in one place." He beamed and strolled closer. "What beautiful toys you have, Phillips. My scientists and technicians will be so excited to take them apart. I believe we have some unfinished business." He twirled his hand. "Take them into custody and search everyone carefully. Have your people stand down and put their weapons on the ground, Branaugh. You don't want to start shooting; you won't win. I have more men, Phillips." He bared his teeth in a smile. "Now, Branaugh."

"What exactly are we being charged with, Busch." Tempest gave him a sweet grin, addressing him the way he was greeting her. He was a little man, in a big position, who got his rocks off throwing his weight around. With the unswerving loyalty of men accustomed to following orders without question, he had distinct advantages in their current situation. She hoped the General they had heard over the datacomp would recall Busch.

"There are unknown ships in our air space and they're heading directly here. Now why is that, Phillips?"

Tempest hid her gulp. Oh, my.

It was as if he called the metal beasts into existence by thought alone. Grey, black and red ships hovered in the sky above them with noses like the beak of a bee-eater and widespread wings. Others zoomed past, wings folded back, playing a lopsided game of tag with once exotic looking jets.

A larger, clunkier version dropped delicately onto the ground. It didn't have the same cruel beauty as the other ships, but it still had a deadly elegance. The fighters projected a more menacing aura, the promise of more than retribution should something befall the craft.

"I believe you're on, Sebastian," Tempest muttered.

"No one fucking moves!" Busch yelled.

Tempest gave him an incredulous look. A hysterical giggle erupted which she quickly swallowed. "Are you fucking nuts? What do you plan to do against that?" She pointed at the looming ships.

The side of the spacecraft split and a ramp surged out. A petite woman dressed in red, black and grey pants and form-fitting top halted in the opening for a moment before two tall men appeared to frame the delicate figure. She strode forward secure in her confidence.

Sebastian laid a hand on Tempest's arm. "Come with me and we will welcome the Mistress together."

She smiled and patted his hand. "She might like to greet the lost Blood Lair Patriarch without an audience. Just give me a call when you're ready."

Something niggled at Sebastian. He had the strongest impulse to take Tempest and some of the others to cover his back. He shook his head at the traitorous thought. These were his people and even though he wasn't at his strongest he was still many thousands of years older than the Mistress and her companions. He leaned over and kissed Tempest's cheek as he had seen Rogan Branaugh do often. "You are right. I will greet our visitors while you attempt to deal with the consequences of this 'rescue'." He gave her a rueful laugh.

She touched his chest and stepped back. "We'll watch your back, Bastian. Just make sure they don't carry you off," she jested. She looked down to hide the tears filling her eyes.

"He'll be okay, Tempe." Strider handed her a white cloth. A watery laugh escaped when she unfolded the old-fashioned handkerchief. She dabbed her eyes, blew her nose half-heartedly with one hand, and attempted to refold it.

Strider raised his hands in front of him in mock horror and stepped back two paces. "I don't want it back, Tempe!" Relief filled him when he saw the light return to her eyes, her shoulders even out, and a smile wing onto her face.

"I wasn't even thinking of that." She stuffed the cloth into her sling.

"No!" Rogan shouted. He signaled the Strike Force teams to cover the military men and sprinted towards the quartet too fucking far away, sensing others straining behind him to reach the fallen Bloodhawk.

Sebastian's spark in Tempest's mind winked out. She staggered and would have collapsed onto the ground if Strider hadn't caught her. The feeling of loss overwhelmed her grinding her down into a black hole. A swelling wave of love, support and comfort rushed into the chasm from all the people bound with her in the tie to Sebastian, relieving the devastating desolation. She was able to take a deep breath, then another and another. She was finally able to stand, and she nudged away from Strider.

In the distance, the tall men dragged an unconscious Sebastian to the oversized barge. The hovering ships pitched forward projecting a high pitched hum covering the people on the ground. The feminine figure matched the men's speed trotting backwards covering their retreat.

In a wide-legged stance, Tempest planted her right hand on her hip, the nails of her fingers biting deep into her left palm. "You traitorous, bitch! You can't have him!" She screamed filling her voice with steel and rock solid certainty. She was Sebastian's Reciprocate. She would find a way to jumpstart their connection. "You can't have him!"

Explosive rage emanated from Tempest when the female flashed a toothy grin and gave Tempest a quick salute tapping her fingers against her forehead.

A hand descended to her shoulder pulling her around. "Get out of my face," she snarled at Busch. She shrugged him off, whirled and ran to the nearest Predator drawing the others in her wake. The alien spacecraft had been beautiful and elegant. The Predators were aggressive, brawny and threatening. Half the fighters aimed their weapons at the stunned Busch and his soldiers, depending on the others to guide them over the rough ground. The teams split between the three Predators and climbed on board.

Tempest kept her face lowered until the ramp closed. She raised her head. Resolve and conviction hardened her eyes. "Is everyone okay? No bad effects yet?"

Rogan sat in the seat beside Tempest, leaning his head against the padding laced between the metal struts of the compartment. "I'm feeling a slight drain of energy and a headache, but it's evening out. You knew she was going to take him. That's why you brought in three Predators."

"Yeah, it was a distinct possibility. If I were in her place with her resources, it's what I'd do. Sebastian is the lynchpin of their Lair, without him the other Lairs will tear them apart." She activated her 'link. "Wraith, are you receiving?"

"Coming in loud and clear, Tempest." Wraith's voice was deep, gruff.

"Are you sure it's still attached to him?" She sagged against Daire's chest, drawing comfort from the feeling of his arms around her waist.

"His energy signature is pulsing nice and steady. It's still on him."

"Good. Round the clock surveillance, please."

"Already on it. There are enough volunteers to cover several weeks without having the same person on twice. We'll be able to track him no matter how far out they go. Royce and Kachina are working on a boost as a failsafe. I put a rush on completion of the orbiter. We should be able to get it into space and hide it from detection in a couple of weeks. With that in place, they won't be able to hide him."

"Thanks, Wraith. I'm contacting Brion. Wait for his signal then send your teams with one of our computer techs to every subcontractor's facility and have the techs wipe everything that might have the plans. If anyone at the companies refuse to allow the techs to enter their premises, pulse the hell out of their building. If they haven't backed up their data to outside servers, it's their problem. Our techs know their business. I'm just rattling because of the situation. Make sure you search for hard copies and remove them. Okay. We're returning to Summerfield. Out."

"They'll find the transmitter eventually." Rogan rolled his head so he could see Tempest.

"I don't think so. The emitters contain a low band signal designed to intercept and confuse tracking devices. And it's in the emblem he wears around his neck. Since it's his sigil, I doubt they'll remove it. However, that's only the backup. He's still here." She tapped the side of her temple. "It doesn't matter where they go, I'll be able to pinpoint his position."

"She doesn't think you're his Reciprocate." Rogan grunted with pain as he shifted slightly in the seat.

"No. I don't believe she does. The connection to everyone is superimposed over my link with Bastian." Her brow furrowed, sadness washing across her face. "Bastian doesn't believe I'm his Reciprocate."

"What!" Rogan sat upright, stopping quickly as pain thudded through his body.

"He feels guilty for joining with me when I was so young. He thinks the cocktail from everyone diminished my link with him so he doesn't need my blood specifically. The Lair has a large base of 'feeders' who are ecstatic to bond with the Patriarch. Who knows? It's possible. With Bastian's needs resolved, Blood Lair can take their time to decide if they want more contact with Earth."

Tempest shuttled through the memories of the emotions Bastian had emitted since his rescue from the medpod. The consciousness that was Timebender emanated pulses of strength, power, support, comradery – and a plethora of other sensations. She sighed. "I want to go after him now but ..." She shook her head. "If he truly wants to separate himself from us, I can circumvent any effects on everyone, including me." With Timebender's willing and enthusiastic assistance, she could either burn out Bastian's node in her mind or encase it in layers and layers of shielding. "He has to decide the type of life he wants – something new with us or follow what the Lairs have done for thousands of years. It's his choice. I won't take away his right to choose since his decision won't adversely affect any of us."

Pulling away from the depths of despair and sorrow, Tempest focused her attention on her family and the life they were creating together. She tapped her fingers against her leg, her eyes squinting in concentration. She nodded. "Contact Brion Kendar. Tell him to collect the prototypes from the subcontractors. I want the lightdrives at Summerfield for testing. With the plans and physical models, our mechanical and technical crews can refine them and add them to our Predators. Mass production of the drives will never happen, and the final specifications will never enter the public domain. We have to move on. There's enough political maneuvering to face with the Covens, military and our new 'allies' without taking our battles outward." For now, Tempest thought.

The Predator rumbled and growled in agreement, its engines revving to settle its occupants on the ground within its protective casing.